Praise for *New York Times* bestselling author Elle James

"James' story rages as strongly as a blizzard, with action blowing fast enough to cause whiteout conditions."
—*RT Book Reviews* on *Hostage to Thunder Horse*

"An action-filled plot mixed with intrigue… Alluring lead characters will keep readers turning the pages."
—*RT Book Reviews* on *Deadly Allure*

Praise for author Debbie Herbert

"With all the paranormal genre books out, Debbie Herbert takes one that is not as popular as vampires and werewolves are and makes it her own."
—*Fresh Fiction* on *Siren's Secret*

"Herbert doesn't skimp on characterization… Nice chemistry and emotions make *Siren's Secret* a solid read."
—*RT Book Reviews*

"I am amazed at the depth and power of this story. Debbie Herbert is well on her way to becoming an established author."
—*Paranormal Romance Writers* on *Siren's Secret*

Elle James, a *New York Times* bestselling author, started writing when her sister challenged her to write a romance novel. She has managed a full-time job and raised three wonderful children, and she and her husband have even tried ranching exotic birds (ostriches, emus and rheas). Ask her, and she'll tell you what it's like to go toe-to-toe with an angry 350-pound bird! Elle loves to hear from fans at ellejames@earthlink.net or ellejames.com.

Books by Elle James

Harlequin Nocturne

The Witch's Initiation
Possessing the Witch

Harlequin Intrigue

Thunder Horse Redemption
Triggered
Taking Aim
Bodyguard Under Fire
Cowboy Resurrected
Christmas at Thunder Horse Ranch

Visit the Author Profile page
at Harlequin.com for more titles.

Elle James
and
Debbie Herbert

POSSESSING THE WITCH

AND

SIREN'S CALL

HARLEQUIN NOCTURNE™

If you purchased this book without a cover you should be aware that this book is stolen property. It was reported as "unsold and destroyed" to the publisher, and neither the author nor the publisher has received any payment for this "stripped book."

Recycling programs
for this product may
not exist in your area.

ISBN-13: 978-0-373-60153-0

Possessing the Witch and Siren's Call

Copyright © 2015 by Harlequin Books S.A.

The publisher acknowledges the copyright holders
of the individual works as follows:

Possessing the Witch
Copyright © 2015 by Mary Jernigan

Siren's Call
Copyright © 2015 by Debbie Herbert

All rights reserved. Except for use in any review, the reproduction or utilization of this work in whole or in part in any form by any electronic, mechanical or other means, now known or hereinafter invented, including xerography, photocopying and recording, or in any information storage or retrieval system, is forbidden without the written permission of the publisher, Harlequin Enterprises Limited, 225 Duncan Mill Road, Don Mills, Ontario, Canada, M3B 3K9.

This is a work of fiction. Names, characters, places and incidents are either the product of the author's imagination or are used fictitiously, and any resemblance to actual persons, living or dead, business establishments, events or locales is entirely coincidental.

This edition published by arrangement with Harlequin Books S.A.

For questions and comments about the quality of this book, please contact us at CustomerService@Harlequin.com.

® and TM are trademarks of the publisher. Trademarks indicated with ® are registered in the United States Patent and Trademark Office, the Canadian Intellectual Property Office and in other countries.

Printed in U.S.A.

CONTENTS

POSSESSING THE WITCH 7
Elle James

SIREN'S CALL 325
Debbie Herbert

POSSESSING THE WITCH
Elle James

For friends and lovers who accept you for who you are, no matter your physical or social flaws.

To Cleve for inspiring my drive and ambition to succeed in this crazy world of publication and for being there when I need a swift kick in the pants to get back to work. You're more than just a husband. You're my cheerleader, coach and team. You love me for all my successes and my flaws and encourage me to push on. I could not have accomplished so much without your love and support.

Chapter 1

She glanced behind her, certain she'd heard something that sounded like a growl. When the sound did not repeat, she shrugged and pulled up the collar of her jacket to block the bite of the chilled autumn air. Now, she wished that she'd accepted an offer of a ride to the garage from her friends. At least then she wouldn't be alone, on a dark street, jumping at every noise.

She knew better than to go anywhere alone in downtown Chicago, especially after dark.

As she entered the parking garage, she let out the breath she'd been holding and laughed. All that worry for nothing. She climbed the stairs to the second level and there, in the middle of the empty bay, stood her car, a shiny, creamy, pearl-white Audi, the heated leather seats beckoning to her.

As she dug in her purse for her keys, she heard it again. This time louder. The deep rumble of an animal's growl sent shivers coursing down her spine.

It sounded as though it was coming from her car.

The growl burst into a roar, echoing off the concrete walls of the garage, so real and frightening she screamed and dropped her purse, keys and all, and ran back toward the stairs.

"No," she cried, her heart in her throat, her breath catching on a sob. "No."

Although hampered by high heels, she made it all the way to the bottom. As she turned toward the street, fifty feet away and still busy with traffic, something big and heavy slammed into her back, knocking her facedown on the concrete.

Too far from the traffic to be seen, she lay pinned beneath the weight of an animal, its heated breath sniffing at the back of her neck.

She whimpered, struggling to crawl from beneath it, her heart racing, her hands scuffed and bleeding. "Please..."

The creature's nose nuzzled the line of her throat, then a long, hot, wet tongue snaked out and licked her skin.

She screamed, renewing her frantic fight to free herself from the faceless beast.

The animal roared again and sank its teeth into the back of her neck, shaking her viciously.

Her arms and legs went numb and she couldn't move any part of her body, but her thoughts were clear and frightened beyond comprehension.

The creature dragged her from the garage into the shadows of an alley, pavement scraping her face. He stopped behind a stack of bound cardboard, dropped her to the ground and roared, the sound reverberating off the walls.

"Please...don't kill me."

* * *

Selene Chattox jerked awake, drenched in sweat, her heart racing.

Please...don't kill me.

She snatched her cell phone from the nightstand and speed-dialed her sister, Deme.

"Yeah...what...who is this?" A loud banging noise was followed by a muttered curse. "Sorry, I dropped my phone. Selene? What's wrong?" Her voice was hoarse, filled with the gravel of sleep.

"She's dying."

"Who's dying?" All raspiness cleared, Deme's words were clear and clipped.

"I don't know."

"Can you tell where?"

"In an alley."

"Can you be more specific? Do you see anything else, a street sign, a building name, something?"

Selene inhaled, closed her eyes and let her mind drift back into the dream. Her cheek stung where the pavement had scraped against her skin in the nightmare—blessedly, the rest of her body felt no pain. Hot breath snorted down on her neck and Selene jerked out of the vision, her hand shaking so hard she could barely hold the cell phone to her ear. "I smelled water. She was in a parking garage, leaving the theater, when she was attacked. It dragged her into a nearby alley."

"A theater near water..." Deme spoke to someone on the other end. "River or lake?"

"River."

"The Civic Opera House on Wacker Drive?"

"Maybe."

"I'm coming over. Cal's calling Lieutenant Warner. We'll have someone there in minutes."

"Hurry," Selene whispered. "It's going to kill her."

* * *

Wind blasted down the back alley as Gryphon Leone emerged from the Civic Opera House, wrapping his long cloak around him. The chill of fall had settled in far sooner than he'd expected. He sniffed the air, his keen sense of smell picking up on the delicate nuances of coming rain and the dampness of the river.

He'd waited until the other theatergoers had departed before leaving the shadows of his box. He arrived early and left late, valuing his anonymity and privacy. The fewer people he encountered, the better. Despite years of exercising his control, he didn't trust himself with the people of the light and didn't put himself in too many situations that required him to remain in the public eye for long.

With the rise of his business and philanthropic ventures, he feared his anonymity would soon be a blessing of the past.

He hurried toward the street, determined to return to his apartment at the base of his office building, a haven beneath the surface of the oldest part of downtown Chicago, before the rain came.

The scent captured him, bringing him to a sudden halt. He lifted his nose to the air, a low rumble rising in his throat.

Blood. Fresh blood and animal musk.

His apartment, and the need to return before the rain, slipped through his thoughts, forgotten as his inner animal pushed to the surface.

Gryph fought back, breathing deeply in and out until the growling abated and all that was left was the scent—blood, tantalizingly fresh, tainted by the musk of another animal and the accompanying stench of fear.

He wanted to turn and walk away, but he couldn't, his

feet moving of their own accord, closer to the source. Rounding a corner, he spied a parking garage and something dark staining the sidewalk near the stairs leading up.

The stain spread like someone had taken a large paintbrush and dragged it along the walkway, until the paint ran out at the entrance to an alley.

Go home. Return to your apartment. Don't get involved.

Balthazar's words echoed in his head, the old man's warnings etched firmly in Gryph's brain since as far back as he could remember.

Still, the trail begged to be followed. He'd go as far as the entrance to the alley, no farther.

Gryph crossed the street, keeping out of the inky liquid staining the concrete, and worked his way quietly to the entrance to the alley.

As he stepped into the opening, a bellow blasted against the brick walls, followed by a woman's scream.

A huge shadow rose up from behind a stack of wooden pallets, the shape that of a giant wolf, rearing back on his hind legs.

Gryph's beast exploded from inside, answering with a deeper, more ferocious roar, thundering into the alley, echoing against the brick walls. His skin and bones moved, spread and stretched as his physical form altered, expanding, his clothing ripping at the seams. He shrugged out of his cloak, the long folds falling to the ground at his feet.

The creature in the alley rumbled again, launching itself toward him.

Caught in midtransformation, Gryph was helpless to defend himself.

The wolf, equal in size to Gryph's inner lion, hit him

full in the chest, knocking him back into the side street. The air slammed from his lungs.

His attacker flew past him and hit the opposite building, his feet glancing off the bricks, then landed on all fours, launching a new attack within seconds.

His transformation complete, Gryph dodged to his side and sprang to all fours, reaching out to pound the animal with a powerful swipe from his forepaw.

The wolf tumbled across pavement, sprang back on his feet and tore into Gryph, his fangs slashing for Gryph's jugular.

Gryph twisted to avoid the worst of the bite, but not all of it. The wolf's teeth sank into his skin, ripping through his shoulder near his collarbone. Pain rocketed through his senses, blinding him briefly.

The wolf pounced on him, pinning him to the ground. Had the creature wanted to finish him off, it could have with one more fatal bite.

Instead it stared down at him, its chest heaving, and it growled low and menacingly, like a warning. Then it leaped over Gryph and disappeared out of the alley and around a corner.

His shoulder bleeding, Gryph pushed to his paws, his racing heartbeat slowing.

A moan alerted him to another being's presence in the alley. With his focus on survival, Gryph hadn't moved on to the source of the long, thick bloodstain.

He staggered toward the banded stack of compressed cardboard boxes, his nostrils filled with the scents of blood, woman and fear.

Before he reached her, his body began its transformation back to man, the change made more difficult given his wounds.

His arms and legs completed before his face and head,

allowing him to reach out to the woman and feel for a pulse.

Her eyes blinked open, widening, a scream bubbling up in her throat.

Gryph tried to reassure her with words, but all that he could emit was a rumbling growl.

The woman's eyes rolled back in her head and she passed out.

The pavement was soaked with her blood from a wound in the back of her neck. If she had any chance at survival, she had to get to a hospital as soon as possible.

He left her on the ground for only a moment to retrieve his cloak, his cell phone tucked in the inside pocket.

Quickly he dialed 911 and gave a description of the victim, her injuries and her location. When the dispatcher asked his name, he clicked the off button and pocketed the phone.

He returned to the woman and applied pressure to her wound to stem the flow of blood from her body, but her face was deathly pale.

As he leaned over her body, blood dripped down on her.

Until now, he hadn't realized how much blood he'd lost. He could tell he was weakening, but he couldn't leave the woman until the police or ambulance were close.

A siren sounded in the distance, growing closer by the second.

Gryph had to leave before the emergency personnel arrived—how else would he explain his tattered clothing? And given his injuries and the pain they caused, he couldn't risk being around surface dwellers should the pain increase, summoning his inner beast.

He stayed until the last possible moment. When the

flashing lights of an emergency vehicle pulled into the side street, Gryph leaped over the chain-link fence behind him, raced for the opposite end of the alley and rounded the corner to the next street.

Keeping to the shadows, he ran until his feet slowed, the blood running in a stream down his arm, dripping onto the sidewalk, draining his strength. The police would follow his trail. He couldn't let that happen, he couldn't let them find him. Then he remembered how close he was to the river, its scent drawing him to the corner of Washington Street and Wacker Drive. Making a sharp left, he stumbled toward the bridge. An ambulance passed him, its lights blinding. A police car followed, slowing as it passed by.

Exhaustion pulled at Gryph—he wanted to sleep, but he knew he couldn't. He leaned against the bridge railing and stared down into the water.

The police car stopped and backed up.

Gryph leaned out and let himself tip over the edge. Then he was falling, racing to meet the black shiny surface of the river.

When he hit the water, the force of the fall sent him deep into the murky black depths.

His shoulder burned, the effort to move it too much. But he kicked his feet, propelling himself upward, hoping the current would carry him far enough away they wouldn't find him.

He surfaced a hundred yards from the Washington Street Bridge. A cop stood at the rails shining a flashlight below, sending a sweeping arc back and forth across the water.

Gryph sucked in a breath and sank below the surface, letting the current carry him farther away. As he flowed downstream with the river, he wondered what it would feel like to drown, to let his lungs fill with water and the river claim him. His chest burned for oxygen and he kicked his feet to send him closer to the river's edge. Dying in a river wasn't in the cards for him tonight.

When he came up again, he had drifted far enough that the cop's light couldn't find him. Tired beyond endurance, he kicked and pulled with one arm to the side of the river, searching for a place he could crawl out. Several minutes later, he found a metal ladder pinned to the concrete walls of the river and dragged himself up the east embankment onto a walkway, where he collapsed, the night sky of the city fading to black.

Chapter 2

Pain...tired...can't breathe.

Selene staggered to the door of her basement apartment below the vintage dress shop she owned that was situated among the quaint little buildings of old-town Chicago.

She could barely breathe and her shoulder ached unbearably, the pain draining her strength, sucking the life from her body.

Holding on to the handrail, she pulled herself up the steps to ground level. Headlights flashed on the street in front of the building.

Once outside the door of her shop, Selene met Deme, as her sister climbed out of her Lexus SUV. "Thank the goddess, you're here."

"Were you going somewhere without me?" Deme asked.

Selene lurched toward the car and leaned against the door. "We need to get there."

"Are you all right, sweetie?" Deme started to round the car.

"I'm okay, but we need to move fast." She opened the car door and slid into the passenger seat. "Hurry."

"Where exactly do we need to get?" Deme climbed back into the driver's seat and inserted the key in the ignition.

"Head toward the Washington Street Bridge."

Deme shifted into gear and spun the SUV around in a tight U-turn, bumping over the curb on the other side of the street. When they'd gone several blocks, she looked across at Selene.

"Is it the girl? The one you called about earlier?"

Selene shook her head. "No. Someone else. He's injured and alone." She closed her eyes, shivering. "And cold. He'll die if we don't get to him soon."

"What about the girl?"

"The EMTs are with her now. But *he's* alone."

Deme's foot sank to the floor, shooting them along the streets, dodging the occasional driver unfortunate enough to be out on the city streets so late into the night.

As they crossed the Washington Street Bridge, Selene leaned forward, her gaze panning the landscape, the steel, glass and concrete buildings rising high into the night sky, blocking the moon. "Turn left on Wacker."

On such short notice, Deme slammed on her brakes and skidded into the turn. The rear end continued around and she goosed the accelerator to keep her SUV from making a complete three-sixty.

As they shot down Wacker, Selene dug her fingers into the dash, leaning so far forward her nose almost touched the windshield. He was near, very near. Selene leaned back in her seat, braced herself and yelled, "Stop!"

Deme hit the brakes, bringing the vehicle to a standstill, tires burning into the asphalt.

Selene burst from the door, rounded the car and raced across the street. So intent on reaching the wounded man, she didn't see the car until almost too late.

A horn blared, tires squealed and an older model Lincoln Town Car swerved, barely missing her.

Without slowing, she ducked between buildings and headed for the river.

"Selene, wait for me," Deme called out behind her.

But she couldn't wait, his need drove her forward, sending her on a headlong rush toward the river. She found a staircase leading down to the walkway along the water's edge.

"Selene!" Deme called out behind her. "Damn it, this area is dangerous at this time of night."

She knew. He'd been injured by a dangerous animal, his blood running into the river. Selene ran along the water's edge, heading north. Something moved in the shadow beneath the next bridge.

Fear had a place in Selene's race to save him. But it wasn't for herself. It was for him. She didn't slow until she reached the bridge.

A moan echoed off the steel supports.

A man lay across the concrete, a soaked cape pulling at the string around his neck, but otherwise he was shirtless in the late autumn chill. His soaked trousers were torn and ragged, as though they'd been through a shredder. No shoes, no jacket, his hair, longish and tousled, was hanging in his face.

Selene ripped the coat from her back and covered him, pulling it up to the wounded shoulder. Blood oozed from a deep gash. Not a gunshot wound, but the vicious bite of a raging animal. She tore the hem of her blouse, wadded the material into a pad and pressed it into the gash, stemming the flow of blood.

His eyes opened and he gasped. A low growl rumbled in his throat and his hand reached out to grab her wrist in a fearsome grip, pulling her hand away from the injury. The strength of his grasp hurt, cutting off her circulation.

Selene bit her lower lip, pushing back the pain. He didn't know what he was doing. "Shh...I'm here to help. We have to stop the bleeding. Let me help." Tears stung her eyes as his grip tightened. She stared into his face, trying to read his expression, the shadows blurring her view.

If he squeezed much harder, he'd snap her bones. Such strength in an injured man was extraordinary.

She sent soothing thoughts into his consciousness.

Deme skidded to a halt behind her. "Let her go," her sister said to the man.

"It's okay, Deme. He's delirious, he doesn't know he's hurting me." Selene sucked in a breath and let it out slowly. "Please, let go. I need to stop the blood. Do you understand? Otherwise you'll die." *Please, I only want to help.*

His eyelids drooped. "Tired. Can't hold on."

"That's right, let go." Selene peeled one finger loose, then another. "We need to get you help."

"No hospital," he whispered. Then his hand slackened and dropped to the ground.

"About damned time he passed out. I was going to have to knock him out so that you could help his stubborn ass." Deme dropped to her haunches and pulled her cell phone from her pocket. "I'll get an ambulance here."

"No!" Selene's response came swift and sure. From where, she didn't know. All she knew was that this man wouldn't want to go to a hospital, no matter how injured he was. "Help me get him back to your vehicle."

"Are you kidding? He must weigh close to two hundred pounds. There are stairs and..."

"Please. We have to get him out of the cold and bandage his wound before shock sets in or it won't matter." She pressed the wad of material to his shoulder. "Give me your scarf."

"But it's my favorite."

Selene held out her hand.

Deme unwound the scarf from around her neck and reluctantly handed it to her, a frown creasing her brow. "You don't even know this guy. What's so special about him?"

Selene didn't answer, instead wrapping the scarf around his shoulder and knotting it over the wound to apply more pressure. Then she stood and grabbed him beneath the injured arm.

Deme took the uninjured side.

The man growled again, guttural and animal-like.

"Get up," Selene said in a strong voice any drill sergeant would envy. "Get up!" With her sister's help and the efforts of the half conscious, half naked man, they got him to his feet and led him to the stairs.

After nearly losing him twice, they got him up the steps and onto the street above. Selene leaned him against a light pole to help hold him up as Deme ran for the vehicle. She pulled up beside them and they guided him into the backseat, bumping his head and shoulder in the process.

A low roar ripped through the car, startling the women.

Deme stared across at Selene. "No man should make that kind of noise, I don't care how delirious."

"Just get him in." Selene lifted one of his legs, shoved

it in and closed the door quickly. She climbed into the passenger seat and twisted around to watch him.

Deme eased into the driver's seat and stared into the rearview mirror at the man. "Sure you don't want me to drop him off at a hospital emergency room?"

"No." Selene's jaw set in a hard line. "Take me home."

Deme shook her head, her lips pressing into a thin line. "I'm not leaving him at your place."

"You have to." Selene shot a pleading glance at her sister. "I'm his only hope."

"Look, Selene, you don't know this guy. He could be a mass murderer or a rapist. He could be the person who jumped the woman from your vision."

"He's not."

"How do you know?"

"I just know."

"He was in the same area, Selene."

"He didn't hurt that woman." Selene's words were low, intense.

Deme stared into her sister's eyes for a long, hard minute. "Okay, then."

Selene breathed a sigh as the SUV pulled away from the curb and headed back across the river toward her apartment. Why she'd insisted on taking him to her home, she didn't know. He'd insisted no hospital. Why?

Selene stretched out her mind to read into his thoughts, but the more she pushed the more frustrated she became. So many questions spun through her own thoughts, she couldn't see into his.

The man in the backseat moaned. He'd lost a lot of blood and from the looks of him, had gone into the river, a very unsanitary place. If he didn't die of exposure, the bacteria from the river water might kill him.

"Could you hurry?" Selene urged.

Deme shook her head, but the SUV's speed picked up. A red light ahead made her slow the vehicle enough to look both ways before blowing through.

In what seemed like an interminable amount of time, but had been less than ten minutes, Deme pulled up in front of Selene's shop.

"We're here, now what?" Deme cast a glance into the backseat, where the man lay semicomatose. "How are we going to get him in the basement? Assuming I agree to this plan of yours."

Selene bit her lip. "I don't know. But we have to."

Deme reached into her purse and pulled out her cell phone. "Cal can be here in fifteen."

"No." Selene put her hand over Deme's phone. "I'd rather we kept this to just you and me."

"What? You and me carrying a large unconscious man into your basement apartment?"

Selene nodded. "Yes. And I don't want Cal to know that he's even here. I don't want anyone else to know. Not even Gina and Aurai. Especially not Brigid."

"We're your sisters. Why keep it from us? Look, just let me take him to the hospital. Let them handle him. They have big strong burly orderlies that—"

"No." A deep voice cut into Deme's words. The back door to the vehicle opened and the man got out.

Selene ripped her door open, but not in time.

One second he was holding on to the door, the next he'd crumpled to the ground.

Her heart beating hard against her ribs, Selene dropped to her knees. "Are you all right?"

"I don't need your help," he said.

Deme stood over them both, her fists planted on her hips. "Like hell you don't."

"I won't go to a..." He lay still with his eyes closed, his breathing shallow, almost nonexistent.

Selene slid one of his arms around her neck. "Help me get him up."

Deme sighed. "Stubborn witch."

Selene's lips twitched. "Shut up and get his other side."

Deme lifted his arm to drape over her shoulder, but as soon as she moved it, he jerked, growling like a rabid animal, his teeth peeled back over sharp incisors. With her head down to get the arm over her shoulder, Deme didn't see the pointed fangs.

But Selene did. Her stomach flip-flopped and she ducked her head to avoid Deme's gaze. "Just get an arm around his waist and help me haul him to the stairs." To him she said, "Could you manage to stay with us long enough to help yourself down a flight of stairs?"

"Must get below," he said through gritted teeth.

"That's where we're going, just help us get you there." Selene glanced across at her sister. "Ready?"

"Whenever you are." Deme's arm tightened around his waist.

Selene stepped forward at the same time as Deme.

The man between them lurched and stiffened, then a low rumble rose in his chest.

"Either stop growling, or I'll drop you here and leave you on the pavement," Selene threatened, her voice sharp, her back straining under his weight.

"You go, sister." Deme grunted, easing toward the building and the next hurdle. The steps.

The rumbling abated, but his grip tightened around Selene. He snorted. "And I thought you were an angel come to rescue me."

Deme laughed out loud.

Selene shot an angry glare at her before she responded.

"Hardly. I'll be your worst nightmare before this night is over." She shuddered thinking of how she needed to clean his wound and how painful it would be for him. She guessed he wouldn't like it in the least.

When they reached the narrow stairs leading down into the basement apartment of the shop, Deme laid the man's hand on the rail and moved down the steps in front of him. "The stairs aren't wide enough for three. You'll have to help yourself down the stairs, big guy."

The man groaned, his eyes rolling to the back of his head, the hand on the rail turning white with the strength of his grip.

Selene turned his face toward her and tried to probe his mind.

His chaotic thoughts were a jumble of pain, darkness and overwhelming sadness.

Unable to bear the ache and sorrow, Selene jerked out of his head and swayed.

"What is it?" Deme asked.

"Nothing. I just can't read his mind." She could sense emotions and pain, but not thoughts or words. She'd have to use other means to get through to him. "Listen, mister, if you want to get off the street and lie down, you have to help me get you down these stairs. Do you hear me?"

He moaned and leaned heavily on her.

"Wake up." She shook his good shoulder. "I need your help."

"No angel," he muttered, his eyes opening.

"I'll be the devil himself if that's what it takes to get you down those steps. Now, move!"

Deme chuckled. "Didn't know you had it in you, sis. Sure you don't want me to get him down here? I'm bigger than you are."

"I got him." Selene fished in her pocket for her keys and tossed them to Deme.

Her sister hurried down in front of Selene and the stranger to open the door to the little apartment.

Straining against his weight, Selene stepped down first. In a combination of deliberate steps and clumsy falling, she got him down the short flight so quickly he slammed into the door frame.

The big man roared, his eyes flashing open, exposing deep, tawny gold irises, like a lion.

Selene gasped.

"What?" Deme leaned past the man to stare out at her sister. "Did he hurt you?"

"No, no." Selene couldn't meet her sister's gaze. "Let's get him to the bedroom." No need to worry her sister. Especially when she wanted her to leave as soon as she got the injured man settled. If Deme had seen what Selene had, she'd have this man out of her apartment so fast his head would be spinning more than it was already.

By the time they reached her antique cast-iron bed, the man teetered on the verge of passing out. He was more a dead weight than a help. Or that's how he felt to Selene, bearing the brunt of his weight. He leaned toward the bed, but she held on.

"Not yet. You're soaked to the skin." Selene pushed him toward Deme. "Hold him up while I get his clothes off."

"You're going to strip a stranger?" Deme asked.

"You want the honors?" Selene quipped. "He's not lying in my bed in those wet, smelly clothes."

"Why is he going to lie in your bed? I'm not liking this arrangement, Selene. You don't know this guy. He could be a serial killer."

"I can't leave him on the streets, Deme." Though her

back hurt, she held on to the man. "Look, if it makes you feel better. I can sense that he won't hurt me."

Deme's lips pressed together and her eyes narrowed. "You said you couldn't read his mind."

"I can't read his individual thoughts, but I can tell he's harmless to me."

Deme stared hard at her sister. "I'm not convinced, but I'll hold on while you do the stripping. I don't think Cal would be thrilled to know I'd stripped a strange man." She took over by sliding beneath the arm Selene had been holding him up by. "Just hurry. He weighs a ton."

The man groaned, his knees buckling.

Selene helped Deme straighten him, then she went back to work, reaching for the waistband of his trousers. She wasn't a virgin, but removing a strange man's tattered pants was…well…disturbing. She quickly flicked the buttons loose and stripped the damp trousers down thick muscular legs coated with a fine layer of tawny hairs.

Her heartbeat quickened when she realized he wore nothing beneath his trousers.

Breath caught in her throat and she hurriedly removed his pants, setting them in a pile on the floor.

"Holy smokes, the man is hung like a frickin' horse!" Deme grunted and almost fell over. "Damn, I think he's out again. It's all I can do to hold him up." She shifted his weight, leaning hard to keep him up.

With her heart already beating a rapid tattoo inside her body, Selene hoped Deme wouldn't mention the man's nakedness again. Her older sister couldn't be happy about this stranger being totally nude in her sister's bed. She'd never leave him alone with Selene at this rate.

Selene knew, by way of her "gift," that she had to get Deme out of the apartment before she tried to clean this man's wounds. Something about him screamed danger.

But not necessarily a danger to her. Those eyes, that growling and the roar, were only the beginning, she feared.

Deme wouldn't understand. She didn't have the gift of spirit like Selene.

Trousers off, completely naked, the man swayed. Selene helped Deme maneuver him to the bed, where they sat him on the edge and laid him back gently, lifting his feet up onto the mattress. Once settled, Selene pulled the sheet up over his legs and hips.

Selene went to work on the padding she'd tied over the wound, pulling it carefully over his shoulders, easing the fabric caked in sticky blood loose from his injury.

He sat straight up, his hand reaching up to grasp hers in a surprisingly strong grasp.

"Easy now. We have to clean it so that it doesn't get infected," she said in a stern but gentle tone.

His grip loosened, his hand falling to his side. Golden eyes, glassy with pain, stared at her before they rolled back in his head again, and he slumped against her.

Selene braced herself to keep from falling over with his weight.

Deme moved forward to steady Selene. "You got him?"

"Yeah. Thanks."

Selene and Deme held on, lowering him back to the mattress. Once there, they stood back and flexed their arms and shoulders.

Selene took a deep breath and let it out. "I'm sure you have to get back to Cal. I can take it from here."

Deme crossed her arms over her chest. "I'm not leaving you alone with him."

"Yes, you are. If I need your help, I'll call you. I have you on speed dial."

"Selene, be serious. You don't know him and what he's capable of."

"I told you. I can sense he won't hurt me. Trust me, Deme. I need you to leave me and go check on the woman who was attacked earlier."

"He could be her attacker." Deme's brows rose and her gaze captured Selene's. "Your sense of spirit has been wrong before, hasn't it?"

Selene shook her head. "Never. And no, he didn't attack the woman." She knew beyond a doubt this man wasn't the girl's attacker.

"Still, I don't feel comfortable leaving you with him." Deme's cell phone buzzed and she pulled it from her back pocket. "Hey, Cal. What's happening?" She listened for a minute, her gaze going from Selene to the man on the bed and back to Selene. "Okay, I'll be there in ten minutes." She clicked the off button.

Selene's brows rose. "Cal wants you at the hospital to question the woman, doesn't he?"

Her sister nodded. "He'd like you to be there, too."

Before Deme could finish the last word, Selene was shaking her head. "I'm not leaving him. His wounds must be treated."

"He's unconscious. We could take him to the hospital with us and let the professionals fix him up."

Selene stared down at the man's pale face. "Even if I wanted to, we couldn't get him back up the stairs."

"The woman regained consciousness. I need to get there before they knock her out completely."

"Go. I'll be fine." Selene didn't wait for her sister to leave—she started gathering supplies to clean and bandage the man's shoulder.

"Well, then, I'll check back here when I'm done at the hospital."

"No need. I tell you, I'll be fine."

Deme snorted. "I'll be here." She touched her sister's arm. "Be careful, and whatever you do, don't trust him. You're my sister and I care about you. I don't want you to be the next woman in the hospital, or dead."

Selene took Deme's hand and squeezed it. "Then trust me. I know what I'm doing."

"Fair enough." With one last pointed stare, Deme left.

As the door closed behind her sister, Selene filled a bowl with hot water and set to work cleaning the wound.

She dabbed at the dried, caked blood all around the jagged, ripped skin, careful not to cause him more pain. But the effort was hopeless. She'd have to scrub to get the dirt and grime off. She applied more pressure, anxious to get the river water off and treat him for infection with one of her mother's poultices made of the dried herbs she kept in her pantry.

After she'd cleaned the skin surrounding the injury, she took a breath and, with a fresh, clean cloth, attacked the wound itself.

Her first dab was hesitant and as gentle as she could be and still get it clean.

The man, whose hair was drying to a tawny gold, jerked with each touch. As she worked toward the center of the jagged, torn skin, his chest rumbled, his body tensed, the muscles in his arms seemed to grow.

Selene tried to hurry but she didn't want to be careless and hurt him further. Her next touch set him off.

He flinched away and a bellow erupted from his throat. His back arched off the bed and his arms and legs writhed against the sheets.

Selene jumped back, tripped over his pile of clothing and fell hard on her butt.

The man rolled to his side, away from her, twisting and jerking, his skin stretching taut over bulging muscles. Thick golden hair sprouted from the skin covering his back, arms and neck. His hair grew longer, thicker and coarser around his head.

The man's back arched again and he roared, falling to the floor on the opposite side of the bed from where Selene sat on the floor in stunned silence.

As soon as he hit the ground, another roar echoed off the walls of the small bedroom and knocked sense back into Selene. She pushed to her feet and threw herself across the bed.

If he continued to thrash around, his wound would start to bleed again.

"Stop it," she yelled. "Whatever's happening to you, stop it now." Selene's heart raced as she stared down at the back of an animal that appeared to be half human, half lion. "What are you?"

He roared again, his back bowing upward.

Selene fell back on the bed, knowing that deep inside, this man was in pain, and the pain wouldn't get better until the injury was tended to. Pushing back her fear, she forced her voice to be calm while she shook inside. "If you don't get back in the bed and lie still, you could die. And I'll be damned if you die on my watch."

The beast's body stilled, the only movement the heaving of his chest as he breathed in and out, his thick, hairy skin twitching.

Taking a deep breath, Selene slid off the bed and crouched on the floor beside the huge creature, touching his uninjured shoulder. "Please. Let me help you."

He flinched away from her.

"You might as well let me help you. I know your secret now. We're past the awkward part. I know why you don't want to go to a hospital. But that doesn't mean your wound can't be treated here." She touched him again.

This time he didn't withdraw.

Taking that as acquiescence, Selene urged him to roll over onto his back.

He laid still, his eyes those of a lion, staring up into hers, unblinking. The hairs on his naked body receded back into his skin, the huge bulk of his lionish muscles reduced to those of a bodybuilding hulk of a human.

Selene reached for his hand, her own shaking. "Come. Get back in the bed where I can clean that wound."

His eyelids fluttered.

She tugged on his uninjured arm. "I can't do it for you and you're not staying on the floor."

He let her help him back into the bed, where he lay completely naked, his skin returning to normal.

Selene's breath caught in her throat as her gaze ran from his toned calves up to thick thighs to the juncture of his legs, where a thick, hard erection, bigger than any Selene had ever witnessed in her limited sexual experiences, jutted upward. As she ran the sheet over his body, she forced her gaze up to his head. The angles in his face eased from the animal he'd become back to the handsome, clean-skinned complexion of the man she'd rescued from beneath the bridge.

Once settled, he lay as still as death, his face pale, his breathing shallow and uneven.

Selene collapsed on the chair beside him, her heart racing, her confidence in the world she'd known shaken even more. What had she gotten herself into? This man obviously wasn't human. Selene laughed shakily. Deme would be livid if she knew what she had in her apartment.

Selene shook her head, staring at the man lying so innocently against her clean white sheets.

What the hell was he?

Chapter 3

Gryph floated in and out of consciousness, pain forcing his beast to the surface more than once. Each time he was coherent enough to realize his body's metamorphosis, he fought the change. A gentle but firm voice led him through the darkness, each time bringing him back from that place so primal and dangerous that he feared he'd go there and never return.

In a burst of pain his body stretched, flexed and altered, his lion surfacing, ready for battle. But an angel's voice cut through his confusion, through the instinct driving him to lash out against the source of his suffering.

Once his eyes opened and he thought he saw a brown-haired beauty hovering over him. A halo of light surrounded her head. A dark angel there to drag his sorry ass back from the grave. She dabbed something cool and moist across his brow, whispering assurances to him. Then she pressed a glob of thick, oozing paste into the angry wound on his shoulder, bringing him fully awake and off the bed. The pain stabbed through his muscles and his jaw tightened. He could feel the lion fighting to break through. He opened his mouth to yell, but the lion's roar erupted from his throat, echoing off the walls.

The angel became the devil, glaring at him, her dark eyes flashing. "Shut up and lie down. That's the second poultice I've applied that you've shaken off." She laid her cool hand on his heated, good shoulder and pushed him down onto the pillow.

A wave of nausea washed over him and he let her guide him back to the mattress. As soon as his head hit the pillow, the lion backed off and his human thoughts became clearer. "Why?"

"Why what?" Her hands dug into a stainless steel bowl on the table beside the bed and came up with a glob of greenish-brown mud. "Let's try this again, and this time don't sit up, or roar. And most of all try not to kill me, will ya?"

Her words cut through his pain, causing him to clench his teeth and focus on maintaining his humanity. "Why did you help me?"

She laid the poultice over his wound.

He gasped, his fingers clenching the sheets at his sides to avoid lashing out at his angel.

The woman shrugged. "I didn't see anyone else coming to your rescue." She adjusted the sheet around his waist and tucked a blanket over him.

For the first time, Gryph realized he was naked. His brows shot up. "My clothes?"

"What's left of them are in the dryer." Her lashes swept down over her deep dark eyes, her cheeks reddening. She pushed a long wavy strand of rich brown hair behind her ear. "They smelled like stinky river water. I washed your trousers, but I'm not sure they'll be fit to be worn." She looked up, her gaze capturing his.

"Did you...?" He nodded toward the sheets covering his body.

"Undress you?" Her chin tipped upward. "You weren't lying on my bed in the soaked clothing. And you weren't cooperating much in a semiconscious state."

Gryph chuckled, and regretted it immediately as the movement shook his shoulder. Pain sliced through him and he growled.

Her eyes narrowed and he stopped.

"Perhaps you can tell me your name." She ripped a white sheet in half, then in half again. Her movements were smooth, capable and graceful. Slim flingers made quick work of reducing the sheet into bandages.

Despite his pain, Gryph found himself fascinated by the firm, capable movements of her slender fingers, wondering what they'd feel like running over his naked skin. The animal in him purred.

Her brows rose. "Is it so hard to tell me your name?"

He hesitated. Having spent his young life avoiding answering questions posed by surface dwellers, he still didn't feel comfortable sharing anything about himself with those above the world he'd grown up in. But something about this woman inspired his confidence. "Gryph."

She nodded. "Gryph." On her lips, his name sounded like the music he listened to with Balthazar in the Lair. "I am Selene."

Her fingers folded the sheet into a neat pad, which she laid gently over his wound. Using white medical adhesive tape, she taped it down firmly, holding the poultice in place.

"What is that foul-smelling stuff you put on me?"

"A poultice my mother used to make when we fell and scraped our knees. Guaranteed to help you heal quickly."

"Was your mother an angel like you?"

The woman's lips tipped upward. "*She* was the angel. I'm not. In case you don't remember, I cleaned your wound earlier. You were somewhat out of it. But not enough that you didn't raise a ruckus several times throughout the procedure."

Gryph cringed, his fists tightening into knots. "Did I say or do anything?"

"You didn't *say* anything. You *growled* and *roared*."

She'd only answered half of his question. Gryph's eyes narrowed.

The woman wouldn't meet his gaze and she busied herself gathering the bowl and washcloths on the nightstand.

Gryph grabbed her wrist.

The bowl upended and fell to the ground. The woman's eyes widened.

"What did I *do*?" His voice came out gravelly and as more of a growl than he'd intended. The flash of fear in her eyes told him everything he needed to know. He dropped her hand.

She stepped back, rubbing at the red marks where his fingers had been.

Gryph sighed. "You didn't turn me over to the authorities." He shook his head, staring hard into her eyes. "Why?"

"Should I have?"

"Any surface dweller would have."

Her brows dipped together. "Surface dweller?" She bent to retrieve the bowl, scooting back out of his reach as soon as she straightened, clutching the bowl to her chest. "What do you mean by surface dweller?"

His lips clamped shut. *Damn*. He'd said too much. The less this woman knew the better off he was, and the safer the community of souls was who lived far below the hustle and bustle of Chicago in the dark tunnels under the oldest part of the city. The scarred, the unusual, the mutants and the physically and mentally disfigured freaks who slid beneath the surface to live out their lives unnoticed by the beautiful, so-called normal people of the light.

"I should leave." He pushed to a sitting position and the room spun so fast, he tilted toward the edge of the bed.

The woman was there to catch him, steadying him against her breast. Her tantalizing scent cut through the gray fog consuming him, bringing him back from the edge of unconsciousness.

"You're not going anywhere in your condition," she said, her voice firm.

As much as he wanted to remain with his cheek leaning into the softness of her breast, he straightened. "I'll be fine. I heal fast." His voice sounded weak, even to his own ears.

"If you let yourself." She held on to his arm, her gentle fingers urging him toward the pillow.

Too exhausted to fight her, Gryph lay back, the slightest movement shooting pain through his shoulder. The gray fog swirled around his peripheral vision, shadows sneaking up to claim him. He closed his eyes, giving in to the darkness. "Why didn't you turn me in?"

As if from the bottom of a deep well he heard her answer, "Because I know what it's like to be different."

Selene stayed by his side through what remained of the night. When it came time to open her dress shop above her apartment, she would leave it closed for the day. The man in her bed needed her more than women needed the vintage and whimsical dresses, beautiful, colorful blouses and artistic jewelry her business was known for in the city.

Gryph's wounds had taken more out of him than he would have admitted. He burned with fever for hours and every time he moved, the pain shot through him, triggering the beast within.

Exhausted from little sleep and the stress of caring for her strange patient, Selene was drifting off in the chair beside the bed when her cell phone rang.

Selene hurried to the kitchen to answer and keep from disturbing her patient.

As soon as she clicked the talk button, Deme's urgent voice asked, "Selene, honey, are you okay?"

"Yes, I'm fine." She laughed softly. "Did you expect anything else?"

"With a strange man in your apartment, I didn't know what to expect. Is he still there?"

Selene turned toward the bedroom.

Gryph lay as still as death, his face flushed with fever.

"Yes, he's still here."

"Do you want me to come over? He hasn't attacked you or anything?"

"No, he's too far out of it to be a danger."

"What about when he comes to? I can be there in five minutes. Just say the word."

"No." Selene was firm. If Gryph changed in front of her, Deme might not understand. She sure as hell wouldn't agree to let him stay in Selene's apartment after that. "What's the status of the woman who was attacked?"

"She regained consciousness for a few minutes, but she was so distraught, we couldn't get her to answer questions or identify what attacked her. We're at the hospital now, hoping she'll come to long enough to describe her attacker." As a member of Chicago PD's Special Investigations Division, Selene's sisters, Deme and Brigid, had an inside track on any case that defied the norm. Last night's attack was right up their ally.

"Let me know what you learn."

"We had the ME examine her wounds."

"Isn't that a bit premature?"

"Her physician wanted a forensic look at what he saw."

"And?"

"They both confirmed it was some kind of animal attack."

Selene's hand tightened on the cell phone. "Did they say what kind of animal?"

"No, only that it was large enough to snap her neck and paralyze her. If she lives, most likely she'll never walk again."

Selene drew in a long breath, empathy for the girl weighing deeply in her mind. What if she was wrong? What if the man in her bed was the beast who'd attacked the woman?

She focused on the man lying against her sheets for a long moment. She could sense no latent savagery in him. No hunger to kill. Even when he'd half shifted in pain, she hadn't sensed that he was capable of killing without cause. He wasn't the one.

"Selene, are you there?"

Selene shook her head and returned her attention to her sister. "I'm sorry, what did you say?"

"Brigid is with me. I can send her over to assess the guy in your apartment, if you'd like me to."

"No, Deme." She gripped the phone. "You didn't tell her about him, did you?"

"No. I respected your wishes. Although if you're comfortable with him in your home, why be secretive? We're sisters. Since when do you keep secrets from any of us?"

Since the man in her bed had a beast inside him. "Please, just let me get him well. I'll tell the others once he's able to get around on his own."

"By that time, he might be well enough to attack you. I tell you, Selene, I'm not happy with the situation. It's bad enough watching over a stranger who's been attacked. I don't want to know what it feels like to stand over one of my sister's hospital bed."

"I'll be okay. I promise."

"Well, I'm coming by later today. Whether you like it or not."

"He's unconscious now. Let him wake before you do."

She snorted. "I'm not liking this."

"Duly noted." Selene sighed. "Don't worry, Deme. I'll be careful."

"Yeah, yeah. I'm sure that's what this woman said as she stepped into that parking garage." Deme hung up.

Selene sagged against the counter.

She could hear the man in her bed moan, the moan changing to a low rumbling growl as he thrashed, the sheets slipping low over his waist.

Tired, but determined, Selene prepared another of her mother's poultices, wet a clean washcloth and filled a basin with fresh water. She laid them on a tray and carried them into the room.

With great care, she removed the bandages and plucked away the old poultice a little at a time. The wound was an angry red around the edges. When she applied the damp washcloth, the man jerked to a sitting position, his gaze wild as he slapped her wrist away as if slapping a paw at her. His eyes were glazed, his cheeks flushed with fever.

"It's okay." She pressed a hand to the uninjured shoulder. Speaking softly, she urged him to lie down.

As if he understood, he eased to his back, grimacing, his lips drawing back over long catlike fangs.

As she removed the poultice from the wound, she talked softly. "I've never met a man quite like you."

He winced and growled, small hairs rising on his neck and arms. Fascinated, she stopped cleaning and reached out to touch the hairs. "What are you? Half man, half beast? I have a million questions for you when you are up to answering." She sang her words, soothing him as she applied the new remedy and bandages.

By the time she finished, his face had paled alarmingly and his body shook so hard his teeth rattled.

She pulled the sheet up over his chest.

"Shh, you'll be okay," she said, worried when he shivered so hard he shook the bed. Even after she'd covered him with a blanket, he trembled and his jaw clenched.

Afraid he would go into shock, Selene did the only thing she knew to do. She stripped down to her panties and slipped beneath the blanket and sheet, pressing her warm body against his cold skin. Careful, so as not to touch his wound, she draped an arm over his belly and a leg over his thigh. Curling her body around his, she held on, praying to the goddess the fever and shock wouldn't be the end of him.

Slowly, the tremors lessened, dropping from constant to intermittent and finally, they stopped altogether.

Warm alongside him, and tired beyond exhaustion, Selene lay her face against his chest and closed her eyes. His deep, even breathing reassured her that he would be okay while she took a short nap. Sleep claimed her instantly and with it began the dreams...

Wandering through the dark, she recognized the tunnels. They were just like the ones she and her sisters had traversed beneath Chicago to save the youngest of her sisters from an evil Chimera a couple of years ago.

So dark...

Selene carried a flashlight, the beam barely lighting the way, pushing against the inky blackness like a hand shoving back heavy drapery.

The longer she walked, the longer the tunnel seemed. She stepped over old railroad tracks, discarded pallets, pipes and debris, searching for...whatever, she wasn't quite certain.

Something clattered behind her. Selene stopped to listen. Nothing but the eerie silence. When she started walking again, she sensed something moving with her, getting closer.

At a T-junction, she ducked to the left, clicked off her flashlight and waited, barely breathing so that she could hear the sound of footsteps treading softly in the passage.

There it was.

The soft steps, moving slowly toward her. Not those of a human but the close succession of patters on the ground like those of a four-legged creature.

The closer it moved the faster her heart beat and the more shallow her breathing. She was afraid if she made even the slightest sound, she'd give away her position.

Just as the creature eased to the junction, Selene flicked her thumb over the on switch, shining her light into the eyes of the predator, hoping to blind it while she made her escape.

The red eyes of a wolf shone back at her like twin

blood orbs in a face so dark it blended into the black of the tunnel.

Selene screamed and backed away, the hand holding the flashlight shaking so badly she almost dropped it.

It was huge, as big as any man, only twice as menacing. Its lips curled back, exposing long, sharp teeth, and it emitted a growl so frightening, Selene spun and ran through the tunnel.

"Help me!" she cried, her voice echoing off the empty walls. No one was there—most sane people didn't venture into the subterranean underworld beneath the city. She was alone, being chased by a wolf. She ran, knowing she couldn't outrun the creature.

Her foot caught on a broken rail and she crashed to her knees.

The wolf caught up, braced its paws on either side of her and breathed its hot breath onto the back of her neck, as if waiting for her to turn over. To face her death.

Selene rolled to her back, clutching her pentagram between her fingers, unable to close her eyes to the wicked gleam in her attacker's face, knowing she would witness her own death.

The wolf's body tensed, his mouth opened and he bunched his muscles.

Then a tawny golden flash of sinew and fur hit him head-on, knocking the wolf onto his back.

Selene scrambled backward, grabbing for her flashlight as a mighty battle for supremacy raged in the beam of her light between the wolf and a glorious male lion.

The wolf lunged at the lion, his teeth sinking into the lion's shoulder.

Selene gasped. "No!" She pushed to her feet and would have thrown herself at the wolf, but hands held her back.

"Let me go. I have to help," she whimpered.

"Shh," a low male voice crooned. "It's okay."

"No, it's not." She wept, struggling to free herself. "He'll die."

"It's only a dream," the voice said. A hand smoothed the hair back from her forehead. "It's only a dream. Come little angel, wake up."

"A dream?" Selene whispered. Rising from the darkness, she blinked her eyes open...

Selene stared at the glow-in-the-dark stars she'd tacked to the ceiling shortly after she'd moved into her small apartment. The stars reminded her of the night sky filled with twinkling stars that dispelled the darkness and gave promise of the vastness of the universe.

A solid warmth pressed against her side. She turned her face, her cheek resting against skin—a lot of skin. Selene tipped up her chin and stared into golden eyes and lips quirked at the corners.

"The angel awakens." His words rumbled in his chest, echoing into her ear. His arm shifted beneath her head, his hand cupping her shoulder.

"I must have fallen asleep," she said.

"I think you and I must have been having the same dream. I woke only moments before you."

"I was being attacked by a—"

"Wolf?" His brows descended. "I saw you."

"But then a lion saved me." Selene's eyes widened. "Was that you?"

His gaze grew guarded. "I should be going." He tried to sit up, growled in pain and fell back against the pillow, wincing at the effort.

"You're in no shape to go anywhere."

"I can't stay here."

"Why not?" Selene leaned up on her elbow before she

realized she was only wearing her bra and panties. She lay back down, her face burning.

His eyes flared, the pupils dilating. He opened his mouth to say something.

Selene placed a finger over his lips. "Don't get any ideas. I only lay here to warm you when you were going into shock." She cupped his cheek. "It seems the fever is gone." Sitting up, she pressed a pillow to her breasts. "You won't need me to keep you warm."

His good hand closed gently around her wrist. "Stay."

"But I'm not dressed."

"I know. And neither am I." His voice had lowered to a warm rumbling purr. "I feel a chill coming on."

Selene frowned. "Yeah, right."

His body shook and his face tightened in pain. "Please. It's your bed, and you need sleep as much as I do."

"I don't know you."

"I'll keep the monsters away from your dreams."

"What if *you're* the monster?"

"You've already proven you can tame my beast."

She wavered, the warmth of his skin tempting her. "I'll need to change your bandages soon."

"They can wait." He tugged on her hand, drawing her back to the bed.

"I *am* tired." She settled against him, trying to read into his mind. She couldn't hear his thoughts, could only feel his emotions or see flashes of images. They weren't malevolent so much as hot and lusty, sparking an answering heat deep in her core. "I shouldn't." Her hand rested on his chest.

His muscles hardened, his skin stretching tight. "You should sleep," he whispered.

Ha! Sleep was the furthest from her mind as she lay almost naked against this ruggedly powerful and mysterious man. The longer she lay there, the more she wondered what it would feel like to press her lips to his skin.

An image of lips brushing the top of her head was followed by a featherlight stirring at her temple. Selene's breath caught in her chest.

Her heart tripped over itself then thundered against her ribs. She shifted until she faced him, staring up into his eyes. "Did you kiss me?" she asked, her voice little more than air.

His mouth quirked upward. "Had I really kissed you, you would know."

Every logical thought in her head screamed for her to get up, get dressed and throw this man out of her apartment. But logic didn't rule when it came to Gryph. Her heart had firm control and was moving forward, the momentum sweeping her with it.

Bolder than she'd ever been in her life, she leaned up until her mouth hovered over his. "Then kiss me so that I'll know."

He chuckled, the mirth dying as his gaze claimed hers and his head rose to close the distance between them. His hand wrapped around her hair and pressed her into him and he claimed her lips, his mouth slanting against hers, his tongue snaking out to dart between her teeth, sliding the length of hers, the surface coarse, sensual, enticing.

Selene slipped her hand behind his head, her fingers threading through the longish, thick, golden mane, tangling and tugging, to get closer still. Half lying on his good side, she inhaled the musky scent of male and something more primal. Her body ignited, her skin on fire from breast to thigh where it met his. Her center tightened, her channel growing slick.

A low purr rumbled in his chest and his hand flexed and skimmed across the small of her back to cup the curve of her buttocks. His fingers massaged the flesh, sliding into her panties and between the seam of her thighs, finding her entrance.

Her insides clenched, a wash of liquid dampening the path as he pressed his finger inside her.

Her mouth consumed his, she sucked his bottom lip between her teeth and moaned as he swirled the digit inside her.

Selene let go of his lip and arched her back, her head tipping back as she basked in the rush of sensations shooting fire through her veins.

Gryph raised his injured shoulder and cried out. "Damn!"

Yanked back to reality, Selene slid off him and stood in her bra, then adjusted her panties, her eyes wide. "That shouldn't have happened."

The man in her bed nodded, his hand pressing gently against the bandage over his shoulder. "You're right. I'd be taking advantage of the situation."

"You? You're the injured party." Selene grabbed a short champagne-colored silk robe and jammed her arms into the sleeves, pulling the edges closed around her. "I'm sorry. I don't know what came over me." She grabbed the washbasin and rag and rushed from the bedroom into her little kitchen, where she stood with her back to the open door, her body trembling. Not from fear, but from coming so close to making love with a stranger, and then pulling back. She still wanted him and—damn it—he was injured, practically a prisoner in her bed until he could get around on his own.

Selene sucked in a deep breath and let it out slowly. She had to get a grip, go back in there and dress his wound. The sooner he was well, the sooner he'd be out of her bed, her apartment and her life.

As she filled the basin with fresh, clean water, mixed more of the magical poultice and grabbed another clean cloth, she squared her shoulders and called herself a fool for falling into bed with a stranger.

With her mental pep talk fresh on her mind, she entered her bedroom.

Gryph lay on the bed, the sheet covering all the right places but it was tented.

By the goddess.

Selene nearly dropped the basin. Her hands shook so badly and her body burned, craving to be beneath the sheet sporting the evidence of his desire.

"You don't have to do this," he said.

"If I don't, your wound will get infected and you could die."

"So?" he said. "You don't owe me anything."

"I owe you human kindness. I'd take care of anyone injured as badly as you."

"Anyone," he said softly. "Selene, what happened a moment ago—"

"Don't." She set the basin on the nightstand. "Let's forget it ever did."

"Problem is...I can't." He nodded toward the tented sheet.

"You can and will." She refused to glance at his groin, focusing on the injured shoulder. "It should never have happened."

"Because I'm different?"

"No, because *I* am."

He frowned and opened his mouth to say something else, but the cell phone in the kitchen rang, saving Selene from further argument. She didn't want to explain why she was different. How would any man like to know she could read his thoughts? What if she could project her thoughts? What if all of Gryph's desire could be a manifestation of what Selene was feeling? Her gift was being able to connect to other's minds. A telepathy of emotions and images.

She ran from the room and grabbed her cell phone.

"We need you at the hospital," Deme said without preamble.

"Why?"

"The victim is awake and we don't know for how long. Hurry."

"I can't leave right now."

"Brigid is already on her way. She should be there to pick you up in less than two minutes." Her sister sighed. "I don't like you being alone in that apartment with that man."

"I'm fine." Selene's gaze shifted to Gryph. "He's not going to hurt me."

"We'll know more as soon as the woman can tell us. We need you here for that, in case she can't speak."

"But—"

"Come, or I'll tell Brigid about your guest."

Her hand clenched around the phone. Her sister wouldn't understand Selene's trust in a stranger. And for that matter, Brigid was more likely to throw a fireball first, ask questions later. With the threat of letting Brigid in on her rescue, Selene had no choice. "Fine. I'll come."

Selene clicked the phone off and scooted back to her bedroom, grabbing her jeans from the floor. "I have to go."

"When will you be back?"

"I don't know." She jammed her legs into her jeans and pulled them up over her hips. Her hands hesitated on the robe. "You won't go anywhere, will you? You're not healed enough."

His gaze met hers, the heat of those golden eyes warming her body all over again. He gave a brief nod. "I'll stay until I'm better."

Selene dropped the robe, without breaking visual contact.

His golden eyes flared, his lips tightened and a low, rumbling purr rose from his chest.

Then she pulled a T-shirt over her head. "I'll be back as soon as I can."

Chapter 4

"I don't know why I had to come." Selene couldn't help worrying about the stranger she was forced to leave behind in the bed, back in her apartment. Alone, injured and sexy as hell.

"I'm sure Deme had good reason. Probably because you can read minds better than any of us." Brigid parked her Harley in the visitors parking area outside the emergency room and kicked the stand down to hold up the big machine.

Selene climbed off, pulling the helmet over her head.

In her biker leathers and with her badass attitude, Brigid was hard enough to stand up against. To keep Brigid from asking questions or entering her apartment, Selene left without inviting her sister in, claiming they'd better hurry. Her Chicago police special detective sister didn't need to know about the man. She'd go ballistic, possibly even fling a fireball or two, if she even knew Selene had him in her apartment.

In the dark hours just before dawn, Selene and Brigid slipped in through the emergency entrance to the hospital. They headed straight for the elevators and the ICU floor where the injured woman was being cared for.

As they rode up in the elevator, Selene let her guard down and stretched her thoughts out, gathering in emotions, thoughts and fears of the people in the hospital. Most were asleep, some dreaming, some having nightmares. Those who lay awake in their beds worried about their loved ones or whether they would live to see another day.

The overall feeling was one of worry and sadness, with one exception. A dark malevolence slithered through Selene's thoughts, skimming at the edges, slipping in and out like a thief. One moment the darkness took shape, the next it pushed her away, making her head hurt with the pressure.

A hand on her elbow made her open her eyes.

Brigid stared at her, her brows furrowed. "Are you all right?"

Selene hadn't realized she'd closed her eyes. Nor had she realized the elevator door had opened onto the ICU floor. She blinked and forced a smile. "Yeah." Then she stepped out onto the highly polished tiles, rolling the strain from her shoulders. Surely she'd imagined the darkness. "Let's get this over with." That way she could get out of this hospital and back to the man called Gryph, lying semiconscious in her bed.

As she rounded the corner of the elevator bank, Selene saw Deme and Cal, Deme's fiancé, standing at the nurses' station, consulting with a doctor.

Deme looked up, the strain in her face easing slightly when she recognized Selene and Brigid. "I'm glad you came." She introduced them to the doctor, who immediately excused himself, leaving the four of them standing beside the nurses' station. Deme tipped her head to the right. "Let's go somewhere we can talk. I could use some coffee." She led them back to the elevator and down to the cafeteria that remained open 24/7.

"Was the woman able to identify her attacker?" Brigid asked.

"The victim's name is Amanda Grant," Cal said.

Selene leaned forward, her breath lodged in her chest. "What did she say?"

Deme's gaze connected with hers and she continued without looking away. "We had a sketch artist draw from her description. Show her what we got, Cal."

Cal Black, the tall, handsome Chicago police officer, pulled a white page from the folder he held and handed it to Brigid. "I've never seen anything like it."

"Me, either," Deme said, her gaze fixed firmly on Selene.

Brigid whistled. "What is it?"

Selene leaned over, her heart beating so fast, it pounded against her eardrums. When the page came into view, she gasped.

Lion eyes stared out at her, and a full mane of hair encircled a half human, half lion face. The same face she'd seen when Gryph had suffered severe pain and changed into something she'd never encountered before. Selene swallowed the lump in her throat. "Miss Grant said this was her attacker?"

Deme nodded. "About that time she passed out. She's been unconscious since. The police chief has a copy of this and will be circulating it to the press."

That dark spirit flitted through Selene's thoughts again and she winced, pressing her fingers to her temples.

"Are you okay?" Deme leaned forward and grabbed

Selene's wrist. "What the hell?" She stared down at where her fingers touched Selene's skin. "Where did you get these bruises?"

Selene pulled her hand free. "Must have hit my arm against my stair rail."

"Like hell you did." Deme reached out and pulled her close to study the marks. "*He* did it, didn't he?"

"He who?" Brigid closed the gap between them and took Selene's hand from Deme. "Who did this?"

"No one." Selene glared at Deme, wishing she'd shut up and left Brigid out of it.

"Selene and I found a man down by the river and took him to her apartment," Deme announced. "Against my better judgment."

"He was injured." Selene tried to pull her hand free form Brigid's grip. "I only wanted to help."

"And a hospital wasn't good enough for him?" Brigid snorted and let Selene have her hand back. She stood with her arms crossed over her chest. "What am I missing here?"

"Yeah. What are we missing?" Gina, followed by Aurai, stepped into the cafeteria. Now all of her sisters were here. "The nurses' station said we could find you here."

Selene stared across at Deme. "You called everyone?"

"I got the feeling this was something that could potentially involve all of us."

"It doesn't. It only involves me." She spun around and paced away from her sisters, turned and marched back. "I only needed assistance getting him into my apartment, or I wouldn't have asked for your help."

"Thanks." Deme's lips twisted. "I thought we were sisters. Aren't you the one always preaching that we shouldn't keep secrets from each other?" she demanded.

"What is it about this man that has you ready to lie by omission to your family?"

With her four sisters staring at her accusingly, Selene had no other choice but to tell the truth. "He's different."

Brigid shook the paper with the sketch at Selene. "Just how different?"

"He…" She shook her head, the dark, painful consciousness stabbed through her mind, closer this time. Selene gasped, clutched her head in her hands and doubled over.

"Selene?" Deme grabbed her arms and helped her straighten. "What's wrong?"

"Something dark…" She pressed fingers to her temple to stop the pain. "Evil."

"Where? At your apartment?"

"No." She looked up, her gaze turning toward the hallway outside the cafeteria. "Here."

"Here? Something evil in the hospital?"

Selene staggered toward the door. "Amanda…must get to her." Without waiting for an answer, she ran to the elevator, stabbed at the button and then waited, her hands twisting together as the elevator made its slow descent to the cafeteria, every second stretching excruciatingly. When the doors finally opened, Selene fell in and jabbed the button for the floor where the ICU was located. Cal jumped in with Deme, Brigid, Aurai and Gina close behind before the doors closed.

"Hurry," Selene whispered as the elevator whisked upward.

"What is it? What do you sense?" Deme asked.

"Amanda's in trouble." The elevator door opened and Selene darted out.

"Selene!" Cal called out. "Wait. Let me go first. It might be dangerous."

Selene couldn't hear him for the roaring in her ears, the pounding of her heart nearly beat out of her chest. The pain throbbed with so much intensity that her breathing grew shallow and she couldn't get enough air into her lungs. She dropped to her knees, clutching at her throat.

"Selene." Cal reached her first.

She pushed him away, pointing to a hallway, unable to push any air past her vocal cords because she couldn't get air into her lungs. When he wouldn't go, she pushed him again.

Brigid squatted in front of her. "What is it, Selene?"

She pushed her away, too, her vision dimming, her head getting light. "Amanda—"

Brigid's eyes widened and she sprang to her feet. "Something's happening to Amanda."

"I'll stay with Selene, you guys go!" Aurai dropped to the tiled floor with Selene and slipped an arm around her sister. "Breathe, Selene. You can do it. Please. Pull yourself out of Amanda and come back to me." Aurai turned Selene's face to her. "Look at me."

Selene stared into her sister's pale blue eyes. The overhead lights glowed off her bright gold hair, almost blinding her with the intensity. A light, a bright light to follow, to drift toward.

"Selene!" Aurai shook her head. "Snap out of it." She raised her hand and slapped Selene across the face.

The contact brought Selene back from the light, back to the cool hard tiles of the hospital floor. She stared into her sister's eyes, seeing her for the first time, kneeling on the ground beside her.

Selene gasped in a huge breath and let it out, her breathing returning to normal, her vision clearing. Then the malevolent presence wavered in her mind, making her jaw tighten and her temple ache. "He's getting away." She lurched to her feet, holding on to Aurai.

"Who's getting away?"

"The one who attacked Amanda." Selene stumbled down a hallway toward a stairwell.

"You can't go after him, Selene." Aurai grabbed her arm and held her back.

Cal ran out of an ICU room shouting, "Get a crash cart in here!" Gina, Deme and Brigid joined him.

Critical-care nurses raced for the woman's room and for the equipment necessary to save her life.

Selene and Aurai ran to join the others in the hallway, staying well out of the way. "What happened?"

Deme shook her head. "Someone smothered Amanda."

Selene pointed to the stairwell. "He went down the stairwell."

Cal ran for the stairwell and shouted over his shoulder, "Deme, call Security, get them to block the exits."

"I'm coming with you," she said.

"I'll make that call." Aurai ran for the nurses' station.

"I'll take the elevator down." Brigid ran in the opposite direction.

Selene started to follow Cal and Deme, but Aurai yelled at her. "No, Selene. Go with Brigid. You're not strong enough yet." She pointed toward the elevator where Brigid waited. The bell rang, announcing the car's arrival, and Brigid stepped in.

Selene dove for the elevator, catching it as the doors closed.

When she turned, she saw Aurai talking on the telephone, a frown denting her smooth young forehead.

The sense of evil was fading, the tightness easing in Selene's head. "He's getting away."

"Not if I have anything to say about it," Brigid said through clenched teeth.

Thankfully, the elevator went all the way down without stopping on even one floor. Whether it was because Selene was willing away anyone who dared to touch the buttons or just luck, she didn't know or care. The main thing was to get to ground level before the killer.

The bell rang, the door opened and Brigid leaped out. Selene followed more slowly. She closed her eyes and felt for the presence. Her senses only picked up on the worry and sadness surrounding the hospital. The evil had gone away…vanished.

"Brigid!" Selene called out as her sister hit the exit door.

Brigid came to a sudden halt and looked back over her shoulder.

Selene shook her head. "He's gone."

Deme and Cal emerged from the stairwell, breathing hard. They stopped in the emergency room lobby, staring across at Selene.

She shook her head. "We're too late."

Brigid cursed. "Well, I'm going out to look anyway."

"I don't even feel him anywhere close. It's as though he dropped off the face of the earth, his presence disappeared so quickly."

Aurai emerged from the bank of elevators and ran across the lobby to join her sisters. "We missed him?"

Deme nodded.

"Damn." Brigid punched a fist into her palm. Then she turned toward Selene, her eyes blazing. "The man you took to your apartment, did you lead him here?"

Selene shook her head, her stomach knotting. "He didn't do this."

"Are you sure?" Brigid crossed to stand in front of

Selene, anger flowing from every pore of her body, her very presence heating the air around them all.

The anger surrounded Selene, filling her senses. She staggered backward. "I'm sure. He didn't do this."

"What about the picture? The one Amanda had drawn before she was murdered." Brigid's lip curled up in a snarl. "Was your guy the one in the picture?"

Selene stared out at the faces of her sisters, all waiting for her answer, all wearing accusing expressions. She couldn't lie to them, but if she answered, she'd damn the man in her apartment. She inhaled and let the breath out before she said, "Yes."

"What do you want to bet when we get back to your apartment, your guest is gone?" Brigid punched out of the hospital, running toward her Harley.

Selene had to sprint to catch up to Brigid or be left behind. She prayed the man was still lying in her bed. Then at least it would prove he wasn't the man who'd attacked Amanda Grant and returned to finish the job.

Gryph's eyes fluttered open. It took him a few moments to comprehend that the puffs of clouds and blue skies were nothing more than a mural painted on the ceiling of the room he found himself in. Stars were tacked amongst the clouds in an odd day-night combination. The soft bed and sweet-scented air contrasted sharply to the musty dampness of the underground he'd grown up in. He sat up, wincing at the soreness in his shoulder.

He must have dozed off or passed out after Selene left. Over an hour had passed, his shoulder already felt better, and his vision had cleared. One of the benefits of being a shifter was that once the injuries had been addressed his body regenerated quickly. He rose, wrapping one of the sheets around his middle, and paced the interior of the tiny two-room apartment, his strength returning with every step, even as the walls closed in around him.

Light, colorful fabrics draped the windows. The furniture, a scattered array of mix-and-match items, most likely found at yard sales, appeared lovingly restored with new fabric and accessorized with bright throw pillows and blankets. Every color in the rainbow was represented, none appearing out of place, as if they all worked to get along in the close confines of the interior.

In the living area, a rich red overstuffed sofa took up most of the space. On a coffee table in front of the sofa stood a candleholder in the shape of a pentagram, each point holding a small tea candle whose wicks had been burned at some point in time. Facing the sofa was an old-fashioned gas fireplace set against one wall and surrounded by a bright mosaic of tiles, adding even more color to the room. Over the fireplace hung a large filigreed pentagram, encased in a circle. Fine images inscribed in the design of each point of the pentagram represented spirit, air, fire, earth and water.

On the wooden mantel stood a photograph of five women, one of whom was Selene with her rich brown hair. Another was the red-haired woman he vaguely remembered, who'd helped get him into the basement apartment. The women held hands as they faced the camera and smiled. Clearly they cared about each other. Sisters, if not biologically, then by their strong connection to each other.

Despite being at the bottom of the stairs and in the basement of an older building with only a couple of windows filtering sunlight into the room, the space breathed of warmth and comfort—what Gryph had always thought a home should be. The atmosphere filled Gryph with a sense of longing he hadn't experienced since he'd been a small child, and was led to the surface at nightfall to experience a sunset so grand and beautiful he'd cried.

Gryph shook off the feeling of home and spied a small television settled on a corner of the breakfast bar between the kitchen and the living area. He switched it to the local news station and rolled his sore shoulder, gritting his teeth at the pain.

A newswoman stood in front of the Chicago trauma-and-critical-care hospital, the wind whipping her hair into her face as she gave her late-breaking report of an attack on the streets of Chicago.

"A young woman was brought to the hospital late last night after being brutally attacked and left to die when leaving the theater in downtown Chicago. Admitted to the trauma center, she only had minutes to speak to the police before she was taken into surgery. A forensic artist was able to compile a rough sketch of her attacker before the surgeon arrived. Just to let you know, the woman made it through surgery and is now in recovery, expected to live. Whether she'll walk again remains in question.

"Folks, as crazy as it appears, were posting the image of her attacker. The police department isn't quite sure what to make of it, and neither am I, but if you see anything like it, call 911 and report the location and time of the sighting. If such an animal is loose in the city, the sooner we capture or kill it, the safer we *all* will be."

A drawing replaced the images of the reporter and the hospital.

Gryph's heart thudded against his ribs as he stared at a crude drawing of a lion's head with a man's face. It was him.

Chapter 5

Gryph continued to watch the television newscast. The sketched image of him was replaced by the reporter. "This just in—the victim was in ICU after surgery when she was attacked again and smothered to death before anyone could get to her." Police units, lights flashing, rolled in beside the newswoman. Officers leaped out of their squad cars and raced into the building.

His blood freezing in his veins, Gryph realized what saving the woman had cost him and the rest of the outcasts who lived their lives beneath the city streets. With an animal like him identified as the beast who'd ravaged a woman on the streets, every police officer would be searching all the nooks and crannies in the city. If they dug too deeply, they would locate the Lair.

He'd put them all at risk of discovery. And whomever had attacked the woman outside the theater in the first place was still running free and had gone back to finish the job.

He had to get out of Selene's apartment. She'd seen him in his half-changed form. She'd know the drawing was of him, and she might return with the police to haul him in for murder. Or if she didn't turn him in, and the police found him there, he'd bring her down with him. The evidence was stacked against him by an eyewitness, who was dead. If Selene chose not to hand him over to the authorities, she could be arrested for aiding and abetting a suspected murderer.

With purposeful strides, he entered the kitchen and pulled open the compact clothes dryer, removing his cloak and the tattered remains of his trousers. He stepped into the ripped pants. The shirt was beyond repair. Rather than leave it there as evidence against Selene, he shoved it into a pocket, slung his cape over his shoulder and hurried toward the door.

Gryph paused by the small window beside the door, pushed aside the frothy mauve curtain and lifted the edge of the blinds to peer out at street level. It wouldn't be long before people ventured out onto the early morning city streets. The sidewalks would fill with workers headed to their jobs.

He unlocked the door and eased it open. The sun had yet to top the horizon and spill over the crowns of the skyscrapers. For the moment, nothing stirred, nothing moved in front of Selene's apartment. Lights remained off in the buildings surrounding the little dress shop and its basement apartment. One by one the streetlights blinked off.

Still weak, but getting stronger, Gryph slipped out the door, up the stairs and eased into the gloom. Years of blending into obscurity had refined his skills at disappearing.

Rounding the corner of the building, he paused and listened. The rumble of an engine grew louder until a dark motorcycle turned onto the street and slowed in front of the dress shop. Two people got off.

He risked being seen or caught, but he had to know if the rider or the passenger was Selene.

Both riders pulled off their helmets. The driver's long, inky-black hair slipped free and fell to her shoulders, the streetlight shining down on it, giving it a blue glow. The second rider struggled with the strap beneath her chin.

Gryph held his breath as she finally loosened the strap and lifted the helmet up and over her head. Long, chocolate-brown hair slipped free and fell in a dark cloud, tumbling down her back. Selene, with her brown hair and deep, brown-black eyes, stood beside the motorcycle.

The driver pulled a gun from a holster beneath her black leather jacket, released the clip, checked her ammunition and then slammed it back into the handle.

Selene laid a hand on the woman's arm. "Brigid, that's not necessary."

"I'd ball up some fire, but I don't want to burn your place down."

"He wasn't the killer. Whoever it was had an enmity, an evil about him that was palpable. I never sensed that with Gryph."

"So his name is Gryph, is it?" The woman with the coal-black hair and ice-blue eyes held out her hand, palm up. "Give me the keys."

Selene dug in her pocket and handed over the keys. "He's not a monster."

"Could have fooled me."

"He's different," Selene insisted.

"I'd say. How many people do you know who look like him? He's a freak and he killed a woman tonight."

Gryph ground his back teeth. *I didn't kill anyone*, he wanted to shout aloud, but he held his tongue.

As the black-haired woman descended the stairs to the basement apartment, Selene turned in his direction. She stared straight at him, as if she could see into the shadows.

His eyesight, keen in the dark, both from experience at moving in the blackness of the underworld and from the inner lion's nocturnal nature, could see the worry lines etched into her brow. He inched backward, ready to run.

A soft sensation brushed across his senses as if someone reassured him that it was okay. At the same time it gave him a gentle mental push, urging him to leave.

Headlights filled the street as an SUV turned the corner and came to a stop behind the motorcycle.

The redhead who'd helped Selene get him down the stairs climbed out of the driver's seat and a man unfolded from the passenger side. A blonde and a brunette emerged from the back doors.

"Is he still here?" the redhead called out.

"About to find out," said the black-haired woman with the key in her hand.

"I tell you, he wouldn't hurt anyone," Selene insisted.

"You saw what he did to that girl in the hospital. We all saw the bruises on your arms. He's dangerous."

"He didn't kill her and he didn't mean to hurt me."

Guilt squeezed Gryph's chest so hard he couldn't breathe. He'd hurt her when all she'd tried to do was help him. Balthazar had been right all those years. The only place for him was below the surface. Up until the past five years, he'd lived his life in the underworld, where the misfits and freaks existed judgment-free, and where he wouldn't be unleashed to hurt innocents. Amassing a fortune and building a business didn't make him any more human.

"You say he didn't hurt her, but the victim had the forensic artist draw a picture of her attacker, which happened to match your guest from what you say." The redhead nodded to the woman at the bottom of the steps. "Sounds pretty damning to me. Let's check out your monster."

The woman at Selene's door unlocked it and pushed it open, her gun held in front of her. A light went on inside the apartment. She disappeared inside. A few moments later, she called out, "He's gone."

It was time to go. Gryph turned to leave. His night vision temporarily compromised by the headlights, he didn't see the soda can until he nudged it with his bare foot. The can skittered across concrete, making a metallic grating sound that echoed against the buildings in the alley.

"What was that?" the man who'd arrived in the SUV said from the top of the stairs.

"Probably the wind," Selene said.

Gryph stood poised to run, out of sight of the group standing near Selene's apartment.

"I'll check it out," the man said.

Gryph took off, aiming for the corner of the building at the end of the alley. If he could get there before the man rounded the side of Selene's building, he could lose him in the maze of downtown structures.

Channeling his inner beast to give him speed and strength, he ran, reaching the corner as a shout rang out.

"Stop or I'll shoot!"

He didn't slow, didn't stop, just ran as fast as his feet could carry him. At the end of another building, he flew around the corner, crossed the street and ducked around another structure.

Before long, he was several blocks away, the sound of pursuit long disappeared.

Careful to ensure he wasn't being followed, he entered a back alley, swung wide around a large trash bin and a stack of decaying pallets, and stopped in front of a solid steel door. He dug his fingers into a chink in one of the bricks beside it and unearthed a key that fit the door.

With practiced efficiency, he twisted the key in the lock. The door opened inward, revealing stairs that led into a basement. Replacing the key in the chinked-out space, he entered, closing the door behind him. On quiet feet, he moved through the darkness, descending to the basement floor.

One of the oldest buildings in downtown Chicago, it had access to the tunnel system beneath the city. Built in the early nineteen hundreds, city planners had hoped the tunnels, with their narrow-gauge rail cars, would allow quick and efficient transportation of cargo to and from the buildings downtown, freeing some of the congestion of the streets above. The plan failed, but the tunnels remained, for the most part. Some had collapsed, others had been filled in when skyscrapers had been built on top of them. The labyrinth provided a warm, safe haven from weather and prying eyes to the inhabitants who called it home.

Having been abandoned as a small baby, unable to fend for himself, Gryph had known no other domicile. If not for the benevolence of Balthazar, he'd have perished in the harsh Chicago streets, unwanted, unloved and unprotected. When he'd discovered a good living in day trading five years ago, he'd accumulated enough wealth to own his own building downtown and he dared to move closer to the light.

Like many who had been forgotten, shunned or thrown away, like himself, he'd lived his life in the shadows of the city, rarely venturing out. Even in his own building, he rarely stepped outside, preferring to limit contact with humans to avoid any mishaps or triggering his inner beast to appear.

Balthazar warned him about the surface dwellers and their lack of compassion or understanding of anything strange or unusual. His adoptive father taught him to sense the rise of his inner beast and control the urge to morph into his animal form. As a child, spikes in emotion had thrown him into animal form.

At those times, for his own protection and the protection of the others in his care, Balthazar had confined Gryph to a cage, letting him out when he'd returned to human form. Those times had marked him deeply. He'd hated the cage and everything it stood for and vowed never to be caged again.

Kindhearted yet firm, Balthazar had taken him into the Lair, brought him up as his own son. The older man collected strays like him, bringing them into the fold, helping them to assimilate into a life in the shadows, finding useful work for them, from running street cleaners to servicing office buildings at night when everyone else slept.

Balthazar raised Gryph and another lost boy who'd been the child of a crack addict with no other family to call her own or to claim the child. Broke, homeless and strung out, his mother had holed up in the basement of a building. When the maintenance super had discovered her temporary lodgings, she'd tied her baby to her back and hidden beneath a trap door, clinging to a ladder to avoid being evicted. She'd descended the metal ladder until her feet touched the bottom of the well.

A light glowing at the end of a long tunnel led her to the center of the underworld city. Balthazar had taken her in, offering food and shelter for her and the baby as long a she resisted the lure of her addiction and promised to keep the community secret.

Not long afterward, her hunger for drugs drove her back to the surface. She never came back.

The baby named Lucas came to live with Balthazar and Gryph when Gryph was eight.

Balthazar, a college professor in his former life amongst the humans, had taught Gryph and Lucas to read and write, instilling in Gryph a love of classic literature and the arts. Determined to give them all the educational advantages of the surface dwellers, he'd set up a computer lab in the Lair, running ethernet cables from above to allow them to learn about the world in the light.

Though he'd never traveled outside the city limits of Chicago, Gryph could name all the countries on earth. He'd learned about finance and day trading, becoming quite good at following the news and anticipating market changes. Using seed money he'd earned cleaning buildings after sundown, he'd amassed a small fortune he kept stashed in banks stateside and abroad. Five years ago, he'd come out of the darkness to buy the building he now lived and worked in.

He'd dreamed of one day visiting other countries.

For now, his home was in the basement of his office building with a shaft that led to the maze of passages beneath the city.

He worked his way to the center of the Lair, passing old Joe Lowenstein, fast asleep in his cubby, blankets tucked up to his chin to ward off the chill and damp of the underworld. Joe had been a chemist until he'd been severely scarred in a chemical accident. Half his face melted off, blind in one eye and his right arm completely useless, he now made a living carving beautiful figurines out of wood, with his good hand and a vise grip Balthazar had appropriated from an abandoned workshop. Each finished figure sold in an upscale art gallery on 35th Street for thousands of dollars. Still Joe slept in the cubby, his money accumulating in a bank.

He rolled over, his good eye opening. "Gryph? That you?" Joe's voice was as mottled as his face, gravelly to the point of almost being unintelligible.

"Go back to sleep, Joe," Gryph whispered.

"Trouble's brewin'," Joe rasped.

"How so?"

"Some say it's you." Joe rubbed a hand across his scarred cheeks. "Don't know what they're talkin' about. Balthazar will know."

"I'm headed there now. Thanks for the heads-up." Gryph continued toward the forgotten city's center, the hairs on the back of his neck spiked, the inner beast clawing at his insides to be released to attack the tension in the air.

A small gathering ringed the entrance to the rooms he, Balthazar and Lucas had called home for so long. It was nothing more than a former storage area beneath the city, where supplies had been kept. It consisted of four large compartments. Gryph, Lucas and Balthazar each claimed one as his own and the fourth was a common area they still gathered in to share the events of their days or nights when time permitted. Balthazar had refused to move in with Gryph in his building nearer the surface, claiming he preferred the darkness to the light after all these years.

Now Balthazar stood at the entrance, his voice ringing out over the angry shouts of the small crowd. "Keep calm, people. I'm sure there's some kind of misunderstanding."

"What if he leads them down here?" someone asked.

Balthazar held up his hand. "He wouldn't. He's much

too smart and cautious to let that happen. Please, go to your homes. Let me talk to Gryphon. I'm sure he can clear it all up."

"Clear up what?" Gryph strode across the wide, open space where the old tracks had switched and turned down the long tunnels leading to the ends of the old city. He clutched his cloak around him, to hide the tattered remains of his clothing beneath.

"There he is!" a woman shouted. "What have you done? What kind of monster are you to attack a defenseless woman?"

"I've done nothing." Gryph stood straight, his shoulders thrown back. "I'm no more a monster than any of you."

"You killed a surface dweller." Raymond Henning, a man with the ability to blend into the surroundings as easily as a chameleon, shook his fist at Gryph. "We all took an oath when we came to live here. No one hurts anyone. Now that you've let your beast kill, it will crave more bloodshed."

"I didn't kill anyone, and I don't crave blood," Gryph said, his voice urgent but calm. These were his people. Most of the money he earned through his day trading and businesses went to providing food and comfort for them. He'd only ever told Balthazar, whom he'd sworn to secrecy.

"How soon before they start a city-wide manhunt for you?" A young woman with blue and green fish scales on her neck and face pulled a scarf up over her head, her eyes darting around the group. "They'll find us and drag us back into the light, or worse, exterminate us."

"Will any of us be safe if the authorities discover what we have built down here?" Raymond asked.

"No!" shouted a mutant man with a bulbous blob completely covering the entire left side of his face spoke up. "We're doomed. The authorities will track him here. They can't have a killer on the loose in Chicago. It's bad for tourism. They had an eyewitness, they know his face, and they won't stop until they string him up for the woman's murder."

"I won't lead the authorities down here. I'm careful to preserve what we have. It's as much my home as yours. You all know me." He waved a hand at Raymond. "Raymond, didn't I lead you here when you'd passed out drunk in an alley and given up hope?"

Raymond frowned. "Yeah, but—"

Gryph continued, "Tara, when you first came to the Lair, didn't I show you around the maze of tunnels until you were comfortable on your own?"

The furry woman nodded. "You did."

"Many of you have known me my whole life. Have I ever hurt anyone?"

Many in the crowd muttered no.

Gryph lowered his voice and said softly, "I wouldn't condemn the people I love to exposure to those who don't understand us."

Lucas, who had long dark hair, draped an arm over Gryph's shoulder. "That's right. You all know Gryph. He's a good man. He might not be able to control his beast, but he'd give his life for any one of you."

Gryph frowned at his brother. "I have control."

Lucas's mouth twisted. "Of course you do, even when you're angry, right?" He clapped his hand on Gryph's back. "Always the hero who could do no wrong." Though he smiled, Lucas's lip pulled back on one side in almost a sneer.

Gryph stared at his brother whose hand on his shoulder was tight, his fingers digging in.

Balthazar held up his hands. "You heard the man, he didn't kill the surface dweller. Go home and get some sleep. Everything will be better by morning."

Reluctantly, the crowd of misfits dispersed, muttering and grumbling as they trudged to their makeshift rooms constructed of abandoned pieces of plywood or cardboard in offshoots of the derelict rail tunnels.

Not long ago, Balthazar had worked with a handful of people to tap in to the electrical grid of the buildings, reactivating the lighting system in select tunnels so that they wouldn't have to live in total darkness. For safety's sake, everyone was required to have a stash of emergency flashlights. Every inhabitant knew that when city workers descended into the underground tunnels, they had to make themselves scarce. If they were discovered, the good surface-dwelling citizens of Chicago would force them to the surface, where they'd be pitied and treated as freaks.

"Where have you been?" Balthazar asked as he led Gryph and Lucas into his chambers.

"Recovering." Gryph whipped the cape off his shoulders exposing his naked chest and the bandage Selene had carefully applied.

Balthazar's lips pressed into a thin line. He peeled back the bandages and examined the ragged scabs over Gryph's shoulder. "Who did this?"

"Question might not be who, but what?" Lucas said. "Looks like an animal attack. Did you do this to yourself?"

Gryph cast a tired glance at Lucas. "What reason would I have to attack myself?" he asked, then turned to Balthazar. "The woman was attacked by a large black wolf. I got to her as he was ripping into her."

Balthazar's brow lowered into a *V*. "Wolf, you say?"

"Since when have there been wolves in downtown Chicago?" Gryph asked. "I thought they stayed well north. Could they be shifters?"

"Are you sure that's what it was?" Lucas lifted the tattered shirt. "You didn't black out when you transformed?"

"I didn't black out," Gryph assured him.

"Were you unconscious at all last night?" Balthazar asked.

Gryph hesitated. "Yes. After I made sure the woman would be okay, I left her for the emergency medical technicians and got away before they could see my face."

"But not before the woman saw yours." Balthazar walked to a bookshelf and selected a brown leather journal. "Unfortunately, the victim was able to describe you in sufficient detail for a sketch artist to draw a reasonable likeness of you in your half-shifted state. And equally unfortunate, the news publicized it. Did anyone else see you? Did you pass anyone while you were running?"

Again Gryph hesitated. "No." The lie came hard to him. But he didn't want any of the otherkin to seek out Selene or the other woman and consider them threats to the Lair's existence. The two women had helped him when he might have died of his wounds or from exposure to the potentially toxic river water. The fewer people who knew he'd spent time in Selene's apartment, the better. He hoped that she wouldn't tell the police he'd been there. If she did, it might hit the news and the inhabitants of the underworld would once again see it on their televisions, even in the depths of the tunnels.

Yes, cable television was another improvement, along with internet connection, that Balthazar had been adamant about bringing to the people who lived below Chicago. Because of his desire to bring technology to the underworld, Balthazar had opened up an entire world of learning to Gryph and Lucas.

Balthazar checked Gryph's wound and bandaging. "Since when did you learn about poultices, son?"

Lucas's pale gray eyes narrowed, watchfully.

"I've been studying the internet for holistic cures. It was one of the remedies."

"Made of what?" Lucas leaned close and sniffed. "Some kind of herb and mud?"

"Something like that." Gryph strode into his old room and dug a shirt out of the dresser, his gaze lingering on the world map tacked to the wall.

"Traveling among the humans is dangerous. You risk your life and anonymity each time you walk among them." Balthazar held up a hand. "I know you've been doing it for the past five years, but this was exactly what I feared might happen." Balthazar stood in the entrance to his room. "Last night you thought you had control of your beast, yet you still transformed."

Gryph stiffened. "What else was I supposed to do? I couldn't let him kill her."

"Indeed, but by transforming and showing yourself as such, you've made yourself a target."

"No one in my office knows."

"But the woman you saved saw you with your face half man and half lion."

"I saw the drawing on the television. They won't link it to Gryphon Leone. The features weren't specific enough. She concentrated on the animal."

Balthazar nodded. "True enough. In the meantime, you're better off taking a leave of absence. Tell your office staff you'll be out of the country."

Already shaking his head, Gryph stepped forward. "I can't."

"What is so important you can't lay low for a few weeks until the furor dies down?"

"The charity ball for the children."

Balthazar's lips formed a thin line. "The charity ball. Why do you have to be there?" Balthazar's eyes narrowed. "Can't you just spend the money and let someone else take the reins on planning?"

"My company is sponsoring it. The money raised will go to the homeless children of Chicago. I've helped sponsor it for the past three. This year, GL Enterprises is the main sponsor. The Women's Aid Organization is demanding that the head of GL Enterprises needs to attend the ball to show his support."

Lucas chuckled. "My brother, a home-grown Chicago celebrity. A wanted man in more ways than one."

"Believe me, I'd let them handle all of it, but they said our donations have dwindled and the public wants to know the man sponsoring the ball is fully committed. They're afraid I'm Mafia or something—you know, dirty money."

"That's right, father, the philanthropic Gryphon needs to put in an appearance, to set the old biddies' minds at ease."

"You can't risk it," Balthazar insisted. "If you transform during the ball, you'll have the entire city on you so fast you won't have a chance to escape."

"The children need me."

"They need you alive. Not dead."

"I'll keep my exposure to a minimum. At least until the ball is over. Perhaps, in the meantime, the police will find the animal responsible for Miss Grant's attack and death."

If the animal was a shifter, there had to be others in the city. Gryphon would put out feelers among his staff.

All his life he'd held on to the dream of traveling to other countries. After the previous night, he was certain he couldn't risk getting too far from his haven beneath the city. Where else would he go if his inner beast emerged unbidden? Where would he hide if his secret was unleashed?

"Son," Balthazar said, "none of this would be an issue if you hadn't transformed."

"I had to transform to save the woman," Gryph said.

"And her attacker came after you." Balthazar spoke like it was a statement instead of a question.

Gryph nodded, his thoughts processing the information and coming up with what lay at the back of his mind during his escape to the Lair. "It had to be a shifter."

"Why do you say that?"

"How else could it have entered the hospital without being detected to finish the job it started? A wolf can't open doors without hands."

"Are you sure it was the same person or creature who attacked the woman in the first place?"

"Why would anyone come back to smother her unless he wanted to make sure she didn't expose the true nature of the animal that attacked her?"

Chapter 6

"Chicago Police Department and animal control have issued a warning for citizens and guests to be on the lookout for a man fitting the forensic artist's rendition of the murder victim's attacker. What more proof do you need?" Brigid drummed her fingers on the bistro table at the local delicatessen, where she'd insisted Selene meet her and Deme.

Selene's salad remained untouched on the plate in front of her. She hadn't had much of an appetite since Gryph had disappeared. If only she knew where to look for him, she could set her mind at ease and quit worrying about his wounds and whether he'd healed properly.

Unlike her siblings, she understood why he'd left. The television in her kitchen had been on when she'd gone inside her apartment. He had to have seen the report on the news about the attack on the victim in the hospital.

He'd been there when she and Brigid rode up on the

motorcycle. Selene felt his presence and had sensed him in the shadows at the corner of her building. While her sisters figured his absence confirmed his guilt, Selene knew he couldn't have been the one to attack the woman in the hospital. He'd barely been able to stand when they'd left. When Cal had gone after him, she'd held her breath, praying to the goddess that he would escape. Injured like he was, he might not have been so lucky. Cal was one of Chicago Police Department's best, was in good shape and hadn't lost several pints of blood in a vicious attack.

"Cal said he just disappeared. One minute he ran down an alley and the next, he was gone. The doors into the buildings on either side had been locked. Unless he had a key to one of them, he couldn't have gotten in."

Yeah, he'd disappeared, after stirring up such intense feelings inside her. How far would they have gone had he not been injured? Could she have stopped herself from making love to the man?

"Selene?" Deme stopped in the middle of her conjecture. "Are you even listening to me?"

"Yes." Selene blinked, her cheeks burning. "What was it you said?"

"Is it possible that we have more shifters in the city?" Deme asked.

Selene glanced from Deme to Brigid. "Shifters? As in half man, half animal?"

"Yes." Brigid leaned forward. "If the stranger you had in your apartment could look like a man one moment and a lion the next, who's to say there aren't other kinds of shifters roaming the streets?"

"Seems reasonable." Selene wasn't sure where the conversation was going.

Brigid dug her smartphone out of her pocket and

tapped the screen. "We know whatever attacked Amanda in the parking garage wasn't human."

"Right," Deme agreed. "The scratches and bite marks could only have been a large animal."

Brigid's thumbs flying over the keypad, she continued talking with her head down. "Whoever entered the hospital and Amanda's room was human. An animal would have certainly been noticed well before making it to her door."

Deme nodded. "Undoubtedly."

Brigid's brows drew together. "At least human at the time he entered the hospital, killed the girl and escaped."

"What do you mean?"

Brigid glanced up. "Amanda was attacked by an animal on the street."

"Agreed," Selene said. "Gryph said it was a wolf."

"Though an animal supposedly attacked her, a human thought it important enough to finish her off, right?"

"Right." Brigid glanced up. "I just got word that the surveillance video showed a man dressed in scrubs with a stolen ID entered her room with a chart. Walked right past the guard we had posted. It was shortly afterward that they found her and informed us.

"Unfortunately, before she died, the description she gave of her attacker was that of a lion with a man's face." Brigid laid a hand over Selene's. "Honey, it's a pretty damning eyewitness account."

"On the video, what did the man look like?" Selene demanded.

Brigid shook her head. "Couldn't tell from the video. He was wearing a surgical mask."

"Gryph said it was a wolf that attacked Amanda in the alley, and I believe him. I don't know who the man was who came in the hospital to kill her, but it wasn't Gryph."

"He could have left your apartment right after you did, come to the hospital, waited for us to leave Amanda's room and sneaked in to kill her."

"I'm telling you, he wouldn't have killed her," Selene insisted.

"If he didn't come to the hospital to kill her, why did he leave your apartment and make a run for it? Why not hang around and tell his side of the story?"

"With a description circulating on the television, knowing I'd seen him like…like that, he had to feel like it was run, or be sent to jail for a crime he didn't commit."

"If it was a wolf, we could have a lot more shifters in the city than any of us can imagine. If they can look human, there's no telling who they are or where we should look to find them." Brigid tipped her head toward the man seated at the table beside them, and she leaned close to whisper, "The guy in the seat beside you could be a shifter and we'd never know until he shifted in front of us."

Deme and Selene both looked left at the same time. The man had lifted a large hoagie to his lips and was just about to take a bite when their gazes met.

He frowned, the frown turning into a glare as he turned his chair, put his back to them and bit into the sandwich.

"Who would know more?"

"We could go to a library and research the news reports," Deme offered. "Or check through the police files of all the reports passed to the special investigations team."

"Or we can go to Byron Crownover." Brigid shoved her phone across the table, the screen displaying an internet page identifying strange and unusual happenings in Chicago.

"Who is Byron Crownover?" Selene leaned over the screen and read the title—Chicago's Secret Inhabitants. "What's this about?"

"We've had loads of calls about strange happenings reported to the police department, from sightings of pumas on the streets to a huge bird flying past the Willis Tower with the wings of a hawk and the face and body of a man."

Deme snorted. "Sounds like the people who report being abducted by alien creatures."

"I know." Brigid leaned forward. "But we know from our experience battling the Chimera beneath the Colyer-Fenton College campus, that otherkin exist."

Selene shivered. She and her sisters had nearly been killed trying to save Aurai, the youngest, from the creature who'd taken up residence in the tunnels deep beneath the city.

"Question is—" Deme leaned closer to the phone "—what kind of shifters and how many live here in the city?"

"We need to contact Byron. He's the area expert, although some suspect he's a kook. But if he's got statistics on where the sightings occur most often, that might narrow our search down to a specific location."

Deme pushed her chair back. "Let's talk to Byron. Where do we find him?"

"He's an anthropology professor at Colyer-Fenton College."

Selene's lips twisted. "Why does that not surprise me?"

"Haven't we suffered enough at that place?" Deme asked.

"I'm just glad Aurai is finished with her studies there.

The place still gives me the creeps." Selene's badass sister Brigid shivered.

They'd all come so close to dying trying to rescue Aurai from the Chimera's clutches. Before that time, Selene had assumed the creature with three heads—a lion, a goat and a snake—had been nothing but a Greek myth. The reality was even more frightening than she could ever have imagined.

"I'm coming with you." Selene stood.

"Shouldn't you be minding your shop?" Brigid asked.

Selene gathered her purse, determined to go with her sisters. "I closed it for the day."

"What about the planning for the Women's Aid Organization charity ball? Weren't you supposed to meet with them at five o'clock?" Deme glanced at her watch. "You have fifteen minutes if you still want to make it."

Selene clapped a hand to her mouth, torn between her obligations to the charitable event and going after information that could help them find out who was responsible for a woman's tragic death. "Damn. I forgot all about that. It seems so inconsequential compared to finding Amanda's killer." And proving Gryph wasn't the one to do it.

"I know, but for some of us, life goes on. And the children will benefit from the money raised." Deme patted Selene's arm. "Let Brigid and me do our jobs and you do yours."

"I want to find the killer just as much as you do." Selene straightened. "Even more so."

Brigid's eyes narrowed. "What's so special about this man you rescued that has you so protective of him?"

"Nothing." Selene looked away. "I just don't like to see the wrong man accused of such a horrific crime."

Brigid and Deme both stared at her for long moments.

The intensity of their glances made Selene squirm.

"Something tells me there's more to it than that," Brigid said.

Unfortunately, there was, and damned if Selene was going to tell her sisters. Not when she didn't know what to make of the feelings she had for a man she'd crawled into bed with after only knowing him for a few hours. "I'd better get to my meeting." She turned and almost ran out of the deli.

Deme's hand on her arm stopped her. "Be careful, Selene. Falling for the wrong man could be painful."

"Especially if he's a killer," Brigid said, her voice tight and edgy.

Her sisters' words hit a little too close to home and left Selene wondering what she'd gotten into by rescuing a man-lion. She couldn't regret her actions. Gryph was worth saving. She knew that in her heart. "He's not a killer." Selene lifted her chin, squaring her shoulders. "And I'm not falling for a man I've only met once."

Once outside the deli, Selene checked the calendar on her smartphone and headed for the downtown building of GL Enterprises, where she was to meet with the Women's Aid Organization. She hoped the meeting wouldn't last long because she wanted to spend some time on her own, searching for her mysterious houseguest.

Gryph returned to his apartment beneath his corporate headquarters, redressed his wound and then crawled into his king-size bed and slept until mid-afternoon the next day. Not until he felt someone watching him did he awaken, then he jerked to a sitting position, his pulse slamming through his veins.

He stared at the man sitting with his legs crossed elegantly in a chair beside him. It took a moment for his eyes to focus and his brain to engage before he relaxed. "Sneaking into a man's bedroom can get a body killed."

"I didn't sneak. I knocked on the door, but you didn't answer, so I let myself in to wait." Lucas stared at Gryph's wound. "Thought you'd never wake up. How's the shoulder?"

"Fine." Gryph shoved a hand through his thick hair, pushing it away from his face. He flexed, a stab of pain shooting through his sore shoulder. "What are you doing here?"

"Father asked me to check on you."

"Tell him I'm okay, and not to worry." Gryph flung the sheet back and rose, naked from the bed.

"Many of the inhabitants of the Lair have been pounding at his door. They're afraid."

Gryph stepped into a pair of sweats and pulled them up over his legs and hips, cinching the drawstring. "Tell him I'll stay clear of the Lair until this all dies down."

"Some are calling for you to turn yourself in to the authorities."

Gryph's brow furrowed. "I haven't done anything." He strode through the apartment to the room containing his workout equipment and stepped up on the treadmill.

Lucas followed. "The picture of you is everywhere. If you turn yourself in, they won't have to worry about being discovered."

Gryph started walking, then adjusted the settings to a steep incline and broke into a jog. "I'm not turning myself in." Every time his heels hit, it jolted his shoulder, reminding him of the attack that had cost a woman her life and almost his own. "I need to be free to find the animal responsible for that woman's murder."

Lucas leaned against the wall, crossing his arms.

"Aren't you afraid you'll cross paths with the police working the case?"

"They can't find me from the picture they have unless I change in front of them. I have no intention of providing that opportunity."

"Are you certain no one saw you?"

He hesitated for a moment before responding. "Yes. No one saw me but the victim."

"The inhabitants of the Lair know you. Aren't you afraid one of them will turn you in?"

"I have to trust them. I have no other choice. I can't change who I am or where I've come from." And he would never completely blend into the world of the surface dwellers. It couldn't happen. Not when he had so much to lose and could potentially harm a human. "You're lucky." He glanced at his brother.

"How do you figure?"

"You are human."

His brows rose. "Your point?"

"You can live anywhere you want and you don't have to worry about changing or hurting others. You have choices in your life."

"And you don't?" Lucas pushed away from the wall.

"No one will call you a freak. You're a good-looking guy with a great future ahead of you." And he could love anyone he wanted—otherkin or human.

An image of Selene's dark brown hair splayed out across his skin, the residual warmth of her leg draped over his and her breasts pressed against his side, made him miss a step and he almost fell off the treadmill. He grabbed the rail, sending stabbing pain through his shoulder. The pain brought him back to reality. He couldn't be with a surface dweller. Although he'd established a tentative place in society, maintaining a certain level of anonymity was required to keep from exposing his true nature.

Lucas nodded toward the healing wound. "That's quite an injury you have there. How'd you manage to get away after you were attacked?"

Gryph snorted. "I threw myself into the river."

"I'm surprised you didn't drown."

"I managed to pull myself out."

"But you were gone quite a while. You had to be freezing."

"I managed."

"Did someone help you?"

"I'd rather not talk about it."

Lucas's eyes narrowed. "Ah, it must have been a woman."

Gryph hit the stop button on the treadmill and climbed down. "I have a meeting to attend. Don't you have to be at work?"

"I'm on a sales call."

"Not if you're with me." Gryph stepped around his brother and returned to his bedroom, shedding his sweats and tennis shoes as he went. "I have a business to run, I'm sure you can find your way out as easily as you found your way in. Tell Father I'll steer clear of the Lair for the time being." He stepped into his shower and turned the spray on cool.

Silence reigned as Gryph let the water wash down his body. His wound stung, but was healing nicely. The poultice Selene had used had done the trick.

Selene.

What a mess. She'd saved his life, going above and beyond the role of nurse to keep him warm when he'd nearly gone into shock.

Trouble was, he couldn't get her scent or the feel of her

body against his off his mind. Even now, his groin tightened, blood flowing south. He twisted the water controls to ice-cold and forced himself to think of something else until he had his body under control, then stepped out of the shower.

He dried off, wrapped a towel around his waist and left his bedroom for the kitchen and a cup of coffee.

"Mr. Leone, you have an appointment with Althea Washburn of the Women's Aid Organization in ten minutes." Marge Reingan, his executive assistant, held out a clipboard with several papers on it. "Sign here." She handed him a pen.

"What am I signing?"

"A letter authorizing the purchase of the building on Wacker."

He scribbled his signature.

Marge flipped a page. "And here." She pointed to a line on the page.

Gryph signed. "I guess you heard about the attack?"

She nodded.

"Do you think I should turn myself in?"

"Not if you didn't do it." She took the pen from him. "Besides, too many people depend on your generosity. What would happen to them?"

"Balthazar can manage my assets."

"Not like you do. He has no desire to rejoin the surface dwellers."

"I've always wondered why. As a human, he could blend in easily."

"Not all who live in the Lair are otherkin."

He smiled at Marge. "Like you?"

She nodded, the gray hairs standing out more in the overhead lighting. "It's a safe haven to many."

"I know and I wouldn't want anyone to be displaced

by my elimination. That's why I have Balthazar on my accounts. If anything should happen to me—" and it almost had "—he will have access to the money from my corporation. He can continue to support the inhabitants of the Lair."

"Why do you let them continue to think Balthazar provides for them when it's the money you make that helps them survive?"

"I owe my life to Balthazar. He took me in when my own mother couldn't take care of me."

Marge nodded. "He has a big heart."

"He's taken in a lot of strays, like me, Lucas and just about everyone in the Lair."

"Many of us wouldn't be alive today if not for him."

"Exactly." His chest swelling, Gryph remembered the many times Balthazar had played with him in the tunnels, how he'd taught him to read and write. Balthazar had been responsible for getting them connected to the internet and online for distance learning. He wanted every person in the Lair to have a chance to provide for themselves should they choose to live amongst the surface dwellers. "Balthazar deserves the credit."

Marge tucked the clipboard against her chest. "Do you want me to cancel your meeting with Mrs. Washburn?"

"No, I'll see her."

"Are you sure that's a good idea?"

"The drawing that's circulating doesn't look enough like my human form to present a danger." His only danger lay in the hands of the woman who'd rescued him. He could only pray she wouldn't turn him in.

Marge's gaze went to the wound on his shoulder. "Did the animal that killed the woman do that?"

He nodded.

"What was it?" she asked.

"I suspect it was a wolf shifter." He paused, waiting for her response to his announcement.

She didn't even blink. "My husband, God rest his soul, was a member of a pack that lived on the edge of the city. I can put out some feelers, if you'd like."

He'd known, but didn't want to ask for her help. Since her husband's death, she'd had no connection with the wolves. "Thank you, Marge. I'd appreciate that." He nodded toward the door. "In the meantime, I'll get dressed and see you up in the office."

"Whatever you do, don't let anyone take you to jail." Her lips formed a thin line. "Shifters don't do well in captivity. My husband's cousin was jailed for stealing. He didn't last long behind bars. Captivity made him crazy."

"I'll bear that in mind." He had no intention of spending time in jail. Metal bars gave him the hives. But if he wanted to clear the air, he had to do something to find the murderer.

Marge spun and headed for the elevator, then stopped and faced him as she waited for the door to slide open. "Oh, and, Mr. Leone, I believe you didn't hurt that girl."

"I'm glad someone does." He smiled.

"A more troubling concern is that whoever did could strike again."

He nodded. "I know." All the more reason to do something before it happened again. "Stall Mrs. Washburn. I'll be up in five minutes."

"Yes, sir."

"And, Marge. Anything you can find out about the shifter packs…"

"I'll get right on it." The elevator door slid open and she stepped inside, turning to face him.

"Hey, Marge." He held a hand over the closing door, forcing it back.

"Sir?"

"What was it like for you, as a human, to be married to a shifter?"

Her gaze drifted to the far wall, her mouth softening. "Like a woman in love. What he was didn't matter. It was *who* he was that I fell in love with." Her attention returned to him. "Why do you ask?"

"No reason." He let go of the door.

This time, Marge put her hand out to stop it from closing. "Gryphon, you know I love you like a son. Okay, a grandson." She cupped his chin. "Life is way too short to squander a chance at love. If you fall in love with someone, look at what you have in common, and don't focus on your differences."

They exchanged glances, then the door closed, leaving Gryph alone.

Marge had been with him since he'd moved closer to the surface. She'd lived among surface dwellers in her youth and part of the time after she'd met and married her husband, Tom.

When Tom had come down with a brain tumor, she'd moved him to the Lair to live out the remainder of his days so he wouldn't be judged if he shifted without warning.

After his death, Marge had gone to work helping Balthazar raise Gryph and Lucas. When Gryph's success in day trading had grown to the point he had to invest what he was making in other businesses, he'd moved closer to the surface and taken Marge with him, giving her an apartment in his building. One with floor-to-ceiling windows to let in as much light as possible. He knew she loved the sun. And he loved her like the grandmother he'd never known.

What he hadn't expected was that she was a wizard at

managing his office and his schedule, and her compact frame was every bit a match to stand up to unwanted visitors.

Gryph hurriedly dressed in a business suit, shirt and tie, hating the constriction around his throat. The suit was his cover. He glanced into the mirror, his skin smooth with no sign of the fine hairs that appeared when he shifted. No one would recognize him in the drawing being circulated. No one but Selene and the other woman who'd helped him into her apartment.

With a deep breath, he stepped into the elevator that whisked him to the top floor of the building. No amount of rationalization could erase the sense of foreboding that went with him.

Chapter 7

"It was nice of GL to offer his conference room for our planning efforts, don't you think?" Mrs. Washburn said.

"Indeed. That and his funding." Mrs. Stockton laughed. "Without it, we'd have had to have the ball in some squalid concert hall instead of at a grand hotel. We've already sold out of tickets and the finest of Chicago society will be in attendance."

"Isn't the ball open to the public?" Selene dared to ask. Surrounded by the matrons of Chicago's wealthiest, she was outnumbered and feeling out of place. Perhaps she wasn't right for the costume-planning portion of this particular event, except she had the most popular dress shop in downtown Chicago and she knew her unique clothing and designs suited the fairy theme the ladies had chosen for this year's charity ball.

Mrs. Washburn's brows rose as she directed a stare down her nose at Selene. "Yes, but who can afford the price of the tickets? Only the most connected."

"And isn't that as it should be?" Mrs. Stockton said. "We want high-dollar contributors to come and give lots of lovely money."

"For the children," Selene reminded them.

"Of course." Mrs. Washburn tapped the paper in front of her. "How are the costumes coming?"

On the spot, Selene straightened. "I pick up the completed fairy costumes after our meeting is over."

"You can have the servants' costumes delivered directly to the hotel, and the Women's Aid Organization's dresses delivered to my house, please."

"Shall I schedule a seamstress to do any last-minute adjustments?"

"No, no." Mrs. Washburn waved her hand. "I'm sure none of us have changed measurements significantly in the past two weeks." She eyed the others in the room, as if sizing them up. "With the ball only days away, it would be foolish to scramble at the last minute."

"Very well." Selene nodded. "Whom do I submit my bill to?"

"Leave it with the man at the front desk on your way out of the building. Security will ensure it gets to GL for payment."

Selene exited, glad to be out of the room of stuffy women, full of themselves and what their husbands made. She would love to go to the charity ball, if only to see her dress designs on display, but she couldn't afford the ten-thousand-dollar ticket price and really didn't want to be stuck with a lot of Chicago's elite snobs, like the elusive GL of GL Enterprises.

Outside the conference room, she waited in front of the elevator. She could hear the car rising up the shaft. As it grew closer, her pulse quickened, her breathing growing shallower. If she wasn't going crazy, she could swear the person inside the elevator was the man she'd rescued from the side of the river. She could sense his presence.

She punched the button several times, but the car didn't stop at her floor. Instead, it continued upward toward the roof of the building.

It had to be him. Selene spun back toward the conference room and burst through the door. "Who owns this building?"

Mrs. Washburn frowned at the interruption. "GL, of course."

"Of GL Enterprises. One of the richest men in the city of Chicago," Mrs. Stockton added.

"What does he look like?" Selene demanded.

"Not many of us have actually had the pleasure of meeting the man. He prefers his privacy."

"However, I have." Mrs. Washburn straightened, lifting her nose to the ceiling. "Why do you ask?"

Her heart beating against her ribs, Selene backed out of the room. "No reason. Excuse me. I apologize for disrupting your meeting."

As she closed the door between her and the ladies, she heard Mrs. Washburn say, "Silly girl. Are you certain she's the best for the costumes?"

"With the ball only a couple of days away, you're asking now?" The other woman laughed. "We'll have to make do."

The woman's words hurt. She'd put a lot of time and effort into the design, planning and construction of the costumes. Not to mention fronting the effort with her own hard-earned funds. If they backed out now, she'd be out thousands of dollars and she still had to pay the seamstresses.

"She came highly recommended—" Mrs. Stockton said.

Selene retreated to the elevator and punched the up

button. When the car opened, she stepped in and glanced at the control panel. The penthouse suite had its own button and a key card slot beside it. The only way she'd get into that suite was with a card, or if she accompanied a person with a card.

She hit the button for the lobby and rode the car to ground level.

At the desk, she paused in front of the security guard. "I'd like to see GL." She frowned, ashamed to admit she didn't know what GL stood for. If she had to guess, the G stood for Gryph.

Her stomach fluttered. Surely this couldn't be only a coincidence. How serendipitous could it be to have a meeting in a building Gryph owned?

She shook her head. Was she thinking right? Gryph, the man she'd found shivering beside the river, half-dead and wounded, was a multimillionaire? A member of Chicago's elite? A man of great wealth and assets? If that was the case, why had she found him wounded by the river?

Unless he'd been wounded by the attacker that killed the woman or…the woman he'd killed.

Her mouth tightening, Selene waited for the guard on duty to respond.

"I'm sorry, he's not available for meetings."

Selene turned away, disappointment and frustration bubbling up inside her. She could walk away and never know if the man passing her in the elevator shaft had been Gryph or she could stay and try again to get to the penthouse. Full of determination and not willing to take no for an answer, she pushed guilt aside and turned back to the guard. Instead of reading his thoughts, she stared into his eyes and said, "You want to take me to GL."

"I do?" The man chuckled, shaking his head. "'Fraid not."

Selene gathered a deep breath, focused all her energy into her next words. "You will take me to GL."

The security guard tipped his chin downward, his gaze clouding. He shook his head and pinched the bridge of his nose. "Let me see if he's in."

She maintained her focus, as if applying steady pressure to get a ball rolling. "He's in."

His hand left the phone and he stood. "If you'll follow me, I'll take you up to meet with GL."

"Thank you." Selene stepped into the elevator and waited for the guard to slide his card into the slot and punch the penthouse button.

"You don't need to go with me," she said.

The guard smiled politely and stepped out of the elevator, saying, "I don't need to go with you."

The door slid closed and Selene was on her way up to the penthouse, guilt, elation and a wicked sense of power flooding her. She'd manipulated the security guard's mind. A thrill shivered across her skin. She'd never done that before. Able to sense thoughts and emotions, she'd never attempted to plant ideas in another person's brain. Until now. Had she pushed the boundaries of right and wrong?

The elevator rocketed to the top. The closer she got, the more certain she was that she'd find Gryph. She could sense his presence, feel his emotions, and knew without a doubt it was him. As the elevator slowed, her feet grew cold, her nerve slipping down the shaft. Though she'd found him irresistible in bed, he might not have been as taken. Not that she was going after him to finish what they'd started. She told herself she only wanted answers. Nothing more.

As the elevator doors slid open to reveal an opulent suite of offices, Selene shrank against the back wall, suddenly afraid of his reaction to seeing her. Would he be angry that she'd found him? Would he deny having ever set eyes on her? Would he call security and have her thrown out?

An older woman rose from behind a large mahogany desk. "Are you lost?" she asked, stepping forward.

"N-no." The elevator doors started to close, sparking life into Selene's limbs, she stepped through into the office suite. "No, I'm not lost," she said with more conviction. "I'm here to see GL."

"I don't have any appointments scheduled on the calendar for him." She stood in front of Selene, her small stature no less intimidating.

When Selene couldn't come up with a reason why she was there without an appointment, she clamped down on her bottom lip.

"I see. Perhaps I should call security." The older woman backed toward her desk and lifted the phone.

"No." Selene stepped forward and focused on the woman, channeling her thoughts toward her.

The older woman frowned and pressed her fingers to her temples. "I'll just call…" She glanced up at Selene, her eyes narrowing, the irises flashing a deep red.

A stabbing pain ripped through her own temples and her mental push slammed back into her, making her stagger backward and hit the closed elevator doors.

What the hell? Selene pressed her fingers against her throbbing temples, but refused to give up. "Please. I need to see your boss. I need to know—"

"Marge, I hear voices out there. What's going on?" A tall man in a black suit stepped through the doorway to the adjoining office. His tawny blond hair, thick and full, was combed back from his forehead and hung down to the top of his collar.

"Gryph." Selene's knees wobbled at the startling pushback from the seemingly gentle Marge, and from seeing the man she'd been thinking about nonstop since she'd found him by the river.

"I was about to call security to escort this woman out of the building." The older woman lifted the phone on her desk.

"No." Gryph held out his hand. "I'll deal with her." His gaze never left Selene's. "Please, come into my office."

Marge stared from her to him and set the phone back in the cradle.

"Aren't you supposed to run an errand or something?" Gryph turned to Marge as Selene gave the other woman a wide berth and slipped by him into his office.

Selene caught the older woman's frown and the dark red that flared in her eyes. What the hell had just happened? She'd never had someone slam her thoughts back at her. Nor had she run in to anyone whose eyes could change from plain gray to bloodred in a heartbeat.

"I guess that means you want me to disappear." Marge rolled her eyes. "Just say so." She grumbled as she gathered her purse from a desk drawer. When she straightened, a small smile played at the corner of her lips. She patted Gryph's face. "I hope you remember what I said." She turned toward Selene and poked a finger at her, her smile fading. "Hurt him, and you'll answer to me." Her back to Gryph, her eyes flared red again, then she stepped up to the elevator, the door slid open and she disappeared inside.

"What did she say that you're supposed to remember?" Selene asked, a shiver shaking her.

"Nothing." Gryph closed the door to the office and stood silent, staring down at her.

Selene's stomach turned cartwheels and her gaze focused on his mouth. Her tongue slipped across to moisten her suddenly dry lips. She wanted him to take her into his arms so badly, she could practically taste him. *Kiss me.*

In one smooth movement, he gathered her into his arms and crushed her lips with a breath-stealing kiss that rocked Selene all the way to her core. She ran her hands up his chest and curled them around his neck, pressing her body as close to his as was possible with her clothes still on.

He cradled the back of her head as he deepened the kiss, his tongue sliding past her teeth to stroke hers in a long sensuous caress. His free hand slipped down her back to cup her bottom, pressing her pelvis against the growing ridge beneath the fly of his trousers.

When he finally set her back on her feet, he was breathing hard and so was she.

"I shouldn't have done that," he said.

"Why not?"

"I'm not the man for you. You have to understand."

A horrible thought insinuated itself into her mind. What if her longing had pressured him to kiss her? And now that he'd done it, he was regretting it.

Her knees shaking, afraid she'd gone too far by following him up to his office and possibly pushing thoughts into his mind, she opened her mouth to apologize but what came out was "You left without saying goodbye."

He leaned his forehead against hers. "I had to. I couldn't let you be accused of harboring a murderer."

"You didn't—"

His finger pressed against her lips, warm and gentle. "I know, but the sketch they're circulating is pretty damning. You and the redhead who helped me into your apartment were the only humans who could identify me and place me close to the scene of the crime."

"I wouldn't have turned you in." She shook her head. "And my sister..." Selene bit her lip. "I'd like to think she wouldn't have, either."

"I couldn't bank on it. I don't know you well enough." He smoothed the hair back from her face. "And I couldn't count on your sister's silence. When everyone showed up at your place, I knew it was time for me to leave."

"Those were my sisters."

"And the guy?"

"My sister's fiancé." Selene's lips quirked. "He's a cop. And two of my sisters are consultants for the Chicago PD."

Gryph pushed a hand through his thick hair. "Wow. I believe I'm in up to my eyeballs in trouble. Are they going to show up any minute to rescue you from me?"

Selene shook her head. "They don't know I'm here. They think I'm at a meeting for a charity ball. Which I was until I...found you." She'd been about to tell him that she'd sensed him.

His thumb brushed across her lips and he bent to sweep his mouth across where his thumb had been. "And will you tell them where you found me?"

"No," she whispered into his mouth. "At least not until we find out who killed the woman."

"And then?"

"If you want me to." Right then she didn't want to tell anyone she was with him. That way she could have Gryph all to herself. Maybe she'd rekindle those feelings he'd inspired, the hot, lush lust she'd never before experienced in any other man's arms. She hadn't been able to push him out of her thoughts since she'd discovered him.

"I haven't stopped thinking about you," he whispered against her lips.

If he hadn't been so close, the heat of his body spreading fire through her veins, she might have paused to consider his words mirroring her own thoughts. But she couldn't think past his lips sliding across hers in a slow, intense attack on her senses.

Coarse hands slipped the strap of her dress over her shoulder and his mouth trailed kisses down the column of her throat to the curve of her neck and across her bared shoulder.

Urgent need drove her to shove his jacket over his shoulders.

He shrugged free and let it drop to the floor.

Selene fumbled with the buttons on his shirt until she had them all loose down to where the tail disappeared into the waistband of his trousers. She yanked it free, finishing the job, and the shirt joined the jacket on the floor.

Gryph's hands found the zipper on the back of her dress and slid it down to the base of her spine.

Without hesitation, she stepped back and slid the straps down her arms. The dress fell, leaving her standing in front of him in a white lacy demi bra and matching white thong panties.

Gryph's gaze raked across her from the tip of her head, caressing her all the way to the apex of her thighs. His golden eyes flashed.

A cool air-conditioned draft brushed across her skin and made her pause for a moment, heat rising up into her cheeks. She raised her hands to cover her breasts. "I'm sorry. I didn't come to seduce you."

He chuckled, lifted her hand and drew her close. "I'm beginning to get a complex. I thought *I* was seducing *you*."

Selene's gaze shifted to the wound on his shoulder and she frowned. "You'd never know you'd been injured so badly such a short time ago."

"Thanks to the magic in that poultice, I'm well on the way to recovery."

Selene stiffened at the reference to magic. Did he know that she was a witch? Did she dare tell him about her ability to sense emotions, sometimes read minds and now push thoughts into others' heads? He should know so that he could make a rational decision about where they were going with whatever it was raging between them. "About the poultice..." Her hands landed on his bare chest, his muscles flexed and all her logic flew out the window.

"Hmm?" Gryph nuzzled her neck, kissing a path down to the swell of her breast.

Intense pleasure washed over her in a tsunami of sensations, rendering her incapable of breathing properly. Her fingers skimmed across his chest, testing the strength and hardness of the muscles beneath the smooth skin.

His hands slipped down her back and grazed the rounded curve of her buttocks. Then he scooped her up, wrapping her legs around his waist, walking her across the room to the huge black desk in the center of the room. Gray light shone through the floor-to-ceiling windows from a storm-laden sky, the clouds dimming the vastness of the Chicago skyline, making the atmosphere more tempestuous, as well as intimate.

One hand balancing her against him, Gryph swept his other hand across the surface of his desk, sending papers and pens flying across the room. Then he settled her bottom on the cool, hard surface, laying her back until she was sprawled across the middle, her legs dangling over the side.

Her body was on fire, her mind caught in the blaze, unable to generate coherent thoughts. Selene rode a wave of lust so powerful she wanted nothing more than to be naked, with Gryph between her legs, riding her hard and fast.

The man-beast bent over her, pushing aside the bra's cup to take a beaded nipple between his teeth and biting gently. He swiped a raspy tongue over the taut nub.

Selene arched her back, pressing closer to his magical mouth.

He wrapped his lips around the taut bud and sucked, drawing it deep into his mouth. His hand slid down over her belly, angling toward the tuft of curls covering her sex.

Selene stilled in anticipation of his fingers finding and stroking her there.

Releasing her breast, he seared a path to the other breast, pushing aside the bra to shower equal attention on the opposite side, then continued his storm of passion across her torso and down to join his hand, sliding between her swollen folds.

Selene moaned, her body writhing against the wooden desk. She wanted more, wanted him inside her, filling her, stretching her channel with the huge member she'd born witness to when she'd undressed him.

Gryph parted her folds and, with one long finger, stroked the small strip of flesh packed with the most sensitive nerve endings in her body.

The force of sensations made her moan, her thighs spreading, welcoming him in. A wash of liquid coated her channel, warm, wet and ready to accept him.

Her fingers joined his and guided them to her aching entrance.

One long finger entered her, then another and another until he had all four fingers easing in and out of her.

It wasn't enough. "Please," she said, her voice raspy with her need. "I want you inside me."

His hand froze for a fraction of a second, then he ripped her panties down her legs and tossed them across the room.

Selene sat up and reached for his belt buckle, while he pulled his wallet from his back pocket and removed a small foil packet. He tore the edge with his teeth and removed the condom.

Selene unbuckled his belt and eased his zipper down. His cock sprang free into her hand, long, thick and hard. Her tummy tightened and her breasts tingled as she gauged his length and girth. Praise the goddess, he was big.

"Are you sure?" he asked, holding back. "What if I'm too big. What if I change?"

Her hands circled him, caressing him from tip to base, reveling in the feel of steel encased in velvet. "I'll take my chances."

His jaw was tight, his breathing ragged. "I don't want to hurt you."

"You won't." She gripped his arm with one hand. "Please," she pleaded, past caring that she begged, anxious to feel all of him inside her. She held out her hand for the condom.

He placed it in her open palm and threaded his fingers through her hair, his gaze capturing hers, the hunger in his eyes so real it burned through her.

Before she rolled the prophylactic over him, she scooted off the desk, dropped to her knees and ran her tongue across the rounded head, poking into the small hole, oozing come. Smooth and musky, he tasted good. Selene flicked the sides, running her tongue the length of him all the way down to the base.

His fingers dug into her scalp, pressing her down over him.

She took him into her mouth, swallowing him until the tip of his member bumped the back of her throat.

He withdrew and she grasped his buttocks, dug her nails into his flesh and pulled him back in, loving the taste, texture and feel of him in her mouth. The intimacy of the moment sparked a desire so powerful she lost herself to it.

He pumped in out until his body jerked to a stop and he yanked free of her lips. In one smooth motion, he had her seated on the desk again, his hands caressing her thighs, spreading them wider. "Tell me no, and it stops here."

She slipped the condom over his cock and guided it to her entrance.

With a low growl rumbling inside his chest, Gryph draped her legs over his sinuous arms and eased inside of her.

Selene struggled to breathe as his length and thickness seemed to push the air from her lungs.

He backed off a little until the muscles of her channel contracted around him, urging him closer. He leaned over her, sliding even deeper as he took one of her nipples between his teeth and bit down. The slight pain made her gasp. She caught his head in her hands and pressed his mouth down over her.

He moved in an out, slowly, at first. As the heat built, his body tensed and his movements became more fervent, ardent and all-consuming.

Rising to the edge, her thoughts jumbled, her being an inferno of lust. She forgot to breathe, forgot where she was, that the windows bared her to the sky and that she'd only known this man for a day.

He rammed into her, slamming hard, his thrusts deep, his grip on her ass bruising.

But she didn't want him to stop. She tightened her legs around his waist and rode the passion, wishing he'd thrust harder, rougher. Maybe even let out some of the animal inside him.

Tiny hairs sprang from his skin, his grunts became more guttural and primitive. As he reached his climax, he threw back his head and roared, his face covered in sweat and tawny hairs.

The large brawny fingers digging into her buttocks grew sharper, the extending claws scraping the flesh.

As the pain and pleasure mixed to fling her over the edge, Selene cried out, rocked by the most powerful orgasm she'd ever experienced. She locked her ankles around his waist and held on until they both returned to earth.

She was the first to take a deep breath and let it out on a sigh. Her legs slid down over his hips and dangled over the edge of the desk. She was shaking and spent.

Gryph's fingers loosened, the sharp pain receding as he let go of her bottom. Her skin felt warm and sticky against the desk.

When Gryph raised his hands, he stared at his fingertips, his eyes widening. "Oh, dear God." He rolled her onto her stomach, his hands smoothing over her rounded bottom. "My God, you're bleeding, and I did that." He backed away, leaving her on the desk.

Selene pushed to her feet and faced him. "I wanted it."

"This can't be." He shook his head, backing farther away, mentally as well as physically. "This can't happen again."

She crossed to stand in front of him, naked and feeling thoroughly satiated, but afraid he'd make good on his promise. "Gryph, they are only scratches." She glanced over her shoulder. "See? They've already stopped bleeding."

He stared down at his hands, the claws having receded, leaving only dried blood on his fingers. "I hurt you."

She cupped his face, her thumb brushing across his lips like he'd done at the beginning. "I wanted you. The pain only made my climax better."

"Making love shouldn't hurt."

"For me, it made it even more intense, more sensual." She smiled. "If we were to make love again, I'd want it the same."

"What if I went too far?" He shook his head. "I can't risk it. This ends now." Grabbing her wrists, he shoved her hands away from him. "Get dressed, I'm taking you home."

Selene could feel his anger and fear and she wanted to reassure him that everything was okay. She'd never been more attracted to another individual or more satisfied with sex than what she'd experienced with him.

The solid line of his jaw, the tightness of his lips and the way his brow furrowed made her clamp down on her words and gather her clothing.

She dressed quickly, her body still tingling in the aftermath of mind-blowing sex, her bottom still burning.

By the time she was clothed, she was ablaze with desire all over again.

Gryph stood at the elevator door, his back to her. "Are you ready?"

Selene walked around to stand in front of him. "I am."

"Then let's go. The sooner you're out of my life, the better for both of us."

Selene stepped into the elevator and leaned her back against the wall, her arms crossed over her chest, her thoughts warring. On one hand, she didn't want this to be the end. But the more she reflected, the more convinced she was that her thoughts and desires had pushed their way into Gryph's mind, causing him to transform. He'd been fine and remained in his human form until the point at which she'd wished he'd let go of the animal inside.

Which begged the question: Had he really wanted to make love to her, or had she overlaid his common sense with her own needs and desires?

Gryph took her to the garage level of the building and exited onto a large open area with only a couple of vehicles taking up the space—a sleek silver Ferrari convertible with the top down and what appeared to be an armor-plated, foreign-model SUV that could be as comfortable on a red carpet as a battlefield. He waved a hand toward the latter.

Selene slid into the passenger seat and waited while he closed the door.

Gryph took the wheel and drove toward a closed overhead door. As he approached, the door slid upward and he drove through and out into the Chicago dusk that had arrived early due to the low-hanging clouds.

Selene sat with her hands in her lap, her insides still simmering from making love. She wanted to say something, but the solid granite of his jaw didn't bode well for conversation.

All too soon, he approached her shop building and came to a halt at the curb.

When he started to get out, she laid a hand on his arm. "I can open my own door."

He ignored her, dropped to the ground and rounded the SUV before she could locate the door handle. The door opened for her and he held out his hand.

She laid hers in his and that spark of desire engaged

and sent a flash of desire through her that made her ache all over again.

When she was safely on the ground, he didn't let go of her hand, instead drawing her into his embrace.

"I don't know what it is about you," he growled. "But I'm finding it impossible to resist."

She smiled up at him, her hand resting on his chest. "Then don't." Whether he was feeling that way himself, or she was putting the thought into his head, Selene didn't want to know. All she wanted was to feel his lips against hers.

Gryph lowered his head, claiming her mouth in a long, hard kiss.

Selene melted against him, her body merging with his. As her hands snaked up to entwine around his neck, an angry darkness pierced the veil of lust surrounding her and Gryph, sending a shard of razor-sharp pain through her head.

Selene gasped and broke the kiss.

If not for Gryph's arms around her, she'd have fallen to her knees.

"What is it?"

"I don't know." She struggled to remain upright and forced a wobbly smile to her lips. "I must be tired."

"Let me help you inside."

"No." She shook her head, fumbling for the keys in her purse. "I'll be fine. I just need something to eat and a chance to rest."

"I'm staying."

"I thought you couldn't get rid of me soon enough."

"You're not well. I can't leave you like this."

"You don't have to bother. My sisters are supposed to be by soon."

He hesitated. "Then I'll stay until they get here."

"And risk being recognized by Deme?" Selene inhaled and let out a slow, cleansing breath. "I'm fine. Really." She stepped out of his arms, ignoring the wicked darkness pushing against her subconscious.

Gryph reached into his wallet and pulled out a business card. "If you need me for anything, that's my cell phone number. Call me." He placed the card in her hand and curled her fingers around it.

Selene wanted to hand it back to him. To tell him she didn't need it or him. That he'd been right when he said what they'd done had been wrong and shouldn't be repeated. She wanted to say she agreed with him, but it would all be a lie. What had happened between them had been so very natural and…right. She pocketed the card and turned away before she broke down and cried, or worse, begged him to take her into his arms and hold her until the evil went away.

Obviously reluctant to leave, Gryph remained standing on the sidewalk until Selene descended the stairs and unlocked her door. With a wave, she entered her apartment, shut the door and collapsed against the wood paneling, waiting for the sound of Gryph's vehicle leaving before she let herself slide to the floor, trembling.

Something heinous and hateful had been watching them kiss and hadn't liked it one bit. Its antagonism had been so palpable, it had sapped the energy from her body. The last time she'd felt something this strong, this life-depleting, she'd been at the hospital near the evil that had killed Amanda.

Chapter 8

If Gryph could have flogged himself for what he'd done, he would have. Seeing Selene's punctured skin, blood oozing from the wounds, had been the cold bucket of ice water he'd needed to douse his passion and bring him back to the stark reality he'd known all his life—he couldn't be with a human.

He was a danger to her. Yes, she'd wanted him as badly as he'd wanted her, but *he* had to end it. He could never forgive himself if he caused her harm.

Slamming his foot to the accelerator, he sped back to his apartment in the basement of the GL Enterprises building. Once inside he flung his keys against the wall, stripped his jacket from his shoulders and sent it in the same direction. Rage ripped through him, making hairs spring forth from his skin. He need to run, to get outside in the darkness and charge through the countryside, roaring. But a lion couldn't be so obvious. A wolf could get away with being seen. A lion would be hunted down and shot, deemed unnatural to the area, and a danger to the human population.

And wasn't that what he was? A danger to humans?

He entered his workout room and stepped up to a large punching bag suspended from the ceiling. Channeling his anger and the beast within, he rammed his bare fist into the canvas, not even wincing at the pain in his knuckles and his sore shoulder—the shoulder *Selene* had nursed back to health.

Her scent still lingered against his skin, the image of her lying naked on his desk seared into his memory.

What good did it do to think about her? He couldn't be with her without wanting to make love to her. And God forbid he made love to her again, and hurt her like he'd already done.

He slammed his hand into the bag, again and again, until his knuckles were bruised and raw. Then he hit it again, welcoming the pain.

"Shouldn't you be using gloves?" Marge's voice forced him to stop.

"I thought you were gone for the day," he said without turning to glance in her direction.

"I did, but I'm back with someone you should talk to."

Gryph slowly turned to face her.

"Gryphon Leone, meet my brother-in-law's son, Rafe Cain, leader of the Kenyon pack from the north side of Chicago."

Gryph extended a bruised hand.

Rafe's gaze narrowed, and his nose twitched as if he was sizing up Gryph's scent and sincerity. Finally, he took the hand and gave it a firm shake. "Marge tells me the woman killed last night was attacked by a wolf."

"Initially, that's right."

Rafe tipped his head, eyeing the healing wound on Gryph's shoulder. "He do that?"

"Yes."

"Shifter?" Rafe asked.

Gryph's heartbeat stuttered and then pushed on. "I am."

Rafe's lips twitched and he sniffed the air. "Lion?"

After a long moment, Gryph nodded his acknowledgment. He hadn't told anyone outside the Lair of his affliction. It felt oddly liberating to admit what he was to a fellow shifter and stranger.

"Thought so." Rafe grinned. "But I really wanted to know if you thought the wolf was a shifter."

If the situation hadn't been so dire, Gryph would have laughed at himself. He had to be reminded that the world wasn't out to expose him for the lion shifter he was. "He managed to get inside the hospital to finish what he'd started. I don't think a wolf could do that without being noticed."

The leader of the wolf pack nodded. "I asked around and I'd stake my reputation that it wasn't one of ours."

"And you came all the way from the north side to tell me that?"

Rafe's mouth twisted. "No."

Gryph waited. Whatever Rafe had to say might prove to be a link to this case that would help them solve it.

"There's a pack on the southwest side of Chicago that call themselves the Devil's Disciples. As part of the initiation rites, they have to attack influential targets."

"To kill?"

A frown dented Rafe's brow. "That's what had me stumped. The pack doesn't usually kill women. They usually go for the offspring of some rich or influential bastard. And they don't kill."

"What *do* they do?"

"They bite or scratch them deep enough to draw blood."

"And you think they went too far with Amanda?" Gryph shook his head. "As far as I know, she's not from a rich or influential family."

"The Disciples don't go for women and don't kill unless in gang warfare. They turn their targets."

"As in make the human a shifter?" Gryph blew out his breath. "Wow. That means there's a growing population of shifters in the city."

Rafe nodded. "The rich are keeping it on the down low. They don't want their status to be impugned by the knowledge they have tainted bloodlines."

"Why did I not know this?" He turned to Marge.

She shrugged. "It's the first I've heard of it."

"It started about six months ago. Their alpha male was murdered by a fresh turn who took over and started the initiation rites."

"Southwest Chicago, huh?"

"Warehouse area, Archer Heights district. They congregate at night at this pool hall." Rafe handed Gryph a slip of paper with the address. "I'd go with you, but that would start a gang war I'm not ready to commit my pack to."

"No," Gryph said. "It's best I handle this alone."

"After nine is the best time to catch a large number of them."

Gryph stared at the address, then glanced at the clock on the wall. Evening had turned to night and he had an hour to kill until nine. He stuck out his hand. "Thanks for the information."

"Don't mention it." Rafe gripped his hand hard. "Really. Don't mention it. You didn't get this information from me. I wouldn't have passed it on if I didn't think it was important to find and stop the shifter who killed the woman. If word gets out to the general population that there are shifters in the city, the humans will go on an extermination hunt."

"Understood."

Marge showed Rafe to the exit and returned a few minutes later. "Are you going there?"

"I am."

"Without backup?" Marge planted her fists on her narrow hips.

"Who would I take?"

"How about some of the misfits you support in the Lair?"

"Most of them are women, children and broken-down men. They wouldn't be of any use standing up to a gang of young shifters."

His assistant clucked her tongue. "You're going to get yourself killed."

"As long as I stop whoever killed Amanda from taking another life."

Marge frowned. "If it's all the same to you, I like my job, and I'd like to keep it."

Gryph wrapped an arm around her shoulders. "I'll keep that in mind."

Marge hugged him around his waist and stared up at him. "What happened with your woman?"

Gryph stiffened. "She's not my woman."

She harrumphed. "Is that your way of avoiding an answer?"

"There are some things that don't bear discussing."

"She ditched you?" Marge's back straightened like a ramrod. "Say the word and I'll scratch her eyes out."

Gryph frowned down at Marge. "You say that like you mean it."

Marge crossed her arms and stood with her feet slightly apart, like a militant grandmother. "I do."

"Well, it wasn't *her* ditching *me*." He shoved a hand through his hair. "I ditched her."

Marge took a step back so that she could face him head-on. "You like this girl?"

Gryph turned toward the punching bag, flexing his sore knuckles. "Too much."

"Then what's stopping you from seeing her again?"

"There's been a BOLO, be on the look out, issued on me, for one. And then there's the other thing I can't just clear up with a phone call."

"What other thing?"

"The beast."

Marge snorted. "It's a part of you. Has she seen it?"

He nodded. "Partially."

"And she didn't run screaming?"

He'd been delirious with pain and infection, but she'd stayed right there with him, even when he'd roared and half changed. "No."

"That's a good sign." Marge nodded approvingly. "She's not afraid."

"Yeah." He slugged the bag again, regretting it as soon as his knuckles hit canvass. "I'm afraid of what the beast will do to her."

"Your beast doesn't control you, Gryphon." Marge laid a hand on his arm. "*You* control *it*."

He stared at her small older hand. "And if I can't?"

"There's no question about it."

"I can't risk her life to prove I can control my beast. There are…situations…that bring it out."

"Hot-and-heavy sex?" Marge grinned. "I'm old, not dead. My husband always half turned in the middle of making love to me. He even bit me a time or two."

The image of Marge and her husband getting naked in the sheets wasn't one Gryph wanted permanently imprinted in his head. "What did you do?"

"I bit him back."

"Did he draw blood?"

"Not much. It was more of a scratch."

"And you didn't turn?"

"Takes more than a scratch. You have to exchange a little blood."

"Assuming shifting to a lion is similar to wolf-shifting, what if I scratch her and mix my blood with hers?"

"Have you ever thought she might want the opportunity to decide if she's willing to risk it?"

"No." Gryph headed for the door. "She's a happy, healthy and well-adjusted human. I won't subject her to the kind of life I lead."

"Who said she's all that? Do you really know who or what she is?" Marge shook a fist at him and walked toward him. "And what's wrong with your life?"

"I'm hiding in plain sight. I don't travel. Chicago is the center of my world."

"And why is that?" She held up her hand. "And don't tell me because of the beast. You have the most control of any shifter I've ever known."

He shook his head. "Not always."

"You do, when it counts."

"Don't you understand?" He grabbed Marge's arms. "I scratched her. My claws came out and sank into her skin. I drew blood." His heart squeezed so hard in his chest, he dropped his grip on Marge and pressed a hand to the pain. "I can't risk it."

"Fine." Marge rubbed her arms. "Go through your life sad and lonely, and miss out on everything love has to offer. It's your choice." She backed toward the door. "I'm going to my apartment, putting my feet up and watching *CSI*."

"Marge."

Gryph's voice stopped her from punching the elevator button. "You gonna yell at me some more?"

"No." He crossed the room and pulled the woman into a gentle hug. "Thanks. You always know how to bring me down off the ceiling."

"Wouldn't have to, if you'd just use your head, not your..." She glanced at his crotch. "You know." She pushed the button and the doors slid open. Once inside, she looked back at him. "And don't think your pretty little girlfriend is all so human. She might have a secret or two she's keeping from you." The elevator door slid closed.

"Huh?" Gryph lunged for the button and pressed it, but the car had already gone.

What the hell did Marge mean by her parting comment? Selene was human. Wasn't she?

Selene stepped out of the shower, feeling clean and refreshed. The oppressive evil had abated and her world had righted itself.

Well, almost. Her thighs still had a delicious ache and the wounds on her fanny stung every time she sat down, a continuous reminder of the intensity of the passion they'd shared on Gryph's office desk.

No amount of cold water in the shower had cooled her desire. How she wished she'd invited Gryph to come in. But he'd been so bipolar in how he'd treated her. One minute he'd been anxious to leave her with the promise to never see her again, the next he'd volunteered to stay until he was sure she was okay. She sensed he really wanted to be with her, but was afraid he was bad for her. The claw marks had been the clincher for him.

So be it. She didn't need him, or his warm caresses, or the raspy tongue licking the insides of her thighs. No, sir.

She checked her cell phone, half hoping he'd called, changing his mind. Disappointment filled her as she noted two calls from Deme, not Gryph.

She played the voice-mail message, her hand tightening.

"Selene, they've taken Amanda to the Cook County morgue. We've located Professor Crownover and he's asked to see the body. Meet us at the morgue at nine o'clock."

Selene rushed into her bedroom and dove into her dress pockets, her pulse speeding until her fingers touched the slick gray card Gryph had given her. Standing with her hair wrapped in a towel and another wrapped around her middle, she debated calling Gryph and asking him to meet them at the morgue. He had a right to know whatever Crownover had to say.

Then again, if there was big news to come out of the meeting, she could relay the information to him. She'd already interrupted his life and busy millionaire schedule enough by dropping in on him with a surprise visit.

She set the card on her nightstand and hurriedly dressed. Twice she almost lifted the phone and called him.

Dressed in jeans, T-shirt and a black leather jacket, her wet hair combed back and secured in a ponytail, she lifted the card from the nightstand, stuck it into her back pocket and headed for the door to her apartment.

Her hand paused on the doorknob and she reached out with her thoughts, searching for the evil she'd felt earlier.

A lingering thickness hung in the air as if the evil hovered, waiting to manifest itself in something more solid, more physical. A faint warning tremor rippled across her.

Selene grabbed the long, black flashlight she kept beside the door in case of emergency. It was solid and heavy, like the ones cops used as a light or a billy club, depending on what was needed at the time.

Armed, in a fashion, she stepped out the door and rounded the building to the driveway at the side, climbing into her compact Prius.

She drove away without incident; the farther from her apartment she went, the less she felt the disturbing and disconcerting feeling of being watched.

At the morgue, she climbed out of her car and entered the building. A night watchman checked her driver's license and led her back to one of the autopsy rooms, where tables stood in a line like a factory waiting for parts to be assembled. Or in this case, to be dissembled.

At the far end of the room, Deme, Brigid, Gina and Aurai stood with Cal, a man in a white lab coat and another man in a brown tweed jacket. They were gathered near a table with a body on it.

As Selene neared, she recognized the woman on the stainless-steel surface as Amanda Grant. Her body had been stripped and she lay on her belly, her long blond hair pulled away from the back of her neck, exposing the bruising and skin trauma of puncture wounds.

Deme glanced up. "Selene, good. I'm glad you're here. You'll want to hear what the professor has to say."

The man in the brown tweed jacket barely acknowledged her, his attention on the woman's body as he pointed with a scalpel to the wounds at the back of the woman's neck.

"As I was saying, these bite marks are from a large canine. A very large dog or a wolf, to be more specific."

"You're sure about that?" Selene asked.

"I've examined cattle killed by wolves on numerous

occasions. Although they usually attack the hindquarters, the spacing between the canine teeth is narrower on a wolf than on a lion. The lion's is noticeably broader. Most likely a wolf attacked this woman. And it had to be a really big wolf."

"Professor, have you heard of wolves of this size in downtown Chicago before?" Brigid asked.

The professor nodded to the ME and stepped back. "Perhaps we should move this discussion outside the morgue so that the medical examiner can finish his work and get home before midnight."

Selene, her sisters and Cal left the autopsy room and stepped out in front of the morgue with the professor before they spoke again.

"I didn't want to say anything to alarm the ME." The professor removed a handkerchief from his pocket and wiped his hands on it, then dragged it over his face. "I've been studying wolf sightings in Chicago for the past five years, tracking the locations and documenting the time, size and colors reported."

"Sightings?" Brigid asked. "How many?"

"Over three hundred, and counting. The trend has become more frequent over the past year." He waved toward the parking lot. "If you'll follow me, I'll show you what I mean on my laptop."

The group gathered around the professor's older model Cadillac as he pulled his laptop from a case, set it on the hood of his vehicle and booted the system.

When the screen came up, he punched several keys and a map filled the display with red flags marking different locations on the Chicago city map. Many overlapped each other.

"All these were wolf sightings?" Selene asked.

"Those were just the *reported* sightings."

"Why don't we hear about it in the news?" Aurai touched the screen. "Look at all of them."

"The mayor is keeping it low-key. As long as no one had sustained injuries from a wolf attack, he didn't want to alarm the citizens."

"Until last night." Selene's fists tightened. "There seems to be a concentration of sightings in the southwest part of the city."

"Right. In the Archer Heights district. I've set up surveillance there several times. Some of the sightings were added from my own observations."

"So there really are wolves in the city?" Selene's heart soared. "And it wasn't a lion that attacked her? You're positive?"

"I saw the picture posted on the news, like everyone else. Just looking at the picture, I can tell you her attacker wasn't whatever she described. The facial structure was all wrong. Frankly I don't know what that was she had the forensic artist draw. Maybe some hallucination."

Selene knew, but she kept the information to herself.

Brigid pointed to the computer. "Can we get a copy of your data?"

"Sure," the professor said. "Got a flash drive?"

"As a matter of fact, I keep one on my keychain." Deme handed over her keychain, the professor plugged the storage device in and downloaded the information and removed the thumb drive.

Deme took her keys and held out her hand to the man. "Thank you for coming out so late at night, Professor."

"Let me know if there's anything else I can do. I have a daughter about Amanda's age. I'd hate to think there was a man-eating wolf roaming the streets close to where she lives on the northeast side."

"We'll let you know," Brigid assured him.

The professor closed his laptop, climbed into his Cadillac and drove away.

"So, what now?" Selene asked.

"I don't know about you, but—" Deme pocketed her keychain with the flash drive "—I'm headed to Archer Heights to see if I can catch me a killer." She spun toward her SUV.

Selene held up her hand and said in a clear and firm voice, "Hold on."

Her sisters and Cal all turned toward her.

"You heard the professor. Amanda was killed by a wolf. Just like Gryph said."

"Yeah, so?" Brigid frowned. "Your point?"

"You all agree then that Gryph didn't do it?"

Deme nodded. "I'd go as far as saying we're ninety-nine percent sure."

"Close enough." Selene took a deep breath. "I found him."

"Your wounded stranger?" Aurai laid her hand on Selene's arm, her eyes sparkling her excitement. "Where?"

"Doesn't matter where. I think he deserves to know about the professor's research. His life and reputation are on the line for trying to help."

Brigid shrugged. "Then call him. Cal, Deme and I are heading for Archer Heights."

"I'm going with them," Gina said.

"And me," Aurai added.

Selene smiled. "Guess we're all going. Who's driving?"

"Me." Deme pulled her keys from her pocket and headed across the parking lot for her SUV. "I can take most of us."

"I'll follow on my bike." Brigid straddled her Harley and glanced at Selene. "You riding with me?"

"Yeah. Just as soon as I place this call." She strode away for privacy, then punched the numbers on the keypad and hit Call. She held her breath, her pulse beating so hard it reverberated against her eardrums.

"Selene?" Gryph's deep, gravelly voice spread over her like warm melted chocolate.

"We're headed for Archer Heights. We think the killer may be there."

"Wait. I got the same information."

Selene glanced across at Deme. "From what source?"

"I can't say, but I have the address of a pool hall where we might start our search. I've mapped out the area. It's mostly warehouses and low-income housing. We should meet somewhere else and form a plan before we go charging in. The locals might not be so ready to answer questions otherwise."

"Good point."

"Where are you?"

"With my sisters at Cook County morgue."

"I'm less than a mile from you. Stay there. I'm coming." He hesitated. "That is, if you sisters aren't going to shoot me as soon as they see me."

A smile curled Selene's lips. "I'll make sure they don't." When he rang off, Selene rejoined her sisters.

"Ready?" Brigid revved the engine on her Harley.

Shaking her head, Selene told them what she'd learned. "Gryph got a tip on the Archer Heights area and, even better, an address of a pool hall where we might get some answers. He's on his way."

"Good," Brigid said. "I have a few questions for him when he gets here."

Selene lifted her phone like a weapon. "If you even think about shooting him or taking him in for questioning. I'll tell him not to come."

Brigid's eyes narrowed. "Fine. But he better not hurt you, or all bets off."

For a long moment, Selene stared at her sister, torn. She trusted her sisters with her life, but could she trust them with Gryph's? Finally, she sighed. "He wants us to wait here."

"The longer we wait the bigger chance of the attacker going after another victim."

"We don't know that. Archer Heights is a big area, are you going to cover the entire district?"

"She's right." Deme crossed her arms. "If this Gryph guy has a specific address, it could save us a lot of time."

"We need him," Selene said. "We'll wait." And pray her sisters didn't harm him.

Chapter 9

Within minutes of Selene's call, Gryphon pulled up in the armor-plated SUV he'd driven Selene home in. He dropped down and crossed to her.

The redhead Selene had identified as one of her sisters and another woman with jet-black hair stepped in front of him, before he reached her.

A growl rumbled up his throat and he fought to keep it from emerging. "I'm not going to hurt her. I came to help find the animal that killed Amanda."

"These two rude women are my sisters, Deme and Brigid." Selene stepped around them and stood beside Gryph, facing the women. "The other two are Gina and Aurai, also my sisters. And the cop is Cal Black. Sisters, this is Gryph." Her cheeks reddened and she glanced up at him. "I'm sorry, I don't know your last name." She'd made love to him, but there were a lot of things she didn't know about him. And a lot he didn't know about her.

"Leone. Gryphon Leone." Gryph's chest swelled at her show of faith as she stood with him in front of her sisters. The heat from her body ignited those embers he'd thought banked by a few hours' separation, reminding him of how beautiful her pale skin was against the black surface of his office desk.

The sandy-haired sister stepped up beside Brigid, the raven-haired one. "*The* Gryphon Leone?"

Gryph cringed. He preferred to maintain his anonymity. That others outside his corporation knew of him always baffled him. Why would they care? He wasn't his business.

"You know him?" Brigid asked.

"I don't *know* him," Gina said. "But I've *heard* about him. I contracted to clean the built-in aquariums in his corporate headquarters. He's one of the richest men in Chicago."

"By the goddess, we have a celebrity among us." Aurai chuckled. "And one of the hardest to get a picture of. The media would kill to get an interview with him." She covered her mouth. "Sorry, I didn't mean to infer someone in the media would have killed Amanda to get an interview with you, Mr. Leone."

"Please, excuse my ignorance." Deme's voice dripped sarcasm. "I'm not up on the rich and famous."

"Maybe not, Deme." Gina faced her sister. "But you've heard of GL Enterprises, haven't you?"

"Who hasn't?" Deme's eyes widened. "You mean to tell me we rescued the owner of GL Enterprises?"

Gryph nodded.

Selene's lips quirked on the corners.

Brigid wasn't laughing. "Rich or not, we know it was you Amanda drew the picture of."

Gryph's mouth firmed into a straight line. "Mine was

the last face she saw. I was leaving the theater when I heard her scream. I found her *after* the wolf had already attacked. I fought him off, or he'd have finished the job then." He touched his shoulder where the wolf had bit him, the pain still all too memorable. "I stayed with her as long as I could until I heard the ambulance. I didn't attack her."

"The ME and a forensic anthropologist said that based on the bite marks, she was attacked from behind," Selene said, filling him in on what the professor had said about the bite being from a large dog or wolf.

"A shifter," he said.

"You know?" Aurai asked.

Brigid laughed. "Hell, *he's* a shifter. I'd guess he'd know if there were others in the city."

"Not necessarily," Gryph responded. "I shift to the form of a lion. I haven't had much contact with many wolves. However, I know they exist."

"And how many lion shifters are there in the city?" Deme asked.

His chin lifted. "I'm the only one I know of."

"You say you know an address of a place in Archer Heights we can start looking?" Brigid asked.

"I have an address of a pool hall where a gang of wolf shifters has been known to hang out."

"Where'd you get it?" Deme asked.

Gryph shook his head. "Sorry, I can't say."

Brigid crossed her arms and glared at him. "Why should we trust you?"

His lips quirked. "Do you have any better ideas?"

"No." Brigid's arms fell to her sides. "Let's look at it."

He pulled out his smartphone and brought up the map location, clicking on the satellite image that displayed the roofs of homes, businesses and warehouses.

"We can't all go barging into the pool hall demanding answers," Cal said.

"You're not leaving me behind," Selene said.

"Or us," Gina added as she nodded to Aurai.

"Some of us can stay in the vehicle outside the building in case we need to make a quick getaway." Deme stared around the group, her gaze landing on Aurai and Gina. "You two will be in the vehicle, at the ready, if we need a bit of sister persuasion."

The two of them nodded, and Gina glanced at the sky and sniffed. "If we're lucky, it'll rain."

Aurai draped an arm across Gina's shoulder. "We can make our own luck with a little help." She winked.

Selene shot what seemed like a nervous glance at Gryph.

His eyes narrowed. "I don't like the idea of any of you going in. It's a wolves' den, not an ice-cream parlor."

Cal chuckled. "You don't know much about the Chattox sisters, do you?"

He shook his head. "It's not safe. If they choose to attack, they'll outnumber us."

"I have my gun." Cal patted the weapon beneath his black leather jacket. "But it's nothing compared to their talents."

"Deme and I can handle anything thrown our way. We've walked into worse situations." Brigid turned to Selene. "Although I don't like the idea of Selene going in, we could use her skills."

"What skills? What do you mean?" Gryph asked.

"Nothing." Selene glared at her black-haired sister. "And don't worry, I'm going in."

"You'll stay in the SUV with Gina and Aurai," Gryph insisted.

Gina laid a hand on Gryph's arm. "Trust her, she can be our best asset inside."

"I'll be okay," Selene said softly. "I know what to do."

"Those are some of the roughest neighborhoods in the city," Gryph argued. "The humans are more like animals."

Gina grinned. "We can hope the animals are more human."

"Look, Gryph, we can be one of the most formidable opponents anyone will ever meet." Deme glanced around the circle. "Right?"

"Right!" Selene and the rest of her sisters all answered as one.

Brigid clapped a hand on Gryph's back. "Guess we're going to the pool hall. Unless you think it's too dangerous. You can stay here until we come back."

He glared at Brigid.

"Cheer up." Cal checked his firearm. "They're a force to be reckoned with."

"I'm beginning to realize that."

"We'll stop two blocks short of the warehouse and let Brigid, Cal and Deme go in first."

Deme pulled a kerchief from her back pocket, tucked her hair back behind her ears and tied the cloth like a do-rag, securing the knots at the back of her head.

She'd transformed from classy detective in a black leather jacket to a thug in seconds.

Brigid, in her kick-ass black leather chaps and well-worn black Harley jacket, already fit the part. She climbed onto her motorcycle and revved the engine. "Selene, you can't go in like that, get dirty or something."

"These are my best jeans."

"Exactly. Roll in the mud or something." Brigid's gaze skimmed across the neatly pressed line down the front.

"They're too new, and switch shirts with Aurai. That white T-shirt will get you killed. You look like a high-school prep."

Selene's cheeks bloomed bright red. "We can change in the SUV."

"Just don't get yourself killed." Aurai grinned, running her hands over her shirt. "It's one of my favorite Smashing Pumpkins T-shirts."

"Nice to know where I rank." Selene hugged her sister. "What are we going in?"

"You're riding with me." Gryph wasn't giving her any other choices. He didn't like that she was going at all. At least if she was with him, he could provide some kind of protection.

"Aurai and I will ride with Deme and Cal," Gina said.

They made plans and synchronized their watches.

Aurai and Selene stepped into Deme's SUV and exchanged shirts, mussing Selene's hair to give her a tougher, more badass look. When she emerged, wearing Aurai's stilettos, her chin high, sunglasses shading her brown eyes and bright red lipstick slashed across her full, luscious lips, Gryph wanted to skip the pool hall and take her straight to his apartment, where his king-size bed would be a lot more comfortable than the top of his desk. He'd make love to her until the sun rose the next day.

She strutted by him, running a finger across his chest. "Ready?"

His cock twitched. Yeah, he was ready.

Aurai giggled. "What a tease."

Brigid roared out of the morgue parking lot, leading the way to Archer Heights.

Before long, Gryph was driving past the pool hall. Several men leaned against the outside wall, smoking cigarettes. A couple of girls in tight jeans and strategically torn jean jackets hung on the arms of two of the men. Motorcycles, tricked-out cars and junkers lined the parking lot and rock music vibrated through the walls of the dilapidated building.

Gryph didn't even slow. He drove past an old bottling company warehouse, turned on the next street and pulled in behind a guard shack. The huge warehouse was surrounded by a chain-link fence, the gate chained and locked.

"Aren't you afraid someone will steal your car?" Selene asked.

"I have insurance."

"I hope you have life insurance. We might need it by the look of that pool hall."

Gryph turned in his seat and captured her hand. "I don't want you to go in."

She squeezed his hand. "I have to do this. They need me, and I need to help find Amanda's killer."

"Stay here. Let me handle it."

Her gentle smile made his insides flutter. "Between me and my sisters, we can handle anything that's thrown our way. We've been in worse situations than a little pool hall."

"Those are shifters in there. If they are anywhere as big as the one that attacked Amanda, they will dominate you and your sisters by sheer size and strength.

Again her smile sent blood rushing straight south. "There are things you don't know about us and that I don't have time to explain. We have to get in there. Deme and Brigid need me."

"I don't like it."

"So noted."

Gryph slid out of the vehicle and rounded the hood to open the door for her. Grasping her around her middle, he lowered her to the ground, sliding her body down the length of his, rubbing her pelvis over the hard ridge beneath his jeans. "We could call this off and go back to my place."

"I thought making love to me was a big mistake." She traced a finger in a swirling pattern across his chest. "Change your mind?"

"I still think it's a mistake, but I'd rather risk me hurting you than that gang of wolves in the pool hall."

"See? You're beginning to make more sense."

"So you'll go with me?"

"No." She stepped back. "You see, I have skills my sisters don't."

"Like?"

She bit her lip and stared to the far right. "I can read people."

Gryph studied her face. Selene wasn't meeting his eyes. Something about what she'd said didn't ring completely true.

"We don't have time to discuss it. Just know, I can tell when it's time to leave, before it's too late."

"I hope so, because we'll be surrounded." He grabbed her hand and guided her past the guard shack to the sidewalk. They rounded the corner two blocks away.

"Brigid just entered."

"How can you tell?"

"I know." She gazed ahead toward the pool hall, where a dingy neon light hung over the door. "Deme and Cal are inside."

"How do you know?" He squinted. "I have good night vision. It's one of the perks of being part lion. But from here, I can't distinguish who's going in or out of the building."

"Trust me." She pushed her sunglasses up on her nose

and put a little more sway in her walk, slipping his arm over her shoulders. "Let's get inside and find us a killer."

Gryph gritted his teeth and went along with the plan. As they neared the pool hall, the men leaning against the building straightened, eyes narrowing, nostrils twitching.

Oh, yeah. They looked like humans, but something about the way their nostrils flared made Gryph think these could be some of the wolf shifters Rafe had said would be here and the whole area reeked of dog.

Without slowing, he tucked Selene close against his side and entered the building.

The guys on the outside followed them inside.

His gut told him things were about to get sticky.

As soon as they stepped through the door, Selene could sense the tension rising in the room. All eyes angled toward Gryph.

They knew he wasn't human and he was on wolf turf.

Perhaps having Gryph along wasn't such a good idea. Humans were expected. She and her sisters might have been better off coming in sans the men. Most men assumed women were helpless and didn't consider them a threat.

Selene could feel the first prickles of hair rising on the backs of the necks of the wolf shifters in the room. A low rumbling built in some of their chests. Too low to be heard over the music, but she sensed it, nonetheless.

Cal and Deme sat at one end of the bar, talking to the bartender. The bartender's lips were moving and his eyes were shifting around the room as if he was afraid of talking to the two.

Brigid stood beside one of the pool tables, observing a game and chugging a mug of beer.

Selene steered Gryph to a table in a shadowy corner and sat, glad for the glasses so that she could browse the room without being too obvious. The tabletop was sticky and the room smelled of old cigarettes and spilled alcohol.

Selene was in no hurry to order drinks she had no intention of drinking. She focused on the thoughts and mental images of the patrons of the pool hall.

Two tattooed men racked the balls on the pool table close to where Brigid stood. They were sizing her up and debating whether or not to let her in on the game.

Selene almost laughed out loud when her kick-ass sister dropped her keys on the floor and bent to retrieve them, hiking her ass in their direction, displaying the smooth curve in the tight jeans beneath her leather chaps.

The men's temperatures rose and a wave of lust flowed over Selene's senses. Two seconds later, they invited Brigid to play a round.

Selene shifted her focus to the bar, where Cal and Deme leaned toward the bartender, their faces purposely relaxed. Inside they were tense. Whatever the man behind the bar was telling them had their full attention.

"I'm going to the bar to order drinks and ask questions." As Gryph started to rise, a scuffle broke out by the pool table.

A third man had joined Brigid and her two pool players, his attitude and vibes shooting off anger and aggression. The man grabbed for Brigid.

The two men she'd been playing with stepped between her and the interloper, spun him and slammed him against the wall, knocking the cue rack over. The man slithered to the floor, a knot the size of a quarter rising on his forehead.

The bartender shouted, "Take it outside."

The two men picked the guy up, dusted him off and

shoved him toward the door. He swayed, steadied and then staggered out the door.

A heavyset waitress, who was wearing a T-shirt with the words Waiting for Mr. Right written across her ample breasts in faded and peeling letters, stopped by their table. "What can I getcha?"

"Information." Gryph slid a one-hundred-dollar bill into the woman's hand.

She stared at the bill, then tucked it into her pocket. "For that kind of money, I'd give you the combination to the safe in the back room."

"I don't want the combination."

Selene didn't sense any animosity from the woman. She was tired from working two jobs, her feet hurt and she wanted the night to end so that she could get four hours sleep before she started all over again. An image of a small boy wove through her thoughts.

"Which one of the people in this bar is the Devil's Disciples pack leader?" Gryph asked, keeping his voice low and conversational, adding a little louder, "We'll have two beers."

Immediately the woman's back stiffened and her hands shook. Fear replaced exhaustion. "Don't know what you're talking about."

"She's lying," Selene said softly. "And she's frightened."

"There's another one hundred dollars in it for you if you point him out," Gryph said.

She backed away. "I got a kid. I don't want no trouble."

"I'm not asking you do anything but point."

She looked left then right. "He's not here."

"Is there a second in command?" Gryph asked.

She leaned over the table and wiped a dirty rag over

the surface. "In the corner at the pool table. The tattoo with the upside-down cross."

Gryph slid another bill into her hand.

The woman hurried away, looking back toward the man beside Brigid with the upside-down cross tattoo on his upper arm.

Selene closed her eyes and sent a warning nudge to her sister.

Brigid gave an almost imperceptible nod and lifted her pool cue to take the shot.

A few moments later, the waitress returned with their two beers and a big burly man with tattoos covering his arms followed.

The waitress set the beers on the table and scurried away, keeping her gaze averted from Gryph and Selene.

The woman was cringing inwardly and envisioning an escape route from the crowded bar, anticipating a fight, as if she'd seen many fights before.

The man who'd followed the waitress moved closer, his arms crossing over his massive chest. "We don't serve the likes of your kind here." Every gaze swung toward him.

Trapped in his seat, with the big guy threatening him, Gryph smiled and leaned back. "And what *kind* would that be?"

Though his words were casual and drawn out, as if he didn't have a care in the world, he was revving up beneath the surface, ready to react to any threat.

Selene could sense the animal inside waking and flexing, preparing to spring, and she marveled at his self-control.

The pack member snarled, canines extending enough to let Gryph know he recognized a shifter when he saw one. "You better leave."

Gryph tapped the bottle in front of him "My girl and I haven't finished our beer."

In a lightning move, the man swiped his tree-trunk-sized arm across the table and the full bottles of beer crashed to the floor. "Looks to me like you're finished now."

Selene jumped, but managed not to squeal. The animosity emanating from the man could only be described as primal. One animal defending his territory against another, the wolf beneath his skin fighting to get out, barely leashed.

Gryph shrugged out of his jacket, folded it neatly and laid it across Selene's lap. "I'll leave when I'm ready."

Her breath lodged in her throat, Selene whispered, "Gryph, don't."

"I'm not starting anything, babe." He patted her hand, then glanced at the guy standing over him, his eyes narrowing.

Selene sent a silent push to her sisters. *Get out. The shit's about to hit the fan.*

Several other men closed ranks behind the tattooed man standing in front of Gryph, all shrugging out of their jackets.

Selene felt the wolves shift a few seconds before it happened, and the tiny hairs springing out of the men's skin almost made her itch.

She touched Gryph's leg and gave him an urgent nudge with her mind. *Shift. Now.*

He leaned over and kissed her cheek, whispering, "Get out while I distract them." Then he lunged from his seat in a flying tackle, hit the man in the gut, sending him crashing backward into the others. All of them landed in a pile on the floor, giving Gryph enough time to transform—the change was almost instantaneous, from man to lion.

He roared, dropped to all fours and pounced on the downed men even as they shifted into wolves. One by one, they were sent flying with a powerful swipe of his massive paw.

With three wolves in front closing in on him, Gryph didn't see the two who'd been playing pool with Brigid shift and spring toward him.

Brigid balled up a fist of flames and flung it at one of them, catching his fur on fire. The wolf howled, dropped and rolled, the scent of singed hair filling the room.

The other wolf bunched his muscles as he prepared to leap, but Selene hit him hard with a mental slap, making him stagger and fall on his face. He lurched to his feet, shook his head and would have leaped into the fray, but vines that snaked out from an ivy growing along a ledge wrapped around all four legs and pulled tight, like in a calf-roping contest. The wolf fell hard on his side and struggled to break free.

More wolves gathered until a dozen circled Gryph. A brief yip from the leader and all of them lunged at once.

If all the wolves ripped into Gryph, he wouldn't make it. What he needed was something like a force field, a wall between him and the enemy.

Fear for Gryph made Selene concentrate her telepathic abilities on him, a chant in her mind calling forth the influence of the goddess. A swell of power built inside her, around her, encompassing the space around Gryph, building an invisible barrier that prevented the wolves from reaching him, but it was more in their minds than grounded in reality.

Wolves charged toward Gryph and, at the last moment, skidded to a halt, their minds refusing to let them cross the invisible line.

Snarling and snapping at the air, they remained back, pacing, waiting for the moment they could pass through a barrier they could not see, but most certainly felt.

Deme dropped from her stool on the bar and raised her hands, sending a twist of vines at the wolf who'd yipped the attack signal, trussing him up like a pig for slaughter. In moments, he transformed back to his human form, the upside-down cross tattoo easily discernible in the dim lighting of the pool hall.

The other wolves backed away, growling.

Selene sent thoughts of fleeing to them. Some shook their heads, backed toward the door and ran. Others glared at her, seeming to know she'd been the one to put the thoughts into their minds.

The tattooed man fought against his bindings. "What do you want with us?"

Gryph allowed himself to transform back to almost human form, retaining enough of his animal to still appear fierce, but not enough he couldn't be understood. "Which one of your pack killed Amanda Grant?"

The wolf on the ground at his feet shook his head and spat on the floor beside Gryph's feet. "You're barking up the wrong tree."

"Lion's don't bark." Gryph's animal came out enough for him to slam a giant paw on the man's chest and he growled against the guy's face, his canines, wickedly long and sharp, pressing into the skin.

Selene shivered, glad Gryph was on their side.

The man flinched. "It wasn't us. Whoever it was went rogue. He's acting on his own. He's not part of the Devil's Disciples."

"You're known for turning humans. Do all the humans you turn join your pack?"

"No."

Selene prodded the man's mind, but couldn't get beyond the image of another wolf. One that had held off his pack in a daring standoff. "He knows who it might be."

Gryph roared and bounced his paw on the man's chest for effect. "Who did it?"

"I wouldn't tell you, even if I knew." He growled, his snout elongating, wicked teeth bared, the effect frightening even with the man securely tied in vines. "You can't fight off the entire pack. You won't get out of here alive."

Selene couldn't help glancing toward the door, half expecting an army of wolves to step through.

Gryph transformed into full lion and opened his jaws wide, his teeth gleaming in the darkness. He dropped his head fast, his teeth connecting with the man's throat, without breaking the skin.

"You better tell him what you know. He's not very good at holding back his beast," Selene warned him.

"Go ahead," the man on the floor snarled. "Kill me."

Gryph roared again.

Selene willed him to spare the man. He might be useful.

The lights in the building blinked out, the music from the sound system died with the lights, leaving the room pitch-black and eerily quiet except for the snarling wolves, and shifting feet and furniture as people and animals shuffled in the darkness.

Then the sound of wind wailed at the building and the pinging of something hard hitting the roof sent a shiver of dread through Selene.

She sensed the urgency in her sisters outside, a silent call to hurry it up, things were getting bad. "Time to go."

Chapter 10

Gryph, his paw firmly planted on the leader's chest, shot a glance toward Selene, blinking to focus his catlike night vision. *How do you know?* he thought.

"I just do." She stood with wide eyes, apparently unable to see the wolves, *knowing* they were creeping closer to her.

Gryph growled low in his throat, a warning to the animals taking advantage of the darkness to press in for the attack.

A flame flared in Brigid's hand, forming a bright glowing circle around her body.

What the hell? For the first time, Gryph noticed the woman had fire in her hands and wasn't burning.

Selene's mouth tipped upward in a lopsided smile. "Brigid likes to play with fire."

"Think that's cool?" Brigid dug her free hand into her jacket pocket. "Get a load of these." She pulled out what appeared to be tiny creatures, tossing them into the air. Soon, the little buggers flew around the room, giving off bursts of fire like fireflies blinking, only with real flames, creating a strobe-like effect over the room and its occupants.

The night couldn't get stranger. Having lived in the Lair most of his life, Gryph knew other animals, magical beings and mythical creatures existed, but he'd never known one to pack fire in her fist like a softball.

Red eyes gleamed in the shadows, the wolves of the pack inching closer, snapping at the fire-belching, flying animals when they came too close and singed their fur.

Already outnumbered eight-to-one, Gryph had to get Selene and her sisters out of the pool hall before the rest of the wolf pack surrounded the building, if they hadn't already.

"Come on, let's go." Gryph, returning to half man, half beast, grabbed their captive from the floor and dragged him out the door.

Selene scrambled after him.

As soon as he emerged into the open, a gale-force wind nearly knocked him off his feet. Pellets of hail rained down on him, stinging against his fur-covered skin. What the hell had happened to the weather? The forecast had been for a clear and cool evening.

Then he saw it, and had to do a double take. A small, tightly wrapped tornado spun in front of him, grabbing up any loose objects, spinning them into the twister and flinging them outward.

On the other side of the funnel cloud stood Deme's SUV, which was supposed to have been parked a couple blocks away. Aurai perched on the running board, her arms raised into the air, as if directing the chaos like a symphony conductor.

First the vine-throwing Deme, then the fire-wielding Brigid, now this... What *were* these women?

Witches. The answer came like a whisper in his mind. One moment he was wondering, the next he knew.

He glanced back at Selene, her body hunched low to remain standing, her gaze shooting to his at that exact moment.

"You, too?" he asked, his words whipped away by the blast.

Again she nodded, as if she heard him, even in the din from the storm.

When they got out of this mess, they sure as hell were going to have a conversation.

In the meantime, a pack of wolves stood in the street, leaning into the wind. Each time the wolves tried to make a dash for the door, hail pounded on them, driving them back. Gina stood on the ground beside Aurai, her hair twisting and dancing around her face.

"Get him to the SUV," Selene called out over the howling of wind and wolves. "My sisters will hold them off."

"Anything else I should know about you?" Gryph snapped, feeling the fool for thinking Selene defenseless.

Selene gave him an apologetic look, squinting as her hair lashed across her face. "I didn't mention that my sisters and I have special talents?"

"Yeah, but I thought you meant self-defense skills, not—" he waved a hand "—this."

"I'd say it's all about self-defense." Selene stepped out into the street, the tornado moving enough to allow her to pass behind it.

The shifter he had in his grip struggled against the restraining vines, his wolf snout jutting out of his human face, grabbing and tearing at the bonds. He jerked hard, ripping through enough to free his arms and lunge at Gryph with razor-sharp teeth.

Gryph dropped him in time to miss being slashed by vicious canines. The man rolled away, ripping at the vines around his legs, his body shifting into wolf form. Gryph dove for him, snagging a leg before he could make a run for it.

Deme, Brigid and Cal backed out of the pool hall at that moment, followed by the flying fire-breathing things.

Cal had drawn his weapon, ready to shoot anyone following them. When they cleared the door, Gryph shouted to Deme, "A little help here."

The wolf twisted and snapped at him.

Gryph let go of one leg and grabbed another to avoid being ripped to shreds.

Deme spun toward Gryph, whipped her hands into the air and, despite the storm raging around her, had their prisoner's four legs bound together so tightly, he toppled over in a snarling heap.

The wolves in the street howled, leaping forward, only to be slapped back by the twister. Several wolves burst through the door.

Brigid was ready with a ball of fire in each palm. As quickly as she launched a ball, another appeared in her hand. She twirled the balls, daring any wolf to make a play for her or any of her sisters.

Once Deme had their prisoner secure, she lassoed the pool hall door and jerked it shut, tying it with heavy vines, blocking the remaining pack members from exiting that direction. "We don't have much time before they'll be coming out the back."

The fireflies flew over the pack of wolves, spitting flames into their fur. Two of them got too close to the funnel cloud and were sucked up inside.

"Damn. Sorry," Brigid called out to the trapped creatures.

Gryph, still in a halfway state, dragged the angry wolf shifter along with him and stuffed him into the backseat of the SUV. Then he turned to help the others.

Wolves raced around the side of the building, joined the other members of the pack and closed ranks in a semicircle around them.

The tornado spun to the ground and disappeared as if it were a balloon that a child had let all the air out of.

"I couldn't hold it any longer," Aurai said.

"We've got it now," Gina called out, raising her hands to the sky. Brigid, Deme, Gina, Aurai and Selene joined hands. Cal stood on one side while Gryph stood on the other, wondering how they'd get out of this mess intact.

Gryph stepped out in front of the sisters and called back over his shoulder. "I can hold them off for a few minutes while you all get into the SUV and make a run for it." He let his inner beast loose, shifted into full lion and dropped to all four paws.

"I'll stay, as well." Cal raised his gun and aimed at the closest wolf. "Go."

"I'm not leaving you." Selene stepped up beside Gryph and put a hand on his shaggy shoulder.

"We're all in this together," Deme said.

Behind them, the SUV door slammed shut.

Gryph looked back in time to see their prisoner in human form, leaning over the steering wheel as he shifted into Drive and hit the accelerator, leaving a streak of rubber on the pavement as he shot forward.

"Hey, that's my car!" Deme started to run after him, but Cal snagged her arm.

"It's just a vehicle."

"Yeah, but it was mine." Deme glared after the retreating SUV.

Tattoo man hadn't gone a block before a commercial semi tractor-trailer rig appeared out of nowhere and broadsided the SUV so hard, it flew through the air. The SUV crashed through a fence and slammed into a building upside down, the roof crushed beneath.

Then the rig barreled toward them, engine revving, a gigantic bull plowing through a ring of amateur matadors.

Wolves scattered as they leaped over each other to get out of the way of the oncoming vehicle.

Aurai and Gina dove one direction, rolling out of the way. Brigid, Cal and Deme dove in the other direction.

Selene stood firm, her gaze on the oncoming monster of a truck, like a deer in the headlights.

Fear shot through Gryph. Fear for Selene. Still in lion form, he rammed into her, knocking her off her feet and out of the way of the truck. He barely cleared the wheels as the killer truck blew by.

Selene jumped to her feet as the sisters regrouped. "Run! Now! While they're still scattered." She led the way to Gryph's vehicle. He and Cal followed, bringing up the rear as the wolves regrouped and started after them.

Selene reached the vehicle first and slid in behind the wheel. The others piled in. Brigid, Cal and Gryph stood guard.

Cal climbed in, the windows down, his gun aimed out at the advancing pack.

"Get in," Selene yelled.

Gryph roared one last time, wanting to attack, not run. But if he wanted to stay alive long enough to figure out who had killed Amanda Grant and now the second in command of the Devil's Disciples, he had to retreat.

Selene pulled up beside him, leaned across the passenger seat and pushed open the door.

Gryph leaped in, the change coming over him slowly, his human side fighting back the lion defending his pride.

Selene hit the accelerator with all the force of a race car driver and sped away from the wolf pack.

After only a block, Brigid yelled, "Whoa! Stop!"

Selene slammed her foot on the brake, throwing everyone forward.

Gryph flung out his arms to keep his head from crashing into the windshield.

"What?" Selene shot a glance at the side mirror.

"My bike." Before Selene had come to a complete stop, Brigid shoved the door open and leaped out of the vehicle. "I wouldn't hang around here for long. See you at the station." With a quick nod toward their rear, she dove behind a bush and rode out on her Harley, leaning low over the handlebars as she sped away from the glowing fire of Deme's burning vehicle.

Selene followed, driving fast.

Gryph kept watch out the side mirror, hoping the members of the Disciples weren't following. Soon the wolves dropped back.

Before all the hair on his body receded, Gryph leaned over the seat. "Deme, if you'd hand me the duffel bag at your feet, I'll get dressed."

"I don't know. I was enjoying the scenery." She grinned, then reached down and came up with a gym bag, handing it across the seat. "Smart to keep spares handy. Does this happen to you often?"

"No." He gritted his teeth. He'd never turned in public. Balthazar had kept him in the tunnels until he'd matured enough to control his changes. He'd sneaked out on occasion as a young teen, but he hadn't officially been allowed to go topside until Balthazar was sure he could handle any situation without changing.

He was almost certain Balthazar hadn't considered a situation like being surrounded by a pack of wolf shifters with nothing but witches and an armed detective to help bail him out.

Selene kept her gaze on the road, slipping up onto the expressway as Gryph shoved his legs into the sweatpants he'd kept in the gym bag, never really expecting to have to use them.

His jacket lay over the console. Despite having to beat a hasty retreat from the pool hall, Selene had held on to it and made sure it came with them. Without his fur, the jacket was welcome. He slipped his arms into it and leaned back. "Who wants to fill me in?"

By the time they pulled into the parking lot of the police station, Deme had called 911 to report the fire, and Brigid was waiting on her motorcycle.

Selene cringed, realizing there was no keeping the truth from Gryph. Much as she'd liked being with him, once he knew what she was able to do, he'd probably never want to see her again.

"Witches, huh?" Gryph asked as he dropped down out of the SUV.

"Yeah." Selene glanced across at him as she pulled the key fob from the ignition and tossed it to him. She was quick to add, "We don't always use our...skills. Only when we need to."

"Some of those magic tricks your sisters pulled made shifting look tame."

"I wouldn't say that." Selene smiled across at him. "You're superstrong and ferocious when you've shifted.

Not that you aren't strong in human form." Her cheeks heated at the memory of him thrusting into her, his taut muscles glistening in the natural lighting from his office windows. "Every gift has its advantages and drawbacks."

"Don't I know it." He turned toward her. "Let me get it all straight in case some of those so-called gifts are used on me. Deme, you, can throw vines."

"I have the ability to influence all things relative to earth." Deme slid out of the SUV and dropped to the ground.

"Not only can she throw vines, she can create a pretty convincing earthquake," Aurai said.

"Among other things," Selene added.

"Good to know." Gryph shoved a hand through his tawny hair. "I'll have to take out earthquake insurance. Never thought I'd need it in Chicago."

"Aurai can influence wind and weather," Selene offered, hoping he'd forget to ask her where her talent lay.

Aurai grinned as she climbed down out of the backseat. "My weather, plus Gina's ability to channel water, made the hail storm pretty handy, don't you think?"

Gryph nodded. "Gina's got water, and Brigid's pyrotechnics were pretty spectacular." Gryph got out of the vehicle and stood beside the others. "And what were those bugs she let loose?"

Aurai's smile brightened. "Not bugs. Miniature dragons."

"Fire-slinging, fire-breathing dragonflies and tornado tossing. What's that leave you?" Gryph stared across at Selene as she joined them in front of the building.

"Selene has the gift of spirit," Brigid said as she climbed off her motorcycle. "She's telepathic."

"She can read minds and feelings of the living and sometimes the dead."

"I can't read all minds. And usually it's more a sense of what the person is feeling." She studied his face, looking for any sign of revulsion and finding none.

His eyes narrowed. "Is that how you found me down by the river?"

"Some thoughts come to me louder than others. I couldn't ignore yours that night."

"So you knew I hadn't attacked Amanda?"

"That's what she kept telling us," Cal said.

Selene nodded. "I didn't exactly read it in your mind. It's more like I sensed it. Again, some thoughts and feelings are more prominent than others."

"Cal, Brigid and I have to report in to the lieutenant." Deme motioned toward the building. "You want to continue this discussion inside?"

"If it's all the same to you, I'd rather not." Gryph's gaze captured Selene's. "The less people know about my…other side, the better."

"We understand." Aurai touched his arm. "For the most part, we like to blend in."

"With mad skills like you all have, that has to be hard."

Brigid shrugged. "We get 'em out and brush them off when we have to."

Gina patted Gryph's back. "Your secret's safe with us."

"Unless you hurt one of us." Brigid's eyes narrowed.

Gryph half expected fire to shoot out of her eyes and burn him for even standing close to Selene. He raised his hands. "Message heard, loud and clear."

Selene glared at Brigid and hooked Gryph's arm. "Can you drop me at my place?"

"Do the rest of you need rides home?"

"That's right." Deme's lips pressed together. "I don't have wheels."

"The lieutenant should authorize a vehicle from the motor pool," Cal said. "We're working a case."

"Think the department will cover the replacement cost of my SUV?"

"If not, your insurance will. It was stolen."

"By a shifter." Deme crossed her arms. "I'm still trying to figure out how to explain stolen, run into and flipped over with a guy still inside."

Cal pulled her against him and kissed her lips. "You don't."

Aurai raised her hand. "I'll ride in the cop car."

"It's unmarked and doesn't have all the whiz-bang stuff the patrol cars have," Deme warned.

"I don't care. I've always wanted to ride in back." She held out her wrists. "Wanna cuff me?"

Deme swatted at her.

Gina rolled her eyes. "I don't know what she's thinking."

Brigid laughed. "Too many erotic romance novels."

"Tattletale," Aurai said, pouting.

"I'll go with Brigid," Gina said. "I could use a little more wind in my hair."

That would leave Selene riding alone with Gryph. Her stomach tightened and her heartbeat kicked up a notch. "Will the lieutenant need statements from us about what happened at the pool hall?"

Deme frowned. "Come to think of it, you never told us whether you read anything in the leader's mind."

"I didn't get much. When you asked him if they'd turned a human that could have gone rogue, I got an image of a pitch-black wolf with green eyes."

"Most of the wolves at the pool hall were gray or brown."

"Think the black wolf was the one who attacked the woman?"

"I'll check with the crime scene investigators," Cal said. "Maybe they recovered black wolf hairs at the scene of the crime."

"If it was a black wolf shifter, how do we find him?" Deme asked. "We can't just line up all the seemingly human men in the city and tell them to shift and see what we get."

"I felt him when he showed up at the hospital. When he smothered Amanda," Selene said. "And I've felt him again since."

"When?" Gryph demanded.

Selene looked away, refusing to meet Gryph's gaze. "When you dropped me off at my apartment earlier today."

Gryph frowned. "When you weren't feeling well?"

"Which means he knows where you live." Gryph's lips pressed together. "Damn."

"I don't like it, Selene," Deme said. "Anywhere else?"

"I felt him again when the truck tried to run us over." Her brow furrowed. "I tried to read his mind, but it was as if he knew, and pushed back."

"And almost made roadkill out of you." Gryph gripped her shoulders. "Promise me you'll let us know the next time you sense his presence."

She nodded, the intensity in Gryph's expression making her very aware of the warmth of his hands on her arms. His jacket swung open, revealing his muscular chest, reminding her of what it felt like to run her hands across his taut skin.

His nostrils flared and his fingers tightened.

"You should stay with one of us tonight," Brigid said.

"Yeah," Aurai agreed. "He finished off Amanda to keep her from talking and ran down the Devil's Disciples dude. If the killer knows you can sense him, he might target you."

"And he knows where you live," Gina pointed out.

Selene shook her head. "I'll be fine in my own place. I have locks on my doors."

"What about when you open your store?" Gina persisted.

"Close it for the next few days," Brigid ordered.

Selene laughed. "I can't close my store for long, or I'll go out of business. And I can't hide in my apartment, I have places to go and people depending on me for the charity ball."

"I'll hire someone else to take care of things," Gryph announced.

"No way." She moved out of Gryph's hands. "I've worked too hard coming up with the costumes for the waitstaff. If you take it away from me, how will I pay the suppliers?"

"*I'll* pay them."

"No, this is a chance for me to get my name and my work seen." Selene crossed her arms over her chest. "I'm not going into hiding because of what *might* happen. It might *not* happen and I will have missed this chance."

Aurai leaned close to Gryph. "You're not going to convince her now. When she gets that look, she's planted her heels in the dirt and she's not going to let you change her mind."

Selene rolled her eyes. "I can hear everything you're saying, Aurai. I'm right here, and I'm not running scared."

"We don't want you to end up like Amanda." Gina slipped an arm around her waist. "You said he pushed back when you tried to read him. What if he attacks you?"

"You can't throw fireballs." Brigid spun a ball of fire in her palm.

"And you don't have the ability to tie him up." Deme stood with her fists on her hips. "What will you do to defend yourself?"

"I have a brain, you know." Selene glanced at her feet, wanting the conversation to end so that she could get home to bed. "I'll think of something."

"That wolf had to be huge and heavy, Selene," Cal said. "How is your brain going to fight him off? It could be like throwing a BB at a fence post. You might hit it, but it's not going to have any effect. You have to go after an animal that large with an elephant gun and blow it out of the water."

"I can handle it without an elephant gun," Selene said quietly.

"What aren't you telling us?" Brigid's eyes narrowed. "Was that you holding back the wolves attacking Gryph in the pool hall? By the goddess, when did you learn how to do that?"

Selene's cheeks burned. "It just happened."

"You did that?" Deme grinned. "I wondered why they couldn't get to Gryph."

"How?" Gina asked.

Gryph's frown deepened. "What are you talking about?"

Selene shrugged, not wanting to make a big deal out of it. Talking about her abilities only made it more apparent that she had some control over others' minds. How soon would it be before Gryph realized she might have the ability to control his thoughts and feelings? Thus the reason for her to stay out of relationships she really cared about. And for some reason, she felt this one had the potential to be one of those. "I can't explain it and, if it's all the same to you, I'd like to go home and get some rest. It's been a stressful night, as it is." To Deme, she added, "Let me know what you learn, if anything, from the lieutenant."

Deme gripped her hand. "Will do."

"Don't try being a hero," Gina added. "We're your sisters. We're in this together."

"Yeah." Aurai extended her other hand to Gina. Soon all the Chattox sisters stood in a circle and, as one, chanted:

"Feel the power,
Free our hearts,
Find our way
Be the one.
With the strength of the earth,
With the rising of the wind,
With the calm of the water,
With the intensity of fire,
With the freedom of spirit,
The goddess is within us.
She is power.
We are her.
We are one.
Blessed be."

They broke apart and Selene joined Gryph. "I'm ready."

It wasn't until they got into his SUV that he sat back against the seat and stared across at her. "Maybe you can fill me in on everything."

She looked away. "You heard it all from my sisters."

"I'd like to hear the part about your controlling a pack of wolves with your mind."

Selene lowered her eyelids and sent a silent prayer to the goddess to help her let this man go. There was no other way.

Chapter 11

Gryph drove away from Selene's sisters, the moon shining bright in the sky. So many thoughts churned in his head with one rising to the top. "Let me get this straight. You can read minds?"

Selene sighed. "Sometimes. If the thought is prominent in the person's mind, sometimes I can hear their thoughts word-for-word. More often, it's a feeling, emotion or sense."

"Can you read my thoughts right now?"

"I can sense you're angry and that you have a lot on your mind. Images are flashing through of the wolves, the truck and the interior of the pool hall."

"And what do you see about you?"

Her cheeks reddened and she glanced at her hands, twisting in her lap. "I sense confusion."

"Anything else?"

"Anger...and...lust." She stared out the window, her

chest rising and falling with shorter, ragged breaths. Her reflection was one of a woman torn by honesty and longing.

Gryph almost pulled to the side of the road and took her into his arms. Instead, he shifted his gaze back to the road in front of him. "I'm not sure I like having someone in my head." His fingers tightened on the wheel. "Granted, if you hadn't sensed my distress the night I went for a swim in the river, I'd most likely be dead. But this mind reading and maneuvering is another thing entirely. Is that how you manipulated the wolves attacking me?"

"Something like that. I didn't even know I could stop those wolves. It just...happened."

"Nothing just *happens* like that. What were you feeling at the time? Was it like a buildup of emotions that manifests itself in a type of force field?"

"I don't know." She pinched the bridge of her nose. "Could we not talk about this?"

He bit back the questions spilling into his head and nodded. For the next few minutes he sat in silence, going over everything that had happened over the past forty-eight hours.

The attack on Amanda, Selene showing up to save him, the intense thought he'd had right before the leader of the wolf pack had transformed from human to animal. In his head, he'd felt the urge to change. As though someone told him to change.

When he pulled up in front of Selene's building, Gryph shifted into Park and stared at the storefront with the pretty sign and dainty vintage and designer clothing display in the window.

Selene reached for the door handle.

He grabbed her hand before she could get out and held on with a firm grip. "Why didn't you tell me?"

She twisted her wrist, trying to slip out of his grasp. "It's not something you announce to strangers."

"Okay, I get why you didn't tell me, at first. Same reason I keep my inner beast secret. But later, you might have given me a hint."

She quit struggling and stared at where his hand held her wrist. After a long pause she said, "I was afraid."

"That I'd be angry?"

She glanced up. "Well, you are, aren't you?"

"Only because you didn't bother to tell me you could be reading my mind and pushing thoughts into my head." He released her hand.

Selene didn't get out right away. "I know. I should have told you. But I didn't expect things to go as fast or as far as they did. I expected to walk away from you before then."

"Instead, we made love in my office." His jaw tightened, a muscle twitching in the hardness. "Did we because *you* wanted to, or because *I* wanted to?"

She flipped her hair back. "That's why I didn't tell you. *I* wanted to and I was afraid *you* might not want to as much as I did. For all I know, I could have pushed the thought into your mind. I'm sorry. It's just that I wanted you, so very badly." Her head dipped again, her gaze shifting away from his. She turned and scrambled for the door handle, missing several times before she found it and jerked it hard to open.

Gryph was out of the SUV and around the front to her side before she could drop to the ground and run. He reached for her waist and slid her down the front of his body, sure to let her know the effect she was having on him. Slowly, he settled her on her feet, his hands resting on her waist. "Are you pushing thoughts into my head now?"

"I don't know," she whispered.

With his thumb, he brushed a stray hair across her cheek. He was so close he could smell her fragrance, a mix of herbal shampoo and shay-butter body lotion. He wanted to taste her, to feel her skin against his. "What are you thinking?"

She chewed her bottom lip before answering. "That I should go inside, and you should go home."

He bent his head, his lips hovering over hers, so close he could feel her breath. "Is that all?"

Her gaze shifted to his lips. "No," she whispered.

The brush of air across his mouth was almost his undoing. His fingers tightened on her hips. "I have the sudden urge to kiss you."

Her brow furrowed. "You see? That's exactly why you should leave and never come back." She pressed her hands against his chest in a weak attempt to push him away.

He caught her fingers in his, bent and pressed his lips to her fingertips. "No, I want that kiss." His mouth slipped across hers, a feathery brush at first, then he was crushing her in his arms, holding her so close, their bodies melded together.

She opened to him, her mouth parting.

His tongue thrust against her, darting and tangling in a warm wet dance, making his blood turn to molten lava, pushing hard through his veins, flowing south to the hard evidence of his lust.

Selene moaned into his mouth, her fingers digging into his shirt, dragging him impossibly closer, her leg circling behind his, her crotch riding his thigh.

Gryph broke off the kiss long enough to say, "Your key."

Selene fumbled in her jeans pocket, and then handed him the key to her apartment. He scooped her into his arms and carried her down the short flight of stairs to her basement home, dropping her to her feet in order to unlock the door.

As Gryph reached for the doorknob, Selene grabbed his wrist. "Wait." Her tone was soft, but intense.

That concentrated nudge of danger rippled through him. He recognized it as the same feeling he'd had just before the wolf leader transformed. He stared down at Selene.

Her brow furrowed and her eyes narrowed as she nudged the door with her fingertips, jerking them back as if they'd been burned. The door swung open without resistance, the doorjamb splintered, the lock broken. "He was here."

Gryph shoved her behind him. "Stay here."

Her hand touched his back. "He's not inside. I can't sense him."

"Fair enough." He turned to face her. "Humor me, and let me check things out before you go inside."

She nodded, shrinking against the walls of the alcove, hidden in the shadows from the streetlights above.

Gryph allowed his inner beast to rise to the surface, just enough to give him good night vision and increase his auditory and olfactory senses. If Selene was wrong, and the intruder was still there, he needed to be ready to defend himself.

Once inside the apartment, he slipped from one room to the next, checking beneath the bed, in the closets and behind the shower curtain. As small as the apartment was, it didn't take long. When he returned to the living room, Selene stood in the doorway and flicked on the light switch.

A soft glow filled the room, chasing away the shadows, revealing a room that appeared to be untouched, other than the shattered doorjamb.

"Is anything missing or out of place?" Gryph asked.

Selene walked silently around the room, touching picture frames, lifting items from tabletops. She entered her bedroom, her frown deepening. "He was in here the longest." Opening the closet, she ran her hands across the clothes, pausing as her fingers touched a gown she'd designed and sewn herself for the upcoming charity ball.

"Are you sure it was Amanda's killer?"

She nodded, a shiver shaking her from her shoulders all the way down her spine.

Gryph sensed her unease, the fear and anger over having had her personal space violated. His heart aching for her, he hooked her arm and turned her to face him, brushing a strand of hair from her face. "Your sisters were right. You're not staying here tonight."

"It's my home." Her gaze skimmed across the furnishings, the artwork on the wall, the candles lining the tabletops.

"Yeah, but it's just a place. And if he's been here once, he knows where you live, and there's a chance he'll return. You can't stay here."

Her body stiffened. "I won't be frightened away."

"Think through this. Your doorjamb is busted, you don't have a way to lock him out, or anyone else for that matter. Not that locks stopped him this time. If you stay here, you're setting yourself up for attack."

She stared at the door, another shiver rattling across her body, vibrating against his grip on her arm. "I can stay with Deme."

"You'll stay with me."

"No!" She jerked free of his hand. "I'll be fine at Deme's place."

"She might not be there yet."

She glanced around as if in a daze. "I'll call. And if she's not home, I'll go to Brigid's."

Gryph's jaw tightened. "Are you afraid to stay with me?"

"Yes." She gazed into his eyes. "Aren't you afraid I'll manipulate your mind—make you do things you had no intention of doing?"

His lips twitched upward. "Like making love to you? I can see where that would be a hardship. Look, if it bothers you that much, I'll sleep on the couch, you can have my bed and I'll resist any urges, yours or mine, to make love to you."

"What if *I* can't?"

"I guess that's the chance we'll have to take." He spun her around and gave her a gentle shove toward the bedroom. "Get whatever you need for tonight and tomorrow. And hurry, I want to make a stop before we settle in for the night."

"All the more reason for me to stay with my sisters. I don't want to be a burden."

"Says the woman who rescued me. Seems to me, I owe you one for saving my life."

She shrugged. "I'd have done it for anyone hurt."

"You're stalling. I want to get there before everyone is asleep."

"Where are you taking me?"

"My place first, and then to where I grew up."

Selene hurried through her bedroom and bathroom, throwing clothing, panties and toiletries into a small duffel bag, her heart skipping beats every time she thought about where they were going. Gryph wanted to take her where he grew up. Curiosity pushed her to move faster.

"Do you happen to have a hammer and nails?" he called out.

"In the kitchen pantry." Within five minutes, she had everything she needed for a night in Gryph's apartment, including a condom. She dug in her stash for another, and another. Her body flushed with warmth. Not that she intended to use them. But a woman never knew when desire would outweigh caution.

Her lower abdomen clenched and lust washed over her like butter melting over a hot potato, sliding into every crevice.

Finally, she emerged from the bedroom, her cheeks flushed, her insides trembling in anticipation of the night to come. She sensed that Gryph didn't share his life easily, and that he was going to show her where he'd grown up was something big.

He'd found the hammer and nails she kept and stood waiting by her damaged front door.

As she passed him, she could sense his body tightening. She prayed to the goddess it wasn't her thoughts creating his automatic response.

Gryph checked outside and then caught her arm before he let her exit. "You don't sense him?"

She shook her head. "No."

Once outside, the night air feathered across her skin, raising gooseflesh and cooling her rising passion. Selene wrapped her arms around herself, as the city that had been her home and sanctuary felt less welcoming and safe.

Gryph's warm hand on the small of her back chased

away some of her hesitation and she let him guide her to his SUV.

Once settled in the passenger seat, she expected him to take her to the suburbs. Instead he drove her to GL Enterprises' corporate headquarters.

"You grew up in your headquarters building?"

He shook his head, his lips thinning. "Not hardly." But he didn't give her more than that. After parking in his secure access parking place in the underground garage, he led her into the building and into an elevator that required an access card and his thumbprint to open the door. They were whisked downward, into the basement, the air growing cooler the lower they descended.

Again, she wrapped her arms around herself to ward off the chill and Gryph didn't offer to wrap her in his warm embrace.

He stood beside her, but he might as well have been somewhere else. The lower they went the colder, more distant and unapproachable he became.

"Why are we going into the basement of your building? I don't get it."

"You will, soon enough." His tone was flat, emotionless.

Selene waited for the elevator to come to a stop and the doors to open. When they did, she expected to see the inner workings of what it took to keep a huge building operational, from pipes and electrical equipment to plumbing and air ducts.

What greeted her was white marble floors, opulent decor and artwork worthy of a museum, in an open, well-lit foyer to what appeared to be a spacious apartment.

"Do you live here?" Selene asked.

He nodded. "This is my home."

She walked out of the elevator onto the smooth marble, her footsteps echoing against the walls. "And you grew up here?"

"No." He hooked her elbow and led her through the foyer, down a long hallway, past a sitting room, a library and a dining room to the back of the apartment and a room equipped with commercial-grade, exercise and weight-training equipment.

Gryph slid a hand across what appeared to be a poster of a world-famous boxer. The poster shifted to the side, revealing a panel beneath with a keypad and retinal scanner. He leaned forward, lining up his eye with the scanner. A beam of light fanned out over his eye, then a soft click sounded, motors engaged and a door slid open, revealing a spiral staircase leading even deeper into the bowels of Chicago.

When Gryph turned toward her, Selene shivered and stepped backward. He held out his hand. "Come with me."

She shook her head. "The only place I know lower than the basement of a Chicago building is the tunnels beneath the city. Been there, didn't like what I found."

"You want to see where I grew up?"

She nodded, bracing herself for what he was about to say, knowing it before the words left his lips.

"I grew up in the tunnels."

"Blessed be." Selene pressed a hand to her chest.

Gryph's hand fell to his side. "I take it you're familiar with the tunnels?"

She nodded. "My sisters and I had an...altercation with a very dangerous...opponent in the tunnels not long ago. We almost lost Aurai to it."

Raising his hand again, he gave her a half smile. "Must have been in one of the lesser-used tunnels. Let me show you mine."

His gaze begged for her trust.

Selene placed her hand in his.

Gryph grabbed a flashlight from a recharger that was plugged into the wall and switched on the beam, the light barely penetrating the inky blackness below. Then he led the way down the long, winding spiral steps. By the time they reached the bottom, Selene was disoriented and dizzy. Like the tunnels beneath Aurai's college in another part of the city, the rails were rusted and dusty, abandoned equipment lay scattered along the way.

"You lived down here?" Appalled at the desolation, darkness and creepy atmosphere, her heart went out to the young Gryph.

"Not right here, but close." With his fingers wrapped around hers, he stepped over the rails and led her through the maze of tunnels, turning left, then right and back to the left. Just when she thought she couldn't get more confused, soft lights appeared high on the walls, sending a golden glow down over the tracks.

Ahead, beneath one of the bulbs lay a stack of cardboard boxes and a bundle of rags, leaning against a wall.

Gryph stopped in front of the rags. "Good evening, Joe."

The rags shifted and a face, tortured by burns, peered up out of them—one eye seemed almost fused shut by scar tissue.

Selene pressed a hand to her mouth to keep from crying out.

"Gryph, what brings you back to the Lair so soon?" Joe said, his voice coarse and scratchy.

"I came to speak with Balthazar," Gryph said.

The old man nodded, his gaze shifting to Selene, who'd been standing in Gryph's shadow. When the man saw her, he ducked his head and pulled the ragged blanket up around his mutilated face.

Gryph ignored his withdrawal and pulled Selene into the light. "This is Selene."

"A surface dweller." The man spat at the floor by Selene's feet. "What's she doing down here? You know the danger."

"I know," Gryph said quietly. "Let's just say she's special. Not like the rest."

The man's head came halfway up, his brows rising. "Like us?"

Gryph nodded. "Like us."

Joe stared at Selene.

Selene wanted him to feel safe with her and projected that thought toward the man.

Joe's eyes narrowed and his brow furrowed toward the bridge of his nose. Slowly, his head dipped in a nod. "Yup. She's special all right. But watch her. We don't want folks followin' her down here."

"I promise to keep your home a secret, Mr....Joe." Selene held out her hand.

Joe thrust out his right arm. Where his right hand should have been was now a scarred stump. Immediately, he yanked it back and held out his normal, left hand.

Selene took it and squeezed his fingers. "Nice to meet you."

He grunted, but squeezed her fingers.

Gryph urged her to continue down the tunnel toward a light at the end.

A soft tapping sounded behind her, and Selene turned.

Joe used a stick to tap against a metal pipe. He seemed to be tapping a pattern.

Selene wondered if it was Morse code and, if so, who

would he be sending it to down here? She shrugged and pushed to stay up with Gryph's longer strides.

As they reached the end of the tunnel, the underground opened into a cavern-like room, where rails crossed, switched and multiplied, disappearing into other dark tunnels. Bulbs cast a soft, warm light from the ceiling down onto the tracks and box-like structures against the walls. Some walls had doors built into them that were painted in bright, cheerful colors.

The box structures were made of plywood, also painted, but with flowers lining the bases like so many gardens with daisies and roses in bloom.

"What is this place?" Selene asked in a hushed whisper. "It's beautiful."

Giggles erupted from a shadowy corner.

Selene spun to face a battered, small railcar, standing against one wall, abandoned decades ago. "Did you hear that?" she whispered.

Gryph chuckled. "It's just the fairies who inhabit the underworld. Pay them no mind." He winked at Selene, let go of her hand and walked lightly toward the railcar. When he got close enough, he dove behind the heavy metal cars and came up with his hands clutching the scruffs of two children's necks. "It's not nice to spy on people," he admonished the two. "And why are you two up so late?"

"Mrs. Martin said we could stay up, since we did so well at our studies this week."

"Well, then come say hello." He turned the children toward Selene.

"What…" Selene clamped down on her tongue to keep from blurting out inane questions of the two catlike creatures who giggled like normal children and struggled half-heartedly to get loose of his grip.

"Let us down, Gryph," the little girl pleaded.

Gryph frowned mightily. "Not unless you promise to greet our guest politely."

"I promise," the girl agreed.

"Being polite is for sissies," the little boy grumbled.

"Nevertheless, you will greet her, and make it nice." Gryph's voice was stern, but gentle. Not until he set the two kids on their feet in front of Selene did she get a good look at the pair.

Both looked almost normal. The girl wore a worn pink dress and had long golden blond hair flowing in wavy locks down her back. The boy's hair was shaggy, hanging in his golden eyes. Each had two arms, two legs and two ears. But that's where normal ended. The children were uniformly covered in short, fine hairs, like the sleek pelt of a cat. Two beautiful, tawny cats.

Chapter 12

What kind of place was this, buried beneath the streets of Chicago? Selene stared at the tawny, fur-covered girl, unable to look away. She was mesmerizingly beautiful as well as strange.

The little girl dropped a quaint curtsy. "I'm Jillian. Nice to meet you."

The boy stuffed his hands into faded blue-jeans pockets and stared at his feet until the girl beside him poked her elbow into his side.

"I'm Jack," he said.

Gryph touched the boy's shoulder. "And?"

The boy scuffed his worn tennis shoe on the uneven surface, then glared up at Selene. "You're a surface dweller. Are you going to rat us out? 'Cause if you are, I'll kill you." He ducked to the side, but not fast enough to escape Gryph.

The big man snatched him up and held the wiggling

child until the boy went still. Then Gryph set him on his feet, maintaining one hand on his narrow shoulder. "Want to try that again?"

"Well, she is, isn't she?" Jack said, glaring at Selene mutinously.

"I'm not going to bring anyone down here." Selene held up her hand like a person in court. "I promise. And a witch's promise is sacred."

Jack's frown slowly eased up. "A witch?"

Selene nodded.

"But you don't have warts," Jillian observed. "And you're not ugly."

"Not all witches have warts or are ugly."

"Will you turn Jack into a rabbit?"

Selene laughed. "I'm not that kind of witch."

"What kind of witch are you?"

Selene thought hard, trying to think of a way to explain what she could do with her powers. "The kind that tries to see things that cannot be seen?"

Jillian's little face screwed up and she thought about what Selene said. "Like dreams?"

"Yes, like dreams." Selene smiled at Jack. "So is it okay if I visit today?"

"I guess."

"Jack…" Gryph squeezed the boy's shoulder.

"I'm Jack." He stuck out his hand. "Nice to meet you."

Selene took his hand with a serious expression. "I'm Selene. Pleased to meet you, Jack."

With the pleasantries over, Jack turned to Gryph. "Will you push us on the merry-go-round?"

Jillian looked up at him with soulful golden eyes. "Please, Gryph?"

"I need to speak to Balthazar first."

"Then hurry." Jack turned Gryph toward a doorway and gave him a shove from behind.

"Pushy little fairies, aren't you?" Gryph ruffled Jack's hair and bent to Jillian. "I'll be there in five minutes."

"Yay!" The two children scampered away.

Selene's heart warmed at how gentle the big man was with the small children. Then another thought occurred to her. Were they his?

Gryph leaned close and whispered, "No, they aren't mine."

Her cheeks heating, Selene wondered if Gryph had read her mind.

"We're two different creatures. I shape-shift. Jack and Jillian are like that always." He straightened, his gaze following the little girl and boy. "But if anything ever happened to Mrs. Martin, the woman who adopted them, I'd raise them as my own. They're wonderful children."

Selene smiled. "Yes, they are." Her heart went out to them. She and her sisters had grown up knowing they were different than other children. Physically, they looked the same. These children, with their beautiful fur, would be teased and tormented by *normal* children in the world above. Surface dwellers.

"Are there more?"

"Like Jack and Jillian?" Gryph shrugged. "Not that we've seen so far. But there are other inhabitants of the Lair with equally unusual characteristics."

"Like Joe?"

"His were scars from an industrial accident."

"And the others?"

"Are a mix of scars or accidents of birth…abnormalities by surface dwellers' standards." He gripped her elbow in his strong hand. "Come, I want you to meet Balthazar."

"Someone looking for me?" A deep, rich voice with a

faint British accent called out, the sound filling the still air of the cavernous space.

Selene spun to face an older man with shaggy white hair, wearing a worn, wool jacket with patches on the elbows. Wire-frame glasses perched on the end of his nose as his gaze skimmed over Selene.

Gryph's lips lifted in a smile. "Father." He engulfed the man, who was stooped with age, in a bear hug.

Father? Selene stared at the older man, trying to see in him traces of Gryph and finding no similarities whatsoever.

Balthazar patted Gryph's back. "Back so soon?"

Gryph's smile faded. "There's been more trouble."

"So much trouble you would forget to introduce me to your beautiful lady-friend?" Balthazar held out his hands to Selene.

Selene immediately trusted the man, placing her hands in his. He had an aura of serenity that made her comfortable with him from the moment her hands touched his. "I'm Selene Chattox. It's nice to meet you."

The gray-haired man waved toward a doorway that was painted a sleek antique blue. "Come inside."

With his hand on Selene's arm, Gryph led her through the door and into what once must have been a kind of warehouse, but was now an open, high-ceilinged room with soft rugs covering a concrete floor and walls painted in shades of cream and the warm gold of wheat. Prints of famous paintings from the ages decorated the walls and antique furniture graced the living areas. There were lamps glowing on tables and track lighting hung from the ceiling. On several walls, murals had been painted of French doors and windows, overlooking lush gardens filled with sunshine, roses and gerbera daisies. The paintings were beautiful and looked almost real, as if you could step through the doors into a garden.

Selene was struck by the beauty and the light and airiness of this underground abode.

"Do you like my home?" Balthazar asked.

"It's stunning."

"I fill it with all the things I love. I have a library with all the classics in multiple languages and many contemporary works."

"I'd love to see it."

"Gryph can show you, while I prepare a pot of tea."

Gryph shook his head. "Father, we don't have time."

"Nonsense. You both look flustered. A bit of tea will calm you so that you can sleep. Show your young lady the library. I'll bring the tea there."

Selene wanted to contradict the older gentleman and tell him that she was not Gryph's lady. But she bit down on her lip and kept her words and thoughts to herself.

Balthazar entered an open kitchen area as Gryph led Selene toward another doorway.

As they stepped into the room, Selene was overwhelmed by the rich reds and golds of the furnishings, and the mahogany bookshelves that stretched to a twelve-foot ceiling and were lined with leather-bound, hardback and paperback novels. A thick Persian carpet filled most of the floor space and a large mahogany desk dominated the room, with a leather sofa placed in front of it.

"This room is amazing," Selene whispered.

"Balthazar encouraged us to read from the moment we could started talking."

"We?" Selene wanted to know more about this enigmatic man.

"My brother and I."

"You have a brother?"

He glanced down at her. "I do."

Selene shook her head. "A father, a brother... Are there any more people in your family I should know about?"

His lips tightened. "That's all of us. And the others who live in the Lair are like my extended family. We look to each other for support."

"Why is it people—surface dwellers—haven't discovered the Lair? I would think the people who've come to explore the underground tunnels would have come across all of you by now."

"We've sealed off most entrances, hidden those that we use and manage to discourage entry by those curious enough to dig beneath Chicago's glitzy surface."

"And Balthazar? I'm sorry, but you two don't look anything alike? Is he like you? A shifter?"

"Balthazar is not my biological father. I've never seen or met either of my parents. My mother left me with Balthazar when I was an infant. She couldn't handle raising me, knowing I was a monster. Balthazar accepted me and raised me. I owe my existence to him."

Selene's heart squeezed. "You and your brother were abandoned?" A woman had to be either heartless or desperate to leave her child.

"My brother came to the Lair with his mother when he was not quite two years old. I was eight at the time. From what I recall, they were homeless, his mother had been an addict, abused and stalked by her former boyfriend and in need of a place to hide out and get clean. Other than the trauma of an unhealthy situation, they were normal. When Lucas's mother couldn't shake the addiction, she disappeared back to the surface, leaving Lucas behind. Balthazar opened our home to him."

"Does Balthazar do that often?"

"Do what?"

"Take in strays?"

Gryph chuckled. "It's who he is."

"How many people live in the Lair?"

"Last count, around forty."

"Forty?" Selene stepped back. "That many?"

"Those who can, work on the surface."

"If they're that...different, how do they get jobs?"

"Balthazar has connections and, as you know, I have businesses."

"You employ them?"

"I try to accommodate as many as possible. It's not always a fit."

Selene let her brows inch upward. "You can't have cat people working for GL Enterprises?"

His mouth tightened. "I'd hire them all, but many don't want to work during daylight hours, where they will be seen, and I don't have as many night-shift opportunities."

"What do you think of my library?" Balthazar entered carrying a silver tray with a silver teapot and cups. "You're lucky—Mrs. Martin brought by scones this morning." He set the tray on the edge of the desk. "Gryphon will you be so good as to fetch the tray of scones from the kitchen?"

Gryph frowned. "Father, we have to discuss an urgent matter."

"Certainly." His father nodded. "After you retrieve the scones."

Gryph's chest rose and fell on a silent sigh and he left the room.

Selene stood in the middle of the Persian carpet, not sure what to say. The entire setting, the underworld society, this home beneath the city—everything was so unusual she struggled to take it all in.

Balthazar poured a cup of tea and turned to hand it to

her. "Gryphon has always been a blessing to me and the other inhabitants of the Lair."

She accepted the cup and sipped carefully before asking, "How so?"

"He was the one who got permanent electricity wired into the homes within the Lair. I managed to get internet here, but he insisted on high-speed access for all those who desired it, wanting our children to take online coursework to enhance their homeschooling, and so that they could learn about the world above from the relative safety of their homes here."

"I don't completely understand. They are people like the rest of the world. They should be allowed to live in peace on the surface." But she knew even as she spoke the words what life on the surface would be like. She'd been bullied as a child when she'd been in public schools.

"You know their reasons. Fear of rejection. Past experiences." Balthazar's shoulders rose and fell. "Has Gryphon told you about how his mother abandoned him?"

Selene nodded.

"It was more than that. She was a young college coed when she was raped by a monster."

"That's terrible. Did they ever catch the man?"

"Maybe you don't understand that when I say she was raped by a monster, it was a true monster, not just a man with evil in his soul."

"Oh." Selene's eyes widened. "Oh."

Balthazar nodded. "You see, Gryphon's mother was human. Her rapist was not. We're not certain what it was, but once Gryphon started shifting, even as early as two months old, she knew she couldn't provide for him and keep him safe from people who would exploit him and turn him into a science experiment.

"Though she loved her baby, she didn't have the

strength or the resources to support him in a private environment, where he would be protected from the ridicule, poking and prodding of people trying to understand what exactly he was.

"I found her outside a church, near one of our hidden entrances. She was bent over a basket, crying softly, tucking blankets around her baby."

"Gryph." Selene's eyes welled with tears, her heart filled with the ache of despair Gryph's mother must have felt to come to the conclusion that only by abandoning her baby could he get the care that he needed.

"She told me her story and how she couldn't keep him in a world that wouldn't understand. She begged me to take good care of him and that she loved him, but couldn't be a part-time parent. When she gave up custody, she didn't want him to come looking for her. I never told him who she was."

"And you took him in."

Balthazar nodded. "He was a fighter then and now. As a toddler, he nearly ripped off my arm."

"Sweet goddess," Selene exclaimed.

"Don't worry. He's learned to control his beast. Now he only calls on the animal inside when danger is present. He would rip anyone apart who tried to hurt someone he loves." Balthazar glanced down at Selene, his gaze softening.

Selene's face heated. "Gryph and I just met," she muttered. She refused to consider their urgent lovemaking as anything more than lust.

"Really, Father, don't fill Selene with tales of monsters and demons," Gryph said as he returned.

"Are there demons in the Lair?" Selene asked.

Gryph chuckled. "No, but there are monsters."

"Only in the eyes of people who won't understand."

"Don't scare her more. I need her to go with me to D'na Ileana."

"The gypsy." Balthazar set his teacup on the desk. "You remember the dangers?"

With dip of his head, Gryph stared hard at his adoptive father. "The animal who attacked the woman outside the theater was a wolf shifter. When we went to question the Devil's Disciples—"

Balthazar reached out and gripped Gryph's arm. "You went into Disciple territory?"

Gryph nodded and the hint of a smile curved his lips. "And lived to tell." Beneath his breath, he added, "Barely."

Balthazar turned and paced away, coming back to stand in front of Gryph. "When you confront a pack, you take your life into your own hands." Balthazar glanced at Selene. "And you? Were you with him?"

"Yes, sir," Selene responded, feeling like a recalcitrant child. "With the help of my sisters, we managed to get away."

"Very fortunate, indeed." He crossed his arms over his chest. "And why must you visit the gypsy?"

"We need to find the rogue werewolf threatening the city." Gryph stepped forward. "Unless you know where we can find him, D'na Ileana may be our only hope."

Balthazar shook his head. "I've only heard rumors of the wolf. Remember, the gypsy sees the future," Gryph's adoptive father said, "not necessarily individuals."

Gryph's eyes narrowed, his jaw tightening. "If she can see where he'll strike next, we can be there."

Selena smiled, now that she understood why Gryph had brought her with him. "We could stop him before he kills again." They might get ahead of the killer and catch him before he harms another. "Where is this gypsy?"

"Deep in the darkest tunnel," Balthazar said.

Like spider legs crawling across her arm, Selena's skin tingled. "I take it where she lives isn't as nice as this place?"

"No," Both Gryph and Balthazar said at once.

"And there are other creatures who live in the maze of tunnels we don't want to anger along the way," Gryph added.

Her knees suddenly shaking, Selena asked, "Would one happen to be a Chimera?"

Balthazar shook his head. "There was legend of such, but none of the inhabitants of the Lair have come across one."

Selene bit down on her tongue. She and her sisters had fought a mighty battle against a Chimera in the tunnels beneath Colyer-Fenton College in another part of the city.

Selene needed to know what the stakes were, how difficult it would be to get to D'na Ileana. "What do we have to aware of?"

Balthazar counted off on his fingers. "Old rusty machinery, possible sinkholes, crumbling bracing and a nasty old troll who threatens to eat you if you pass through his tunnel."

"Don't worry." Gryph's lips twitched. "He has no teeth."

"Let me guess," Selene said. "Although he has no teeth, he's strong enough to grind my bones to mush?"

Gryph shrugged. "He's big, but I won't let him hurt you. He's slow and not very bright."

"Anything else?" Selene asked, though she wasn't sure she wanted the answer.

"We might run into Kobaloi."

"And that is…?"

"Spritely creatures who like to deceive people and

lead them into danger." Gryph pushed a hand through his tawny mane. "As a child, I followed one who'd disguised itself as a firefly. I almost fell into a sinkhole. If I hadn't shifted at the last minute, I might still be at the bottom of that hole. I believe the drop fell all the way to the reservoir deep beneath the city."

A huge tremor shook Selene and she was afraid to ask, but had to know… "Is D'na Ileana somewhere near this Kobaloi and that sinkhole?"

"Unfortunately, yes." Gryph drew in a long breath. "I shouldn't have brought you. But I thought—"

"I might be able to see what the gypsy sees?" Selene pushed aside her fear of the dark and dangerous tunnels that had nearly been the death of her and her sisters. "If this helps us find the one responsible for that woman's death, we should get going. The sooner, the better."

"You'll need a flashlight." Balthazar reached for one in a recharging unit plugged into the wall. "You think she's up for the journey?" he asked Gryph as he handed the light to Selene.

Gryph's lips curled upward at the corners. "Absolutely."

Selene's heart swelled at the confidence Gryph had in her. After the episode at the bar, she'd been more shaken than she cared to admit.

She'd always considered herself the weak link among her sisters. Not anymore. She'd just begun to realize the extent of her powers.

And what could be worse than battling an evil Chimera, or a pool hall full of angry werewolves?

Chapter 13

Gryph stopped to play with Jack and Jillian for a brief moment, then promised he'd be back when he had more time.

"Oh, don't go, Gryph. You hardly visit us anymore," Jillian cried.

Being a busy businessman meant staying at the office more than he preferred and the relationships he cared about had suffered. The ones with the man who'd raised him as a son, his brother, Lucas, and the people of the Lair had all taken a hit lately.

"I promise. I'll be back to play soon." Gryph grabbed Selene's hand and headed back the way they'd come.

Jack ran ahead of them. "Can I go where you're going? Are you going to the surface? When can I go? Are the people up there as mean as everyone says? Why can't we live in the light?"

"Not everyone is mean who lives on the surface."

Gryph rubbed the boy's head. "Selene is from the surface and she's not mean."

"Only when I haven't had my morning coffee." She smiled down at the boy.

Jillian raced up behind them. "Are you taking Jack? May I come, too?"

Gryph stopped, blocking the way ahead. "You two have to stay here. It's not safe where we're going. Besides it's way past your bedtime."

Jack puffed out his chest. "I'm strong and brave. I've gone all the way to the sinkhole on my own. And I can stay up very late and never get tired."

Gryph gave the boy a stern look. "You should never go that far without an adult. You know the tunnels can be tricky. You could get lost."

"But I didn't and I looked down into the sinkhole, and I could see all the way to China."

"Could not," Jillian said. "It was just a dark hole."

Gryph gripped her arms, his pulse pounding at the thought of these small children teetering on the edge of the sinkhole's abyss. "You went with him?"

Contrite, Jillian nodded, her eyes round. "Yes, sir."

Squatting in front of the two children, Gryph stared hard at them. "Promise me you will not go back to the sinkhole without an adult."

"Ah, Gryph." Jack rolled his eyes. "It was easy."

"And you probably didn't run in to any Kobaloi."

Jillian shook her head. "No, we didn't. Jack said he saw a light, but I didn't."

"Promise." Gryph stared from Jack to Jillian and back to Jack, the older of the two kids.

Jack ducked his chin and scuffed his sneaker on the ground in front of him. "I promise."

"I promise, Gryph. I didn't want to go anyway." Jillian flung her arms around Gryph's neck. "I'll be good."

"Thank you." Gryph stood, with Jillian on his arm. He hugged her tight, then set her on her feet and touched Jack's shoulder. "You have to protect your little sister. She's younger and smaller and needs a big brother to make sure she doesn't get into trouble."

"I didn't want her taggin' along, but she always does." The boy glared at his sister.

Jillian crossed her arms. "I don't, either."

"Enough. You two stay in the Lair. Selene and I have an errand to run and can't be worried about two hooligans following us through the tunnels." He turned them around, gave them a pat and sent them on their way. "Go back home to bed."

"Are they always so precocious?" Selene smiled after the children.

The twinkle in her deep brown eyes made Gryph look again. "You're beautiful when you smile."

"Thanks." Her lids closed over her eyes, hiding the shine. "And you're good with children." She straightened and looked him in the eye. "We should be going. The wolf could be planning another attack as we speak."

"Right." Gryph took her empty hand, liking the feel of it in his. Smaller, more delicate, yet strong. She'd surprised him in the pool hall. He'd never known someone who could stop an attack by thinking it.

One thing he'd learned in the Lair was that there were all kinds of people and creatures living on or beneath the surface. He shouldn't have been surprised.

Wanting to get their meeting with D'na Ileana over with, he hurried through the tunnel, wishing he could shift to his lion form. He was much more sure-footed on all four feet.

"You should make the change," Selene suggested, her warm voice echoing softly off the cool brick walls.

He slowed and shot a glance her way. "Were you reading my mind?"

She shook her head. "No, but if I had the ability to shift, I would. You'd be able to see better in the dark and four feet are steadier than two."

He hesitated, knowing he would be in a better position to protect her as a lion, but not willing to shift when he had to lose his clothes in order to do it unrestrained. Finally, he nodded. "Okay, but only halfway. Enough to see better in the dark and sniff out trouble ahead of time." He stopped in the middle of the rail track they'd been walking along, slipped out of his leather jacket and handed it to her, his hands tugging the T-shirt from the waistband of his jeans.

Her gaze followed as he lifted the shirt up over his head.

Gryph's pulse quickened and jumped into overdrive when her tongue came out to moisten pretty pink lips. "Stop that."

She glanced up, her gaze meeting his. "Stop what?"

He reached out and ran his thumb over her bottom lip. "That."

She swayed, her hand reaching toward his naked chest. "Do you want me to take that?"

He wanted her to take him, all right. Instead, he handed her the jacket and shirt, and then grasped her hands in his. "When we get close to D'na Ileana's we can't lose focus."

Her knuckles rested on his naked chest. "Unfortunately, I'm completely focused." Her voice was low and gravelly and so damned sexy.

Gryph dragged her closer, his hands circling to the

small of her back and downward to cup the curve of her bottom. "What is it about you that makes me forget everything?"

"I could say the same." Her mouth was so close, her breath warm against his chin.

Before he could think through his actions, question his sanity, he lowered his head and claimed her lips. At first tender, the animal inside surged and demanded more. The gentle kiss hardened, changing with the flash of molten blood coursing through his veins. He crushed her to him, lifting her legs to wrap around his middle.

Selene dropped the items in her arms, the flashlight clattering against the metal tracks, the beam flickering, then shining down the rail into the pitch-black. She intertwined her arms around the back of his head and deepened her connection, her tongue lashing out, thrusting through his lips and teeth to tangle with his.

He ground the ridge of his erection against the apex of her thighs, not satisfied to mimic the motions of making love, wanting all of her now, against the cool brick walls of the tunnel.

Out of the corner of his vision, Gryph saw the glimmer of a pinprick of light. At first he ignored it, unable to drag his lips from the sorceress consuming him. When it twinkled again, then again, he slowly came back to his senses and broke the mind-numbing kiss, resting his forehead against hers. "Now is not the time, nor the place."

As her legs slid down his sides, he eased her to the ground. She was breathing hard, her hands resting against his chest. "You're right. We need to move."

"And if I'm not mistaken, one of the Kobaloi have found us."

Selene jerked her head to the right, staring into the darkness. "I thought I felt something else here with us."

"Watch," he whispered, gathering her into the curve of his arm.

A moment of silence passed and the flash of light recurred—it was like a firefly, only bigger.

"Did you—"

She gasped and pointed. "There!"

He nodded. "Don't try to follow it. They're known to be mesmerizing."

"But it's so pretty."

"When you live in the darkness, you tend to appreciate anything that gives light. Except the Kobaloi. Now that they know we're here, they won't leave us alone." He gathered the clothing and flashlight she'd dropped and handed them to her. Then he concentrated all his control on transforming just enough to allow him the nocturnal advantages of the lion. Fine hairs sprouted from his skin and his muscles bulged, stretching, changing. He willed his metamorphosis to slow and stop before he dropped to all fours.

His night vision sharpened and he could smell the sticky sweet scent of the Kobaloi ahead in the tunnel. Unfortunately, he and Selene had to pass the Kobaloi and the sinkhole before they reached Ileana's cave, carved out of the oldest tunnel in the maze beneath Chicago.

"Hold my hand and whatever happens, do not let go," he said, his voice coarse, almost the growling rumble of a lion. He held out his hairy hand, not quite human, nor lion.

She stared at it for a brief moment.

Gryph didn't realize he held his breath until she placed her hand in his. The air rushed from his lungs and he curled his thick fingers around her thin, hairless ones. That she would place her trust in a beast made him want to prove to her that he could protect her. That he wasn't just an animal.

He continued on, leading her away from the relative safety of the Lair and into the darkness and danger of the outer tunnels inhabited by all manners of creatures less human, and less benevolent, than himself.

As he neared a turn, he slowed, trying to remember exactly where the sinkhole was. He sensed it was close and could smell the water of the reservoir beneath the city. Gryph rounded the corner.

The single Kobaloi was joined by another, and another, until there were three small blinking lights farther along the tunnel, luring them with their cheerful promise of illumination in the darkness.

Selene stepped up beside Gryph. "Oh, look, now there are three." She started forward, eagerly continuing the journey.

Gryph's hand tightened on hers, jerking her back.

Her foot slipped on loose gravel and she fell, nearly jerking him off his feet. He braced himself, her hand slipping through the fur on his.

"Help!" she cried, shining the flashlight beam into the black abyss of the sinkhole below her dangling feet.

Willing his fur to recede, he laid back on the track, pulling her body up and over his. For a long moment, she lay on top of him, breathing hard. She released the flashlight and it clattered against metal, settling on the ground beside him. Her fingers curled into the hairs on his chest as if she was afraid to let go, lest she slip back into the hole.

"Are you all right?" he growled.

"I think so," she said, her breath warm on his body. Selene made no move to roll off him, still clinging to him like a lifeline.

He closed his eyes briefly, liking the feel of her body on his, her soft curves pressed into the hardness of his muscles, her legs tangled with his. If only the train rail wasn't digging into his back and the Kobaloi weren't waiting to tempt them into more danger.

"I should have remembered exactly where the hole was."

She laughed shakily. "And you were right about the Kobaloi. They're like the dragonflies my sister keeps. Always looking for trouble." Finally, she leaned up, her hands pressing against him, and glanced over her shoulder at the hole that had almost taken her. A shiver rippled across her body. "I shouldn't have been so careless. Are there any more sinkholes we should be worried about?"

"I haven't been deep in the tunnels for years."

When she moved to get up, his hands reached out to grasp her face, dragging her down to his, which was distorted into that of half lion, half man. "I want to kiss you."

"Then why don't you?"

"I'm not myself."

"I think you are." She cupped his face and leaned down, pressing her lips against his mouth. "Your fur tickles me," she whispered before her tongue slid between his lips and slipped along the length of his. When her head came up, she smiled. "And your tongue is raspier."

"I'm sorry."

"Don't be. I think it's very sexy and could be a definite asset in other areas." She winked and rolled carefully to the side.

If he was not mistaken, the color in her cheeks had darkened to a deep rosy hue.

She grabbed the flashlight and stood well away from the hole, refusing to lock gazes with him.

Gryph climbed to his feet.

"How do we get around it?" Her beam circled the edges of the hole, then shone down into the center, barely penetrating the blackness. Another shiver shook her body.

Gryph slipped an arm around her waist. "We should go back."

"No." She stood straighter. "If the gypsy can help us, we need to get to her."

"She might not be willing."

"Then we'll convince her." Selene pointed the light toward the far left of the sinkhole. "I believe there's a ledge along the side."

"If my memory serves me right, it's wide enough for a person to traverse and there are pipes above to hold on to for balance." He held out his hand. "Stay close. I'm not sure how sturdy the sides will be. They could have sloughed off since my last visit."

"Reassuring." Selene gaze moved ahead. "Let's do this." She aimed the light at the nearest edge of the hole.

Gryph inched his way around to the left, gripped a pipe secured to the ceiling above and sidestepped with his back to the wall.

Selene followed his lead, juggling her flashlight and reaching for the pipe overhead. She was too short to grab it and held even tighter to Gryph's fingers.

The Kobaloi danced in the air on the other side of the sinkhole as if laughing. If Gryph wasn't mistaken, they moved closer each time he glanced up.

"Those things don't bite, do they?" Selene's whisper was like a shout in the complete silence of the tunnel.

"No. They're like a pesky mosquito. They irritate." When they were only halfway around the hole, one daring Kobaloi darted across and buzzed Gryph's face, the flutter of its wings causing him to blink. His foot slipped and he clung to the pipe above him.

"Gryph!" Selene pulled hard on his hand to keep him from dropping into the gaping maw.

He regained his balance and chuckled. "Like I said, irritating."

The Kobaloi flickered past Selene's nose. "No kidding."

Gryph continued on, swatting at the Kobaloi, careful not to lose his balance again. If he fell, he'd take Selene with him. And if she didn't fall to her death, she could be lost in the tunnel and have to face the troll on her own.

No, he didn't have time or the desire to disappear into a black abyss. It could be only a short drop, or all the way into the reservoir. As dark as the hole was, even his excellent nocturnal vision couldn't see down into it very far.

Finally, he stepped onto solid ground past the hole and into the tunnel on the other side. He helped Selene the last couple steps and continued on.

"How much farther?"

"Not too far. Try to keep the noise down. The troll will be nearby. He guards the entrance to her cave."

"Oh, goody." Selene swatted at the three Kobaloi hovering around her face. Now that she had time to examine them, she realized they had tiny little humanoid bodies with wicked gargoyle faces. And they didn't want to let up their attack on them. "I think these little buggers must work for the gypsy, as well."

"Could be. I've only run across them in this tunnel."

"Wait just a moment. Let me try something." She stopped in the middle of the old rail tracks and closed her eyes.

After a moment or two, the three Kobaloi stopped their frenzied fluttering and backed away.

Gryph shook his head. Amazed. "What did you do?"

"I let them know we weren't there to harm the gypsy and that we only wanted information."

"That's it?"

She shrugged. "I'm glad they were receptive. Not all creatures are."

"I just hope that if we run across the troll, he's as easily persuaded."

"You and me both." Selene shined the light down the tunnel, the beam only reaching five feet ahead of them. "I like the lighting you had installed in the Lair."

"The people of the Lair should live in light."

"Then why don't they move to the surface?"

"Many of them would like nothing better. But they also want to live their lives free of the kind of torment some have been subjected to on the surface."

"Why can't people accept others for who they are inside instead of what they look like?"

"Unfortunately, it's part of nature. Birds are attracted to the most beautiful of their species. Some animals shun those of their kind that aren't strong or appealing. It's survival of the prettiest, strongest, most genetically sound."

A resonant thumping sound broke into their whispered words. Gryph raised his hand and stepped in front of Selene, urging her back against the tunnel wall. "Shh."

"What?" Selene asked.

"I heard something," he said softly, pressing a finger to his lips. "Turn out the light."

She hesitated. "Will you be able to see?"

"Yes."

She hit the off switch and the light blinked out. Only the Kobaloi provided any kind of illumination, but it was barely enough to surround them and not sufficient to see anything coming.

Selene rested a hand on Gryph's arm. "I can sense it."

"The troll?" he asked.

"I'm not sure, but it's confused and angry and headed this way."

The thumping grew louder and the ground beneath them shook.

"When it gets closer, be ready to flash the light in his eyes. It will blind him temporarily and give us the chance to run past him. Trolls are generally slow," Gryph said, his voice barely a whisper. "Once you blind him, keep the beam focused on his face."

"Can he see in the dark?"

"As well as I can." Gryph touched her arm. "There he is."

"I don't see him."

Thumping became loud pounding against the ground, vibrating up through Gryph's feet into his body.

"Now."

Selene fumbled with the flashlight beside him and the beam flashed into the tunnel ahead, filling it with light and bouncing off the giant form of the troll.

"Run." He grabbed her hand and raced straight for the troll, praying they could get around him before the creature's eyes adjusted to the bright light.

Selene's heart beat frantically against her ribs as she ran, tripping and stumbling over the rails and discarded debris in the tunnel. The closer she came to the troll, the stronger her panic mingled with the fear and anger of the troll.

His huge bulky body stooped beneath the ceiling, filling a majority of the narrow tunnel. He shouted, swinging his beefy arms right and left.

Gryph waited for the troll to swing away from them,

then practically jerked her arm out of the socket dragging her past the creature.

Once past, Selene's light no longer blinded the troll. He spun, knocking his shoulders against the tunnel walls, roared and thundered after them.

Selene ran, her feet flying over equipment left behind. A few steps ahead, Gryph stopped. "Keep going."

"What are you going to do?" She slowed as she passed him. "You can't fight him. He's huge."

"I'm not going to." As soon as Selene ran past him, Gryph pushed a big rotting crate into the middle of the tracks, turned and continued to run. "Go!"

Selene turned and ran, tripped over a rail and fell, hitting her forehead on the hard metal track. Pain shot through her temples. The flashlight's beam dimmed where it lay on the ground just out of her reach.

"Selene!" Gryph dropped down beside her at the same time the troll crashed through the wooden crate and reduced it to splintered kindling.

Selene tried to rise, to get to her feet and run, but her head spun every time she lifted it.

Gryph leaped to his feet, changed the rest of the way into his most ferocious form and leaped at the troll.

The troll swung a club-sized arm, backhanding Gryph, sending him flying through the air. He slammed into the brick wall of the tunnel's interior and slid to the ground. Shaking himself off, he scrambled to his feet as the troll threw a ham-hock-sized fist at him.

Gryph dodged the blow and sprang to the troll's side and onto his back, sinking his teeth into the giant's neck.

With an eardrum-shattering roar, the troll reached over his head, snagged Gryph by his mane and threw him down the tunnel.

Selene shook her head and pushed to her hands and

knees, forcing back the gray cloud. She reached for the only weapon she could find, the flashlight. Heavy at one end, she balanced the lighter end in her hand.

When the troll started toward Gryph, Selene went after him, tiptoeing so as not to alert him to her presence.

Ahead of the troll, Gryph staggered to his feet. He spotted Selene as she raised the flashlight over her head.

"No!" he yelled.

The troll ground to a stop and braced to turn around and look behind him. Only he didn't get that far.

Selene wielded the flashlight like a baseball bat, aiming for the back of the troll's thick skull. She nailed the swing, connecting with his head.

Her arms jolted and vibrated with the force of her swing. The glass over the bulb cracked, but the metal remained intact. And a good thing, because the blow didn't fell the troll. However, it made him angrier.

He spun on clumsy feet, swatting at the back of his neck as if the flashlight had impacted him as nothing more than an irritating bee sting. The troll spotted her, his heavy brows dropping low over his eyes. Then he snarled and snorted through his nose like a bull in a bullfighting ring.

"Uh-oh." Selene stared down at the flashlight in her hands, debating, for a split second, whether it would help to hit him again. It wasn't going to be the weapon she'd hoped for. Perhaps it was time to run. She turned and sprinted back the way she'd come.

A lion's roar echoed through the tunnels.

Selene shot a glance over her shoulder. The troll had switched direction and was headed back toward Gryph.

"Oh, no you don't." Selene stared at the troll's back, concentrating all her effort, all her inner strength, and even called on the power of her sisters to help her stop the troll before he ground Gryph into mush.

The troll's steps faltered, but he didn't stop and just plowed forward, like a runaway train on a downhill slope, picking up speed as he lumbered on.

"Stop!" A woman's voice sounded in Selene's head. She glanced around, but the answering echo never reverberated against the tunnel walls.

The troll skidded to a stop and stared past Gryph to a shadowy figure in a flowing skirt, standing in the middle of the track.

Selene moved closer, despite the danger of being within range of the troll's mighty hands. She sensed the troll was being controlled by this creature in the darkness. As she stepped past the giant, he grunted and tightened his fists. But he stood so still it was as if he was cemented to the floor.

Who are you? Selene wondered.

I am who you seek.

Gryph, his body slipping back into human form, stood and glanced over his shoulder. "D'na Ileana." He turned fully and bowed.

"What brings you to disturb my sentries and privacy?"

The Kobaloi flitted around her head and landed in the thick, flowing hair that piled high on her head and tumbled down her back in long loose jet-black curls.

"We need to see the future," Gryph said.

"I do not tell fortunes anymore. Go away." Her words were for Gryph, but her gaze remained on Selene.

Selene returned her gaze with a steadfast one of her own. *We need your help. Lives are at stake.*

"Please," Selene begged aloud. "We need to know where a wolf will try to kill again. We have to catch him before he takes another innocent life."

The gypsy's gaze ran the length of Selene and her lip curled in a snarl. "Why should I care?"

"Your gifts come with responsibility to help others."

"And you share your gifts?"

Selene nodded. "I do."

"More fool you."

"D'na Ileana, will you help us?" Gryph asked.

Ileana's lips curled upward, her gaze zeroing in on Gryph.

Selene blinked, and in that short moment, Ileana had closed the four yards distance between herself and Gryph. How she'd moved so fast, Selene didn't know. She suspected Ileana was more than a simple fortune-teller.

The gypsy ran a long fingernail down Gryph's jawline. "I will help you, my dear Gryphon." She drew a line down his bare chest to the waistband of his tattered trousers, which had been ripped by his instant shift into his lion form and back again. "What will you give me in return?"

"What do you want?" he asked.

Her gaze shot to Selene and back to him. "A night alone with you." Her ruby lips trailed along the curve of his muscled shoulder.

Selene's hackles rose and she stiffened, ready to rip the gypsy apart.

The other woman cast a sly glance her way. "You wouldn't mind, would you?"

Selene wanted to scream and scratch her eyes out. But she had no hold on Gryph. He wasn't hers to claim. If he wanted to give the gypsy a night in the sack, he could. Never mind they'd made love less than twenty-four hours ago.

"No." Gryph caught the gypsy's hand and held it in his fur-covered one. "I'm not here to trade sexual favors."

The gypsy tsked. "Such a shame. It's been a long time since I've had a worthy bed partner."

"Find someone else."

"Very well. I will help you, if it is in my power to do so." She glanced at Selene. "But why did you not ask the witch to help you?"

Gryph didn't glance Selene's way, his jaw tight, the muscle beneath the skin twitching with his effort to control his anger. "She cannot see into the future. You can."

"Then why bring her along? She is of no use to you." Ileana leaned into his body. "Which brings us back to me and you. I'll make your body sing."

"Enough. Time is running out. We have to find the wolf responsible for a woman's death before he strikes again."

"I cannot see the present. Only the near future."

"Then tell me where he'll strike again in the near future so that I might catch him before he succeeds in killing another innocent."

"Follow me." Ileana turned, the length of her colorful skirt swirling around her ankles.

Gryph followed D'na Ileana and Selene brought up the rear, not liking that they would be at the gypsy's mercy once inside her home.

Selene shot a glance at the troll. The giant creature glared down at her, his gaze following her every move as she entered the door leading into the dark depths of the cave.

Selene hoped they'd be able to leave unharmed. If they happened to anger the gypsy, would she sic the troll on them as they left?

Chapter 14

Gryph had been inside D'na Ileana's cave only once before. He'd been in his early twenties when he'd come with Balthazar, seeking information about the whereabouts of Jack and Jillian's mother, who'd disappeared a day earlier, leaving her small children with Mrs. Martin.

Ileana had seen Rebecca Miller huddled on a street in the cold, her body wrapped in newspapers and cardboard. Her descriptions hadn't been detailed enough to find the woman in time to save her from hypothermia or the ups and downs of her mental condition. Rebecca had been bipolar and completely incapable of dealing with small unusual children like Jack and Jillian.

By stepping out of the Lair into the blasting cold of a Chicago winter, she'd resigned herself to death.

Between Mrs. Martin and Balthazar, the children had grown up pretty normal for who and what they were. Better off in the Lair than on the surface, where, at the least, children their own age would have harangued them for being so very different. Worse, scientists would have poked, prodded and examined them to discover how this cross-species mutation could have occurred.

They were getting the best education possible under Balthazar's tutelage and when they were old enough, they could study at any college that would provide courses via the internet.

Ileana had been distraught when her future prediction hadn't led to finding Rebecca until too late. She'd withdrawn deeper into her cave and refused to join the people of the Lair for company or even celebrations.

Too caught up in building an empire and enough wealth to care for his extended family in the Lair, Gryph hadn't been back to visit the gypsy. Balthazar made an annual trek into the tunnels to check on her and make sure she was okay and wanted for nothing. She'd chosen to reject any of Gryph's improvements, preferring to live in the near dark, using more primitive means to chase back the shadows.

As they stepped into Ileana's cave, Selene switched off the flashlight. Candles burned on every flat surface, casting soft, warm circles of flickering light, calming in their quiet intensity. By the items scattered around the interior of the gypsy's home, it was clear she had a way of accessing the surface to acquire things. How she acquired them was her business.

Ileana pointed to a round wrought-iron bistro-style table with a dark red tablecloth draped over it. "Sit," she ordered.

Selene perched on one of the two mismatched chairs and Gryph sat across from her in the other.

Ileana dragged a cushioned straight-back wooden chair up between them. "Tell me about the wolf," she said.

Gryph explained what had happened on the streets of Chicago and in the hospital.

All the while Ileana remained silent, studying Gryph, then Selene.

"We need to find the wolf before he hurts another," Gryph said, ending his tale.

Ileana's eyes closed and her head tipped back slightly as if she basked in a warm ray of light.

Gryph glanced across at Selene. Her gaze was on him. She blinked and refocused on Ileana.

The gypsy swayed gently from side to side, a low hum rising up her throat. The more she swayed the faster she moved, until she was rocking back and forth, the humming turning to a distressed keening.

Gryph's pulse quickened.

Selene's brows drew together, her eyes narrowing. "I can't see what she's seeing," she said.

She reached out to touch the gypsy's arm.

Ileana screamed, a bright flash blinded Gryph's mind and the next thing he knew both women toppled out of their chairs, crashing to the floor.

Pain shot through the back of Selene's head where she hit the hard stone of the cave's floor. She lay for a moment, her head spinning with images, trying to make sense of them all.

"Damn you," Ileana stormed. "You shouldn't have come." She pushed to her knees, her long dark tresses hanging in her face, her eyes wide and wild. "Leave." She waved toward the doorway. "Go away!" She turned her focus on Gryph. "You shouldn't have brought her here. She'll die. They'll all die. Mark my words, hurry, before there's nothing you can do. Nothing." She buried her face in her hands and rocked back and forth, wailing.

Selene rolled over and pushed to a sitting position, her vision blurring.

Gryph kneeled on the floor beside her. "Are you okay?"

"Yes. No." She shook her head, as, one by one, the images shifted, bringing into focus the most prevalent and urgent.

She gripped Gryph's arm and her heart seemed to stop beating for a second, then leaped ahead, pounding so hard, her pulse banged against her eardrums. "We have to get back."

"Back where?"

Selene didn't wait to answer, she grabbed her flashlight from where it had landed on the floor, lurched to her feet and staggered toward the door.

Gryph ran after her. "Where?"

"The Lair!" Ileana screamed. "It's too late." She resumed her rocking and keening. "It's too late."

Selene burst through the doorway into the tunnel.

The troll stood as sentry to the gypsy's abode.

When she passed him, all he did was grunt. He did nothing to stop her or Gryph, who emerged on her heels.

Selene ran back the way they'd come, careless of the rails, the abandoned equipment and debris littering her path. She fell, dropped the flashlight, scraped her hands and knees, but got up and ran some more.

"Selene, wait!" Gryph called out.

She couldn't. She had to get to the Lair before... before...

A flash of tawny fur dashed beside her. Gryph, half changed, stood in her path, blocking her from going any farther, forcing her to stop.

Tears streamed from her eyes. "We have to get back."

"Why?" His growling, deep voice demanded an answer.

"They're coming." She tried to push around him.

His furry hand on her arm halted her movement. "Who is coming?"

"The authorities. They'll find the people, they'll drag them to the surface and expose them to the world."

"You saw this?"

"Yes!" She fought to free her wrist. "We have to get back and warn them. There isn't much time, the police are on their way. They're going to shoot anything that moves." She gulped back a sob. "Including Jack and Jillian."

His lion-man mouth tightened, the long incisors flashing in the beam of her flashlight. "Let me lead the way."

She nodded and took his hand, and they ran together. As they approached the sinkhole, Gryph slowed and edged to one side, holding tight to the pipe overhead and to her hand.

Frustrated by how slowly they had to move past the obstacle, Selene bit down on her lip and forced herself to focus on putting one foot in front of the other.

Midway across the abyss, Gryph's foot slipped.

Selene held tight to his hand, leaning hard against the wall to keep him balanced and to avoid being pulled into the dark depths.

"Thanks." He pushed on to emerge on the other side.

As soon as they'd passed the gaping hole, they ran again. Thirty minutes later, they emerged into the Lair.

Gryph ran to the center of the track switch, where a pole held up an old bell with a rope dangling from the middle. He rang it three times and moved to the side. In moments several men emerged from buildings, wearing pajamas, rubbing their eyes.

A large man whose face was normal and human on

one side and more ape than human on the other, stepped forward. "What's wrong, Gryph?"

Gryph stared hard into the other man's eyes. "Nelson, help me evacuate the Lair. We may only have minutes before surface dwellers arrive bearing arms."

"Why?" Nelson asked.

"It doesn't matter why, just get everyone out. Now!" Gryph ran to the nearest doorway and banged.

"Keep your pants on." An elderly lady emerged. "Where's the fire?"

"Mrs. Martin, it's a Code Red."

"Oh, dear." She pressed her knuckles to her lips.

"This is not a drill. Surface dwellers are on their way down. We have to get out before we're destroyed.

"Oh, dear." Her eyes widened. "Oh, dear! The children."

Gryph gripped her arm. "Where are Jillian and Jack?"

"I don't know. They were out playing and didn't come in when I called. I must have lost track of time. Where could they have gotten to?"

"Pack only your essentials, hide what you can and retreat into the tunnels."

She pulled back. "I can't leave without the children."

"You can and will. I'll find them." Gryph frowned down at her. "I promise, I'll take care of them. We'll find them, Mrs. Martin." He gripped her elbow. "Now, go to the shelter. Hurry."

She flapped her hands, looking right and left. "I need to pack up my belongings."

"No, you need to go."

"Now," Selene insisted.

"But who will take care of hiding my home? What if they destroy it?"

"I'll hide it. If they find it and destroy it, we'll build again."

"They need to hurry," Selene whispered.

"I'm too old to start over. What if I get lost?"

Despite the urgency, Gryph hugged the older woman. "You're younger than you think." He turned her toward a woman hurrying by, carrying a tote stuffed full of clothes, books, yarn and knitting needles. "Please, Mrs. Martin, go with Jen Cramer. She'll make sure you take the right tunnels."

Jen Cramer, a woman with the glittering scales of a colorful fish glowing in the lights along her neck and face, overheard her name. She detoured to hook Mrs. Martin's arm and steered her down a tunnel, shining a flashlight into the darkness.

Mothers gathered their children and herded them after the disappearing Jen Cramer and Mrs. Martin.

Gryph ran to the doorway into Balthazar's home and flung it open. "Father!" He ran inside, Selene on his heels. "Father!"

No one answered.

"Father!" Gryph called out, searching from room to room. When they turned up empty, he ran for the doorway, hustling Selene with him. Once outside Balthazar's home, he pressed a brick on the wall and a panel slid in place, covering the doorway. He pressed another brick, extinguishing the overhead lights and those leading down the main tunnels.

Flashlights blinked on and men pushed heavy metal sliding doors over the otherwise normal wooden doorways. When they were in place, the panels blended into the tunnel walls, with a facade of old brick the same color and texture as the old tunnel walls.

By the time the last door was covered, Selene couldn't

tell what was real and what was facade, allaying some of Selene's fear of the Lair's detection.

The sound of men shouting reached Selene's ears and her anxiety level pitched upward. "It's them." She stared at one of the dark tunnels. A light glowed far into the darkness. "They're almost here."

"Come, I think I know where Jillian and Jack might have gone to play."

Gryph led the way toward one of the half-dozen tunnels leading out of the Lair. They slipped into the darkness as the light from the other tunnel grew brighter.

Selene followed, glancing behind her every step she took.

"Turn off the flashlight."

A ripple of fear tightened her belly.

"Trust me," he said.

The crunch of dozens of feet on the gravel floor made her hit the button on her flashlight before they were seen.

Gryph grabbed her hand and continued down the tunnel until they rounded a bend in the tracks. Only then did he stop and turn back to see what was going on.

Over a dozen SWAT team members filled the Lair, semiautomatic rifles at the ready, headlamps shining from their helmets, the red of laser sights bouncing off the dull gray of the tunnel walls.

She could hear a dozen thoughts streaming through her head, as tension and adrenaline raged through each of the men. "Someone tipped them off," she whispered. "They think Amanda's killer is hiding out in the tunnels."

"You can read their minds?" Gryph asked.

"A little. And that's the overall impression I'm getting," Selene said. "Whoever tipped them off told them to be ready. The suspect is considered very dangerous.

They're loaded for bear, and were told to shoot anything that moves."

His hand tightened on hers. "We have to find the children."

Selene let him lead her away from the little bit of light filtering through the tunnel from the SWAT team headlamps.

They moved slowly. Selene carefully placed her feet, afraid to make a noise, but unable to see anything. She prayed Gryph could see well enough to guide them to the children. If Jack and Jillian returned to the Lair while the SWAT team was there…

It didn't bear thinking about. The men wouldn't know what they were and would shoot first, clean up the mess later.

Her heart lodged in her throat, Selene sent out a fervent message to the children to stay hidden where they were. Gryph was coming to find them.

A shout from the tunnel behind her made Selene jump. She tripped over the rail and fell to her knees. Her extinguished flashlight banged against the metal tracks, the sound echoing against the tunnel walls.

"I heard something over here," a voice called out. Light shone at the corner they'd left behind, growing stronger.

"Run." Gryph hauled her to her feet and dragged her along behind him, racing over the uneven ground.

Struggling to keep up, Selene did her best, her lungs burning, her heartbeat banging against her chest. Another turn and the darkness consumed them yet again.

Gryph came to a halt and grabbed the flashlight from Selene's fingers.

A soft click sounded then he flicked the switch. Red light glowed from the flashlight, illuminating what was in front of them enough that Selene could make out a stack of pallets, an old bucket railcar that had probably been used to haul coal beneath the city. Behind all this, two small furry faces peered out, eyes wide.

Relieved they'd found the children, Selene didn't have time to waste.

Gryph dragged her back behind the stack of wooden pallets, where the little girl and little boy crouched. Gryph dropped to his belly and pulled Selene down with him, switching off the light as the SWAT team rounded the corner, their headlamps glowing brightly. Three men stood with their hands on the triggers of their wicked-looking weapons, the red laser sight tracking through the tunnel until it landed on the pallets and railcar.

Jillian shrank against her, so scared, Selene had difficulty telling where the child's thoughts ended and hers began. As the adult, Selene couldn't let fear take control.

The men approached, their headlamp beams swaying right, then left.

Selene's arm slipped around Jillian, tightening enough to be reassuring.

At one point, one of them nudged the pallets with the tip of his rifle.

Jack, who was beside Gryph, let out a soft gasp, masked by the scuffling of the boots.

Selene stared hard at the three headlamps, the men's faces barely visible in the shadows. She concentrated on projecting her thoughts, not certain it would work. These men were focused, on a mission. If she could make her thoughts theirs, they had a chance. *The suspect is not here. There is nothing of interest in this tunnel.*

The more she thought it, the more her head hurt, until she thought it might explode.

Finally, one of the men touched his empty hand to his

temple and shook his head. "There's nothing of interest in this tunnel. The suspect isn't here."

One by one the other two agreed and backed away from the pile of debris behind which the man they were searching for lay.

As soon as the SWAT team members backtracked around the corner of the tunnel, Selene let go of the thought and lay her cheek against the back of her hand, her body and mind drained.

For twenty or thirty minutes more Selene, Gryph, Jillian and Jack lay still, listening to the sounds of footsteps and voices echoing from the Lair. Nothing indicated the team had found anything that would show Gryph had been there.

Too far away now to read their minds, Selene contented herself with soothing the two children. Jillian's furry body snuggled up to hers. After a while the little girl fell asleep from inactivity.

Selene wasn't sure how long they'd been there. Finally, Gryph stirred and whispered, "I'm going to check things out."

"No." She reached out where she'd last seen him, touching his arm.

"I need you to watch out for the children. Keep them safe. Stay here—don't make a sound until I give the all clear."

She knew it was the right thing to do, but she didn't like the idea of him getting caught in the crosshairs. "I'm not the one they're looking for. Wouldn't it be better if I went?"

"I'm going to shift. I move quietly on all fours."

Not happy, but aware of how important it was to the people of the Lair to maintain their secret existence, Selene bit down on her tongue and let him go.

The *shoosh* of clothing falling to the ground was followed by complete silence.

Selene counted to three hundred, waiting for whatever all-clear sign Gryph would give. She'd about given up when the tunnel lights flickered on.

At first blinded by the glare, she blinked several times.

Jack was up and running toward the Lair before she could stop him. Jillian stirred beside her, yawning. "Is it over?" she asked.

"I suppose so," Selene responded. "The lights are back on."

Jillian rubbed her eyes and sat up. "That's the all-clear sign. We can go home now."

Selene climbed to her feet and stepped around the pallet and railcar.

Jillian slipped her furry hand into hers and led the way back to the Lair.

The inhabitants returned, one by one or in groups, carrying what few belongings they'd escaped with and talking in low, hushed tones.

With Jack coming to a stop beside him, Gryph stood at the open doorway to Balthazar's home, wearing trousers and a clean white shirt. He was buttoning the cuffs. "I was about to come get you."

"Thankfully, it wasn't necessary. My capable helpers knew what the all-clear sign was, and got me back here safely." She ran her hand across Jillian's smooth golden hair. "You all act as if you've run this drill before."

"Quite a few times. The people of the Lair like things the way they are. They've gone to a lot of trouble to keep their secret for the past thirty years."

"I'm impressed."

Mrs. Martin emerged with Jen Cramer. Her worried frown cleared as soon as she spied Jillian and Jack. She opened her arms and the little girl and boy ran into them, hugging her tightly.

Balthazar emerged from one of the tunnels, hurrying through the throng of people, talking softly, reassuringly. When he reached the door to his home, where Gryph stood, he raised his hand above the crowd. "If I may have you attention, please."

The talking ceased and all eyes turned to their leader.

"I know you all are worried about the return of the police. And rightly so. Our emergency procedures are in place for that very reason. As you can see, the protocol served us well. I ask that we all remain aware and diligent in assessing outside contacts to insure no one leads others into the Lair. Rest assured I will look into the construction of additional barriers to close off little-used tunnels and installing more early warning devices so that we can evacuate sooner should this happen again. In the meantime, you can all go home."

When Balthazar finished, he turned toward Gryph and Selene. "From what I gathered as I hid in the tunnel, the SWAT team was looking for Amanda's killer, and apparently they know something about our little community. This is the first time we've had an actual breach. People are scared."

Hell, Selene was scared down to the depths of her soul.

"They blame us." Gryph's mouth closed in a tight line.

"Did you get what you needed from the gypsy?" Balthazar asked.

Gryph nodded. "I think so."

"You know I love you, but right now there are so many more people at risk than you. Come inside and tell me all you learned. Then you and your friend must leave."

"I understand." Gryph took Selene's hand and led her into Balthazar's home.

Now that she had time to breathe and think back through what had happened, her thoughts whirled.

She'd seen what was going to happen with the SWAT team, but getting back to the Lair before they did precluded an all-out attack. Though D'na Ileana could see the future, it was only one *possible* future.

It gave Selene hope. Because the other image was of a huge attack by a pack of wolves, led by one big black wolf with green eyes. In that attack, she, her sisters and Gryph were all killed.

Chapter 15

Balthazar insisted on Gryph and Selene taking tea and wouldn't let them talk until they'd settled in chairs with their teacups in hand. "Now, tell me what happened with D'na Ileana."

The images Selene had seen when she'd touched Ileana's arm shot through her mind like balls in a pinball machine, each bouncing off other ones in a disjointed pattern.

Gryph filled in Balthazar about what he knew, Kobaloi, the troll and even D'na Ileana's reluctance to reveal their future. His gaze stayed her, warming Selene with his concern at the same time it chilled her with the possible outcome of what she'd seen in Ileana's prediction.

"We haven't had time to discuss anything. Apparently Ileana predicted the SWAT team raid."

"Apparently?" Balthazar's brows rose.

Gryph turned to Selene. "What did you see?"

"It wasn't so much what I saw as the overwhelming feeling that troops were on their way to raid the Lair."

Balthazar's brows descended. "All who are aware of our little community are sworn to secrecy. The only way the police could know about us is if they followed someone here."

Selene shook her head. She didn't want to contradict the older man. In her heart, she knew there was a traitor among the people of the Lair, she just wasn't sure who it was. Whoever it might be wasn't there. She hadn't sensed sinister thoughts from any of the evacuees. Only surprise and concern. "The thoughts and images I gathered from the SWAT team leader were that they'd received a tip to check out the tunnels beneath the city. Not just a tip, but also an entry location and direction once down under."

Balthazar's face darkened. "Who would have told?"

Selene shook her head. "I don't know, and I didn't get a name out of my eavesdropping on the SWAT leader's mind."

"Did you get anything else out of your connection with Ileana?" Gryph asked. "What happened when you touched her? Whatever it was knocked both of you out of your seats. It must have been something big."

Her chest tightened and the air left her lungs, the fog of a faint threatened to steal the light from her vision. It took several moments of concentration to sort through the overwhelming flood of images that moment had brought with it. "All I know is that what Ileana sees is what *could* happen. Today I sensed the SWAT team raiding the Lair and all the people being herded to the surface. Because we were here before the police, we altered that possible outcome."

"That's an interesting hypothesis and a good one to

know. However, you avoided my question." Gryph pinned her with his stare. "What else did you see?"

Selene paced faster, refusing to meet Gryph's gaze. "Vague images, situations, scenarios."

Suddenly Gryph was standing in front of her. "What images, situations, scenarios? Whatever they are, we can handle them together."

"That's just it. We *are* together in the images I got from Ileana. You, me, my sisters. And we're all killed." Selene threw her hands in the air. "We were surrounded by wolves. And they were led by a big black wolf with bright green eyes."

Gryph gripped her arms. "Did you recognize any of the wolves as those from the pool hall?"

Selene shook her head. "No. But that doesn't mean it couldn't be one of them."

"What about the surroundings?" His fingers tightened. "Do you have an image of where we were?"

She shook her head, straining her memory to clarify the image. "All I got was the glare of bright lighting and…diamonds. A lot of diamonds, maybe crystals, sparkling everywhere I turned. Other than that, it's all pretty much a blur."

"Indoors or outdoors?" Balthazar asked.

Selene frowned. "Inside."

"That narrows it down." Gryph's lips twisted. "Not really, but it's a start."

"I'm sorry. I wasn't prepared to see you or me die. The whole scene was bad. Bloody. Horrible." Selene pinched the bridge of her nose. "I wasn't prepared."

Gryph's hands smoothed down her arms. "You did good."

"I wish I'd done better. I wish I'd seen the scenario where we won the fight."

"We asked for what our killer would do next. At least he won't be targeting another woman."

"No." Her heart rose to clog her throat and her eyes burned. "He'll be targeting you, me and my sisters."

Gryph's lips curled. "Now we know what to expect and we have a fighting chance."

"I hope so." Selene had the uncontrollable urge to get out of the tunnels and up into the open air of the city. "If it's all right with you, I'd like to get some sleep. I'm sure I'll be better able to handle a full-scale attack when I've had a few hours of sleep."

Balthazar rested a hand on Gryph's shoulder. "Take her home. We could all do with some sleep."

Selene's heart hurt with Balthazar's words. She couldn't go home. Her apartment had been breached. Gryph's plan was to take her to his home. The thought of being alone with him had her torn. On the one hand, she didn't want to be alone. Not after all that had happened. On the other hand, she didn't want to be alone with Gryph and the inevitable outcome of falling into bed with the handsome shifter. At the moment, their destinies were entwined and pretty shaky.

Her blood pounded through her veins—fear of SWAT team raids or trolls having nothing to do with it. Images of their naked bodies lying against the sheets pushed to the forefront of her mind.

Tension built inside her as Gryph led her back the way they'd originally entered the Lair, in what felt like a lifetime ago.

Once they emerged into his basement apartment, Selene was wound up tighter than a drawn bowstring.

"I should go stay the night with my sister Brigid." She headed straight for the door, without waiting for his response.

Before she reached for the knob, a hand on her shoulder stopped her, sealing her fate.

"You're not going to your sister's." Gryph growled low in his throat.

The sound sent fingers of lightning shooting across her nerves, angling toward her core. "You can't keep me here like a prisoner." The image of being bound was positively titillating and she almost groaned.

"You know you want to stay," he said, his golden gaze mesmerizing in its intensity.

"So now you're the mind reader?"

"I study body language. And yours is telling me you want this." Gryph leaned close, captured the back of her neck in his big hand and bent to claim her lips.

"I don't want—" she began.

Gryph swallowed her words, slipping his tongue inside her mouth, sliding it against hers in a warm, wet assault she couldn't resist.

Her arms circled his neck and her calf curled around the back of his. Whatever words she might have said flew from her mind as his kiss stole her thoughts and her will to resist.

Without breaking their kiss, Gryph scooped her into his arms and carried her through the apartment to the bedroom, where he set her on her feet and slowly peeled the layers of clothing off her. First her jacket. He unzipped it and pushed it over her shoulders, letting it slide down her back to drop to the floor.

He tugged the shirt from the waistband of her jeans and lifted it up over her torso.

Selene raised her arms and the shirt came off and was tossed to the side. In her bra and jeans, she could feel the stress of the encounter with Ileana leaving her to be replaced by a different kind of tension. One that began at her center and radiated outward.

She reached for the button on her jeans, only to have her hand brushed aside.

Gryph flicked the button loose and dragged the zipper down, parting the edges. He slipped his hand inside the jeans and her panties to cup her sex, a finger sliding between her folds.

Selene sucked in an unsteady breath, aching to be naked and lying in the sheets with this man. "Too slow," she said and grabbed his T-shirt, ripped it up over his head and tossed it aside. While he pushed her jeans over her hips, she yanked the button loose on his and pushed them down over his bulging thighs.

In a few frenzied movements, they were rid of their jeans and shoes.

Gryph scooped her up again and laid her across the shiny gold-and-black satin duvet.

The fabric felt cool against Selene's feverish skin, but did nothing to temper the torrid heat burgeoning inside as Gryph stood beside the bed, gorgeous, naked and dangerous, his golden eyes sultry and dark. "You're beautiful."

"You're not so bad yourself," she said, her voice low and gravelly. She leaned up, grabbed his hand and drew him onto the bed beside her, amazed at her own hunger and eagerness to consummate their shared desire in what promised to be a fiery conclusion to a very long night. With no windows to let the sunlight in, Selene couldn't tell if it was night or day and really didn't care. All her focus centered on this man-beast and what he was about to do to her and with her.

Her channel slicked in anticipation, her heartbeat racing, blood pounding through her veins as she trailed a hand across his broad chest and down his ribs to the hot, stiff member jutting upward, thick and proud. She wrapped her fingers around him, sliding them slowly up and down the velvety smoothness.

He captured the back of her neck and leaned over her, his lips descending on hers, the force of his assault pressing her into the mattress. Then his hand skimmed down her throat, over one shoulder and across a breast to tweak the distended nipple.

Selene arched her back, pressing into his hand.

With his large capable hand, he cupped the breast, rolling the peaked tip between his thumb and forefinger. He broke the seal of their lips and feathered kisses down the column of her throat to the swell of her breast, replacing his fingers with his tongue. At first stroking across the bud with a strangely rough tongue, he made the tip even tighter, then he sucked it into his mouth, pulling hard on it, unleashing a lust so powerful Selene squirmed.

Her legs fell open, her hand guiding his cock to her opening. "Please."

"Patience," Gryph whispered, blowing a warm stream of air across her damp breast. Then he blazed a trail of kisses and nips down her torso to the apex of her thighs, parting her legs to settle between them.

Selene lay back against the comforter, her breath caught in her lungs, waiting for the moment.

With care and calculation, he parted her folds and touched the tip of his coarse tongue to the bundle of electric nerves, setting off an explosion of sensations that had Selene rocking her hips high above the mattress.

He chuckled. "Like that?"

"By the goddess, yes!" she screamed, her fingers threading into his tawny hair, pulling him back to the goal for more of the same.

Flicking her again, he treated her to long, sexy strokes

that left her gasping, her knees tightening around his ears and her world coming apart with an explosion of brightly colored fireworks.

Spasms of electrical shocks racked her body until she was begging him, "Please, come inside me. Now!" Selene tugged on his hair, urging him to climb up her body.

Gryph lapped once more then rolled off her and reached into his nightstand for a condom.

"Let me," Selene said, her voice strained, her body poised for what came next, her anticipation even more pronounced after he'd brought her to an earth-shattering orgasm. It wasn't enough. She wanted more.

With shaking hands, she tore open the packet, slipped the rubber over his member and rolled it down the sides, loving how thick and hard he was, imagining what he'd feel like buried inside her.

Then he was between her legs, where he pushed her knees up, pressed his cock against her opening and paused.

Selene almost came unglued. She wrapped her legs around his waist and dug her heels into his buttocks, urging him into her.

He held back. "There is no way we're going to die anytime soon."

"You bring that up now?" she wailed.

"Damn right. I won't let it happen." He stared down into her eyes, his cock nudging against her wetness. "We have far too much to live for." With those words, he drove into her, stretching her inside, filling her with a fullness she'd never experienced before him. It went beyond lust to a sense of coming home.

Then Gryph moved in a steady, pounding rhythm, driving into her, again and again.

She dropped her heels to the mattress and met him

thrust for thrust, loving how deep and fierce his movements were, craving more with each stroke.

Once again, she rocketed to the crest and soared into the atmosphere.

At that moment, Gryph sank deep and held it there, his member twitching, throbbing, hot and thick inside her.

When Selene finally returned to earth, she lay spent, satiated and complete.

Gryph rolled over, taking her with him, without breaking their intimate connection, his shaft still hard inside her.

Her eyelids drifted closed, her body relaxing in the safety of Gryph's arms.

"Sleep," he said, his breath warm on her cheek as he brushed strands of hair from her face.

Exhausted from all the events of the past few days, Selene let the worry of what might happen soon fade from her mind. She basked in the afterglow of the best sex she'd ever had and she slipped into warm, blessed oblivion.

Gryph lay on his side with Selene nestled in the crook of his arm and marveled at the strength and resilience of this witch who'd stormed into his world, saved his life and refused to sit on the sidelines when the odds were stacked against them. What troubled Gryph was the anguish he'd seen in her face after she'd experienced Ileana's view of what the future had in store for him, herself and her sisters. He didn't want this woman to die. She had so much to offer, so much to give, and a life worth living. And he wanted to be a part of it.

Thinking back to her description of the place the attack would take place, he tried to picture it himself—lots of light, stars, diamonds. Was she referring to a sunrise on Lake Michigan when the angle of the sun makes the water look like it's coated in diamonds? No. She'd mentioned that it was inside. Was there a place bright with lights that sparkled like diamonds? In a city the size of Chicago, that could be just about anywhere. The hotels had rooms with high ceilings and great lighting. Maybe.

Dread threatened to take the joy out of what he'd just shared with Selene. Somehow he had to figure it out and come up with a plan to stack the odds in their favor. If they were to be attacked by wolves, they had to have their plan in place to defend themselves. Surely even witches with the incredible talents of the Chattox sisters couldn't keep up with an overwhelming numbers of wolves. Ileana's vision proved that. One potential outcome was for the six of them to die.

Gryph's arm tightened around Selene's shoulders and he stared down at her face, her creamy cheek pale against his golden tanned arm. Her dark brown hair splayed out across the sheets in rich, luxurious waves. He had such a feeling of belonging, he couldn't imagine her with anyone else.

When had she come to mean so much to him? And how could he ask her to be a part of his life when he wasn't free to be who he was in public? She deserved to find love with someone who wasn't a monster like him. If he wasn't so caught up in his own desires, he'd let her go. Let her live her life without the challenge he faced on a daily basis—namely, hiding his true identity. If the public learned what he was, the empire he'd built would crumble. And he refused to take Selene down with him.

In that moment, he chose to let time stand still. He didn't want to let her go—he wanted to hold her and protect her from whatever horrible event Ileana had predicted. Until they lived through that—overcoming their enemies—he was going to stick to her like a fly on flypaper.

He drifted into a restless sleep, plagued with horrific dreams of rabid wolves surrounding Selene, cutting her off from him and her sisters. As they edged nearer, Gryph tapped into his inner beast, his muscles expanding, changing, morphing into his alter ego, the massive lion that could rip off a man's head in a single swipe of his paw. As he landed on all fours, he let out a roar and stalked toward the wolf pack, squaring off with the leader, a jet-black wolf with bright green eyes.

With a sparkling gleam in its eyes, it lunged. Not at Gryph, but at Selene, knocking her onto her back, pinning her against the floor.

Gryph leaped at the wolf, too late to stop its wicked canines from slashing into Selene's throat, ripping away flesh.

With the force of a Mack truck, Gryph hit the black wolf. The two of them rolled across the ground, teeth flashing, claws tearing into fur.

Gryph suffered a vicious bite to his shoulder, his muscles seizing. With renewed anger, he bit into the wolf's neck, severing the carotid artery. The wolf staggered, blood pouring from the open wound. He stumbled and crashed to the ground, facedown, blood forming a thick copper-scented pool beneath him.

Gryph turned to Selene and gathered her in his arms. She lay as still as death, her skin cool, her eyes open and vacant.

"No!" he cried in his dream. "No!"

A hand shook his shoulder. "Gryph. Wake up." Again someone shook him. "Gryph! Wake up."

He blinked his eyes open and stared into the dark chocolate of Selene's bright irises. He sat up and gripped her arms, the soft skin reassuring him that she was not a figment of his imagination. Then he noticed the deep cuts on her arms and neck. "Good Lord, Selene, what happened?"

She smiled softly at him. "You were having a bad dream."

Gryph recoiled, horrified. "I did that, didn't I?"

Chapter 16

Selene raised her hands. "They're just scratches."

"I could have killed you."

"No, you wouldn't have," she said, though the look in his sleep-glazed eyes had been murderous when he'd pinned her to the mattress, roaring in his half-human form.

Gryph left the bed, grabbed trousers from the closet and slid his legs into them. By the time he returned, his face had changed completely back to his human form, worry and self-reproach etching lines into his forehead.

Selene sat up, letting the sheet fall down around her waist, exposing her breasts. "Please, Gryph, lie down. We can pick up where we left off before we went to sleep."

"Are you insane?" He ran his hand through his hair. "I almost killed you."

She shrugged, both breasts bobbing with the slight movement. "I'm okay."

"No, you're not." He scooped her into his arms, the sheet falling to the floor. "We're going to clean up those wounds before they get infected, then I'm taking you to your sisters."

She wrapped her arms around his neck, pressing her breasts to his chest. "I don't want to go to my sisters. I want to stay here with you."

"Tough. It's not up for discussion."

Selene, unused to flirting with men, tried her best interpretation of a vamp. "Can't we just stay here and make love? Or don't you want me?" She tightened her hold around his neck and nibbled the corner of his lip. "Please, Gryph. I mean it. I'm okay."

Without another word, he carried her to the bathroom, set her naked bottom on the cool granite countertop and rummaged in a cabinet for a first-aid kit.

When he advanced on her with a wet washcloth, she held up her hand. "I can take care of it myself."

He growled. "Move your hands."

For a moment, she contemplated defying him, but the stern hardness of his jaw told her he was in no mood to argue.

Selene tipped her chin up, exposing the long line of her neck.

Gryph gently applied the clean, damp cloth to her torn skin. Though it stung a little, it was the water trickling down her neck that captured her attention. It rolled across the swell of her breast to drip down the valley between, skirting past her belly button to be captured in her mound of curls.

Lust flared like a spark to dry kindling, sending her blood speeding through her veins. She captured his hand and dragged it, cloth and all, over her breasts and down the same path as the drop of water.

His nostrils flared, his hand gripping the cloth so tightly, his knuckles turned white. When she reached the juncture of her thighs, his hand stilled and his breathing grew more labored.

"I can't stop myself," he groaned through gritted teeth.

His words were like a cold slap in her face, a wake-up call to reality. "What did you say?"

"I don't want to hurt you again, but I can't make myself stop this insanity."

"You won't hurt me." Part of her wanted him to continue on and make mad, passionate love to her. The other side of her didn't want to admit what was happening.

"I...can't...control...the beast," he said, his hand moving lower. "Why can't I stop?"

"Because I want it." Pushing aside the nudge of guilt, Selene took the cloth from his fingers and set it aside, urging his hand to take the place of the fabric, to slide through the curls to the folds beneath.

Gryph closed his eyes, his hand cupping her sex, a single finger dipping into her warmth. "You tempt me, witch."

She knew she did more than that and couldn't bring herself to stop. Instead, she wrapped her legs around his waist, tightening to pull him closer, trapping his hand between them.

The hard ridge of his cock pushed against his knuckles, pressing his finger deeper. She lifted his other hand and laid it over her breast.

"This is wrong." He squeezed the flesh between his fingers. Once, twice, his finger pumped in and out of her. When his gaze shifted back to the scratches on her arm, his lips thinned.

Selene wanted him so badly it hurt her to realize she was manipulating him into making love to her. He obviously didn't want it to happen. Her mental push was forcing him into it.

What kind of witch was she? The cool, calculating, dark witch without a conscience?

No way.

With a great deal of effort, she tamped down her base urge to fall back into the bed with this man-beast.

As soon as she backed off her own longing, Gryph's finger left her channel and he unhooked her ankles from behind his back. "You need to clean those scratches yourself."

"Why?" Selene scooted off the counter and stood before him, fighting an inner battle to subdue her lust.

Gryph backed out of the bathroom. "I won't touch you again. I can't risk it. It's too dangerous."

"That's too bad. I was willing to take the risk." She reached up, sliding her body against his one last time.

His eyes glazed with desire.

Damn, she was doing it again. How could she get out of his head, if she couldn't get out of her own?

He captured her wrists in his big hands and held her away. "No, Selene. The risk isn't worth it."

"Maybe it is to me," she whispered, her cheeks heated, disappointment and sadness filling her. "Okay, then." When he let go of her, she let her arms fall to her sides. Pushing her shoulders back, she didn't try to hide her nakedness. If anything, she wanted him to see her, to know what he was giving up. "If we're done here, I have a job to do." With the ball only a day away, she had a dozen things to check on. It had to go off without a hitch or her reputation as a designer and clothier would take a huge hit.

His gaze raked over her. "I'll have my assistant bring you fresh clothing, and my driver can take you to whichever sister you want to stay with."

"Don't bother." She marched past him, purposely rubbing her hip against his thigh. "I can call a taxi."

"With the wolf out there, it's not safe. I insist," he said behind her.

Selene ignored him and snatched her clothing from the floor, where it had landed in their frenzy to get naked earlier. By focusing on her work, she was able to push her longing to the side, apply antiseptic and bandages to her wounds and dress in record time, knowing the sooner she left Gryph's apartment the better off both of them would be. When she was ready, she went in search of Gryph, stopping long enough to place a call to Aurai.

"Selene, where have you been?" Aurai demanded.

"It's a long story," she answered. "Could you pick me up?"

"Where?"

"At the GL Enterprises building."

A long pause met her request. "You were with him all night and half the day?"

Selene closed her eyes and counted to ten to maintain her patience. "Yes. Now, are you going to come get me, or do I need to call a cab?"

"We'll be there in ten minutes."

"We?" Selene gripped the phone harder. "What do you mean *we*?"

The phone had gone dead. Great. The *we* Aurai mentioned could be another sister or all of them, and she wasn't ready to face her entire family. Not yet.

Selene wandered through the spacious apartment to the kitchen, where the scent of coffee filled the air, reviving her.

Gryph stood at the gas stove, wearing a crisp white, long-sleeved shirt and a tie, looking naturally gorgeous, vibrant and more distant than ever. "Do you like eggs?"

Saddened by his remoteness, Selene resisted pouting, something she never thought she'd do but wanted to at that point. "No, thank you. I'm not hungry."

"You haven't eaten anything in at least twenty-four hours." He sighed. "Look, I'm sorry I was so short with you. I just don't want to hurt you."

Bread popped out of a toaster on the counter. Selene's stomach rumbled despite her claim that she wasn't hungry. She decided it was foolish to refuse his offer. "I'll have a slice of toast, if you have enough."

Gryph's brows dipped, then smoothed. "Fine." He placed two pieces of toast on a small plate and set it on the bar. "Have a seat."

Selene settled on a cushioned bar stool and studied Gryph over a mug of coffee. "I'm sorry."

He glanced over his shoulder as he cracked eggs into a small skillet. "For what?"

"Pushing thoughts into your head."

"I'm beginning to recognize when you do that. And believe me when I say, it wasn't all you." He adjusted the heat on the stove and opened the refrigerator. "For your information, I didn't stop because you wanted me to stop. I stopped because I didn't want to hurt you again." He set a jar of strawberry preserves in front of her and stared into her eyes. "My desire to keep you unharmed trumped the desire to make love to you."

As much as she wanted to believe him, Selene couldn't. She feared her telepathic abilities were growing stronger each day.

He brought his eggs to the bar and sat beside her.

Selene chewed the toast dry, if for no other reason than to give her an excuse not to talk. She found herself wishing she wasn't a witch with the ability to influence others. Instead of choking down her food, they'd be rocking the bedsprings. Maybe. She wondered if Gryph truly found her desirable, not just because she planted the thought. Then there was his reluctance to hurt her.

"You think too much." The man of her thoughts took her plate of half-eaten toast, piled it on his empty plate and stood. "If you're ready, I'll take you to one of your sister's houses."

"I'm going back to my shop. I have work to do."

"I can't leave you there alone."

"It's still daylight and my shop can't remain closed forever. I'll lose customers and ultimately my business. Besides, I have a gala to prepare for and no one will attack me in broad daylight."

"You can't be certain."

"I'll take my chances. Besides, I need to arrange for someone to fix my door and locks."

His lips pressing together, he walked past her and laid the dirty dishes in the sink before facing her again. "At least inform your sisters."

"Done. Aurai's on her way. I won't need you to take me."

"Good. And I've already arranged to have your door repaired. The contractor will have a key there for you."

"Then we're done here," she said with finality. Hollowness settled in her belly as she headed for the elevator. Before she reached it, an alarm went off, the sound reverberating through Gryph's apartment. Her heart pounded as she glanced around for the source of the noise. "What's that?"

Gryph raced across the room and snatched the bell-shaped antique phone from the wall and pressed it to his ear. "What happened?"

Selene closed the distance between them, the worry on Gryph's face drawing her nearer.

"When?" He listened, his face growing tighter, grimmer. "I'm on my way." Gryph slammed the phone on its hook. "Jillian's missing."

"Little Jillian?" Selene ran after him. "I'm coming with you."

"Your sister will be here to pick you up. We don't need your help." He hit the switch on the wall, stripping out of his shirt as the door slid back. His chest bare, his hand on the top rail, he glanced back at her. "Go."

His words hit her in the gut, knocking the air from her lungs. Gryph started down the long spiral staircase leading down into the tunnels. He was gone, a little girl was missing and Selene stood staring at the empty staircase, her heart on its way into the bowels of the city with Gryph.

She stepped back and the panel started to slide over the opening. Before the hidden door could close, Selene jammed a fifteen-pound weight into the gap, bracing it open. She couldn't stand back and pretend she didn't care. Jillian was missing and Gryph needed all the help he could get to find her.

A buzzing sound penetrated her thoughts as she stepped over the threshold and onto the metal stairs. It jerked her back to the workout room. "Mr. Leone, you have guests," a voice called out.

Aurai.

Selene followed the sound to an intercom mounted on the wall, found the talk switch, poked it and said, "Send them down."

"I'm sorry, only Mr. Leone has authority to send people into his private quarters."

"Mr. Leone is otherwise occupied," Selene said. Then she closed her eyes and tried again. "You will send them down." This time, she focused on the guard's thoughts, wiping out his orders to defend the private sanctuary of his employer, replacing it with the order to allow the sisters to enter.

"Sending them down" was the guard's response.

Minutes later, the elevator doors opened and all four of her sisters piled out.

"What's going on?" Brigid asked.

"Where's Gryph?" Deme demanded.

"Why are you still here?" Aurai queried.

"Are you okay?" Gina placed a hand on Selene's arm.

Selene fought the urge to cry, knowing there wasn't time to give in to her emotions. "I don't have much time to explain, so listen carefully." She told them of the community of people living in the tunnels below the city and how Gryph had been raised among them. "He feels responsible for them and now one of the children has gone missing. We have to help."

Gina clapped her hands together. "Then let's go."

"How do we get down there?" Brigid asked.

"Follow me." Selene led them to the exercise room, where the panel remained open, jammed on the barbell.

Deme stepped over the weight and stood at the top, her hand on the rail, a frown denting her brow. "I remember the last time we went below."

"To save me from the Chimera." Aurai started to push past Deme. "If there's a little girl down there, lost in that maze of tunnels, we can't just stand around and talk about the past."

"Let me go first," Selene said. "I know the way to the Lair. We can spread out from there."

"Wait." Deme blocked the staircase. "We need a protection spell."

Selene shook her head, a sense of doom urging her to follow Gryph. "We don't have time."

"We *make* time," Deme insisted, her eyes narrowed. She reached out one hand to take Selene's and the other to take Aurai's.

She led off, the others chiming in on the chant they knew so well:

"Feel the power.
Free our hearts.
Find our way.
Be the one.
With the strength of the earth,
With the rising of the wind,
With the calm of the water,
With the intensity of fire,
With the freedom of spirit."

Deme, still holding tight to her sisters' hands continued, "Should evil dwell within this place, banish it with the power of earth."

She nodded toward Brigid.

Brigid picked up the chant. "Banish it with the power of fire."

She turned to Aurai, who said, "Banish it with the power of wind."

Aurai turned to Gina. "Banish it with the power of water."

All her sisters turned to Selene, who added, "Banish it with the power of spirit."

Together they ended with:

"So sayeth, so let it be.
The goddess is within us.
She is power.
We are her.
We are one.
Blessed be."

Once the chant ended, Selene plucked a flashlight from the charger on the wall. Each of her sisters grabbed one, as well. Then she descended into the darkness once again, a chill slithering down the length of her spine.

Gryph arrived at Balthazar's door, half transformed, his sense of smell and eyesight heightened, ready to do what it took to retrieve the child and bring her home safely.

Balthazar was waiting for him, holding a sheet of paper in his hand. "I don't understand."

"What don't you understand? Show me."

He held out the paper with a tear in the top of it. On it typed in block letters were the words "The days of the Lair are at an end."

"Who gave you this?" Gryph demanded.

"It was stuck to my door with these." Balthazar held up a small stuffed bunny and an elaborate knife with brushed silver scrollwork and an emerald set in the silver.

Gryph grabbed the bunny. "I gave this to Jillian."

Balthazar nodded, his old, lined face pale. "I know."

"Where's Jack?"

"With Mrs. Martin. He was beside himself and quite upset."

"What happened?"

"From what I gathered, they were playing hide-and-seek in the south tunnel when Jack heard Jillian scream, and then nothing. He ran to find her, but she was gone. He searched for a few minutes, calling out her name, hoping she was playing the game still. When she didn't respond, he came running back, straight to me. He was the one to find the note on my door."

"No one saw who put it there?"

Balthazar shook his head. "No. Most of the people of

the Lair were inside their homes or gone to the surface for food or to work."

"Someone was bold enough to stick that on your door during daytime hours?" Gryph shook his head. "It has to be someone amongst us. Someone we all know for him to slip in like that."

"No one saw anything."

"Where's Jack now?"

"He wanted to go back out and search for his sister, but I have Mrs. Martin keeping a tight leash on him. It's bad enough one of them is missing."

Gryph nodded. "Who else knows?"

"I haven't alerted the rest of the folks of the Lair. I wanted your take on it. When they realize there is a traitor among us, no one will feel safe again. At the same time, the longer we wait to find Jillian's abductor, the less chance we'll be successful."

"I'm here, now. We need volunteers to search the tunnels."

"There aren't enough folks around."

"Then we bring in more."

"You know the rules."

"Look, rules were meant to be broken and finding Jillian is the best reason I can think of." He glanced back the way he'd come. "I'm going for help. I'll be back as soon as I can."

"Hurry."

To move quicker, Gryph changed into lion form and sped back to the staircase leading up into his apartment. Halfway up, he spied a beam from a flashlight. He slowed his ascent and willed his change back halfway to human, all in a matter of seconds. His trousers shredded and his shoes were lost in the tunnel. Barefoot, he continued upward to meet the person with the flashlight coming down.

Even before he saw her, he knew it was Selene. When she spotted him, she stopped, her eyes widening. "I couldn't stand by and do nothing. And I brought—"

"Us." Brigid leaned over Selene's shoulder. "If you'd told me I'd come willingly back into the tunnels yesterday, I'd have called you a big fat liar and singed you with a fireball."

Gryph's gaze captured Selene's. "I'm glad you came."

Selene touched his arm. "We came to help."

Gryph smiled. "I was coming to ask you if there was some spell you could use to help find her."

Selene nodded. "I might be able to help you with that."

"Can you sense her thoughts?"

"Selene found a child lost in a big department store once," Aurai offered.

Gryph took Selene's hand. "Do you think you can find Jillian?"

"All we can do is try." She glanced over her shoulder at her sisters on the stairs above. "Do you mind if my sisters know about…"

"The Lair?" He shook his head. "I've always trusted my instincts and they're telling me to trust you and your sisters."

Deme added, "The most important thing right now is to find the child."

"Come." Gryph led the way to the Lair.

A small crowd gathered around Balthazar's home.

Gryph introduced the sisters and explained, "They're here to help find Jillian."

A pale woman with jet-black hair and a streak of white at her temple shook her fist. "We don't need surface dwellers helping us."

Gryph raised his hand. "Please, Layla, give them a chance. They have special talents we hope will help us find Jillian faster."

"Please, bring back Jillian." Mrs. Martin sobbed, holding Jack against her side.

The boy's eyes were red-rimmed and his bottom lip trembled. "He took her and I couldn't save her."

Gryph bent to eye level with Jack. "Did you see him?"

Jack shook his head. "No, but I think I heard something. I should have stopped him." Tears trickled down the boy's face.

Selene kneeled beside him, her resolve strengthening. "We'll get her back."

Jack flung his arms around her neck and cried—his tears, his fear and images of dark tunnels flitted through Selene's mind.

When Jack had calmed, Selene handed him over to Mrs. Martin and stood back.

Gryph took charge, assigning certain tunnels to the few able-bodied adult inhabitants who were available and sent them on their way.

Then he turned to Selene and her sisters. "What can I do to help?"

"I'll need something of Jillian's," Selene answered.

He pulled a stuffed bunny from his back pocket and handed it to her. "This is her favorite toy."

Selene held it in her hand and closed her eyes. Images filled her mind of a happy Jillian holding the stuffed animal, having tea with it and sleeping peacefully in her bed, the bunny tucked under her arm.

"Sisters," Selene declared.

All four of her sisters gathered close, reaching out to touch her. Then together, they chanted:

"Goddess of the sun, earth and the moon,
Show us the way to bring the lost home.
So we pray, so mote it be.

With the strength of the earth,
With the rising of the wind,
With the calm of the water,
With the intensity of fire,
With the freedom of spirit,
Blessed be."

Her sisters dropped hands and stepped away from Selene, watching for her next move.

At first, she balked, her mind a blank, nothing surfacing to tell her where to find the girl. A jolt of fear made her close her eyes again and focus. She couldn't fall apart now. Not when a little girl needed her.

Selene clutched the bunny, absorbing the aura of the girl still clinging to the fake fur. An image flitted across her consciousness, one of crumbling walls and dust choking the already dark tunnels. Something was banging, hammering, pounding.

Selene raised her hands to her ears, the pounding beating against her eardrums.

Gryph touched her arm. "What is it?"

"The noise," she whispered. "It's loud, it's loud like a jackhammer, beating against concrete and the dust—" She coughed, trying to clear her lungs. "So dark. Alone. Rocks falling around my feet." Then a hand reached out of the darkness, a pale hand with a light coat of fur covered in a dust.

Help me, a tiny voice cried, the sound reverberating with the pounding in her head.

Selene reached out to take the hand, but it popped out of sight like a balloon with a pin stuck into it.

She opened her eyes and stared down, expecting to see the rocks, hoping to see the hand, but all she saw were her tennis shoes and jeans. Not the choking, dusty darkness or the girl.

Hurry. The whisper of a voice raised gooseflesh on her skin. "Hurry," Selene echoed. "We have to hurry."

"Which way?" Deme asked.

Selene didn't answer, her feet already moving, carrying her where, she didn't know. All she did know was that Jillian was in danger, the walls around her crumbling. If they didn't reach her soon, she'd be buried alive.

Chapter 17

Gryph ran to keep up with Selene, her sisters not far behind. She'd taken the tunnel leading toward the sinkhole. If he didn't catch her soon, she'd fall to her death in the reservoir beneath the city.

When they arrived at the turn in the tunnel that would have led her to the sinkhole, the troll and D'na Ileana, she continued straight, her flashlight bouncing light off the walls, her breathing growing more labored.

The dust grew thicker the farther along they went until Selene slowed to pull her shirt up over her nose. Then she ran on, the beam of her flashlight barely penetrating the swirling dust filling the tunnel.

A distant pounding reached them. If he wasn't mistaken, this section of the tunnels had been declared off-limits to the inhabitants of the Lair long ago. The walls were breaking up, water leakage from the older city streets above ate away at the mortar between the bricks and weakened the support beams.

Gryph racked his memory for where they were in relation to the city above. He recalled a construction site in downtown Chicago.

Oh, hell. His company was tearing down an old hotel that had fallen into a terrible state of disrepair. Even the historical society had deemed it unsalvageable. He'd hired a demolition team to take the building down. They were due to set off explosions to implode the building in place. His assistant had marked the day on his calendar in case he wanted to be present for the event.

It was as clear in his mind now as if he read the calendar all over again. Today was the scheduled date. There would be police barricades set up for several blocks surrounding the building, but none in the tunnels. Most people thought the tunnels too deep to worry about, and uninhabited. Just like the folks of the Lair liked it. He'd informed Balthazar to keep people away from the forbidden zone.

If Selene's abilities were taking them directly to Jillian, there was a good possibility this was all a trap.

It didn't matter. They couldn't stop now, not when a little girl's life was at stake. At the very least, the sisters should know what they were up against.

Gryph caught up with Selene, grabbed her and pulled her to a stop. "Wait."

"No time." Selene sucked in air. "Jillian's in danger."

"I know." When she tried to pull away, he tightened his grip.

Her sisters stopped behind him, breathing hard into their shirts to keep from inhaling all the dust.

Gryph spoke loud enough to be heard by all five of them. "The noise you were hearing is from the surface. They're preparing a building for demolition. They're going to set off explosives today."

"Damn." Selene's eyes rounded and glanced from him to her sisters. "I'll go in alone. You should all stay here."

"Like hell." Brigid sucked in a lungful of dust and coughed.

"I agree," Gina said. "You can't continue on your own."

Aurai nodded. "It's all or none."

"A child wouldn't have wandered this far," Selene said. "Whoever did this wanted someone to come after her."

Gryph's jaw tightened. "It smells like a trap."

"Who are they trying to catch?"

"Me," Gryph said. "I can't let you all go in after the girl. We could be up against more than collapsing tunnels and debris."

"You won't find her without me." Selene touched his arm. "Not in time to save her and possibly yourself."

Where her fingers rested on his arm, warmth spread throughout his body. At least he knew she cared and that grounded him, giving him hope.

"I have to go. Jillian's fate is my responsibility. Someone is using her to get to me." His hands clenched into fists. "I mean to find him, and when I do, I'll kill him."

"*After* we get Jillian out." Selene started forward, moving as quickly as she could with limited visibility. Her flashlight beam only lit two feet ahead. Navigating over old rails, crumbled bricks and debris became increasingly difficult.

When they arrived at a junction, Selene stopped, closing her eyes.

Gryph and her sisters waited silently, the sounds of collapsing rubble and dripping water the only noises. The pounding had stilled.

Selene opened her eyes and stared at the ceiling. "They're about to set off the charges."

"We don't have time. We have to get out of here," Deme said.

"Not without Jillian." Selene turned left and took off at a run, tripping and stumbling as she went.

Gryph forced the change, dropping down on all fours, and ran ahead of Selene, his vision no better than hers with all the dust, but he was more sure-footed on four feet instead of two.

At another junction, not far from the previous one, he paused and listened. Was that a whimper? He glanced back as a fuzzy light pushed through the murky passage. Then he ran in the direction he'd heard the sound coming from.

He hadn't gone ten yards when he practically tripped over Jillian, lying on the rail tracks, her arms duct-taped to her sides, her legs bound together in tape, as well, a rag tied around her eyes. She was sobbing quietly, coughing every time she took in a breath of air.

As Gryph came to a halt, Jillian grew still. "Hello? Who's there? Please, help me."

Gryph changed back to human, his skin and muscles stretching, reshaping until he could stand. "It's me—Gryph."

Her sobbing began anew. "I knew you'd come. I knew."

Gently, he pulled the rag off her eyes and extended a sharp claw to slice through the tape on her legs and around her arms.

Selene and her sisters reached him as he gathered Jillian into his arms. "We have to get out of here."

"Now," Selene agreed. "They've begun the countdown. Even if they want to stop, they can't."

"Move!" Gryph followed the sisters down the long tunnels. On their way back, they didn't have the directional pull that had led them to Jillian. Twice they hesitated at junctions, until Gryph pushed past them and followed his feline sense of smell, clouded by the fog of dust.

"Get down, everyone! Cover your heads and brace yourselves," Selene called out and dropped to her belly. "The charges are about to go off."

Gryph lowered Jillian to the ground and between him and Selene, they covered her body with theirs.

Several rumbling booms shook the earth as, one after the other, the charges above went off. Bricks fell from the ceiling, crashing on and around them.

Gryph used his body and hands to cover Selene and Jillian, protecting them from the debris as it fell. Several large bricks pummeled his back, the pain nothing compared to the thought of losing Jillian or Selene.

As soon as the resonant booming stopped and the earth stilled again, he was on his feet.

"We have to move fast. The second round of explosives will go off in ten seconds." Selene staggered, helped Jillian up into Gryph's arms. Together, they ran back the way they'd come.

The second round of charges went off, pitching Gryph forward. He turned and hit the ground on his back, quickly rolling over to cover Jillian's body.

Selene stumbled to her belly beside him, her flashlight gripped in her hand but shedding so little light in the gloom as to be ineffective.

A brick fell with a soft thud.

Selene grunted beside him.

"Are you okay?" he said as more shaking loosened additional bricks.

"Yes." With her hand over her head and neck, she shined the light back toward her sisters. "Deme?"

"I'm still with the living." She called out, "Aurai?"

"I'm okay. Might have a shiner tomorrow, but I'll be okay, if this doesn't get any worse."

"Gina, Brigid?" Deme continued.

"I'm good," Gina said.

Brigid moaned. "I think I sprained my wrist, but I'll live."

"Are they done?" Aurai asked, her disembodied voice seeming to hover in the murk. She'd climbed to her feet and was shining her light upward. "If not, we could be in a heap of trouble. Get a load of that ceiling."

Selene glanced up. The beam barely penetrated the dust cloud filling the tunnel. They were all covered in a fine layer of dust, appearing like so many ghosts.

Another string of rumbling booms shimmied the earth.

"Get down, Aurai!" Deme shouted as loosened bricks gave way.

Gina swept her hands in the air, directing a wall of stagnant water over their heads, knocking the bricks to the side.

Deme followed with a movement that wove a tight web of vines covering the remaining masonry, stabilizing it long enough for them to get out from under the collapsing tunnel.

Gryph stood, clutching Jillian to his chest. He hunched over her as a stray piece of brick found its way through the blanket of vegetation and bounced off his shoulder. "We need to keep moving. If the falling bricks don't hurt us, breathing the dust will."

"We're right behind you." Selene touched her hand to his back as they moved single-file over the rails and fallen bricks.

He liked knowing she was there. Her compassion for a child, almost a stranger to her, captured Gryph's heart and refused to let go.

The farther they moved away from the demolition site, the easier it was to see, and soon they left the thickest dust behind and were able to breathe more freely.

When they emerged into the switching station that was the Lair, a crowd gathered around them.

Mrs. Martin reached out for Jillian, but the little girl wasn't ready to let go of Gryph. She hugged his neck so tightly, he was afraid he might choke yet again.

When she finally loosened up enough to lean back and look into his face, her tears were making trails through the dust on her cheeks. "You saved me." She kissed his dirty face.

"Not me…" He turned to Selene and pulled her into the curve of his arm. "Selene was the one who led us to you."

Jillian tipped out of his arms into Selene's. "Thank you."

Selene chuckled and held the child, her own tears trickling, making mud tracks down her face. "I'm just glad I could help."

Mrs. Martin engulfed Selene and Gryph in a bear hug.

Gryph handed Jillian off to Mrs. Martin and stepped up to Balthazar's door, where the older man stood, regarding the dispersing crowd, his face grim. "Who would do that to a child?"

"It had to be someone we know," Gryph said. "Someone familiar with the tunnels and what's going on at the surface."

"But, why?"

The why baffled Gryph, as well. "It has something to do with me." Who had he angered so much so that he'd use a child to get to him?

"Why do you think that?"

"Why else would he leave the note on *your* door?"

Balthazar rubbed his chin. "He could have been targeting me."

Shaking his head, Gryph said, "No. He took Jillian to the forbidden zone. The very area I warned you would be unsafe while demolition and construction is going on at the surface. It's one of the construction sites *my* company is responsible for. He did it deliberately to get me there at that exact time, knowing the demolition team would blow the building today. He knew *I'd* go and *you* would stay here to keep the people calm." He stared out at the emptying space. "I don't know who did it, but I intend to find out."

"It has to be someone who knows the people of the Lair and your business on the surface. Someone privy to your warning to stay clear of the forbidden zone."

His back stiffening, Gryph stared out at the junction station that had been his home since before he was old enough to remember. Though he'd thought it before, it was clear, now. "It's one of our own."

Selene stood with her sisters as the people of the Lair thanked them for helping rescue Jillian. The whole time, her head hurt and she had difficulty forcing a smile.

At first she thought the pain an aftereffect of breathing too much dust. But the longer it persisted, the more convinced she was that it was something else. Something evil and so angry it created a darkness that threatened to cloud her mind. She glanced around, trying to figure out where it was coming from. Her gaze was drawn to the mouth of one of the unlit tunnels. Something moved in the shadows. Or at least she thought something moved. She stepped toward it, but a hand gripped her arm.

"Selene, are you okay?" Aurai leaned close. "You're

shaking." She lifted one of Selene's hands. "And your hands are so cold."

Deme, Brigid and Gina gathered around, each of them examining her as if she was under a microscope.

The pressure of hatred increased at her temples. With as much conviction as she could muster, she said, "I'm fine." Her focus was drawn once again to the dark tunnel.

"Let's get you home and into the shower. Then you can take a long, much-needed nap."

Selene wanted to push away from her sisters and investigate the tunnel, but her siblings weren't going to take no for an answer, and after all they'd just been through, Selene didn't want to alarm them.

Before she knew it, they were hustling her back toward the tunnel they'd navigated from the stairs to the Lair.

Gryph fell in step beside her and took over, letting her lean on his arm. "Did that brick hit you harder than I thought? I can have a doctor pay a house call."

"No, no, I'm okay, really. It's just a bruise and barely hurts."

"Then why are you so quiet and weak?" He stopped, bringing her and her sisters to an abrupt halt.

"I..." She glanced back over her shoulder. The evil presence, filled with so much hatred that she'd sensed before, was gone. She straightened, her strength returning. "I felt something...but now it's gone."

Gryph gripped her arm and pulled her to a stop. "What did you feel?"

She shrugged. "Anger. Hatred." Selene grimaced. "Malevolence."

"Should I check the tunnel?" Gryph turned to do that.

Selene grabbed his arm. "No. Whatever it was is long gone. I need to get home and check on a few things before it gets any later."

"If you're worried about the charity ball, don't. I can have anyone you need sent to assist you."

"I don't need help. I just need to be back at my home."

Gryph hesitated a moment longer and then led them up the steps into his apartment.

Brigid tapped her fist into the punching bag hanging from the ceiling in the exercise room. "Quite a place you have here, Mr. Leone."

"Call me Gryph." He shrugged. "It's okay."

"Who drove?" Selene asked.

"I did," Deme responded. "Ready?"

"I am." Selene headed for the elevator, without turning back. After all that had happened between her and Gryph, the angry presence in the tunnel and with her sisters there in Gryph's apartment with them, their parting could be nothing but awkward.

As she stepped into the elevator car, Gryph's hand reached out and stopped her. "Selene, promise me you'll stay with your sisters."

She stared into his deep golden eyes, the electricity crackling between them.

"Don't worry, Gryph. One of us will be with her at all times," Deme said.

Gryph didn't let go of Selene's arm, his gaze never left hers.

"I promise," she whispered, her glance dropping to his lips, the urge to kiss him more than she could hide.

His hand slipped to the back of her head. "I'm going to kiss you, but not because *you* want me to, which I know you do. I'm going to kiss you because *I* want to."

Despite the dust, the muddy tear tracks and dirty hair, his lips claimed hers, bearing down on her mouth, the pressure soft at first then increasing in its intensity.

Selene leaned into him, all will to resist gone. She

wanted him, and to hell with her reservations. She couldn't get enough of him and didn't want the kiss to ever end.

Someone cleared her throat behind Selene.

"You want us to wait in the car?" Brigid asked.

Selene pushed away from Gryph and brushed her dust-caked hair back from her face. "No, I'm ready." He let go of her arm and she stepped out of the doorway and back into the elevator. The doors closed and the car rose.

"Want to tell us what's going on between you two?" Gina asked.

What was going on and where would it go? Selene wasn't sure herself. She touched a hand to her lips and shook her head. "No."

Gryph showered, dressed in jeans and a T-shirt and hurried back down into the tunnels. Whoever was causing him problems, threatening the people he loved, would pay.

Jillian had been the pawn in this latest game. Amanda had only lived long enough to identify Gryph as her attacker. The killer had finished her off after she'd had the police forensics artist draw a sketch of him. Almost being run over by a truck at the pool hall hadn't seemed like an attack by the Devil's Disciples, either.

Since the attack on Amanda, the more recent attacks had hit closer to home. Closer to Gryph, making it more personal. And when he entered the Lair, he went directly to Balthazar's house. Balthazar had been his father, his mentor and the man he went to whenever he had a question or problem he couldn't resolve himself. Now was no different. In fact it was even more important. The people around him were in danger for just being around him. It had to stop.

He entered without knocking, Balthazar's home was just as much his as when he was a child. Voices sounded from the den on the opposite side of the home. Gryph followed.

"Gryph, I'm glad you came back." Balthazar waved toward the man standing behind him and stepped aside.

His brother, Lucas, sat at the table, his lip curled up on one side. "I understand I missed all the excitement."

The anger Gryph had held in check bubbled up and spilled over. "Damn it! This isn't a game. Someone is targeting me and the people around me for some very sick reason."

"And yet you always manage to come up smelling like a rose." Lucas grinned. "My big brother, the hero."

"I'd rather none of these things were happening. There's a dead woman and a terrified child who suffered because of me." Gryph paced the length of the den, across a red-and-gold Persian rug, without seeing the beautiful Victorian antiques Balthazar had collected over the years.

The room was a warm study in the culture and taste of a bygone era, a contradiction to the gloom and darkness of the tunnels, where it was located.

"Why would someone want to hurt these people? What have *they* done to deserve it?"

"Come, brother." Lucas rose from the table and draped an arm around his shoulders. "You've conquered every obstacle in your rise to power. Surely a little mystery won't stump you for long."

Gryph shook the arm from his shoulder, his jaw clenched so hard it twitched. "I *will* find the one responsible."

"Now you're talking." Lucas grinned. "That's the self-assured brother I know and love. It's that certainty that has made you the man you are today. The rich philanthropist that gives all his wealth to the needy."

Gryph stared at his brother. Had there been a thread of contempt in his tone? "Is there something bothering you, Lucas?"

"Of course not. My life is just the way I like it."

Gryph had spent a considerable amount of time counseling Lucas on college and course work that would help him land a good job that would pay for the things he loved, like fast cars and expensive restaurants.

So far Lucas had been as human as any of the surface dwellers. Regrettably, he'd been raised in the Lair with little connection with the world above until he was a teen, venturing to street level at night when no one was looking. He'd fallen in with a gang of miscreants who'd rather deal in drugs than do an honest day's work. "Have you finished those online college courses I helped you sign up for?"

"I'm working on it. You and Father won't have to put up with me much longer."

"We don't *put up with you*. You're family. And a degree will go a long way toward building a career."

"With you as my role model, how can I go wrong?" Lucas smiled, which looked more like a sneer. "Now, if you'll excuse me, I have to go to work."

"You might check in on occasion," Balthazar said. "Things haven't been right lately and people are getting scared."

"Of what? That their safe little hiding place isn't so safe anymore?" Lucas shook his head. "We can't hide forever. Sooner or later, the world will know we exist."

Gryph knew it was only a matter of time, but the folks living in the Lair didn't want to be exposed any sooner than they had to be. The surface dwellers tended to be cruel when it came to people who were different on the outside.

What they didn't know was that while they might look very different on the outside, they were all the same on the inside, with emotions, fears and desires that transcended gender and species. An image of Selene filled his consciousness and his desire spiked and was immediately squelched as another thought hit him.

If he was the target of all that was happening, and the people around him were the collateral damage, Selene could be caught in the crossfire. He couldn't let that happen. Gryph left the Lair and headed back to his apartment. There was only one way to ensure Selene's safety.

Chapter 18

Back at her shop, Selene and her sisters took turns in the shower, then scrambled through Selene's closet for clean clothes. Then they crowded in the store with her, hovering like a bunch of mother hens. "I don't need five babysitters. You all can go home," she said, more irritably than she'd intended.

"We made a promise to have someone with you at all times," Deme said.

Aurai slipped her arm around Selene's waist and hugged her close. "If there's any chance someone might target you, he'll have to go through one or all of us."

"If you're trying to scare me," Selene grumbled, "it's working."

"Be serious, Selene." Brigid tossed a fireball in her palm. "We won't let what happened to Aurai, happen to you."

Selene gave her flame-throwing sister a pointed look.

"We defeated the Chimera. The chances are pretty slim that there's another lurking beneath the city."

"That might be true. But this family sticks together." Gina stuck her hand in the center of the circle of sisters. "No witch left behind."

Brigid, Deme and Aurai covered Gina's hand with ones of their own.

Selene sighed and laid her hand over top for a brief show of force, then dropped it to her side. "I appreciate your concern, but right now, I could use a little *alone* time to gather my thoughts."

"And think about the dreamy Gryphon Leone?" Aurai grinned. "He's very handsome without his shirt, what with all those lovely muscles and those six-pack abs." She fanned herself with her hand. "How does the rest of him stack up?"

"Aurai!" Selene's cheeks burned. "That's not something we discuss."

"Don't be such a prude, Selene." Aurai planted a fist on her hip. "I'm twenty-one and not a virgin. We all know you and the shifter are doing the nasty."

Her cheeks on fire, Selene turned away and punched the button on the shop's answering machine.

Selene had no fewer than fifteen messages from the combined forces of Mrs. Stockton and Mrs. Washburn. Each woman demanded to know why the costumes hadn't been delivered to the hotel with the charity ball only a day away.

"Damn." Selene clapped a hand to her forehead.

"What's wrong?"

"In all the excitement, I forgot to deliver the costumes. They were supposed to be at the hotel yesterday afternoon."

"We can deliver them," Gina offered.

Selene shook her head. "Deme, you and Brigid have a murderer to find. I would think your time would be better served out beating the streets to find the black wolf."

Brigid's cell phone buzzed and she glanced down at the display screen. "Speak of the devil, it's the boss." She punched the talk button, turned and walked a few steps away.

"We can't leave you alone," Deme said softly, but in that firm tone of an oldest sister used to giving orders. "Even if we can't all stay, at least one of us will be with you at all times."

Selene knew they were hanging around because they cared. "Thanks."

Brigid ended her call and turned back to the group. "Well, Deme, that was our cue. The lieutenant got a tip on a secret meeting location of an unnamed wolf pack. We're to meet Cal at the station and go from there back to Archer Heights."

Deme gave Selene a stern look. "Stay with one of your sisters. Having backup isn't a sign of weakness."

"Tell me about it." Brigid snorted. "Deme saved my ass on our last assignment against that telepathic demon who tried to get me into his car. If she hadn't been there, who knows what he'd have done."

Selene nodded. "I get it. I'll keep a backup. Now go. We need to find that wolf before he attacks again. Call me if you need me to help with the investigation. And don't forget, I need help tomorrow night getting the waitstaff ready for the charity ball."

"We won't forget," Deme said over her shoulder as she followed Brigid out.

Gina and Aurai stuck to Selene like glue. They rode with her to the seamstress's shop to collect the costumes and back to Selene's to unpack and check over each garment. She ended up pulling five costumes of the hundred for rework. She and her sisters delivered the rest to the hotel in ten boxes.

When they returned to Selene's apartment, all three women flopped into chairs, exhausted.

"I think I could sleep for days," Aurai said, yawning into her palm.

"Nothing like fighting wolves and escaping a tunnel collapse to get your blood humming." Gina leaned her head back, closing her eyes. "But I think delivering costumes wore me out even more." She tipped her head up and stared at Selene. "How do you do it?"

"How do you clean fish tanks all the time?" Selene shivered. "All that slime and fish poop gives me the heebie-jeebies."

Gina shrugged. "I love the finished product—clean water and happy fish."

"Same here. I like the finished product of beautifully dressed people."

"Speaking of beautifully dressed people..." Gina's eyes narrowed. "What are you wearing to the ball? Are you keeping your gown a surprise or something?"

Selene blinked. "I haven't got a gown because I'm not attending the ball. You know how expensive the tickets are."

"Let me get this straight..." Aurai's brows rose. "You don't get in free for all the work you've done?"

"I'm getting paid for my work. That's enough for me. Besides, the ticket money goes to a children's charity. It's a good cause."

"Oh, come on, admit it," Gina said. "You'd love to go to that ball."

"Think of the hundreds of yards of expensive fabric and gowns made by the world's top designers," Aurai continued, painting a picture with her words. "Sparkling jewels, gorgeous hairstyles, the crème de la crème of Chicago society decked out in their finest. A ball fit for royalty." She swung out her arm with dramatic flourish.

Selene had dreamed about attending, imagining the beauty of the decorations and the people dressed in their finest. It would be truly magical. But even with the money she'd make with the fairy costumes she'd designed for the staff, she couldn't afford to plunk down thousands for a ticket. "It's just a ball. They're only people. I have no interest in going," she lied.

"Aren't you in the least interested in seeing Gryphon in a tux?" Aurai's sly smile didn't fool Selene a bit. The girl was digging for information.

Again, Selene felt it necessary to lie. "No."

"Oh, come on, can't you imagine all those fabulous muscles contained in a tailored black tux." Aurai smacked her lips. "Yum."

Hell, yeah, she'd imagined Gryph in a tux. But she'd seen him in a whole lot less, leaning over her in the bed, making love to her until she cried out. Heat spread down her neck into her chest and lower, pooling between her legs.

As tired as she was, Selene pushed out of her chair and paced the floor. Sure, like any woman who loved fashion and beautiful clothes, she'd dreamed of attending a beautiful ball with music, dancing and men dressed in tuxedoes.

But this was different. Gryph was sponsoring the event and he hadn't invited her or expressed a desire for her to be there. It was a charity event he would barely tolerate and at which he'd probably make a five-minute appearance. Why should she want to be there with the backbiting society matrons picking apart every woman's outfit and hairstyle like the fashion police of Chicago? Besides, I'm sure it's too late to purchase a ticket anyway."

"Ah ha!" Aurai sat up straight and pointed a finger at Selene. "I *knew* you wanted to go." She pulled her smart phone out of her pocket and clicked buttons.

Selene frowned. "What are you doing?"

"Going online to find a ticket for you," she said in a matter-of-fact tone.

"Oh, no you don't." Selene snatched the phone from her hands.

Aurai lunged for it.

Gina plucked the phone from Selene's hand and swung away. "Here's the website."

Aurai wrapped Selene in a hug, trapping her arms against her sides.

Selene struggled to free herself. "Let go. I'm not going to the ball. There are more important things to be concerned about."

Ignoring her protests, Aurai asked, "Any tickets left?"

A long pause and Gina looked up, her lips turning down on the corners. "Sold out."

Aurai released Selene.

"See?" Selene stepped away from her sister, hiding her disappointment. "It wasn't meant to be.

Not as convinced she should give up, Aurai touched a finger to her chin. "We have to think of a way to get her in."

"I'm not going."

Aurai grinned at Gina. "She doth protest too much, methinks."

"Me, too."

Selene rolled her eyes then pinched the bridge of her nose to force back the growing headache. "I need rest.

Tomorrow is a busy day. I have five costumes to alter and deliver, and I want to be in the staff area before it starts to make sure everything fits and looks right." And maybe she'd catch a glimpse of Gryph. Selene glanced at her wristwatch and swallowed a groan. She hadn't been with him for all of six hours and she was counting the minutes until she saw him again.

Damn. She had a business, a home and her sisters. She didn't need the complication of falling for a man, much less falling for a man who wasn't human.

Gina's eyes narrowed. "Are you in love with him?"

Damn. Was everyone becoming a mind reader? Selene shook her head. "No, no, I'm not. Other than an animal attraction—no pun intended—he's not my type."

"You mean your type isn't tall, broad-shouldered and gorgeous?"

"Look, I'm not in the market for happily ever after."

"So, you're in the market for miserable and lonely?"

"Of course not. I'm not miserable, and I'm not lonely."

"Then why have you been checking the time ever since we left the Lair?"

Her cheeks burned and the heat spread down her neck. "I'm not watching the clock." Unable to stop herself, she glanced at her watch again. This time she did groan. "Okay, so I'm clock-watching. The ball isn't very far off. I'm tense, keyed-up and second-guessing my work."

Gina snorted. "Yeah."

"Honey…" Aurai crossed her arms over her chest, her lips twisting into a wry grin. "You're wondering when Gryph will walk through that door, sweep you off your feet and kiss you like there's not gonna be a tomorrow."

"No, I'm not." Though the thought made her knees weak. She had to admit she was disappointed he hadn't come by to check on her. The sun had set and still he hadn't dropped in or called. "I'm going to get a shower and go to bed."

"I call dibs on the couch," Gina said.

Aurai shrugged. "Fine. I'll take the chaise. I feel decadent when I sit on it." The piece was in a rose-and-burgundy red fabric, an antique from a 1930s boudoir. Selene had found it scuffed and torn in a flea market. She'd brought it home and lovingly restored it to its former glory.

"You two do whatever makes you happy. Good night."

Selene grabbed clean underwear and her favorite, worn nightgown and headed down the hallway to the only bathroom, closing the door behind her.

As she stripped out of her clothing, she couldn't help thinking about Gryph. Standing naked in front of the tub, she touched her fingers to her breasts, imagining Gryph's hands there instead of her own. So sensitized by her imagination, her nipples tightened into hard little buds. The least little flick set off electrical charges, bursting along her skin and sending a rush of liquid lust to her core.

She stepped beneath the shower's spray and let the water wash down her chest to the mound of curls over her sex. A soft moan left her throat.

"Are you all right in there?" Gina asked.

Selene raised hands to her taut nipples and said, "Yes." More than all right, she was well on her way to one-handed sex. It would be every bit as good as the real deal she'd shared with Gryph.

Yeah, right.

"Let us know if you need anything," Gina called out.

She needed something, all right—a man. And not just any man. Gryphon Leone was the only man who knew exactly how to scratch her itch. But he had too much on his mind to think about her. Lives depended on him. Sex was only a distraction.

She built a foaming lather with the bar of soap and slid her hands down over her breasts, plumping them in the warm water, continuing the descent to her nether regions. Her channel clenched in anticipation. If only her hands weren't so soft. If only they were the big coarse hands of a man who did more than push paper for a living.

She parted her folds and stroked herself with the tip of her finger, sending shards of sensations shooting across her nerves, lighting a fire deep in her core. Her breath caught in her throat and she stroked again. She wished Gryph was there. He was so much better at this. But in a pinch…

Dipping a finger into her channel, she swirled it around, testing how wet and ready she was.

For what? Her battery-powered pleasure device? Who was she kidding? Nothing was better than the real thing. Yet, she'd been as guilty about pushing Gryph away as he'd been. By the goddess, she wanted him!

She rinsed the suds and lathered her hair with the sweet scented shampoo, scrubbing hard as if to wash the man out of her head before she ducked under the water.

A scraping sound penetrated the blast of water in her ears. She pulled back out of the water to listen.

At the same time, big rough hands slipped around her belly and pulled her back against a hard, muscular body.

She tensed, sucked in enough air to scream.

"Shh. It's me," Gryph whispered against her ear.

Leaning into him she let go of the tension of the day, reveling in a different kind of tautness blossoming in her belly and spreading outward. She reached behind her and grasped his buttocks, pressing him into her, his member nudging her behind.

"How did you avoid the gauntlet of my sisters?"

"What gauntlet? The minute I arrived, they disappeared."

"Some protection they were."

"They did tell me to call them if you needed anything. Do you want me to call them?" He nibbled her earlobe then trailed kisses along the curve of her neck.

"No."

"Do you want me to leave?"

"No."

"What do you want, Selene?"

She curled her fingers around his and pushed them lower, to cup her sex. "This." With her hands guiding him, she pushed one of his big fingers into her channel. "Touch me."

"My pleasure." With one finger sliding into her folds, the other rising up to cup her breast, Gryph had her complete attention.

"Holy hell, I missed you," he breathed against her skin.

"Ditto," she rasped as he flicked that highly sensitive bundle of nerves and sent her body and mind shooting skyward.

"How much?" he asked, his rough tongue sliding down her shoulder, his teeth nipping along the way.

"Enough." She turned, pressed against him, chest to chest, wrapped her arms around his neck and drew his head down until her breath mingled with his. "What took you so long?" She claimed his lips.

Laughter rumbled up his chest, dying off before it could escape his throat. He lifted her, pushing her up against the cold shower tiles, circling her legs around his waist. Nothing could cool the heat raging inside her.

Selene locked her ankles, her wet entrance rubbing against his erection. "What's taking you so long now?"

He grasped her face in his hands and then kissed her long and hard, his hips rocking against hers, yet he refused to penetrate. When he tore his lips from hers he spoke in a low growl. "Promise me…"

"Anything."

"Stop me when I get too rough." He held her motionless, his gaze glued to hers.

Selene could tell by the intensity of his expression, this meant a lot to him. She laid a hand against his cheek and brushed a kiss across his lips. "I promise."

With her gathered in his arms, he swiped the curtain aside and grabbed a foil pack from the counter. Water sprayed out on the floor.

Selene didn't care, desperate for him to slide the condom over his engorged manhood and enter her in one long powerful thrust. She ached to feel him deep inside, filling her, stretching her, making her scream with desire.

With painfully slow movements, he took his time, centering then rolling the prophylactic down.

With a tight huff, she brushed his hands aside and finished the job.

His laughter echoed against the bathroom walls, but he didn't prolong her torture, entering her like she wanted, fast and hard, driving deep, her back banging against the wall. That little bit of pain, coupled with his intense hammering, rocketed her to the edge of reason.

She dug her fingers into his shoulders and screamed out his name as her body shook with the force of her release.

Gryph rammed into her once more and held, his face tight, half-morphed into the beast. When he came back to earth, he looked down at his hands, his claws extended, digging into her buttocks, trickles of blood dripping into the shower's spray.

"Damn!" He lifted her off him and set her on her feet, turning her so that he could assess the damage, his heart squeezing hard in his chest. "You promised to stop me."

She tried to hide the puncture wounds. "They're just scratches."

"I did that."

"Yeah, and that was the best sex I've ever experienced." She reached up to cup his face, a face he knew would be half man, half beast.

Gryph knocked her hand away, regretting his anger as soon as he let loose. "I'm sorry." He stepped out of the tub onto the bath mat and reached for his clothing. "I keep saying never again, but then I can't seem to keep my hands off you."

"Then don't." She climbed out and stood in front of him, pressing a finger to his lips. "I enjoyed every moment. And if I'm not imagining it, so did you."

"I don't enjoy hurting you."

"You didn't."

"For the love of heaven, woman, you're bleeding!" He jammed his feet into his jeans and flung his shirt over his shoulder. "I'll understand if you want me to leave. Aurai said call her if you wanted her to come back tonight."

"Don't make me call her." Selene reached out with her mind. He could feel her strong pull. "Stay." She leaned into him, her hands circling his neck.

He shook his head, and dragged her arms down to her sides. "I shouldn't. Every time we make love, I hurt you."

Selene's jaw firmed. "It's okay."

"No, it's not. I don't want to." He brushed a thumb across her lips and bent to kiss her.

His phone buzzed from where he'd left it on the counter. Ignoring it, he deepened the kiss. But it buzzed again. Finally, Gryph lifted his head and stared down at Selene. "Hold that thought." Then he reached for his phone. Two text messages glowed on the screen.

The first from the lieutenant at the police department. "Got a lead on the black wolf. Call me."

Gryph's heartbeat ratcheted up and his jaw tightened. A lead on the black wolf was what he'd needed, but he didn't want Selene involved.

Selene wrapped her arms around his waist and laid her cheek against his back. "What is it?"

"I'm needed at the office."

Her arms tightened. "Now?"

He turned in her arms and pressed a kiss against her soft brown hair. "'Fraid so."

"Sure it can't wait?" she asked, her hands splaying out across his back and sinking lower.

Gryph captured her arms and pulled them away from him. "As much as I'd like to stay, I have to go. Duty calls."

"Then I'll come with you."

"No. You have a gala to prepare for."

Her lips firmed. "If I didn't, I'd go with you."

As he dressed, Gryph shot a glance at her. "I'll call Aurai and have her come stay with you."

"I'm okay on my own."

"I'd feel better if she came."

"I'd feel better if you stayed." She wrapped her arms around his waist and buried her face against his chest. "I wish you didn't have to go."

"Me, too." He kissed her one last time. "But I have to."

He hurried out the door and up the stairs to the street above. Night had enveloped the city in darkness, broken up by streetlights dotting every other corner. Neon lights blinked to life, advertising beer and vacancies.

Gryphon's heart throbbed with a heaviness he couldn't dispel. Reluctant to leave Selene unaccompanied, he called Aurai.

She answered with a bright "Hello."

"It's Gryph."

"Oh. Everything all right?"

"Can you stay with Selene tonight?"

"Of course," she answered. "You two have a fight?"

His hand tightened around his cell phone. "No. I want to find the black wolf."

"So you're going to join Deme, Brigid and Cal?"

"Why?" he asked, his curiosity peaked. "Where did they go?"

"Somewhere in Archer Heights. The lieutenant got a tip that the black wolf had been spotted with a pack of rogues. They went to investigate."

"Without backup?"

"I don't know. They left Gina and I in charge of being Selene's backup until you showed up."

"Why didn't they call me before they left?"

"Ha!" Her bark of laughter grated on Gryph's nerves. "You seemed to have other things on your mind."

He ignored her innuendo, focusing on what needed to be done versus what he wanted to do. "Do you know the exact location your sisters were headed?"

"No. And I don't understand why they didn't take all of us sisters. We're stronger together."

Gryph figured he'd only seen the tip of the iceberg that was the power of the five witches. "Are you good with staying with Selene?"

"I'd rather be out looking for the black wolf," Aurai admitted. "But if Selene needs me, I'm there."

"She needs you."

Aurai sighed. "Okay. I'll be there in a few minutes."

Gryph clicked the off button and walked to the end of the block, keeping to the shadows. He wouldn't leave until Aurai arrived.

While he waited, he checked in with the lieutenant and got the same information he had passed on to Cal, Deme and Brigid.

"Deme said you were a big help the other night," the lieutenant said. "They could use your assistance again, tonight."

He assured him he'd be on it as soon as he was sure Selene was safe.

As he leaned against a brick building, his gaze returned to the apartment where Selene lived. Why couldn't he control his inner beast? All his life, he'd worked hard to know the signs, to suppress the animal when it rose to the surface. With Selene, he lost all sense of time and presence. He became one with her, forgetting who and what he was.

And each time, he'd drawn blood.

Aurai arrived, parking against the curb in front of the building.

Gryph remained in the shadows until Aurai made it safely into the apartment. Then he stripped off his shirt and shoes and let his beast free.

On all fours, he ran through the streets, avoiding people, staying in the deepest shadows, out of sight. He ran until he could run no more, clearing his thoughts, grounding himself in what must be.

When he looked up to see where he was, he found himself in Archer Heights, several blocks over from the pool hall they'd barely escaped from the other night. For thirty minutes, he ran through the streets, checking any suspicious locations until he came to a group of warehouses surrounded by a run-down chain-link fence.

Slipping through the darkness, moving from shadow to shadow, he inched closer, recognizing the scent of wolves.

After studying the building for a full fifteen minutes, he located all the sentries. Wolves stood at each corner, two on the roof and one near a door at the rear of the building.

Keeping back and downwind to remain undetected, Gryph wondered what was going on inside that required guards and so many standing watch.

About the time he decided to move in, the door opened and several wolves strutted out, and then broke into a run.

Five or six men dressed in jeans and dark shirts emerged, looking back over their shoulders. The men mounted motorcycles and raced away from the building.

Gryph thought that was all of them, but then a woman in a short sexy dress and killer heels stepped out of the building and held the door.

Moments later, a large black wolf exited, head up. He paused for a moment, sniffing the air, his head moving slowly in a 180-degree turn until it stopped, his nose pointed directly at Gryph.

The hackles rose on the scruff of Gryph's neck, his muscles bunching, ready to defend his position.

After a long moment staring in Gryph's direction, the black wolf's shoulders gave what could only be considered a shrug and he turned toward the female, following her to a limousine. Again, she held the door for him. He jumped in and she climbed in beside him.

The limousine left the warehouse through an open gate, headed north.

A shiny new SUV burst from a side street. Gryph recognized Deme in the driver's seat and he leaped into the middle of the road, blocking its path, roaring so loud the sound echoed off the buildings.

The SUV screeched to a halt and Cal and Brigid dropped out, Deme remaining behind the wheel.

Cal pointed a nine-millimeter pistol at Gryph.

Brigid held a fireball in her hand, cocked and ready to throw. "You better be Gryph or you're going to get a mouthful of fire from one angry witch. I nearly wet my pants."

As proof, Gryph partially transformed to human.

Deme jerked her head and shouted, "Get in."

Cal claimed shotgun, Brigid held the back door open.

Gryph jumped in and Brigid slid in next to him.

Deme slammed her foot to the accelerator and sped after the limousine, taking a corner so fast, Brigid was thrown against him.

Brigid righted herself, a frown denting her brows. "I don't know if I'll ever get used to sitting so close to a lion shifter."

Within seconds, Gryph completed his change to human. "Better?"

She nodded. "Much." She smirked. "Though I don't know what's more disturbing. Sitting next to a changeling or a hot-bodied, naked male. I see why Selene is smitten."

Deme raced to the end of the street, where it T-junctioned, and let the SUV drift halfway past the stop sign. Everyone glanced in both directions.

The limousine was a quarter of a mile to the south, turning onto a street Gryph knew to ramp up onto the expressway.

"Hurry. If they get on the expressway too far ahead of us, we might miss what exit they take."

Deme gunned it, turning the wheel hard to the right. The back end of the SUV fishtailed and straightened before the tires got enough traction to propel the vehicle forward.

With the limousine turning farther ahead, Gryph could only hold his breath and pray they didn't lose it.

As they neared the turn the limousine had made, the SUV was rammed from behind, jolting them forward.

A black sedan with dark tinted windows slid up beside them and swerved over, broadsiding their vehicle.

"Hey!" Deme yelled. "I just got issued this SUV."

"Yeah, but now you're pissed off. What are you gonna do?" Brigid prompted as she crawled across Gryph to hit the button that slid the window downward. "I know what I'm gonna do." She balled up a flame and slung it like a professional baseball pitcher, straight at the windshield. The fireball landed and scattered, making no difference to the driver, who slammed into them again, throwing Brigid back onto her side of the vehicle.

The passenger seat window lowered and a deadly looking rifle barrel poked out.

"They have guns!" Gryph shouted.

Deme swerved toward the attacking vehicle, slamming into the passenger door.

The gunman ducked backward, the rifle barrel disappearing for a moment.

Gryph knew it wouldn't be for long. He rolled his window all the way down and, using his great balance as a feline, crawled out on the edge of the window, holding on to the oh-shit handle. When the rifle barrel poked out again, Deme jerked her steering wheel, aiming the SUV at the side of the sedan.

Gryph seized his opportunity and leaped across the small gap, grabbed the top of the other vehicle and held on as the driver jerked back and forth in an attempt to dislodge him. It only made him angrier and even more determined to bring the vehicle to a halt. The gunman leaned out, trying to get a bead on the half man, half cat clinging to the roof.

Grabbing the barrel of the weapon, Gryph yanked it out of the gunman's hands, threw it to the street and sank his claws into the man's arm, dragging him halfway out of the vehicle.

The man screamed in pain, his face elongating, his nose stretching into that of a wolf.

Before he could fully transition, Gryph jerked him the rest of the way out of the car and dropped him to the pavement.

He rolled into the path of the vehicle still trailing them, causing the driver to slam on his brakes too late to avoid the body.

The car hit the shifter and bumped over him before it came to a halt straddling the limp form. Another gunman leaned out the passenger seat window aiming at Gryph, who was still clinging to the rooftop.

A bullet pinged into the metal roof near his hand. Another shattered the back windshield.

The driver continued to swerve back and forth as they neared the ramp to the expressway. The limousine had pulled way ahead, cleared the ramp and shot into the ever-present Chicago traffic.

Deme rammed the sedan with the heavier SUV, forcing the car up on a sidewalk, headed straight for a telephone pole.

Gryph saw it and leaped to the side at the last minute, hit the ground and rolled to his feet as metal crashed into wood.

Deme brought the SUV to a halt and all three passengers jumped out.

"You okay?" Deme asked.

Gryph straightened and dusted himself off before going back to the vehicle wrapped around the pole.

"Quite the acrobat." Brigid chuckled as she caught up to him. "Kind of handy to have around, ya know?"

"Deme, call for an ambulance and also have them run the license plate while we check for survivors and take care of the tail vehicle," Cal ordered.

Gryph glanced into the vehicle—the people inside weren't moving. A driver, and a passenger in the backseat. The vehicle that had run over the gunman wasn't going anywhere and the occupants were bailing.

Gryph roared, dropped to all four paws and ran after them, catching the slowest man, letting the others go. They'd lost heart in shooting him, preferring to sacrifice one of their own to guarantee their escape.

Gryph pounced on the slowest man, slamming him face-first into the pavement. When the man tried to get up, he planted a foot in the middle of his back and applied enough pressure to keep him immobile.

Cal and Brigid gathered around in time to see the man's attempt to shift into a wolf.

Leaning close to the man's ear, Gryph growled—a low, dangerous sound. "I wouldn't do that, if I were you."

The man's transformation receded and he lay still. "What do you want?"

"To know why you tried to kill us?"

He snorted and refused to answer.

"Perhaps you need a little persuasion." Gryph grabbed the man's arm and yanked it up the middle of his back.

His captive grunted, sweat popping out on his forehead, but refused to enlighten them.

"Let me give it a shot." Brigid dropped to her haunches. "Do you know what it feels like to have your flesh burn until it melts off your body? Every nerve in your body screaming for it to stop?" She twisted her wrist and brought up a ball of wicked-looking flame.

The man's eyes widened and his face paled.

"Maybe I'll just go for the eyes and burn them out of your head." Brigid gave him an evil grin and moved the ball of fire so close the heat turned his cheeks red.

"No! Please, don't!" The man squirmed and bucked in an attempt to throw Gryph off his back.

Gryph leaned harder on the arm until the man almost passed out.

"Okay, okay! I'll talk!" He lay with his face pressed into the asphalt, his eyes on the fireball. "Want do you want to know?"

"Who's in charge?"

"Black Wolf."

"That's it? That's all you've got for me?" Gryph tightened up on the arm. "His name."

"That's what he calls himself. I swear," the man cried.

"Where can I find him?"

"We don't find *him*, he finds *us*."

"That limousine has to park somewhere."

"It's rented."

Gryph glanced up at Deme. "Did anyone get the license plate?"

Deme shook her head. "Got away too fast."

"Someone has to know how to get in touch with Black Wolf." Gryph growled. "A second in command? The woman? Who are they? My patience is wearing very thin."

"Brayden. Brayden Sellers is his second, now. Miriam Crestley is the woman. They arrange for his transportation. Ask them."

"If you know anything else, now's the time to tell. And

if you're lying to us—" Gryph dropped his voice into a menacing whisper "—we'll kill you."

The man closed his eyes, his body shaking. "It doesn't matter. They'll kill me anyway for what I just told you."

Gryph let go of the man's arm and straightened. "Then get out of here. Get out of town. Just don't let me catch you anywhere near Archer Heights or Black Wolf again."

Deme was on the phone with the lieutenant, relaying the names and the location of the wrecked car and the dead man. When she hung up, she tipped her head toward the SUV. "Let's go. We have an address. And, Gryph, Cal's gym bag is on the floorboard."

Cal chuckled. "There's a pair of sweatpants in it."

Gryph left the informant lying in the middle of the street, barely feeling sorry for the shifter who'd tried to kill him. He should never have fallen into the group of rogue werewolves to begin with.

The team climbed into the SUV. Gryph found the bag and the pants, pulling them up over his naked legs. They headed to an area Gryph was familiar with. Lincoln Park, filled with some of the most luxurious homes in the city and on top of some of the oldest tunnels. The homes here were as old as the money.

"Why are we here?" he asked.

"Miriam Crestley lives here. Or at least her father and mother do," Deme said. "She's the daughter of a man whose family helped establish Chicago."

"I'm sure they'll be pleased to know who their daughter is hanging out with."

They parked in front of a stately white stone mansion with towering oaks and lush landscaping. Deme turned to the others. "Let me and Cal handle this."

Without a shirt and shoes, Gryph was more than willing to take a backseat to this part of the investigation.

When Cal and Deme returned, they were both frowning.

"Thomas Crestley said that Miriam is staying with her boyfriend in a loft in the Gold Coast area. He wasn't sure where. He did, however, say that she was expected to be at the charity ball, and suggested we talk to her there."

"Did the lieutenant have an address for Brayden Sellers?"

"No. Seems the address on his license is old and he's moved around since."

"Damn. We're back to square one."

"No, we have tomorrow night at the ball to corner Miriam," Brigid argued. "*If* we had tickets to get in."

"I can get tickets. How many do you need? Three?" Gryph asked.

"Yes," Deme said.

"No. We need six." Brigid gave Deme a sharp glare.

Deme cleared her throat. "Right. We need six."

"Okay. I'll have a courier send them over in the morning." Gryph leaned back in his seat, tired to the bone. They had been so close to finding out the identity of Black Wolf.

"Do you want me to drop you off at Selene's?" Deme asked.

He wanted to go back to Selene's. But he couldn't risk it. "No. Take me to my building. Please."

Brigid crossed her arms. "I thought you liked my sister."

"I do. But that's beside the point."

Deme pulled up to the GL Enterprises building and Gryph hopped out, thankful the interrogation was over and he could get on with his life…without the complication of falling for a witch with four very concerned and nosy sisters. He slammed the door and walked away.

If only it was easy to walk away from Selene.

Chapter 19

"Get up, we have a lot to do today and no time to waste."

Aurai's cheerful voice blasted Selene out of a lovely dream where she and Gryph were making love on the tropical island of St. Croix, away from the noise and traffic of Chicago, surrounded by sun and sand.

She'd been there once to visit Deme when she'd been working as a private investigator. The climate was idyllic, the beach clean and beautiful and the sun so bright it could blind you and you wouldn't care.

Selene raised her arm to shield her eyes from the overhead light. "I don't have to be up until eight."

"Honey, it's nine."

"What?" Selene sat up straight, flinging back the covers. "Why did you let me oversleep?"

"You were smiling and moaning. It must have been a pretty good dream. Were you with Gryph?"

"No." Selene's cheeks heated with her lie and she regretted it immediately. "Yes."

"Is he as good in bed as he looks like he'd be?" Aurai lifted one of the pillows and plumped it.

Selene's thighs clenched, her body warming to the memory of him inside her. "Yes."

Crushing the pillow to her chest, Aurai sighed. "I hope I find someone that makes me look that dreamy."

"Yeah, well, it's not all roses and sunshine." Selene climbed out of bed.

"Why not?" Her sister followed her through to the bathroom.

"Do you mind?" Selene shut the door and leaned her forehead against it, tears pooling in her eyes when she thought about how quickly Gryph had run out the door last night. And she'd been the one to worry about influencing him—using her powers to make him want to stay. Apparently he had enough willpower to resist. He probably wasn't that into her.

"So you like him, huh?" Aurai said through the door.

Selene moaned and refused to answer, going through her morning routine, relieving herself, then climbing into the tub for a stimulatingly cool shower that did nothing to quench the embers burning low in her belly. With Gryph on her mind, she couldn't eliminate thoughts of him down the drain with mere water.

She washed her hair, applied conditioner and rinsed, then turned off the water, grateful for that little bit of time she'd had without having to answer her sister's questions. Wrapping a towel around her body, she left the bathroom and entered her bedroom.

Aurai stood with her eyes shining, a smile spread across her face and something in her hand.

"Why the silly grin?" Selene wasn't in the mood for happiness. Not when she'd been rejected by the only man she'd found interesting in a very long time. Interesting *hell*. Possibly the only man she'd *ever* found so intensely attractive and captivating.

Aurai squealed and hopped up and down. "We're going to the ball!"

Selene frowned. "I know we're going to the ball, preferably early enough to get the staff ready in their costumes."

"No, silly. We're going to the charity ball as guests." She waved two tickets in Selene's face, her hand shaking.

Selene had to grab it to make her stay still.

"How can that be? These tickets are worth ten-thousand dollars each."

"That's right." Aurai grinned. "And there were two of them."

"This must be a mistake." She turned them over. "Where did you get these?"

"A courier just delivered them in this." Aurai handed her an envelope.

Her stomach fluttered and her pulse kicked into panic mode as she turned the packet over and read the return address. GL Enterprises. Her heart beat faster then settled like a lump of lead in her belly. "I'm not going."

"What?" Aurai stared at her like she'd grown two heads. "You most certainly are."

"You take my ticket. Invite a friend." She handed the ticket to Aurai. "I'm not one of Chicago's elite."

"Neither am I. But we have tickets." Her sister held up her hands. "We're *both* going, and I won't take no for an answer." Aurai marched to Selene's closet and riffled through her dresses. "Don't you have a ball gown you can wear?"

"I don't go to balls. Why would I keep a ball gown in my closet?" Selene shook her head. "I'm not going.

I don't have a dress. I don't have time to shop, and it wouldn't matter if I did. I couldn't afford the kind of dress they wear."

Aurai faced her, a frown pulling her brows together.

"Look, Gina just texted me that she, Deme, Brigid and Cal all received tickets this morning, courtesy of GL Enterprises. We're all going, so you can't back out."

Selene's heart beat faster and her palms grew clammy. To be seen in a ball gown, dressed to the nines in the company of the man she feared she was already in love with would be too much like Cinderella going to meet Prince Charming. It was too surreal. She couldn't go.

"Don't even think it." Aurai shook her finger. "You're going. We'll find a dress for you and you'll be absolutely the prettiest girl at the ball."

"While a killer roams the streets." Selene snorted. "Seems kind of frivolous."

Aurai planted her fists on her hips, looking so much like their mother, it made Selene's heart hurt. "Who's to say that killer won't be at the ball tonight. With all those people there, someone would make a prime target. You and I both know Deme and Brigid will be close by, if not there. You also know our powers work better when we're all together. Gina said as much. We all need to go to support each other."

Damned if Aurai didn't have a point. Still, Selene didn't bother arguing. With five costumes to oversee the alterations of and a store to open, she had her work cut out for her. She didn't have time to shop for a dress and she was getting too close to Gryph. Now would be a good time to back off, play it cool. Not see him. Especially if he was to show up in a tuxedo, so handsome he was sure to melt her heart.

No. She didn't want to see Gryph.

Liar.

Truth was, she wanted to see him more than she could stand.

Selene worked with the seamstress and customers needing last-minute alterations, waited on customers and cleaned her shop through the morning and afternoon. She had Gina deliver the costumes to the hotel on her way to one of her jobs cleaning aquariums for a law firm near the hotel.

By keeping busy, Selene had little time to think about Gryph, the killer or anything else, until two hours before she was due to be at the hotel. Funny how the world continued to turn, even after the loss of one woman's life.

Selene had promised the waitstaff she'd be on hand for any last-minute adjustments to their costumes and come hell or collapsing buildings, she'd be there.

Gina arrived five minutes before closing, carrying five long garment bags. "I figured you wouldn't have time to go shopping and Aurai wouldn't have time to stop by her apartment. So, I did, and brought several of her gowns for us to choose from."

"Oh, thank goodness." Aurai hurried to take some of the bags from her sister. "We have just enough time to go through the dresses, run a quick iron over them, do our hair and get to the hotel if we hurry."

Selene waved a hand over her calculator. "You two have fun. I'm still working."

"Come on, Selene," Gina said. "We need to get ready for the ball."

Selene stuck to her guns, refusing to consider Gryph, the tickets and the ball. Even though they'd been on her mind all day long. "It seems so frivolous to go to a ball when there's a killer out on the street."

"I was just getting to that," Gina said. "Deme, Brigid, Cal and Gryph almost caught up to the black wolf last night."

"What?" Selene glanced at her phone to see if there were any messages she'd missed. "I didn't get a call, no one let me know."

"He got away."

So after Gryph had left her place he'd gone on the hunt. Selene pinched the bridge of her nose. "Why didn't anyone tell me?"

Gina hefted the dresses in her arms, glancing around the shop. "Well, they weren't going to call anyone in the middle of the night. And I guess they've been busy chasing down leads all day. I just got a call from Deme a little while ago."

"Any progress?"

"They discovered the name of a woman who was seen with the wolf. She's supposed to be at the ball tonight. That's why we all got tickets. Gryph made it happen."

With a glance at the clock and down at her receipts and ledger, Selene muttered, "I wonder if I have time to call Deme for an update on the investigation."

"You can talk to her at the ball, she'll be there with Cal and Brigid." Gina hung the dresses on a hook on the wall. "Now hurry up, we have to get dressed."

"I'm dressed in what I'm going in."

Gina glanced at Aurai.

Their youngest sister shrugged. "You know how stubborn she can be."

"*She* is still in the same room." Selene gave them her best schoolmarm glare. "And I'm not stubborn. I'll be at the hotel, I'm just not going in to the ball other than to make sure my costumes fit."

Gina let go of a long steady breath, and then removed the garment bags from each, one at a time.

Despite her protestations, Selene couldn't help glancing at them, her heart twisting as Gina unveiled each dress. Aurai had been right. Selene had been the dreamer, imagining herself the scullery maid turned princess for the ball, and falling in love with a handsome prince. Only life didn't turn out that way. She was falling in love with a shifter. He was afraid of hurting her, and she was afraid of manipulating him with her psychic abilities to stay with her.

Secretly she was glad that so far he couldn't be pushed by her thoughts. But she'd lain awake all night wishing he was lying beside her, his arms wrapped around her, holding her close.

Selene shook away the mental images, prepared her receipts and locked her cash register. She was headed for the door to lock it when a delivery van pulled up outside.

"I don't have time for this," she muttered.

Aurai hung the dress she'd chosen on the hook and turned. "Do you want me to get it?"

"No, I'm here. I'll handle it." She opened the door as the deliveryman stepped down from the truck carrying a large box.

The sender's address read Mira Bella.

"I don't remember ordering anything from Mira Bella."

Shoving the pen and an electronic pad toward her, the delivery driver asked, "Are you Selene Chattox?"

"Yes."

"Then this box is for you. Sign here."

Selene scribbled her name and handed the device back to the man, who then shoved the box into her hands and left before she could protest again.

"What is it?" Gina leaned over her shoulder.

"I don't know."

"Oh, it's from Mira Bella!" Aurai clapped her hands, her eyes sparkling. "Only the most exclusive designer couture in Chicago."

"I know, but why did they send me a box."

"Open it and find out," Gina suggested.

Selene laid the box on the counter and slit the tape holding it together with a letter opener. Lifting the lid, a layer of tissue paper rose with it and fluttered to the ground, revealing a dress of exquisite lace and shear fabric that was the pale blue-green of glacier ice.

Her breath hitched in her throat, Selene lifted the gown out of the box and layers of glacier-ice taffeta and feather-soft gossamer curled around her legs, drifting across the floor like clouds.

"It's the most beautiful gown I've ever seen," Aurai whispered.

A small card fell from the folds and Gina bent to pick it up. "It's definitely for you."

"Selene" was written across the envelope in bold strokes. She handed the dress to Aurai, who held it as if it was magic and might disappear if she blinked her eyes.

The card read "Please come to the ball" with the initials GL scrawled beneath.

"That's it?" She turned the card over. What did she expect? A declaration of love?

Well, she wasn't getting it. Nor did she want it. He was a rich, influential recluse who happened to shift into a lion whenever he felt like it, and sometimes when he got carried away.

Her body tingled at the remembered feel of his cat-like tongue laving the inside of her thigh and flicking her special nubbin of tightly packed nerves. Instantly, her insides were awash with desire.

She was a witch with the ability to push thoughts, read some minds and, on occasion, throw up a force field of sorts. Why did she think she needed him? They had nothing in common.

Nothing but mind-blowing sex.

Okay there was that. And he had gone to a great deal of trouble to choose a gown for her that suited her to perfection. She couldn't have come up with a better selection.

"Try it on." Aurai shoved the dress into Selene's hands.

The only reason she agreed was to answer the burning question: What were the chances he'd get the right size?

She locked the shop door and descended the back stairs into her apartment, her sisters on her heels.

"Just because I try this dress on doesn't mean I'm going to the ball." She said the words aloud to keep firm in her stance, though her resolve was definitely crumbling.

Laying the dress over her bed, she stripped out of the broomstick skirt and peasant blouse she'd thrown on that morning.

"Lose the bra, too," Aurai insisted. The bodice was sheer in all the right places with thick lace of the same glacier ice hue as the rest of the dress strategically layered over the breast area.

Selene unhooked her bra and, wearing only a pair of

bikini panties, she stepped into the dress and pulled it up over her hips and torso.

Aurai zipped the back to just above the curve of her bottom, the back neckline plunging low, bearing so much skin, Selene felt positively naked.

"Sweet goddess, it's..." Gina began.

"Perfect," Aurai proclaimed on a sigh. "Look for yourself."

Aurai angled her in front of the full-length mirror hanging on her closet door.

Selene gasped. Was that really her? She looked so... surreal...almost ethereal, as if she was otherworldly. And more of her skin showed through the sheer bodice than she'd ever exposed in public when not on a beach.

If the dress wasn't so incredibly beautiful, it might be considered obscene.

Gina stood with her mouth open and her eyes wide. "Wow."

"No kidding, wow." Aurai took charge. "Get out of the dress and let's do your makeup and hair. You can't be seen in a dress like that without the face and hair to match.

"I'm not going," Selene muttered, although much less convincing this time.

Gina and Aurai glared at her, Gina speaking first. "Like hell you're not."

"It would be an absolute crime to let that dress go to waste," Aurai said.

"Then you wear it." Selene slipped the zip down and stepped out of, feeling as thought she'd lost part of herself in the process.

Aurai shook her head. "I'm shorter. The dress would drag and be ruined."

When Selene turned to Gina, her sister held up her hand. "It's not my color. Face it, Selene, it was made for you."

"Don't be silly." Selene stood in her underwear staring at a dress that practically called to her, trying to come up with any other excuse she could possibly live with. When it came right down to it, she *wanted* to wear that dress.

For Gryph.

Maybe he'd changed his mind. Or maybe he *would* if he saw her in a dress fit for a fairy princess.

"Come on, into the bathroom." Gina handed her a button-up blouse to wear while they applied makeup to her cheeks and eyes. Once they were satisfied with her makeup, Aurai swept Selene's hair up on the sides and let it fall in long, loose ringlets down her back, the rich brown shining in the lights from the mirror.

Selene stared into the looking glass feeling more like Alice having fallen down the rabbit hole. "That doesn't even look like me."

"Oh, honey, it does, and better." Aurai hugged her and applied her own makeup in a hurry, brushing her long blond hair back on one side and draping it over the opposite shoulder in loose waves.

Gina combed her straight hair back from her face and secured it in a sexy messy bun at her nape.

Selene smiled in the mirror at Gina and Aurai. "I have such beautiful sisters."

"If only you could see yourself as we do." Aurai flapped her hands. "Now, get into your dress, we have to catch a cab or we'll be late."

"Don't forget, I promised I'd help with the last-minute adjustments to the costumes." As Selene shoved her keys, driver's license and some cash into a slim silver clutch, her cell phone chirped with a text message from the event coordinator at the hotel.

Costumes are perfect, no need to come early.

Well, then, she was stuck in the dress, with no excuse to sneak in through the back of the ballroom.

Gina held up her cell phone. "Ready for me to call a cab?"

The buzzer on her apartment door rang.

"Another delivery?" Selene headed for the door, but Aurai beat her to it and peered through the peephole. "There's a man in a suit out there."

"Open the door and see what he wants."

Aurai opened the door.

"Pardon me, ma'am. Mr. Leone sent the limousine to collect you and your sisters and take you all to the charity ball."

Aurai squealed and hugged Gina. "We're going to the ball!"

Selene frowned. "What *didn't* he remember?"

"Please, Selene, stop looking the gift horse in the mouth." Gina rolled her eyes as she walked past her and up the stairs to the street, like a society debutante.

"Come." Aurai hooked her arm. "Our chariot awaits."

With a resigned sigh and a rising sense of anticipation, Selene stepped out of her apartment, gathered her skirt and climbed the steps. As she slid into the plush leather seats, a stabbing pain shot through her temples like a searing poker and a flash of another's anger overwhelmed her thoughts with its intensity.

She pressed her fingers to her temple and closed her eyes.

Aurai touched her arm. "Something wrong?"

The limo slid into traffic, leaving her street and the pressure of that someone else's powerful malice behind.

"I don't know. For a moment, I felt something. But now it's gone."

Aurai hugged her. "Hopefully, it will stay gone through the ball."

Selene stared out the window, trying to see into the shadows. Who had been watching them? And why? She prayed to the goddess whoever it was didn't follow them to the ball.

Gryph paced the floor of the penthouse suite on the top floor of the downtown Chicago hotel. The ball had begun over an hour ago. He'd had his bodyguard call no less than six times to the detail at the door, and still the limousine carrying the Chattox sisters had not arrived. He paced once more across the expensive carpet, arriving at the door, ready to hit the streets and look for them.

As he reached for the doorknob, the phone in his pocket vibrated.

He scrambled for it and read the incoming text message.

Chattox sisters have arrived.

The air rushed out of his lungs. He grabbed his tuxedo jacket and hurried for the elevator.

He punched the button that would whisk him straight to the ballroom level. Gryph counted the floor numbers, willing them to go by faster. The soft ping announcing his arrival at his destination couldn't come fast enough.

At last he stepped out of the elevator and into the ballroom's hallway, inhaling a mixture of the most expensive perfumes and colognes, none of which smelled as good as Selene's fresh, natural scent.

If someone had told him ten years ago that he'd be hosting a highly publicized event with thousands of people in attendance and that he'd actually make an appearance, he'd have laughed in his face. Now, he eagerly entered the ballroom teeming with the richest people of Chicago, dressed in their finest, not at all worried about shifting at an awkward moment and scaring these people out of their minds.

No, he worried more about where Selene was and if she would actually show up to the event after he'd run out on her.

His hands were clammy and his beast paced internally, anxious to see her as much as his human self.

Then a waft of her essence filtered through all the other warring aromas from the buffet of finger foods to the layers of hair spray used in each coiffure.

Was it her? He lifted his nose and inhaled deeply.

Yes.

Across the crowded floor, she practically floated into the room, the light from the crystal chandeliers glancing off her beautiful, rich brown hair, her eyes sparkling brighter than the diamonds in his breast pocket. And the dress fit her to perfection, just as he'd known it would, the delicate pale lace and filmy layers clinging to her curves. She turned around to say something to Deme behind her and Gryph's breath lodged in his throat.

He hadn't realized just how revealing the back of the dress was, dipping low enough to tempt a saint into naughty thoughts, hoping for a glimpse of the crevice between her buttocks.

His member jerked to attention, swelling beneath the soft folds of his tuxedo trousers. To hell with the ball. He wanted to spirit her away to the top of the hotel and make sweet love to her with the starlight shining through the floor-to-ceiling windows, moonlight the only thing covering her pale skin.

An older woman with blue-white hair and a pinkish gray gown stepped into his path.

He tried to go around her, but she moved to block him.

"Mr. Leone, may I have a word with you?"

Gryph dragged his gaze away from the beautiful Selene and looked down at the woman, who was vaguely familiar to him. "I'm sorry, who are you?"

She sniffed, her nose climbing a bit higher. "Mrs. Stockton. One of the organizers of this illustrious event."

"Oh, yes. I remember. You and your partner did a wonderful job pulling it together." Again he tried to step around her.

Her hand snaked out, snagging his elbow. "Yes, well, thank you. There is one other thing we need from you."

"My assistant will see to your needs. I really must go."

"Mr. Leone, your assistant cannot perform the function of giving the main speech and leading off the dancing. Only the sponsor of this event has that responsibility. And that, sir, is you."

He stared across the room where Selene had been standing and didn't see her. He frowned down at Mrs. Stockton. "What did you say?"

Her brow puckered. "It's time to make the speech thanking all the contributors and to lead off the first dance."

"I'm sorry. I thought I'd made myself clear. I don't give speeches."

"I suggest you make an exception. After all, it's tradition."

He opened his mouth to tell her what she could do with her traditions, but the orchestra in the corner played an introductory tune and the room grew silent, all gazes on him.

Damn.

A hotel employee appeared beside him and held out a microphone, clicking the on button.

Never having given a speech in public, Gryph stared down at the mic for a long moment then up into the eyes of the woman he'd been searching for in the crowds.

Selene stood ten feet in front of him, an absolute vision. Gryph was afraid to blink lest she disappear.

She smiled at him and nodded toward him.

Mrs. Stockton took the proffered microphone, and tapped it before saying. "Ladies and gentlemen, it's my pleasure to introduce your host and sponsor for this event, Mr. Gryphon Leone." Then she placed the microphone in his hand and stood back.

Though he'd rather go talk to Selene, Gryph lifted the mic to his lips. A dozen flashbulbs went off, blinking like so many strobes, blinding him and making it impossible for him to see Selene. "Thank you all for attending the annual Children's Charity Ball. Your contributions will help the children of Chicago live better lives. I'm not one for long speeches so, if the orchestra will play, we should dance." He handed the mic to the appalled Mrs. Stockton, pushed through the reporters and strode across the floor to the only woman he cared to see in the roomful of people.

He bowed and held out his hand, a spark of apprehension assailing him when she hesitated to take it.

Then she smiled up at him, took his hand and stepped into his arms, moving with his steps to the swelling strains of a beautiful waltz.

For the first minute, they were alone in the middle of the dance floor, floating around the room. Even as others joined them, Gryph could only see Selene.

They moved in silent unison, him leading, her following, effortlessly as if their bodies were in tune with each other.

As the song ended and another began, he led her off the floor and to the refreshments table, handing her a glass of champagne.

"Thank you for coming."

"Why did you invite us as guests? We could have waited in the wings in case you needed us. Those tickets cost a small fortune."

He waved his hand. "The money isn't important. I wanted to see you again."

Her heart warmed. "And the dress?" She sipped her champagne, pinning him with her stare over the rim of the glass.

"I knew you wouldn't have time to shop, and when I saw it, I knew it was meant for you."

"Thank you. It's perfect." She sucked in a breath and let it out before saying, "Gryph, every time we've been together, you've claimed it was a mistake. Why do you keep coming back? Why do you do nice things for me when you know it'll only make me want to be with you more?"

"Because, saying I shouldn't see you and following through has proven harder than I anticipated."

"That makes two of us." Her face softened. "So, what are we going to do about it?"

"I don't want to hurt you."

"You haven't so far."

He frowned. "What if I go too far?"

"I'll take my chances."

"I'm not willing to risk it."

"Then why did you invite me here?"

"One: I wanted to see you again. Two, I think the black wolf might show up, or at least the woman who has been reported with him. And though I didn't want to involve you, I need you and your sisters to help me find him."

"Fair enough. Maybe once we nail the black wolf, you and I could figure out our situation?"

He nodded.

Before he could say anything more, Deme and Cal stepped up beside her.

"She's here," Cal said.

"Who's here?" Selene asked.

"Miriam Crestley." Brigid joined them from behind Deme and Cal, Aurai and Gina close behind. "The woman we saw with Black Wolf last night."

"Where?" Gryph stared over their heads, his gaze scanning the crowd.

"By the entrance." Cal glanced that way. "And she's with a man."

"You think he's the shifter?" Selene asked.

"I don't know, but he has black hair."

"So do about fifty people in the ballroom. It could be a coincidence," Aurai offered.

"True." Cal stared around the room. "But I don't believe in coincidence."

Gryph's jaw hardened. "Neither do I."

"Well, we can't all converge on them at once." Brigid flexed her hand sans the usual fireball.

"Why not?" Selene asked.

"If they get spooked, they might bolt," Deme said. "Like they did last night."

Cal led the way. "It's our job, let Deme, Brigid and I handle it." Deme and Brigid fell in step with him.

"We've got your back," Gina called out. "The rest of us can circle around."

"Gina and I can cover the door." Aurai, dressed in a soft rose-colored gown, looked no less bold than a soldier headed into battle.

"They could be dangerous," Deme warned. "If they make a run for it, don't do anything that will get you hurt, or that will hurt the guests."

Gina nodded. "Got it."

Cal clapped his hands once. "Then let's go."

Gryph grabbed Selene's elbow. "Stay with me."

"Wouldn't it be better if we spread out?" She tugged at her arm, but he refused to release her. He wanted to know where she was in case things got dicey.

"Humor me, will ya?"

"You want me, and you don't. Make up your mind. You're making my head hurt," she muttered, pressing her fingers to her temples, but she didn't pull away as she let him lead her around the huge ballroom.

The closer they moved toward the entrance, the more Selene's feet dragged and her shoulders hunched.

Gryph came to a halt. "What's wrong?"

"I can feel…"

"Feel what?"

"Anger, resentment…so strong. Like…" She looked up, her eyes wide. "Like I did the other night. When I could feel someone watching us."

Gryph looked around, searching each face for one that stuck out as malevolent, dangerous and sinister. People laughed, talked and went on about the business of enjoying the ball, unaware of something menacing among them.

Then he spotted the girl. Blond hair piled high. A black dress slit up to her hip. Several men stood in front of her escort, blocking Gryph's view.

"He's here," Selene said softly, her head coming up, her stricken gaze straight ahead.

The crowd parted, revealing the man next to Miriam. A man Gryph recognized immediately.

His brother.

"What the hell is Lucas doing here?" He marched forward, wanting answers.

Selene gripped his arm. "That man, you know him?"

"Yes, he's my brother, Lucas."

Selene pressed her hand to her chest. "Oh, no."

"What?" Gryph was torn between the look on Selene's face and demanding to know why his brother had come to the ball with a woman who'd been consorting with the wolf who'd killed Amanda Grant.

He took another step, practically dragging Selene along with him.

"Gryph, he's not..."

"Not what?" He didn't slow, didn't stop when her hand squeezed his arm.

"Don't go there, Gryph. He's dangerous."

"If that's the case, then I want to know why."

Gryph stopped in front of Miriam and Lucas. "Why are you here?" he said, keeping his voice low to avoid disturbing the people around them.

Lucas waved a hand. "I have just as much of a right to attend this event as anyone who's paid good money to be here. It *is* a public event, is it not?"

"Why are you here with her?" Gryph nodded toward Miriam.

"Please, *dear* brother." Lucas's arm circled the woman's waist, dragging her against his side. "Miss Crestley is my date."

"And she was seen last night with a black wolf shifter. One we suspect killed Amanda Grant."

"Have you taken up spying?" Lucas's brows rose high on his forehead.

"I have since a shifter has taken to killing innocents. This woman is known to consort with a possible killer."

Miriam Crestley laughed, the sound harsh in Gryph's ears. "Lucas, darling. You didn't tell me your brother was so old fashioned. So now I'm a consort?" She laughed again.

Gryph's eyes narrowed into slits as his gaze shifted from the woman back to his brother. "I take it you knew she was hanging out with the black wolf." His gut clenched as it became clear. "Oh, brother, please tell me you're not involved with him, too."

Anger radiated from Lucas like a heat wave, his green eyes darkening to black, then red. "Since when do you care who I'm with?"

"I've always cared." Gryph laid a hand on his brother's arm.

Lucas shook it off. "You've been very busy making a fortune to squander on people who are too useless to live. The Lair should be destroyed. It's outlived its purpose."

Gryph stared back, refusing to back down. "What are you talking about?"

"It's time for the people of Chicago to know of the other creatures who walk among us." He snapped his fingers.

The doors burst open at the end of the ballroom and

at the emergency exits on each side and wolves of all shapes, colors and sizes entered the ballroom.

Panic ensued with women screaming and people rushing toward the exits only to be stopped by a growling wolves. The crowd was herded into a huddle of scared humans at the center of the floor.

Gryph refused to break eye contact with his brother. "It was you all along."

"Took you long enough to figure it out." Lucas's lip curled up on one side. "You're not as smart as Father gives you credit for."

"I trusted you. I saw no need to suspect a man who I'd considered family."

"You left me in that sewer of a Lair." Lucas poked a finger into Gryph's chest. "But while you were topside making a name for yourself, I was struggling to find myself. When I was bitten and turned, it came to me. I needed to make a name of my own."

"We're brothers."

Lucas waved his hand at the wolves. "*These* are my brothers.

Holding Selene behind him, shielding her body with his, he warned, "This can only end badly. These guests don't deserve to be frightened and your pack will only die."

"So be it." Lucas's face changed so quickly Gryph wasn't prepared. His brother lashed out at him with wicked teeth, ripping into his arm.

Lucas's beast burst out, his muscles and sinews ripping through the tuxedo, shredding it beyond repair. He swiped a giant paw at the animal he'd called brother. No more. This creature was cruel, inhuman, had killed innocents and was now out for blood. His blood.

* * *

At first, the anger pressing against Selene's mind worked to cripple her, to weaken her in a way she didn't know how to fight.

She could only watch as Gryph, fully transformed, lunged at Lucas, hitting him hard and knocking him on his back. They rolled toward the crowd of frightened people.

Screams filled the air. Men and women fell, trying to escape the ferocious battle between them. Wolves snapped at the guests, ripping through tuxedos and expensive gowns.

The woman who'd come with Lucas sneered at Selene. "You're all going to die. These people are so fake, pretentious and backstabbing. They deserve it."

"They do a lot of good for the children this charity supports."

"Only for the recognition they get, not because they're altruistic or give a damn about anyone but themselves."

"Right or wrong, it takes all kinds to make things work."

"Not all kinds. Our kind is shunned. But not anymore. And I might as well start with you." Miriam's face stretched, her nose elongating into the snout of a wolf.

Before she could fully transform, Selene shoved the woman backward so hard, she landed on her butt on the hardwood flooring and slid several feet away.

Selene turned and ran toward her sisters, who were trapped in the middle of the screaming humans.

Behind her Miriam growled.

Selene wouldn't make it to safety. She had to defend herself or die trying.

She ground to a stop, turned and focused all her thoughts on stopping Miriam.

Transformed into a white wolf, Miriam launched herself at Selene.

"Selene, look out!" Aurai cried, having worked her way to the edge of the crowd.

Selene could see her sister in her peripheral vision, but didn't acknowledge her, refusing to back down or let Miriam win.

The she-wolf flew through the air. A hair's breadth from Selene's face, she crashed in midair, sliding to the ground in an unconscious heap.

The room went wild. Wolves leaped at the guests, snarling and tearing at them with razor-sharp teeth.

Deme spun a web of vines from a nearby pot, throwing it over a group of six wolves, immobilizing them long enough for Selene to send out a thought for the crowd to part and allow Deme, Brigid, Aurai and Gina to stumble their way free.

With her sisters gathered around her, Selene concentrated on putting a halt to the madness, sending one thought after another into the minds of the crazed wolves.

At first they disregarded her push. Gina blasted their eyes with stinging spray from the lovely water fountain set up specifically for the event. Deme's clinging vines tangled around their feet and sent them sprawling and Brigid singed the hair and whiskers on more than a dozen. The wolves' fanatical attack waned, their strength draining in response to Selene's suggestions that they were tired and would never win this fight.

When Selene thought they had a good handle on most of them, she broke away from her sisters and went in search of Gryph and Lucas. The door into the garden gaped wide open. Selene could sense a powerful struggle taking place among the manicured bushes and flower beds.

Gryph had Lucas pinned to the ground. No matter how much the big wolf struggled, he couldn't work his way loose of the massive lion.

Slowly Lucas returned to human form, his struggles abating.

Gryph half changed, still pressing his weight into his brother. "Give up, Lucas. You're not going to win."

"I can't let you win. Not again. You always win."

"This is not a contest of who should win or lose. We are brothers."

"Father loved you more."

"Father loves all the people of the Lair."

"No. He loved your mother and he swore he'd take care of you and never reveal her secret. All because he loved her and wanted her to have a decent life."

"You're wrong."

"Ask him."

"Lucas, you're my brother, whether by blood or not doesn't matter."

"You'll never be my brother." Lucas turned his face away from Gryph, refusing to look him in the eye.

Selene could sense the loss and hurt in Gryph and wanted to go to him as he rose to stand on two feet. She could also feel the anger still churning in Lucas, and a sudden shift to an eruption of uncontrollable hatred.

"Gryph, look out!" Selene ran toward Gryph.

Lucas sprang to his feet, hit Gryph in the midsection and knocked him on his back, morphed into a wolf and lunged for Gryph's throat.

Selene threw herself at Lucas, wrapping her arms around his hairy neck and squeezing with all her might, physically and mentally.

Lucas fought her, stretching his lethal jaws toward

Gryph's throat. Unable to reach his goal, Lucas rolled over, taking Selene with him, shaking loose of her hold.

Then he attacked her.

She threw her arm over her face, the wolf's teeth tearing into her flesh.

No sooner had he bitten her, he was flung across the room with the mighty sweep of Gryph's big paw.

Lucas slammed into the wall headfirst with a loud thud and a snap. He lay still at an awkward angle, his eyes open, his body returning to human.

Gryph gave him no more than a glance before he dropped down beside Selene. "You're bleeding."

"Now, that's a real scratch." She laughed shakily, her eyes filling with tears. "I'm sorry."

"For what?"

"Your brother."

"You don't have to be sorry." He removed the tattered remains of his jacket and ripped what was left of his shirt into long strips, making quick work of applying a pressure bandage to the torn skin of her arm. His tuxedo trousers hung around his waist, shredded during his transformation from man to beast. He didn't care. "I need to get you to a hospital."

"No. You have guests to help. My sisters—"

"Can help the guests." He lifted her in his arms and held her tightly against his battered body.

Selene didn't have the strength to argue, just leaned her face against his furry chest and sighed. "This is where I want to be."

"And where I want you to be," he whispered against her hair.

"Then why fight it?" She wasn't sure she spoke the words out loud or in her mind.

"I surrender."

A smile curved her lips and her eyelids slid downward. The loss of blood and the strain of fighting to protect the ones she loved had taken their toll. In the warmth of Gryph's arms, the black wolf dead and no longer a threat, his minions scattering to the winds, Selene succumbed to darkness.

Chapter 20

EMTs from all over the city converged on the hotel, treating the wounded and sedating the hysterical. Gryph left the hotel in the back of the ambulance with Selene, her sisters promising to wrap things up and meet him at the hospital.

All the way to the trauma center Gryph had too much time to think and imagine the worst. Selene had slipped into unconsciousness and had yet to wake up. She'd been injured worse than he first thought. The bite had ripped several veins and she was bleeding tremendously. Her loss of so much blood scared Gryph more than anything he'd encountered in his entire life. Gryph pressed Selene's hand to his cheek, praying to every god he'd ever had need to pray to that Selene would live. She had saved him from the river and captured his heart with her warmth and understanding of his family in the Lair. She aroused in him a desire so rare and beautiful he could not imagine living life without her in it. And as soon as she awakened, he'd tell her. If she'd have him, he'd do his best to quell his beast and be gentle with her the rest of their lives.

The EMTs unloaded the gurney at the hospital and wheeled Selene into a room. When Gryph followed, a nurse blocked his path. "You'll need to stay in the waiting room."

He wanted to roar and tell the woman to get the hell out of his way.

But she smiled and laid a hand on his arm. "Trust us and let us do our jobs. She's in good hands."

Gryph backed into the waiting room and paced.

Within minutes, the rest of the Chattox sisters arrived, explaining that Cal had remained behind to help sort through the mess of guests and shifters, identifying those who'd changed back into their human form before they mixed with the guests and could escape.

"How's our girl?" Brigid asked, peering through the window of the swinging door leading to the back.

"I don't know. She wasn't conscious going in." Gryph spun and walked to the end of the room and back. "I should have done more. I should have seen it, suspected him. I should have known it was Lucas."

"We heard the black wolf was your brother." Aurai laid a hand on his arm. "I'm sorry."

Gryph shook her hand off and closed his eyes, the image of Lucas lying against the wall not nearly as painful as Selene slipping away in his arms. "He might have killed her."

"The doctors will save her," Deme said.

"We have to believe." Gina took Deme's hand and held her hand out to Brigid. The sisters came together in a circle, each holding a hand.

Gryph stood on the outside, wishing he could add to their power to save their sister.

Aurai broke the chain and extended her hand to him. "Come."

Gryph took it, and Brigid's, and stood with them as they chanted:

"Feel the power.
Free our hearts.
Save our sister.
Bring her home.
With the strength of the earth,
With the rising of the wind,
With the calm of the water,
With the intensity of fire,
With the freedom of spirit,
The goddess is within us.
She is power.
We are her.
We are one
Blessed be."

Something swelled inside him, lifting his spirit, giving him the confidence to face what would be, and the whole-hearted belief that Selene would be all right.

After a moment of silence, they dropped hands and stepped back.

Gryph walked toward the exit and out into the hallway and almost ran into Balthazar.

He gripped the man's arms, his heart squeezing so hard in his chest he could barely breathe. "Father, I'm sorry."

Balthazar raised his hand. "I know. Word travels fast in the underground. Lucas is dead." For a moment his lips pressed into a tight line, his eyes filling with weary tears. "I'm sorry it came to this. I knew I was losing him, I just didn't realize how badly."

Gryph hugged the man who'd raised him his entire life, who'd shown him more love and care than most biological fathers ever did. This man had opened his home and his heart equally to Lucas.

Gryph stood back from his adoptive father. "What I don't understand is why he was so angry with me. Why he thought I was the favored son."

"Probably because he knew you weren't abandoned like he was. You see, his mother didn't love him. Wanted nothing to do with him."

"So? My mother didn't want me, either."

"No, that isn't true. I told you long ago that your mother brought you to me when you were an infant. She loved you and didn't want you to be exposed to the ridicule and hatred of living your life among humans who wouldn't understand when you shifted to lion and back. And in the early years, you did, without warning. Even as an infant.

"When your mother was raped, her parents threatened to cut her off if she didn't abort you. She told her parents she had, but hid her pregnancy from them. When she gave birth in her apartment, she knew the moment you came out, your condition would be impossible to hide.

"She loved you, but to ensure you lived a happier life, she gave you to me, knowing I could raise you better than she could and in a place that would accept you for who and what you were."

"Why didn't she come to live among us?"

"She wanted to, but she was prone to depression and living in the tunnels wouldn't have been conducive to a happy life for her."

"But she never came to visit."

"We thought it best that you not be tempted by the surface until you had your beast under control."

"And when I did attain that goal?" Gryph prompted, trying to grasp what his father was saying.

Balthazar shrugged. "It was just easier."

"Is she—"

"Still alive?" Balthazar nodded. "And she'd like very much to meet you."

Gryph's stomach churned, his palms were sweaty and his beast surged, threatening to unfurl. "When?"

Balthazar patted his arm. "Soon. In the meantime, we need to make sure no harm comes to your little witch."

"She's not mine."

"Then convince her."

"How?"

"Trust your instincts."

"I'm dangerous. I can't control my beast when I'm with her."

"Give her the choice," Balthazar said softly.

Footsteps rang out in the hallway and Gryph turned.

A man in blue scrubs pushed a surgical mask down from his face. "Are you all with Miss Chattox?"

The sisters filed out of the waiting room to join Gryph and Balthazar.

"We're her sisters," Deme said. "How is she?"

"She'll live. It was a nasty wound, severing several veins, but we were able to stop the flow of blood and stitch her back together. You can go in to see her once she's settled in her room. She should be ready to go home tomorrow, if she has someone who'll stay with her."

"She does," Deme assured the doctor. Once he'd left, she held out her hands to her sisters and they gathered in a tight hug, opening their family embrace to Gryph and Balthazar, who gladly accepted.

A nurse found them in the waiting room and led them to the floor and room where they'd moved Selene.

They gathered around Selene's sleeping form, hooked up to monitors and an IV.

Gryph's chest hurt and the scent of antiseptic made him want to vomit. Selene looked so small and helpless against the clean white sheets.

"She probably won't wake until morning," the nurse was saying. "You all might as well get some rest."

"I'm staying," Gryph informed her.

The nurse's gaze ran his length. "Someone put your tux through a blender, sir? You might want to go home, shower and change. You don't want to frighten our patient."

For the first time since he'd left the hotel, Gryph glanced down at his tattered clothing. It didn't matter. "I'm staying."

Her nose wrinkled and she crossed her arms over her chest. "Are you family?"

Deme, Brigid, Aurai and Gina all answered as one, "Yes!"

The nurse relaxed. "Then I guess you're staying. I'll get a spare pillow and blanket and see if I can't find a shirt."

"That won't be necessary," Gryph assured her.

The woman shook her head. "If I want the nurses to do their jobs and not duck in every five minutes to stare, I'll be finding you a shirt and you will by golly wear it!"

Gryph smiled. "Thank you."

The woman snorted. "That's more like it."

"I'm for that shower and fresh clothing the nurse suggested," Deme said. She touched a hand to Selene's pale cheek. "Be safe, sister." Then she pressed a kiss to her sister's forehead.

The others followed suit.

Deme stopped in front of Gryph. "I'll only be gone for an hour. Call me if she wakes or if you need anything."

"I will."

Brigid faced Gryph. "You're all right for a shifter." She glanced back at her sister lying in the bed. "Selene could do worse," she said, her voice gruff. She touched his arm. "Point is, I trust you to look out for her."

"Thank you."

Gina and Aurai both kissed Selene and turned to leave.

Aurai was at the door when she spun and ran back to Gryph, throwing her arms around him. "Thanks for saving her. We couldn't live without Selene."

Acceptance from the tight-knit family of sisters warmed Gryph's insides, making his chest swell. He hoped he could live up to their expectations and protect their sister from any threats. He'd almost lost her this time. If she gave him a chance, he'd sure as hell do a better job the next time.

Balthazar was the last to leave, laying a hand on Gryph's shoulder. "She's special."

"Yes, she is."

"And so are you. You're as human as anyone, where it counts." His father pressed a hand to his chest.

Gryph nodded. Animals came in all forms, both physical and mental. He prayed he could be the man and beast Selene deserved.

When everyone left but him, he settled in the chair beside Selene and held her hand through the night, praying the bite of the wolf didn't impact her and if it had, that she'd be up for the challenge.

No matter the outcome, he'd accept her for who she was. Because he loved her.

Chapter 21

Selene pulled herself out of the gray fog clouding her brain and opened her eyes to sunshine streaming through the open curtain. She blinked and stared around at the sterile walls and surroundings before she realized she was in a hospital.

"About time you woke up." Deme leaned over the bed and brushed a strand of hair out of her face.

"How long have I been asleep?"

"Just through the night. The doctor was pleased with your recovery and is sending a nurse by to brief you on your release."

"Oh." Selene glanced around the room.

"If you're looking for the others, Gina and Aurai are bringing the rental car around. Brigid is at the station with Cal filling out the mountain of paperwork that comes from an all-out attack by paranorms at a downtown grand hotel."

Selene grimaced. "How many were hurt?"

"A couple dozen, but only one death."

"Lucas?"

Deme nodded.

Selene's chest tightened. Gryph must have been devastated by his brother's betrayal. She glanced toward the door, wondering where he was.

"Gryph's not here."

"Oh."

Deme smiled. "He was here all night. I ran him home to get a shower and some presentable clothes. He was scaring the staff."

Selene's heart skipped several beats. "He was here."

"Honey, he didn't leave your side all night. The rest of us went to bed. He didn't. Looked like hell this morning."

Selene sat up, a little light-headed, and her neck and arm were sore. She stared down at the bandages and stiffened, remembering Lucas's teeth tearing into her flesh. She touched the bandages. "He bit me."

"Yes." Deme ran a brush through Selene's hair, smoothing the tangles. "The good news is that I did a little checking with the local coven. Apparently, witches are immune to werewolf bites, and it takes more than a mere scratch or bite to change a human to a wolf."

Selene let go of the tension knotting her muscles, the steady brushstrokes calming. "It's bad enough being a witch, but a shifter witch?" When Deme finished, Selene leaned back, shaking her head. "At least D'na Ileana's view of the future didn't come to pass."

"No, it didn't." Gryph's deep voice sounded from the doorway. "Her prediction didn't take into account the power of love and family."

Selene's pulse quickened, her cheeks heating. She

lifted a hand to her face, wishing she'd had time to shower and apply some makeup before seeing him.

He carried a vase of red and white roses and set them on the table beside the bed. "You've got some color back in your cheeks."

"It's warm in here," she said.

"I brought you a visitor."

"Really? I'm not even dressed."

"She won't care."

"She?" Selene straightened the sheet in her lap and tugged at the hospital gown.

He turned toward door. "Dr. Richardson?"

An older woman with salt-and-pepper hair, wearing a tasteful business suit, entered the room, her steps hesitant. "Hi."

A spark of recognition teetered on the edge of Selene's memory. She stared from the woman to Gryph. "Don't I know you?"

She nodded. "I'm the president of Colyer-Fenton College, where your sister Aurai studied."

"Oh, yes. I remember now." Not only was she the president during the struggle to free Aurai, but this woman had also been a student at the college when the Chimera had first struck over thirty years ago.

Her frown deepening, Selene's glance shifted to Gryph. What had Balthazar said? Gryph's mother had been attacked by a monster.

Could she be? Her gaze swung back to Dr. Richardson. "Are you—"

"Gryphon's mother?" She held out her hand to her son.

He took it, nodding. "She is. Balthazar introduced us this morning. I wanted her to meet you."

"It's my pleasure." She held out a hand to Selene. "I regret that I wasn't strong enough to raise Gryph on my own. However, Balthazar knew what he was doing. My son is a good man."

Selene squeezed the woman's hand. "Yes, he is."

"Well, I don't want to wear you out and I have to get back to work. I just wanted to meet the woman who captured my son's heart." With tears shimmering in her eyes, she bent and gave Selene a hug. "Grab for love and hold as tightly as you can," she whispered into Selene's ear. Then she was gone, leaving Selene alone with Gryph.

Suddenly shy and at a definite disadvantage, Selene shifted in the sheets, refusing to look at Gryph, afraid she wouldn't see what she wanted to see in his expression. They'd been off again, on again and frankly, she didn't know where they stood anymore or where they were heading.

"I heard what Dr. Richardson said to you." Gryph finally broke the silence, striding across the room.

"You did?" Heat suffused Selene's cheeks and spread down her neck and onto her chest. "And?"

"I agree."

Selene's eyes narrowed. "Just so we're both on the same page...she said grab for love and hold on as tightly as you can. Is that what you heard?"

He nodded, a smile spreading across his face. "Question is, do you agree?"

Afraid of more rejection and too tired to fight about it, Selene gazed up at the man she was growing to love more with each day they were together. "Are you going to push me away again? Because I'm not sure I can handle it. A girl can only handle so much rejection before—"

He gathered her in his arms, his lips crashing down over hers.

She melted against him, recognizing this as the place she wanted to be. In his arms, with his lips on hers.

Several long, delicious minutes later, he came up for air. "I don't ever want to hurt you."

"Then don't give up on me or what we have together."

"I can't always control my beast."

"I'll help you." She smoothed a strand of his tawny hair from his forehead. "Are you sure you want to be with a witch?"

"One who can read minds and manipulate people at will?" He nodded. "I told you, I can recognize when you're doing it to me. I won't do anything I don't want to."

"Promise?"

He raised a hand. "Promise."

"Then there's only one thing left to do?" she said.

"What's that?" His arms tightened around her.

"Kiss me."

And he did.

* * * * *

Debbie Herbert writes paranormal romance novels reflecting her belief that love, like magic, casts its own spell of enchantment. She's always been fascinated by magic, romance and gothic stories. Married and living in Alabama, she roots for the Crimson Tide football team. Her oldest son, like many of her characters, has autism. Her youngest son is in the US Army. A past Maggie Award finalist in both young-adult and paranormal romance, she's a member of the Georgia Romance Writers of America. Visit her website at debbieherbert.com.

Books by Debbie Herbert

Harlequin Nocturne

The Dark Seas Series
Siren's Secret
Siren's Treasure
Siren's Call

SIREN'S CALL

Debbie Herbert

First and always, for my husband, Tim, who has always believed in me. For my father, J. W. Gainey, who takes such pride in my accomplishments. And I want to mention several special friends who have helped me on my writing journey with either their support, or the brainstorming of ideas, or critique of this book as it was written: Sandra Wilson Cummins, Sherrie Lea Morgan and Becky Rawnsley.

Chapter 1

"Look at her..."

Snicker. "Thinks she's somethin'..."

"Heard about her latest?"

Lily ignored the whispers and kept the corners of her lips slightly upturned as she studied the dead fish on display. Her insides churned as cold and slushy as the fishes' beds of ice.

"Miss Bosarge!" The portly seafood manager beamed behind the counter. "What can I get ya?"

She pointed to her selection and he wrapped it in white paper, all the while looking her up and down, a lecherous glimmer in his eyes. He winked. "I'll make a special deal for you."

The buzzing from behind grew louder.

"Disgusting."

"Slut."

That was going too far. Lily placed the fish in her cart

and withdrew her makeup compact. She held it up and dabbed on a touch of lip gloss, checking out her latest tormentors. Yep, Twyla Fae was with a couple of friends and no doubt the ringleader. Twyla still smarted from the time her then-boyfriend-now-husband briefly dumped her to pursue Lily. You'd think the woman would be over something that happened two years ago.

Lily composed the habitual all-is-well smile as she faced Twyla. "How's J.P. doing?" she asked with double-sugar-fudge politeness. "I haven't heard from him in the *longest*. I *really* should drop by and say 'hey'."

Twyla paled beneath her tan but quickly recovered and glowered. "You stay away from J.P." She shifted the whining toddler in her arms. "We're a family now."

Lily moved her cart straight at the trio. They jumped out of the way.

"Maybe I will, maybe I won't," she threatened in honeyed tones, strolling down the aisle. *Never let them see you care*—her mantra since puberty, when her siren's voice had developed and unleashed its power over the entire male population of Bayou La Siryna.

Lily took her time filling the cart with dozens of cans of sardine and tuna and cases of bottled water. The usual fare.

An explosion of green bean tins hit the floor, but she didn't flinch. A teenaged stock boy gathered the spillage, so focused on Lily he made a worse mess and cans rolled in all directions. Almost without fail, men ran into stuff or dropped what they were doing when she walked by. She would have helped the boy, but experience proved it would make matters worse. He'd say something stupid or his girlfriend would see them and get mad, or he'd continue to bumble on or... It was always something.

The grocery store's sliding glass doors opened, bringing in a wave of humid Alabama air. A tanned stranger walked in with an aura as hot and powerful as the bayou breeze. He didn't look around the store to get his bearings, but immediately turned right and went to the produce department. He had a patrician vibe, as if he were Mr. Darcy strolling across English moors, not a local good ole boy grocery shopping at Winn-Dixie.

Lily leaned against the cart and watched as he efficiently grabbed a sack of potatoes and loaded it in his cart, paying no attention to the admiring glances of all the women. Something about the angle of his jaw and the gleam of his long, dark hair looked familiar.

Tingles of awareness prickled her arms and legs. She *had* to get closer. He drew her like a thirsty traveler to an oasis. Is this how men felt around her? The same clawing need for contact? It was a new experience, and Lily wasn't sure she liked the loss of control—no matter how exciting the sensations.

Ignoring the dirty looks from other women, she approached. Bettina, once an elementary school friend, rolled her eyes and deliberately jostled against Lily.

"Fresh meat, huh?" Bettina whispered, breath whooshing against Lily's neck like a poisonous vapor. "Can't you leave one guy for the rest of us?"

Lily refused to glance at her old friend, afraid of losing it. Bett had deserted her like all the other jealous bitches. She lifted her chin and continued toward the stranger, who was culling through vegetables. What to say? The only opening line running through her brain— *Hey, haven't we met before?*—was way tacky. But really, it didn't matter *what* she said. The mere sound of her voice would be enough.

"Hello," she purred, pulling her cart alongside Mr. Darcy-cum-Brad Pitt.

He threw some corn in his cart without looking up. "Hi," he answered in a voice so clipped he might as well have said *back off*.

Shock disconnected Lily's brain from her limbs and she stood immobile while pounding blood made her ears ring. How odd. He acted impervious to the dulcet tones that made other men cross-eyed. Lily stiffened her spine. She'd bowl him over with more talking, would force him to look into her ocean-blue eyes. That ought to do the trick.

"Are you from around here?" she asked.

"No." He pushed away and started down the dairy aisle, his back to her.

What the hell? Lily froze again as she tried to grasp the foreign concept of being snubbed by the opposite sex. It really kind of sucked. Snickering noises from all around sent heat rushing to the back of her neck.

"About time she had a comeuppance," Bettina said with a loud snort.

Lily faced her directly. "What's your problem?" she snapped. "What have I ever done to you?"

Bettina's lips curled. "You really don't get it, do you? How about stealing Johnny Adams in junior high? And then Tommy Beckham in high school?"

It's not my fault, she wanted to scream. But they would never understand. Their dislike and mistrust ran as deep as the Gulf waters, their tears and anger as salty and bitter as the sea that encompassed the bayou. *Forget them.*

Lily shoved away in a huff, turning her attention once again to the handsome stranger's retreating figure. Her fingers gripped the cart handle until her knuckles were white as sea foam against her already pale skin. She lifted her chin. Nobody ignored her. Envied, yes. Lusted, of course. Later left humiliated and angry at her inevitable rebuff, check. But never this total lack of interest.

Lily hurried toward the mystery man. "Hey, you. Wait a minute."

He slackened his pace but didn't stop as she drew close.

"Have we met before?" She'd thought so at first, but she must be wrong. This brutal disregard would have been memorable.

The man turned so slowly, Lily had a sense of inevitability as the seconds wound down into a series of freeze-frames. One: broad shoulders flexing under a dove-gray T-shirt. Two: a profile of a strong chin and deep facial planes. Three: a lock of obsidian hair falling across high, prominent cheekbones.

It wasn't a tan after all; his skin was the shade of light cinnamon from Native American heritage. Leaf-green eyes lit upon her, so shot through with a golden starburst they were startling in their brightness. Not a speck of recognition sparked in them, though.

But, oh, Lily knew those eyes. "Nash," she breathed. "Nashoba Bowman."

He frowned slightly. "Do I know you?"

She swallowed down the burn at the back of her throat. Not only was he immune to her siren's voice and unaffected by her physical beauty, but also he didn't even remember her. A riptide of humiliation washed over Lily. Only years of hiding her emotions kept her from betraying hurt. She licked her parched lips. "You used to spend summers here with your grandfather when you were little."

Nash stared long and hard. The brightness of his pupils deepened to a darker hue as the seconds—minutes?—sped by.

He *had* to remember. She held up her right hand and twirled her wrist. His gaze shifted to the colorful beaded bracelet he'd given her when they were children. *Friends forever*, he'd said when he'd tied it on her wrist. Lily willed him to recall those long-ago walks on the shore, the jaunts in the woods, the picnics and bike rides and… A glimmer of warmth lit his face.

"Lily?"

"Yes," she whooshed in an exhale of relief.

He gave her the once-over, a slow appraisal that left her hot and breathless. His dilated pupils and smoldering aura suggested he might not be as indifferent to her as he tried to act. Or it might be wishful thinking on her part.

Did Nash also remember that chaste, sweet kiss they'd once shared as curious twelve-year-olds?

His eyes met hers again, blazing green and gold. Yet the stoic, expressionless face more resembled Nash's inscrutable grandfather than the kid she used to know. The heat from his skin and a faint, familiar scent drew her closer, strong as the full moon's pull on the tide. The same odd compulsion to approach Nash now drove her to touch him. Lily dropped her gaze and rested her pale hand against his bronzed forearm, admiring the contrast of fair and dark. Her gaze swept lower, noting that no gold band adorned his fingers.

Nash's skin was hot as the Southern sun and his muscles rumbled and flickered under her touch, like thunder over deep waters. His jaw tightened at the brazen contact, but he didn't pull away. His fingers curled tightly on his cart. *Indifferent, my ass.* Lily closed her eyes and inhaled, using her heightened senses to identify Nash's enticing scent—a woodsy, sandalwood base with wisps of pine and cedar and perhaps a touch of oak moss. He smelled like the backwoods they used to roam together.

Bet his kiss was anything but chaste now.

"There you are!" a trilling voice bore down upon them.

She opened her eyes and watched a tall redhead grin as she lifted a couple of plastic bags. "I picked up the last of what we need for the shoot. Doughnuts and dozens of protein bars while we stalk the elusive mating habits of Alabama clapper rails."

Lily blinked and glanced at Nash as he subtly inched away from her touch. The loss of contact left her oddly disoriented. "Elusive... What did you say?" she asked the woman, feeling stupid.

"They're birds. Also known as marsh chickens or clappers." The redhead held out a hand. "I'm Opal Wallace, Nash's photographic assistant." Opal's face was sprinkled with freckles, and a faint scar marred one cheek. A bit plain overall, but her wide smile and merry eyes made up for any lack of sculptured perfection.

A flush of pleasure shot through Lily at Opal's kind greeting. It had been a long time since a female, outside of family, had bestowed a genuine smile her way. She shook the proffered hand, pathetically grateful for the friendly gesture.

Opal winked. "Figured I'd introduce myself since Nash appears speechless."

Nash cleared his throat. "You didn't give me a chance to introduce you," he answered, frowning slightly. He lifted a hand in Lily's direction. "This is Lily Bosarge, an old friend."

"Hey, ole buddy Lily." Opal waggled her eyebrows. "How close of *friends* were you two?"

"Purely platonic," Lily joked. *Well, mostly. Except for one experimental kiss.* "Can't get into too much trouble before the teen years." Nash had been long gone by the time she'd developed her siren voice. Not that it mattered; he seemed unaffected by its magic. This time, *she* was the one flushed and bewildered in the presence of the opposite sex.

And she didn't like it one little bit.

"Let's get together one evening, okay?" Opal whipped out a business card from one of the many pockets on her khaki vest and pressed it into Lily's palm. "Gotta run. There's a ton of stuff I need to set up before we get to work." She gave Nash a brisk wave. "See you on the island in a couple days, boss. I'll have the area scouted out and set up, the usual."

As suddenly as she'd intruded, Opal disappeared in a swirl of red hair and a cheerful smile.

Awkward silence descended and Lily felt an odd jolt of dismay when Nash glanced down at his watch. She didn't want to say goodbye. If he walked out now, would she ever see him again, ever discover why he acted immune to her enchantment? Besides, he was the last good friend she'd ever had, and certainly the only one in the male species. Everything had turned to shit in junior high when the guys started chasing her unmercifully. At first it had been tremendous fun—for maybe half a year. Until the girls turned as one against her like a tsunami of destruction.

Lily grasped at the first conversational thread that popped into her head. "I hear you're a famous wildlife photographer now. I remember how you used to carry around an old 35 mm camera your grandfather bought at a thrift store."

"Most of the time I didn't have enough money to actually load it with film." The taut muscles in his jaw and chin relaxed and the green eyes grew cloudy. He shook his head slightly, and the corners of his mouth twitched in a semismile.

Warmth spread inside at this glimpse of the boy she used to know.

"And you were never without your sketchpad," Nash said. "You were damn good, too. The detail of your drawings impressed me. Please tell me you still draw."

Lily returned the smile, delighted she'd drawn him into a real conversation. "I do some. Mostly, though, I paint with watercolors." She kept her tone deliberately light and casual, as if painting were a mere hobby and not a passion.

His brow furrowed. "Watercolors?"

"It's not like the kiddie paintings you make with cheap dime-store kits," she answered quickly. Too quickly, judging from his knowing expression, as if he'd guessed her art was more than a casual hobby.

"I see. Didn't mean to belittle your art."

Lily shrugged, let her facial features smooth into its familiar mask. Nash wasn't the only one who'd learned to hide emotion over the years. "I'm no artist."

"So you say."

Perceptive eyes drilled into her, as if he saw past the pretty, past the superficial shell she presented to everyone in town who only viewed her as the slutty dumb blonde who'd worked as a hairdresser until a few months ago.

It was exhilarating.

It was scary.

Lily retreated like a trembling turtle, so different from the young girl who had scouted the piney woods and shoreline with Nash. Deflection time. "I'm not surprised you photograph animals. You have some kind of… rapport…or something with all living creatures. It was downright eerie."

Nash shrugged and the warmth left his eyes. "Not really."

"Yes, you do," Lily insisted. "Anytime we were in the woods it seemed the trees would fill with birds and we'd almost always startle a deer or raccoon by getting so near them. Once we even found that den of baby foxes—"

"So what?" Nash cut in, lips set in a harsh, pinched line. "This place is so isolated even the animals are bored out of their minds. Makes them overly excited when anyone draws close."

Ouch. What kind of nerve had she hit with her innocent remark? "You used to love coming here in the summers," she reminded Nash. "Said it was an escape from the city and a chance to run free."

"I get it." His lips curled. "I'm Indian, so I must have a special communication with nature, right? Since we live so close to nature and worship Mother Earth and the Great Spirit and all. Well, that's bullshit."

Damn. Her own temper rose at the unjust accusation. "I don't deserve that. We used to be friends and I thought we still could be. Guess I was wrong. You're nothing like the guy I used to hang out with every summer."

First Twyla and Bett, and now this. Lily jerked her cart forward, eager to escape the grocery trip from hell. Sexy or not, some men weren't worth the trouble.

Warmth and weight settled on her right shoulder. Fingers curled into her flesh, halting her steps. "Hey," Nash said. "Look at me."

Lily turned. The harsh stranger melted and his face softened.

"I'm sorry."

Anger deflated in a whoosh. If Nash was anything like his grandfather or the guy she used to know, he spoke the truth. Lily nodded. "Well, okay, then. Let's start over." She took a deep breath and plunged on. "How about dinner at my place tonight or whenever you're free? Your grandfather's invited too, of course."

Nash rubbed his jaw, as if debating whether to accept the invitation. Any other man would have followed her home then and there. Any other man wouldn't have picked a fight or brushed off her advances.

But Nash wasn't like any other man she'd ever met. And Lily was more than a little intrigued.

"Sorry," he said, dropping his hand to his side. "I'm pretty busy right now. Maybe after I finish this assignment on Herb Island we can get together. Grandfather always liked you. He'd enjoy seeing you again."

The novelty of male rejection left Lily nonplussed until the sting of it burned through the haze of disbelief. "You're turning me down?" she squeaked.

Nash retreated a step. "Like I said, I'm swamped at the moment. Good running into you again, though. Take care."

Unbelievable. Lily mustered her tattered pride. "Okay, then," she said in a high falsetto, gripping the cart. "Tell your grandfather I said 'hey.'"

She hurried down the aisle, not daring to look back and risk exposing her feelings. The air pressed in around her, leaving her a bit dizzy. She scrambled through the line, paid the cashier and stumbled out of the refrigerated environment into the untamed, sizzling bayou air that always held the droning of insects and an echo of the ocean's wave. First thing when she got home, she'd go for a long, cool swim underwater, get her bearings.

Instead of heading immediately to the car, Lily strode down the boiling sidewalk to the drugstore next door. She left the cart by its front door—it would be safe for a minute. Inside the store, Lily hurried to the makeup aisle and gathered up half a dozen lipsticks in every color from baby-doll-pink to siren-red. She peeked at the mirrored glass lining behind the shelves, half expecting to see some glaring new imperfection marring her appearance. But no—same long, flaxen hair, creamy skin and large blue eyes.

So what had gone wrong with Nash? Why hadn't he been attracted to her?

Lily grabbed some blush and a tube of mascara. She'd have to try harder. She hastened over to the cashier and dumped her ammunition on the counter. *I'll go see him. Pay a visit looking my best.* She dug into her pocketbook for a credit card, but the purse lining blurred and morphed into a pool of filmy sludge.

"Are ya crying?" the elderly lady behind the counter asked.

"I'm not—" Lily paused, hands touching her damp cheeks. "Guess so," she admitted in surprise.

The lady handed over an opened box of tissue. "Yer a pretty little thing. Some man ain't treating ya right, get you another."

"Right," Lily sniffed, swiping her cheeks. She had to get out, get herself together before she ran into anyone she knew. Twyla Fae and Bettina would find the tears a hoot. "Um, thanks. I'll take the tissue, too." She paid, retrieved her grocery cart and got to the car. Another five minutes and she could be alone with her thoughts and cry as much as her heart desired. Lily carelessly shoved in the bottled water, bags of seafood and tuna cans. Almost home free.

She corralled the cart and returned to her car, not noticing anything amiss until she almost stepped on it.

A dead, bloody rat lay directly outside the driver's door. The entrails were fresh, and blood was seeping into the shelled pavement. Its skin was precisely cut down the tender underbelly.

Lily pressed a hand to her mouth as bile threatened to creep up her throat. *It's only a rat. No big deal. Just an accident.*

She clutched her purse tightly against her side and glanced around the parking lot. The few people around paid her no attention, yet the tingles shooting along her spine alerted Lily that someone was indeed watching.

Watching and enjoying her fear.

She turned back to the car and noticed the long key scratch that started from the front left tire all the way down to the fender. Anger outweighed fear as she read the large, childlike scrawl etched on the car door.

D-i-e S-l-u-t.

Chapter 2

The whir of electric grinder against metal grated on Lily's ears. She whistled and waved her arms to get her sister's attention.

Jet frowned and switched off the grinder. "What?"

"Are you almost done? You've been at it long enough I'm surprised you haven't sanded a hole through my car."

They stared at the long, narrow patch of bare metal on the red Audi S4. Lily ran a finger over the warmed surface, perfectly manicured nails and graceful fingers a stark contrast against the ugly gash. She tried to joke. "Sure can't see those words now."

Jet scowled, not amused. "'Bout time I had a word with Twyla Fae and her posse of bitches."

"Don't. You'll make it worse."

"Can it get much worse? They're crossing the line into criminal territory with this latest harassment." Jet gripped the sander so tight in her right arm, her biceps bulged and a network of veins popped against taut flesh.

Her sister was strong enough to best any man in a fist fight, courtesy of the supernatural strength from her paternal Blue Clan merblood. But against the verbal warfare of scorned women, Lily considered her own reserved veil of indifference a superior tactical maneuver. "Ignore them like I do."

"Don't see your plan working," Jet grumbled. The fierce glow in her dark eyes contrasted with the large, womanly bump at her waist. Lily shook her head in bemusement. On the surface, their beauty and temperament appeared leagues apart. If she was the ethereal one—silver sparkles drifting on moon-drenched water, soft and shifting and subtle—Jet was more like the oft-admired coral undersea—brittle, bedazzling, with razor-sharp edges that wounded the unwary.

Down deep, they could each be deadly in their own way.

Lily placed a hand on Jet's belly bulge. "Don't get worked up and disturb the baby."

"And don't you try distracting me." Yet Jet's harsh features softened. "Seriously, how about we get Landry and Tillman involved? File a formal complaint."

"I'll think about it." She had no intention of seeking help from her cop brothers-in-law. Lily sensed their wariness of her, their suspicions about her morals.

Jet returned the grinder to a shelf. "Translation—you're too proud to seek help." She dug into her baggy, denim jeans and produced a set of keys. "Drive this until the body shop in Mobile repairs the damage. I'll rent something in the meantime." Jet tossed the keys.

"Or you could buy a soccer-mom van." Lily caught the keys and cast a sly smile. No way Jet would forego her clinker of a truck. They could afford anything, thanks to a tidy trust fund built from pawned sea treasure sold by generations of Bosarge mermaids. Why Jet chose to drive the monstrosity was a mystery. Lily's own aesthetic sensibilities ran along a selective, pricey line. She'd drive something even flashier, but the bayou brine rusted everything eventually.

Besides, Lily drew enough attention from her voice. No need to give the locals more fodder. They'd be convinced she had a rich sugar daddy in hiding.

"Maybe I will." Jet grinned. "But it won't be as funny as you driving my truck."

"Got me there," Lily conceded. She started the truck, wincing at the beater's clickety-clackety rumbling. She fumbled with the clutch and, with a loud screech, backed out of the driveway, nearly sideswiping the mailbox. Jet's smirk faded and her brows knitted.

The beater's ornery procession out of town matched Lily's fitful mood. She'd had a restless night. Not even a long swim beneath the slithering roots of sea grass last night had calmed her restless spirit. The twin mysteries of Nash's indifference and the anonymous etching on her car both tossed and swirled in her mind like a lingering storm.

Today, she would confront both issues directly. If Twyla wanted to get nastier, she had to up her own game. As far as Nash went…perhaps there *had* been some flicker of interest in her siren charm, but like her, he'd learned to hide emotion. At least that theory made a little sense.

Houses grew sparser and paved town roads ceded to red-packed clay lanes as she headed out of town. Live oaks and palmetto shrubs spilled over from the side and encroached until only one vehicle could pass at a time on the narrow lane. She hadn't traveled this way in years and didn't recall it being so forsaken. A curlicue of claustrophobia flickered at the edges of her mind as the choking foliage strangled the open air. It was as if the bayou's wilderness soul were slowly clamping down and reclaiming its territory from human invasion.

Good thing she'd driven the truck after all. Lily's jaw clamped at the jarring scrape of branches against metal. The high-pitched squall set her nerves pulsing and she cursed the siren nature that made her so sensitive to sound vibration. Although excellent for detecting predators at sea, it was hell on land with certain tones and pitches.

A log cabin came into view. In spite of its rustic nature, Lily appreciated the way it seamlessly blended into the landscape. The scene would make a cool picture.

She got out of the truck and lifted her cell phone for a photo, eyeing the detail of the log pine's myriad grooves and knots. This piece wouldn't be a watercolor like her ocean scenes. Only a detailed pen-and-ink composition would do it justice.

Disappointed, she noted that there was no other vehicle in the driveway. Nash had mentioned he wouldn't start the job on Herb Island for a couple of days. Maybe he and his grandfather were in town and would return shortly. Lily scanned the backyard and found the small opening for an old trail she and Nash had hiked often. She'd take a little walk, and with luck, Nash would be back when she finished. Lily ditched her silk scarf and switched from designer sandals to a pair of old Keds that Jet kept on the back floorboard. They were a size too large but doable.

Lily hiked the narrow trail, the ground as familiar as when they'd explored the area as children. Pine needles cushioned the sandy soil and released bracing wisps of fragrance as her feet crushed them, a smell she'd forever associate with Nash.

At the clearing, Lily leaned against a large oak and listened to bird calls—the distant screech of seagulls, thrush and coots. He'd taught her so much, passed on everything his grandfather had taught him, including Choctaw animal folklore and legends.

How she'd longed to share her undersea world in return, show him their sea vegetable garden and swim past the salt marshes and explore a different, equally fascinating new world. But her family's vow of secrecy was absolute. If one mermaid was exposed, their entire race was in danger.

Her eyes swept the clearing, then doubled back to the far edge of the tree line.

A coyote fixed its gaze on her, unmoving, eyes gleaming with intelligence and feral hunger. Lily didn't move either and didn't break eye contact. *Coyote is a trickster*, she remembered, *a sign of an ending and a new beginning*. She wasn't alarmed, but aware. Nash used to say that was the most important thing—to stay aware. He'd even admitted once that he could sense what animals were thinking. Become one with them or some such thing.

The coyote lowered its head and took a step closer, still staring. Its copper eyes held a feral sheen that made Lily quiver from her scalp to the soles of her borrowed sneakers.

To hell with spiritual communication.

Lily turned and ran back down the trail. Twilight had deepened and the trees cast long shadows. Spanish moss hung from live oaks, fluttering in the breeze like ghosts. The cushioned, pine-needled ground gave way to a labyrinth of twisted, jutting tree roots. Lily stumbled but stayed on her feet. *I'm being ridiculous. It isn't after me.*

Yet she ran on. The sound of blood roared in her ears as if she were swimming undersea against a powerful current. Lily wanted to peek over her shoulder but didn't dare divert her attention from avoiding the tree roots, which now appeared as black and deadly as the moccasins that slithered through the swamps.

She ran and ran and ran until the accelerated beat of her heart matched the panicked cadence of her thoughts. *Coyote is the end. Coyote is the end.*

The end, the end, the end.

A violent cracking of twigs, the rustle of leaves and snapping branches, a vibration under his bare feet—Nash stilled and searched the woods. Something was spooked and running toward the cabin. He focused on the dark edge of the tree line and felt to his right for the shotgun. Smooth metal cooled his fingers. *Found it.*

He soundlessly exited the porch, shotgun at the ready. Unlikely it was a chased animal—he hadn't sensed that faint odor of musk and sweat or picked up the panicked energy of an animal hell-bent on escape.

An apparition of white burst into the clearing, like flood waters over a dam. A ghost? Grandfather told tales of the kwanokasha, or Kowi Anukasha—the tiny, fairy people of the forest. But this was no pygmy-sized being. His eyes narrowed, and like a camera lens focusing on a subject, the wall of white morphed into detail: a tall woman with waist-length, pale hair lifted in every direction by the sea breeze.

"Lily?" he called out, his voice sharp and biting. It was as if his own brooding melancholy had summoned her from the forest's darkness. He scanned her white shorts and T-shirt and the scratches decorating her arms and legs like tattoos.

But no blood; she was unharmed. His relief quickly gave way to anger. Was someone after her? Nash's right index finger curled on the shotgun trigger and he searched behind Lily for the danger.

Nothing was there.

He hurried forward. "What happened? Is someone chasing you?"

Lily looked back. "I don't know." She turned to him with a sheepish half smile on her paler-than-usual face. She drew a jagged, uneven breath. "It may not have even followed me."

"It?"

She rubbed her arms, stomach heaving with labored breath. "A coyote."

He raised a brow. "I've never known coyote to chase humans. It's probably more afraid of you than you of it."

"Not this coyote." She shook her head. "The way it looked at me…" She bit her lip. "As if he were sizing me up for dinner. Instead of running off, it lowered its head and stepped toward me. I didn't hang around to see if it chased me or not."

He'd accuse Lily of making a ploy for attention, but she didn't know he'd returned to the cabin and he could see her fear was real. "Go up on the porch and I'll take a look around."

"Why?"

"If a coyote really chased you, it must be eat-up with rabies. It's not normal behavior. If it's got rabies, the kindest thing would be to put it out of its misery. And it sure as hell doesn't need to infect other animals and cause an epidemic."

"Be careful," she said in a trembling, faint voice.

Lily's vulnerability left him flushed with an overwhelming desire to protect her from all danger. And he didn't like the feeling a bit, didn't like the peculiar pull she had on his senses. He stalked toward the woods and tried to concentrate on the immediate problem. If the animal was sick or deadly, he'd pick up on it easily. He'd been near infected, diseased creatures before. Rabies had a metallic smell of pus combined with sweaty musk from an animal's scrambling terror over its changed condition.

Nash entered the tangle of trees and shrubs, into a world he was uniquely attuned and equipped to master. A world where sound was amplified and the energy of every living thing—animal, mineral and insect—vibrated inside him at a cellular level. Even the energy of trees, moss and stone whispered its presence. The rustling of the wind in branches and leaves was nature's murmur and sigh.

He used to struggle more against this odd communion, creeped out by the immersion of his senses. He'd even tried staying indoors most of the time, only emerging to go places in the city surrounded by people and the noisy clutter of civilization. But it was no use. The abstinence made him restless and edgy. Midway through college he changed from a business degree to photography, determined to put his skills to use as a wildlife photographer.

But it was an uneasy compromise. Yes, he worked outdoors. But he erected strict mental barriers to keep from being entirely sucked in by his senses. Lily disturbed this equilibrium. Something about her was too different... too intense. She drew him to her like a force of nature.

Nash inhaled deeply and slipped into the woods' living essence. Beneath the pervasive undercurrent of sea brine nestled the scent of pine and leaf mold. He paused, listening. A faint crackle of dry leaves, a bit of rustling of branches from above, a squirrel several yards away scrambling up an oak. He went farther up the trail, which he well-remembered traversing with Lily. What had she been doing out here? Was the woman determined to hound him? He'd come home to escape that kind of attention.

There. Faint, but detectable, was the smell of sickness. A rabid animal had indeed run along the trail. But the scent was so subtle, he knew it was no longer in the area. He'd have to be on the lookout for the coyote and alert a wildlife management officer of the potential danger.

Nash trudged back down to the cabin where Lily waited on the steps, eyes troubled.

"Did you see it? I didn't hear a shot."

"It was long gone." Nash walked past her and put the shotgun away. "I did pick up a trace of something, though."

"How do you do that?"

He shrugged. "You get a feel for it when you're in the woods for long stretches all your life." Nobody's business about his freakish talent.

"Hmm," Lily said, cocking her head, as if assessing something left unsaid between them.

Nash crossed his arms, daring her to challenge his answer.

"So you say," she drawled.

He stared into mesmerizing blue eyes that he was sure had enticed many a man. The world narrowed until every detail of Lily enveloped his senses. He felt the rise and fall of her chest as she breathed, found his own breath synchronizing to hers.

No. This won't do. If you get involved, you'll only hurt her in the end. Just like all the others. Nash's fingers curled into his palm. Lily was too alluring for her own damn good. He suspected no one had ever rebuffed her advances or broken her heart.

Lily spoke, breaking the spell. "Your grandfather used to say the coyote was a clever trickster. It probably made me more afraid than it should have."

"You can't be too careful when you're alone in the woods." He regarded her sternly. "Especially when you're alone and unarmed."

Lily laughed, not intimidated. "Didn't think I'd run into anything more ominous than the fairy forest dwellers."

Grandfather and his wild, crazy stories. "His old Choctaw tales did a number on you, huh?"

"They're fascinating. Where is he, by the way?" She stood on her tiptoes and peered around his right shoulder.

"He works at the animal shelter on Fridays. I expect him home for supper any minute."

Damn. He shouldn't have said that. Now the woman would stick around and try to wrangle an invitation. He narrowed his eyes. "What were you doing on our property?"

She didn't flush or look away. "Don't see any harm in it. I've walked here over the years and your grandfather's never complained."

Nash opened the screen door and went into the house, Lily close on his heels. He snatched his car keys from the kitchen table.

"Where are you going?" she asked quizzically.

"I've got errands to run." He lowered his chin and stared at her without smiling. "I really don't have time for your friendship. Sorry to be so abrupt, but I'm busy." And the last thing he needed was a gorgeous woman hitting on him—again.

"Who doesn't have time for friends?" She tilted her face to the side and studied him.

Damn, he felt like a jerk. But she was far too beautiful. What if it became more than friendship? He couldn't let anything happen to her. Two women were already dead because of him.

"Look, you're better off forgetting you ever knew me. I'm poison. Okay?"

Her eyes widened. "What are you talking about?"

Nash ran a hand through his long hair. "Drop it."

"No way. I can't believe you'd say something like that. What's happened to you over the years?"

"Life happened," he said past the raw burning at the back of his throat.

"More like a woman is what I'd guess." She arched one perfectly groomed eyebrow. "Someone break your heart?"

Other way around. An image of Rebecca, broken and bleeding, the steel frame of her car bent in two, flashed in his mind, immediately followed by an image of Connie, ashen-skinned and lifeless, a bottle of pills by her side.

"Maybe I don't have a heart to break," he rasped. Nash rubbed his forehead, as if by doing so he could erase the deathly images. "Besides, I'm not the only one who's changed."

Lily's impossibly large eyes widened a fraction more. "How have I changed?" She swept a hand down her body. "Other than the obvious physical development, I mean. I was a flat-chested twelve-year-old girl last time we were together."

He considered. "You used to be…more open. Easier to read. Now it's hard to tell what you're thinking. Except for the obvious fear on your face when you hightailed it out of the woods just now."

She gave a snort that contrasted with her pristine, angelic features. "*I'm* hard to figure out?"

His lips twitched involuntarily. Even as a child, his nature was to retreat to silence when disturbed. And Lily would bug him until she unearthed the problem. "Guess you're as outspoken now as when you were a kid. Always pestering me about things I didn't want to talk about."

"And you used to answer all my questions. How come you stopped coming every summer? I asked your grandfather, but he only said it was a family matter."

The woman was relentless. And shameless. Better to answer what he could and get her off his back. "My parents divorced and Mom got custody. She wasn't too hip about me spending so much time away from her, much less with my paternal grandfather." He continued walking to the front of the house, Lily close in tow. Parents were a safe topic. Events of the past four years overshadowed painful childhood memories.

"Your mom ever remarry?"

"Nope. Don't see that happening. She's not the marrying sort." After his father's numerous affairs, his mother had soured on marriage.

They reached the front door, and Nash opened it, beckoning her out with a grand sweep of one arm. She slowly, reluctantly stepped outside.

Another twenty yards and he'd be rid of her and her questions. She made him uncomfortable and want things he had no right to want anymore. Time to turn Twenty Questions on her. "Did your mother ever remarry?"

"No. She's not interested in marriage, just like your mom."

Lily's reply was quick enough, but he'd always sensed there was much left unsaid, even when they were young. She'd been an open book about most everything except her family. When they weren't outside, they were at the cabin listening to his grandfather's stories.

But he had met her family a few times. Lily had grown into her mother's beauty. He remembered going into their house was like stepping into fairyland. Their huge home had an old-world, rich vibe with carelessly cluttered gold coins, heirloom pottery and solid pieces of antique furniture.

A pair of elliptical beams pierced the twilight. Nash wanted to groan. He was only a few feet away from escaping in his truck. But his grandfather would disapprove at the lack of hospitality. The old man was bound to invite Lily for dinner.

"Your grandfather," Lily squealed. "I haven't seen him in ages."

Sam Bowman exited his truck and approached, eyes focused on Lily. "We have a guest tonight," his baritone boomed, half statement, half question. "Hope you're staying for dinner."

"She was leaving. Maybe next—"

"Why yes, that would be lovely," Lily interrupted, cutting mischievous eyes at him.

Nash stifled a groan. The more he was around Lily, the more she seemed determined to snag him. And the greater his temptation to let her.

His grandfather raised an eyebrow. "You're the little Lily that used to run around here in pigtails with my grandson?"

"The one and only."

"Please, come inside," he invited. Even dressed in worn khakis and an old University of Alabama T-shirt proclaiming national championship number 12, Samuel Bowman garnered respect.

As a kid, he might have sassed his parents all day long,

but when his grandfather laid down the law, he unquestioningly obeyed. Not from threat of punishment, but because of his grandfather's unfailing politeness and show of respect to everyone, including smartass kids.

"This will be like old times." She had a hop in her step that took Nash by surprise. Such a contrast to her guarded nature at the grocery store this morning when he'd asked about her paintings. There was something mystical about her, like she was fae or one of Grandfather's mystical creatures come to life. For the first time he noticed her voice held a musical quality—as if several voices were harmonized into one melody. A bell tone of fairies singing in the woods, beckoning small children and the unwary to enter their realm.

Nash shook his head at the fanciful images. He wanted no part of anything that smacked of otherworldly. He had enough weirdness on his own without adding more to the mix.

If he wasn't careful, Lily Bosarge could be trouble.

Chapter 3

Ugly.
Hideous.
Monstrous.

Opal scrubbed the wet washcloth against her right cheek, leaving a skid of pigmented foundation on the yellow terrycloth. With the tip of her left index finger, she traced the white scar that ran from under her right ear to the corner of her mouth. Three plastic surgeries had smoothed the ridge of keloid tissue, yet the white pigmentation of dead skin would always remain.

Scarred for life. If she could only get the last of it gone... But the doctors assured her this was as good as it would get.

She threw the washcloth against the shower wall. The abomination was a curse. A person as perfect as Nash deserved so much more. Opal pictured his smooth, unmarred olive skin and grimaced at her reflection.

It's okay, love, Nash whispered in her mind, the way he did every night. *Soon I can declare my love for you in person.*

The moist heat from the shower was like his hot breath caressing her skin with endearments. *You're all I ever wanted, Opal. The others meant nothing to me. It was always you I secretly wanted. Always you.*

Opal's fury evaporated, the scent of soap morphed to Nash's scent of sandalwood and musk. He was here, caressing her. Opal cupped her breasts and moaned. Yes. Yes! One hand sank lower and the wet heat between her thighs was as scalding as the hot water pounding her skin.

Nash wanted her as much as she wanted him. Her hands were his hands, touching the soft folds of her womanhood. A finger slipped inside and she clenched as it went in and out. Harder, faster. An orgasm violently racked her body and she slid down the shower stall, weak and sated. Only he could do this, make her crazy in dreams.

Dreams that would soon be reality. He spoke to her like this, and more frequently since she'd taken care of Rebecca and Connie. He hadn't been with a woman in almost a year now.

Now it was her turn. Her time to show Nash that she was his one true love. He'd open his eyes. The veil would lift. *Oh, Opal. How could I not see it? How you must have suffered. No more, my darling. From now on, you are mine. I'll adore you forever.*

Opal rose unsteadily and shut off the water. The signs all pointed to this island assignment as the right time to make her move. And when she did, Nash would remember every conversation, every murmur of endearment he'd been whispering in her brain for the past five years.

He'd never loved those other women, or so he claimed.

But she didn't believe Nash and couldn't stand the thought of another woman in his arms. So she'd done them both a favor getting rid of Rebecca and Connie. No one could love him as much as she did. She alone knew his secret, had watched him meld into nature and mesmerize wild beasts with a whisper. Nash was extraordinary, otherworldly, and she wanted him to tame the wild storms of her internal landscape. No other man could understand the violent, explosive yearnings in her soul. No one else could save her from this crushing isolation. Only one other man had ever come close.

And he was dead.

Opal dried off, caught another glimpse of herself in the mirror and drew in a sharp breath. That slightly overweight woman—with muddy-red hair plastered like rotten seaweed around her head and neck and that hideous scar—wasn't the real Opal. The real Opal, the one Nash would see, was impeccable. Like…that Lily woman.

She scowled in the mirror—making her image that much more repulsive. The ghost of an old nursery rhyme skittered through her brain.

Mirror, mirror on the wall, who's the fairest of them all?

Lily. The slut bitch.

She was the most beautiful woman Opal had ever seen. That hair, with its pastel strands and silver-blond shine; creamy skin unmarred by any scar; and lush body all combined into an irresistible package. Worse, something about Lily's voice was almost…magical.

It wasn't fair.

And the looks that had passed between her and Nash. You could feel a sensual alchemy brewing between them. Plus, they were old childhood friends—which meant they had a history together, an old bond to explore.

This was supposed to be *her* time. He should be here at the island cabin with her instead of spending so much time in the bayou with his grandfather. She'd taken care of Nash's old girlfriends, had undergone all that plastic surgery, arranged and finagled assignments so they worked alone together on a beautiful, practically deserted island, and then this Lily had come along, upsetting her careful plans.

Opal tried to resist, but the compulsive need to again scrub the facial scar festered in her fingers. They twitched and tingled until she caved, soaping up yet another washcloth and scrubbing at the old wound. If only she could get rid of it, her problems would be solved. But no, the damn thing would haunt her forever. Opal flung the washcloth against the mirror and soapy water dripped down, distorting her scar into a mélange of distorted pixels.

Bet Lily had been brought up like a little adorable princess while she'd been shuffled around in foster care. Just when she'd gotten used to one place, she'd be uprooted. The only childhood constant was the fantasy Norman Rockwell world in her mind. A safe retreat.

At least she'd had a little luck today. What a coup to catch that woman keying the car with the "Lily" vanity tag. How convenient that Lily already had an enemy. If it became necessary to kill the blond whore, a suspect was ready for framing. Opal hoped it didn't come to that, hoped that Nash would have no time or inclination for a dalliance. She'd gotten away with two eliminations; a third might be pushing it.

Still, sluts needed to be warned and punished. As the woman and her brat-in-arms tore it out of the parking lot, Opal had dashed over and carved "Die Slut" alongside the gash the other woman had made. In a burst of inspiration, she'd run into the nearby pet store, bought a rat and disemboweled it by Lily's car.

A cache of stainless-steel razor blades were always stashed in her purse.

Cutting open the rat's tender flesh had relieved some of the tension and anxiety from seeing Nash and Lily together. Just like cutting her arms and wrists eased pain in those moments when memories clamored and gnawed.

She'd have to find out more about this Lily. This time, unlike the others, there wouldn't be weeks of warnings and warfare. Time was precious. This assignment was only for a month or so and Nash would be hers by the time it was through. Nobody would stand in her way.

Earlier, she'd driven by Nash's grandfather's home, saw the light from the curtain-less window, saw the cozy bunch at the table eating. Stabs of jealousy prickled her skin all over like leprosy. She was in the dark, on the outside looking in. Her childhood repeated. The ugly redheaded foster kid no one wanted.

Lily bit into the hot, buttered corn bread and forced the crumbly mixture down her throat. "Delicious," she lied, chasing it down with a sip of sweet tea. *More like wet sawdust.* Determined not to offend her hosts, Lily swirled a mound of pinto beans around the plate and lifted a forkful to her mouth. This tangy rotten mush was worse than the tasteless corn bread. *Human food—bleh.* Soon as she got home she'd eat a real meal—a bowl of seaweed salad and a barely blanched lobster. Still, she enjoyed sitting in their cozy kitchen with its rustic pine cabinets and table. This place had been a second home for her growing up.

"Nash says you volunteer at the animal shelter," she

said, diverting attention from the uneaten, rearranged food on her plate.

Sam nodded. "Every Friday."

"What do you do there?"

He chewed a piece of venison and put down his fork and knife. He always spoke carefully, as if mindful of the power of words. "Clean cages, bathe them, take them for walks."

"That's admirable." She didn't care for animals all that much. She loathed cats and the way they licked their chops around her, as if she were a delectable morsel they wanted to devour. "Jet has a dog that's around a lot. Ugliest thing you ever saw."

Neither man responded. Lily wanted to stamp her foot in frustration, but instead she surreptitiously studied the two.

They were similar: tall and large-boned with prominent cheekbones and the same aura of strength. Both had long black hair, although Sam's was streaked with silver. Each had olive-colored skin, Sam's a shade darker. Nash was a younger, more virile version of his grandfather. The only other striking difference between them was the green eyes Nash had inherited from his mother.

Those eyes that avoided her own at every opportunity. How could he resist her siren's voice? The more he retreated, the more determined she became to get answers.

Lily took another stab at starting a dinner conversation. "The dog's name is Rebel, and he's supposedly a Chinese crested, but I say he's a mutt. Got the ugliest yellow teeth and mangiest fur ever."

Sam lifted an eyebrow. "You aren't fond of animals?"

Rats. They would find that odd. Nash worked photographing wildlife and Sam was devoted to all kinds of animals, even nursing wild ones back to health. She remembered an orphaned squirrel he'd fed from a dropper bottle that had hung around their backyard for years before disappearing.

Lily lied for the second time. "They're okay."

A corner of Nash's mouth turned up, as if realizing she wasn't being truthful.

"I have a saltwater aquarium," she said in defense. "It's like an undersea rainbow of colors. I've got violet dottybacks, blue damselfish, spotted dragonets and orange pipefish—" Lily broke off, aware she was rambling.

Nash nodded at his grandfather. "She still fits the name you gave her long ago." He fixed his gaze on her. "Chattering Magpie."

"I am *not*—" Lily closed her mouth abruptly. Defending herself with more words was a trap. She smiled sweetly at Nash's smirk. "Perhaps a bit." She didn't often have much opportunity for conversation. Truth was, she didn't often have anyone to talk *to*. No girlfriends. And Mom gallivanted at sea most of the time. Jet and Shelly, her cousin, had their own lives now, complete with adoring husbands. Jet had a baby on the way and Shelly helped her husband care for his teenage brother, who had autism.

Damn, so much had changed the past two years, and not all of it in a good way. She'd always been the special one of the family, the youngest and fairest and most beloved. Now she felt alone and outcast, taking refuge in her painting. Why the hell didn't she leave Bayou La Siryna? Undersea with the merfolk, her siren's ability made her special—admired by male and female alike—not despised, like in this place.

"He teases you," Sam said. "Your voice is most engaging. This old cabin's been too quiet for too long."

A flicker of something—guilt or annoyance?—crossed Nash's face, and she sensed the tension between them.

"I've invited you to go on assignments with me," Nash said to his grandfather, a muscle working above his jawline. "Get away from the bayou. It wouldn't kill you to take a trip once a decade."

"I can't leave."

"You don't *want* to leave. Big difference."

"My home is here," Sam insisted with a trace of stubbornness.

"Home can be anywhere you want."

"I have no need for traveling the world, nor the time. I provide healings for our tribe. And I have my shelter work and my fishing."

"You can fish and work with animals anywhere," Nash countered.

"This is my place. Bowmans have lived here since the Choctaw first claimed this land as theirs. It means something to me to walk the land of my ancestors."

Was that a veiled jab at his grandson's wanderlust? Sam must be lonely living so far from town. A nicer person, like Shelly, would have been thoughtful enough to visit occasionally. Lily bit her lip. It had never occurred to her. Lily took advantage of their absorption in each other to rise from the table and scrape out her almost-uneaten meal in the garbage can.

She spotted a pie on the counter. "Who's ready for dessert?" she asked brightly. "Smells heavenly." The third lie at dinner. She was on a roll. Lily set the pie between the men. "Is this pumpkin or sweet potato?" she asked.

"Sweet potato. Nash's favorite."

The tension eased at Sam's olive branch of peace.

"Thank you, Grandfather." Nash cut a slice. "I haven't eaten this in…" He paused. "I guess it's been decades."

Lily cut a piece for Sam.

"Aren't you having a slice?" Nash asked.

"I'm stuffed," she said, waving a hand to dismiss his comment. She beamed at Sam. "Dinner was wonderful."

His deep wrinkles settled into a frown as he folded his arms and nodded at the scratches on her arms and legs. "What happened?"

"Got them walking on that trail behind the cabin." She sipped more tea, reluctant to tell more.

Neither man said anything but their unblinking stares meant they were waiting for her to elaborate. Lily flushed and twirled a tendril of pale pink hair near her neck. "I got spooked by a coyote," she admitted.

Sam glanced at Nash.

He nodded. "I checked it out. We may have a rabies outbreak."

Sam turned back to her. "Why did it spook you?"

"It…it stared at me weird. After a few seconds—or maybe minutes—I don't know—it lowered its head and started toward me. I took off. Was I wrong to be scared?"

Sam frowned. "Normally a coyote is more afraid of you than the other way around. But rabies can make animals do strange things."

"That's what Nash said, too."

Sam pushed away from the table. "Think I'll sit on the back porch a spell. I'm sure the two of you have lots of catching up to do."

Nash rose immediately. "Actually, I'm retiring early. Got to get up before dawn to catch the first ferry to Herb Island."

Lily sighed inwardly. No gracious way to stay longer and probe for clues to explain Nash's strange indifference to her voice and his cryptic remarks about poison. She stood also. "I'll clean up in here and head on out."

"You are an honored guest." Sam held up a hand. "I'll take care of the kitchen later." He nodded at Nash. "You should walk Lily to her car. Just to be safe."

"Of course," Nash said stiffly, in a way that meant he'd rather not.

Too bad. She lifted her chin and forced a smile at Sam. "Thanks for the delicious dinner."

"You are most welcome."

She edged past Nash, brushing against his right arm and shoulder. Heated energy danced between them. On her end, anyway. His face was as rigid and inscrutable as ever.

"Wait," Sam called out. "I must warn you. Although it could be aberrant behavior from rabies, consider another possibility. If a coyote singles you out in the woods. It is a sign."

Nash gave a low growl.

Lily frowned at Nash's rudeness. "What kind of sign?" she asked. "I remembered you once said the coyote was a mischievous, sly trickster and that it could mark an ending or beginning."

"In this case, I would say your coyote sighting was meant as a warning."

Her throat went dry. "Warning?"

Sam's brown eyes held the wisdom of experience and secret knowledge. "You are being deceived."

Chills crept up her spine as she pictured the precisely vivisected rat by her car, the *Die Slut* etching. Not hard to figure out the enemy. "I know who it is."

"You do?" Nash narrowed his eyes.

"There's this petty woman in town who hates me over something that happened years ago."

"Why would anyone hate you?" Nash asked.

If Nash stayed around the bayou all summer, he was

bound to hear the rumors of her loose morals. But she'd rather he learned it later, after he knew her better. That way, perhaps he wouldn't judge her too quickly or unfairly. Lily shrugged, watching Sam rummage through a kitchen drawer. She hoped Sam's isolation had kept him from hearing talk of her in town.

"There's one," he muttered, returning with a smudge stick in his hand. "This is for protection."

Nash rolled his eyes.

"White sage?" Lily guessed.

"Smudge your car and your home every day. It may help keep away trouble."

"Thank you." And she meant it. It might not even hurt to pay Tia Henrietta a visit and get some backup voodoo protection; if nothing else, the woman was entertaining. She hadn't seen the crusty old hag in ages.

Impulsively, Lily gave Sam a quick hug for his kindness. When she'd first met him as a child, she'd found the man intimidating with his stern features and the Native American symbols tattooed on both sides of his neck and forearms. But she'd quickly come to realize his gentle heart.

She and Nash slipped out into the humid soup that marked bayou summers. A fine coat of perspiration popped all over her body, making the scratches on her arms and leg itch.

They said nothing until she reached Jet's truck.

"I don't like all this talk of danger and deception," Nash said, leaning sideways against the Chevy truck. "Grandfather's superstitious, but you believe you really have an enemy. Who is this woman you mentioned?"

Lily sighed. Should have known Nash wouldn't let it go. "Her name's Twyla Fae." Warmth flamed her face and she was thankful for the cover of darkness. "She thinks I'm after her husband, J.P."

A beat passed. "Are you?"

"No! I have no interest in married men."

"Then why does she think you want her husband?"

"Because J.P. dumped her for a few weeks and dated me. This was *before* they got married," she hastened to explain.

"Sounds like you were the injured party."

"No. I realized we weren't suited before they got back together." It had started out like all the others. She began each new relationship with hope that it would lead to love. The men groveled and proclaimed undying love—but only because of her voice and looks. No one saw *her*. It was always kindest to say goodbye sooner rather than later. A fact that no man appreciated and that had lead to her name turning into the town joke. Lily was *that* girl in the bayou. The one men were sure was an easy lay and the one women condemned as guilty.

"I don't understand why this Twyla is still angry."

"J.P. broke off with me when she told him she was pregnant with his child. Guess Twyla suspects he married her out of a sense of obligation."

"That behavior's juvenile. What's the woman done to you?" he demanded.

"Usually she and her friends settle for whispering behind my back or giving me the cold shoulder. But yesterday morning was different. One of them called me a slut and when I went outside they'd left me a nasty surprise." She quickly filled him in on the details.

"That's beyond petty. She needs to be prosecuted." His green eyes darkened to the color of an Amazon rain forest at midnight.

"You sound like my sister," she said lightly.

"Maybe I should talk to this Twyla."

Lily's heart lightened at his defense. He had to care about her—at least a little bit. "No, I can handle this," she said hastily. If Nash talked to Twyla, the woman would cast her in the worst possible light. "I was going to confront her today, but it's too late tonight. When I do, I'll carry the sage your grandfather gave me—as a precaution."

Nash snorted. "The old man must be the last Choctaw who takes all the old stories and ways as truth."

"And you don't?" His attitude surprised her. They used to sit around for hours listening to Sam's stories. Back then, Nash was proud of his tribe and its traditions.

"Let's say he takes it too far. Besides, we were talking about you and your problem."

Lily leaned into him and gave in to the urge to touch him again. She lightly ran a finger along the stern edge of his jaw. A delicious frisson of awareness shot down her spine at the contact. Nash didn't move. Did he truly feel *nothing* between them?

"Don't," he said in a harsh, tight voice.

"Why? You don't really believe you're cursed, do you?" And he accused Sam of being superstitious? Her hand crept to the back of his neck, fingers combing his black, smooth hair.

Abruptly, Nash pulled her to him, lips crushing against hers. Heat flared and liquid warmth pulsed through her body. His strength was more than the physical, unyielding planes of his mouth, chest and arms. It was an aura as primal and mysterious as nature's spring fever erupting in every creature and living organism to mate and bring forth new life. Lily parted her mouth, inviting him to deepen the kiss.

Nash thrust her away. "Goodnight, Lily."

Shock doused her like a blanket of snow. "Wh—Why did you stop?"

He didn't answer or look at her, but walked back to the porch, hands thrust in his jeans pockets.

"Of all the rude, inconsiderate…" Lily sputtered, at a loss. She was the one who walked away from men, not the other way around. She folded her arms and smiled grimly at his fading figure.

You can run, Nashoba Bowman, but we aren't done. I'll find out all your secrets. And in the end, I'll be the one to decide when it's over.

Chapter 4

Nash crept closer, honing in on the low, slow snorting. *Bup-bup-bup.* Definitely not the high-pitched clattering of the common *Rallus longirostris*. Ever so carefully, he raised his binoculars. There... This bird was the size of a chicken, rusty-feathered, long-beaked. It lifted its head, revealing chestnut-hued cheeks instead of the gray of its close relative, the common clapper. He'd found the species he'd come to photograph.

Camera replaced binoculars. Nash focused the telescopic lens and started snapping away. Good enough shots, but he wanted something spectacular, more worthy of the Nashoba Bowman standard he'd developed over the years. He crept ahead on all fours, the razor-sharp sea grass edges cutting his fingers and palms. It didn't matter.

His heart fluttered faster, like that of the bird. For every yard forward, Nash halted five seconds, until he drew so close the bird lifted its beak and black, wary eyes focused on him.

Not here to hurt. I'm admiring you. Nothing to fear. Nash pushed the thoughts toward the Clapper Rail before raising his camera again and taking one incredible close-up.

A haunting melody sounded through the brackish bayou island, disrupting their connection. Startled, the clapper opened its beak. *Bup-bup-bup-bup.* In a bustle of feathers and churned water, the bird half flew, half swam in a mad scramble for safety.

Damn. He'd been so close to connecting with the bird, so close to slipping into its essence and establishing trust.

The singing grew louder, sounding like a chorus of perfectly blended tones. Did Opal have a hidden talent for singing? He'd never heard her sing before. But she knew better than to interrupt a shot. Besides, she was supposed to be on the other side of the island photographing another species.

Lily emerged from a clump of cypress trees. Only this time when she came out of the woods she was smiling, not running from a demented coyote. She wore a wide-brimmed straw hat and grinned and waved, holding up a wicker picnic basket.

"Hello," she sang out.

Nash frowned. He should have guessed it was Lily. Looking as damn beautiful in the summer sun as she had last night under the moonlight. "What are you doing here?" he asked gruffly, tamping down the memory of that scorching kiss.

Her smile faltered. "Didn't you hear me sing?"

What a strange response; the woman made no sense. "Of course I heard. You were so loud you scared off the bird I was stalking."

"Loud?" Lily's eyes widened. "That's all you have to say about my voice?"

He cocked a brow. She sounded mildly outraged when he was the injured party here. Although to be fair, Lily might not have realized she was interrupting. "It was… uh…nice, I suppose."

"Nice?"

"Are you going to keep repeating everything I say? 'Cause I've got lots of work to do."

Blue eyes blinked and she breathed deeply, as if to regain her composure. "You are an unusual man, Nashoba."

She didn't know the half of it. Only Opal might have an inkling that he'd gained fame as a wildlife photographer because of his unnatural ability to sense animals' thoughts and calm them with his own form of mental telepathy—or whatever the hell it was that gained their trust for the few nanoseconds it took to get the perfect picture.

Lily held up the basket. "Figured working outside would make you hungry, so I brought us a lunch."

She assumed too much from that short kiss. It meant nothing. Nash pointed to the sketchpad in her other hand. "What's that for?"

"I come out to the island often and sketch. We'll probably run into each other lots while you're here."

Nash stifled a groan. "I was—" he held up a thumb and index finger an inch apart "—this close to getting some incredible shots. You scared off my bird."

"Ah." Lily muttered a sound of sympathy but kept smiling. "It'll come back." She gave him a coy sideways glance. "You sure you didn't think my singing was more than *nice*? I've been told my voice is quite…enchanting."

"I noticed my shoot was ruined."

She tapped a finger on the edge of her cupid's-bow lips. "Hmm… Sorry, I suppose."

An unexpected chuckle rumbled in his throat, like a

motor sputtering to life after months of neglect. "You don't have any self-confidence issues, do you?"

"Not until you started giving me a complex."

"If people say your voice is enchanting, maybe you should have taken up the opera instead of painting." He imagined Lily onstage—the limelight highlighting that mass of blond hair and white skin.

"I could have become a prima donna, but it didn't seem fair."

Again, Lily threw him off with an odd answer. The woman was either incredibly conceited or mentally defective. Perhaps both.

Fair. Was it unfair of him to compete in his field? He'd always thought he'd made a brilliant career choice. Now Lily made him wonder if he exploited his natural gifts.

"Really, your ego—" He stopped abruptly and bit back his annoyance. Lily was an old friend. He could let it go. A few weeks and he'd be on the road somewhere again. "Never mind," he said with a casual flick of his wrist. "Who am I to shake your wonderful self-esteem? More power to you."

"Power, indeed," she mumbled, so faintly he wondered if he'd heard correctly.

She beckoned him with a crook of his finger. "This way."

Nash hesitated, scowling. No harm in taking a short break, though. Now that his prey had scattered anyway. He fell in step behind Lily, his gaze involuntarily dropping to the womanly curves of her hips and luscious ass. Now *that* was impressive. *That* was power and a temptation he didn't know if he could resist. It had been too long… His breath hitched like that of a hormonally charged adolescent. *Stop it. Old friends make complicated lovers.* Next assignment he'd have to do something about his self-imposed celibacy. Find some uncomplicated part-time lover with no expectations of commitment.

Lily spread out a blanket beneath a gigantic oak and began unpacking plastic containers.

He hadn't realized until now he was hungry. And thirsty. "Got some water in there?"

"Even better. Sweet tea." She handed him a sealed mason jar with ice cubes floating like crystals in an amber ambrosia.

Nash removed the canning lid and downed half of it in one swallow. "That's good," he admitted. "I'd forgotten how hot it is down here. How do you stand the heat and humidity?"

"You'll acclimate to it again. I would think you'd be used to all kind of conditions in your line of work."

"Nothing like Southern humidity." He took off his shirt and used it to wipe sweat from his face and eyes.

He glimpsed Lily getting an eyeful of his chest and abs. The lady was definitely interested. Nash groaned inwardly. But what did he expect? He'd been a fool to kiss her last night. Of course she thought he was interested in her. Especially since— Well, he didn't want to think of the last two women he'd dated. Guilt rose in his throat like bile.

"What you got?" he asked as she opened containers.

"Fried chicken, pimento cheese sandwiches, pecan pie, shrimp cocktail and lobster salad."

He picked up a chicken wing. "I'm going to gain twenty pounds this summer," he predicted. Nash bit into the buttermilk-soaked and flour-coated goodness and sighed. "But I'll enjoy every damn minute along the way."

Lily laughed and ate a spoonful of lobster salad. "Live in the moment, I always say."

Ocean-blue eyes fixated on him and Nash couldn't move, couldn't do anything but stare into those eyes. Energy crackled between them, every bit as scalding as the noon sun.

This wouldn't do. "Show me your drawings," he commanded, opening her sketchpad without waiting for permission.

Lily's hand rested on his forearm and his skin tingled at the light touch.

"Just so you know, I'm mostly self-taught. I'm still learning and hoping to find a professional tutor at some point. If I can find one that deems me worthy of his time."

So the lady's armor of self-confidence had a chink. "Understood." A self-taught amateur? He braced himself for convoluted drawings of fruit still lifes, paint-by-number ocean scenes or Victorian-looking flowers and hearts.

"Let me see what you got there," he said huskily, conscious of her fingers over his knuckles working magic on his libido.

Lily released her hand and the tingling ceased. Nash opened the sketchpad and gave a low whistle at the detailed pen-and-ink drawings of birds, sea grass, fish and trees. This was more than mere talent. It was…seeing the bayou through Lily's eyes. Each composition was vibrant and unique as a thumbprint.

"What do you think?" Her voice was high and reedy, anxious. She gave a self-deprecating laugh. "If you don't like them, it's okay. Like I said, I'm—"

"I don't like them." He paused at a watercolor depicting swirls of light in dark liquid. "I love them." He studied it closer—saw an outline of individual fishes swimming in a school spiraling upward, their bodies incandescent in an inky darkness, like a lamp lit undersea. At the bottom of the painting was a large chunk of coral, the top alit in a violet haze and underneath gray shadows bottomed out to black. He flipped the painting toward Lily. "What kind of fish are these?"

"Myctophids, also known as lantern fish. They're as common under the sea as squirrels in a cove of oaks."

"Amazing." As much as Nash's soul longed to traverse the world, seeing new landscapes and animals, so it now also longed to be undersea, to capture the ocean's deep magic—an unexplored galaxy. Again, he had the oddest tingling that something about Lily was different. Too perfect. Too powerful. He looked up from the sketchpad and caught her twirling the ends of her hair—a nervous gesture she'd had when they were kids. Underneath her confident exterior was a sensitive artist. He returned his gaze to the sketchpad and examined the drawings.

In the midst of shades of gray pencil drawings, he came upon another watercolor popping with vibrancy. Striated bands of blue and green progressed from deep to lighter hues as if Lily's perspective originated on the ocean floor, looking toward the sky as the sun's reflection filtered down. The perspective was unusual.

"How did you capture this image?" He opened the book to the watercolor and laid it open between them. "Do you visualize the scenes in your mind or do you paint from photos?"

Lily took a long swallow of tea, canting her long neck upward, exposing the vulnerable hollow of her throat. Damn. He'd never before admired a woman's neck, for Pete's sake.

Her head tilted forward and she delicately patted her upper lip before speaking. "That one was inspired by a picture Jet took swimming one day. Have you done underwater shoots?"

"No. But I'd love to." Would he be any good? His talent came from an unnatural connection to the earth and its creatures. But fish? Undersea life? He didn't have a clue.

"I stopped by and saw your grandfather this morning," she said, turning the conversation. "He showed me a collection of your work. Very impressive."

Nash shrugged, but his gut warmed that his grandfather was so proud of him. "Did he give you any more sinister warnings?"

"No." A shuttered look crossed her face and she glanced sideways, as if expecting another coyote to leap from behind a tree.

"Old man got to you, huh? Used to scare me as a kid sometimes with his tales of the supernatural."

Lily giggled. "Every rustle I hear in the woods, I look for the Little People sneaking up on me."

"Ah, the Kowi Anukasha," he nodded. "They're mischievous and like scaring humans, but they aren't evil. Not like the Nalusa Falaya."

Lily's smile dropped. "The Soul Eater."

"Our Choctaw version of the bogeyman." Nash scooped up a couple of shrimp and popped them into his mouth. "Grandfather has plenty of tall tales."

"Who's to say they aren't true?" She set down her plate and gave him another of her unnerving stares.

Nash shifted, uncomfortable with the question. He didn't want to believe. Life was tough enough without looking for monsters in the shadows. And despite his gift, he'd never seen anything to support the old Native American legends. "You can't be serious."

"Oh, but I am. The bayou's full of magic and mystery." Lily leaned into him, so close her breath flamed his jaw and neck. "Can't you feel it?" she whispered.

He felt something, all right—a fierce longing to meld

into her essence. The need was even stronger than it had been last night. Nash closed his eyes, let the inevitable happen. Lily's lips brushed his. *Talk about magic.* His body thrummed at the contact.

"How do I wrangle an invitation to this picnic?" a cheery voice called out.

Nash winced at Opal's abrupt appearance. Normally, he heard others approach from great distances. It was a real testament to how Lily engrossed his senses. He squelched a renewed flush of irritation—this time because he wanted to be alone with Lily, wanted to explore her curves and secret places. He shouldn't feel this way. He should welcome the interruption.

Opal plopped onto the blanket between them so that the three formed a triangle.

"Thought you were miles away," he said, relieved Opal didn't mention seeing them kiss.

"Started that way this morning, but steadily edged closer here, following a blue heron." Her smile was toothy and catching. "And then I heard this…angelic singing."

Lily waved a hand. No blush stained her face and her manner gave no indication of embarrassment at being caught kissing. "Sorry I interrupted everyone's work. I come here occasionally to draw," she told Opal.

Opal leaned his way and glanced at the open sketchpad.

"Wow. You can paint *and* sing *and* look like a goddess. It's so not fair." Her smile stayed intact and the words didn't seem malicious. That's what he liked about Opal—she was an open book and was never catty.

"Your job must be fun. Bet there's not many women who can do what you do," Lily said.

"There's a few." Opal lifted her face to the sun and

raised both arms by her sides. "I love working outdoors. The more primitive, the better."

"Can I see the pictures you took this morning?" Lily asked.

"Sure." Opal shifted her weight toward Lily and unhooked the camera cord from her neck. She tapped a button on the digital screen, revealing a dozen close-ups of a blue-gray crane.

Lily scanned the photos. "These are beautiful."

Opal grinned at him. "Hear that, boss? Remember that at my next performance evaluation." She turned back to Lily. "Nash takes the superhard shots, though, catching wildlife at intimate or rare moments hardly ever witnessed by humans."

Lily handed the container of chicken wings to Opal. "His grandfather showed me his work this morning, and I was impressed."

Nash finished another chicken wing and polished off a few more shrimp while the two exchanged pleasantries. It allowed him time to cool off and regain his composure. If a mere kiss made him fevered, what would it be like to make love to Lily? *Don't even think about it.* He scrambled to his feet.

"You can't be going back to work already." Lily pointed to the pie. "You haven't had dessert yet."

A few more minutes alone and *she* would have been dessert. Nash studied the slight upturn at the corners of Lily's mouth but couldn't decide if her remark was a deliberate sexual innuendo. "Been fun, ladies, but time for me to go hunt that clapper rail again." He took off his bandana and swiped the sweat from his face again.

"Why don't we take a quick swim and cool off?" Opal suggested. "The heat's brutal."

Lily shook her head. "I can't swim."

Opal gaped at her. "You practically live on an island and can't swim?"

"I had a bad experience as a child. Went to swim before a storm and an undertow almost swept me away. Been afraid of the water ever since."

He'd forgotten that. When they were young, Lily had gamely kept up with him on the hiking and biking but refused to ever get in the water. "Yet you paint it so much—one as if you were actually undersea," he mused aloud.

Lily set aside her plate of lobster salad. "Our fears become our obsessions."

"But couldn't you go in the water up to your knees and splash yourself if we stand with you?" Opal pleaded. "It would be fun."

"'Fraid not."

"Later, ladies." He pulled back on his T-shirt, slung the camera carrier around his neck and took several steps before remembering his manners. He turned around and waved. "Oh, and thanks for lunch, Lily."

Nash sucked in a breath of hot air laced with a bracing, salty tang. Good thing Opal had come along when she had. He'd taken this assignment not only to visit Grandfather, but also to escape from women constantly chasing him and from the memory of his last two disastrous relationships.

From here on, Lily was off-limits.

Lily touched her lips and sighed as he walked away. That kiss had been pure magic.

Opal gave a little laugh. "Enjoying the view? I totally see why the ladies all go for him. He's a hunk, all right."

Lily gazed at her curiously, wondering if Opal had feelings for Nash. "What about you?"

"Nah, I've got someone in my life. And it's never

a good idea to date anyone you work with, especially your boss."

Lily prodded for more details. "So women swoon over him?"

"Breaks hearts everywhere he goes. Women constantly fall at his feet."

And I'm behaving like every other woman. "He have anyone serious in his life?" She put lids on some of the containers and returned them to the basket.

"Not anymore. Not since—" Opal broke off, staring out at sea.

"Not since what?"

"Not since his last girlfriend, Connie, died." Opal dug into the lobster salad. "Mmm…de-lish."

Lily gasped and stopped packing up food. "That's awful. What happened?"

"Suicide. Connie was found dead one morning, an empty bottle of pills on her nightstand." Opal downed a long swig of tea. "Sad, huh?"

Poor Nash. No wonder he's bitter. "Tragic," Lily quietly agreed. "Did she leave a note?"

Opal nibbled on a chicken wing and delicately wiped her mouth before answering. "None was ever found. But he'd broken up with her a couple days before."

"How long ago did she…did this happen?"

"About a year ago. It wouldn't have been so bad, except…" Her voice trailed off.

Lily didn't see how the story could get any worse. "Except what?"

"I really shouldn't say anything. It kind of slipped out, ya know?"

"C'mon. Don't leave me hanging."

Opal spooned up more salad and chewed, as if mulling over the answer. "Thing is," she said at last, setting down the plate, "two years earlier, another of his girlfriends died. Rebecca."

The knot of dread in Lily's stomach grew. "How?" she whispered.

"They had an argument—probably over his lack of commitment—and she drove home. Hours later, apparently drunk, she got back in her car but lost control of it, ran off into a ditch and hit a tree."

Goose bumps pricked Lily's arms and legs and a chill set in that no blistering Southern sun could warm. *I'm poison.* Nash's clipped words echoed round her brain like gunshots in a canyon. No wonder the guy was aloof. She'd be bitter, too.

"That's—that's horrible," Lily said, putting her face in her hands. How the hell did someone cope with that much pain? One death was bad enough. But two? She shuddered.

"Sure." Opal sighed. "The doctors said Rebecca died instantly. So there's that."

Lily didn't want to hear any more details. It was too much to take in all at once. She wanted to be alone and deal with the knowledge of all Nash had suffered, was still suffering. Lily abruptly gathered up food containers and stuffed them in the picnic basket; even the smell of it nauseated her. "Don't say anything else." Lily shut the picnic basket with a snap. "Nash will tell me when he's ready."

"Sorry to spoil your lunch." Opal eyed the pie. "Mind if I keep a piece for later this afternoon?"

Lily wrapped the whole thing in aluminum foil, her movements jerky with haste. She thrust it at Opal. "Take it."

"Thanks. I'll share it with Nash."

They both rose unsteadily to their feet.

Opal frowned. "Look, I hope I didn't scare you off Nash. He's a great guy who's had a bit of bad luck lately."

"A bit of bad luck?" Lily snorted. "I'd say it's more serious than that."

Opal flushed. "Absolutely. You're right. It's— I like you, Lily. I don't want to see anything bad happen to *you*."

"No need for the warning. Nothing is going to happen to me," she said curtly, wanting to end the conversation.

"Of course not." Opal squeezed Lily's shoulder and dropped her hand to her side. "Just thought you should know. I'd hate to see him break your heart."

"Some would say I have no heart to break," Lily muttered.

"Why would they say that?"

"Not important."

Opal's face crumbled. "You don't trust me to keep my mouth shut. Which I can totally understand, given how I blabbed Nash's history during lunch."

"It's not that." Lily's fingers rubbed an itchy scratch on her leg leftover from the run in the woods. She supposed this was what girlfriends did, exchanged secrets and confided in one another. Maybe Opal had done her a favor in revealing Nash's painful past. At least now she knew the problem and could be mentally prepared when Nash brought up the news himself.

And it would be wonderful to have a real friend because Jet and Shelly were busy now with their own lives. She drew a deep breath. "Okay, you'll probably hear this anyway if you meet people in town, but I don't have a great reputation."

"Why's that?"

"I went through a bit of a wild stage years ago and no one will let me forget it. That's a small town for you.

You're doomed to never live down your past. Although, in my defense, rumors of my promiscuity are greatly exaggerated."

Opal patted her shoulder. "Poor Lily. Don't worry—I won't say anything to Nash."

Lily shifted uncomfortably. Opal made her feel… beholden. Guilty. As if they shared something dirty. "Doesn't matter. He's bound to hear the talk, too."

"Maybe not. He and his grandfather live pretty isolated. And Nash has been reclusive the past couple of years. He doesn't get out much." Opal winked. "So you see, probably nothing to worry about."

Again, a prickly unease settled over Lily. She smiled uncertainly. "If you say so," she agreed. Her family had grown up secluded from the townsfolk, making it easier to keep their shape-shifting abilities a secret.

Secrecy was a habit she'd have to let slip if she wanted a girlfriend.

Chapter 5

Sunset through the pines cast coral and mauve spears of light across land and sea. Nash had returned to the cabin on the evening ferry, bent on a mission. Now he trudged through mosquito-infested lowland, shotgun at his side. Diseased or not, the coyote was clever at eluding him. In spite of pain and fear, the will to live was strong in the animal. Nash respected that.

The wind shifted, hot air rippling across his sweaty skin. The fresh scent of pine needles had an underlying taint. Nash followed it, back on the coyote's track. Another fifty yards ahead, the smell of sickness grew thicker and obliterated the pine odor.

Black energy seeped inward as he drew near. Most likely the unfortunate coyote had been ousted from his pack, a threat to the group's survival. Cold fingers of loneliness fidgeted along his spine as he sensed the animal's toxic miasma. Nash picked up a faint, rumbling groan. Not the growl of an aggressive animal, but the mewling of one suffering.

Nash emitted a calming message. *Your time has come. Let's end the pain.*

An answering whine came from behind a dense clump of saw palmetto trees not a dozen yards to his right. The coyote emerged, trembling, its amber eyes dull and flat. Mottled gray fur encased an emaciated body. Telltale foam bubbled along its tapered muzzle. Rabies had rendered the animal unable to swallow its own saliva.

Nash ever so slowly raised the shotgun, not wanting to provoke the animal. *I'm sorry. This will be quick, I promise you.* His right index finger crooked onto the metal trigger.

The coyote leapt, snarling and baring sharp teeth, amber eyes alit in a last-shot bid to escape death. Fur, fear and fury hurled toward Nash and he pulled the trigger.

An explosive boom rang out. The reverberation from the shot was still echoing as the dead coyote's body hit the ground with a thump. Nash closed his eyes and drank in the silence until peace washed through the woods.

It was done.

He took out the garbage bag and latex gloves he'd tucked into the waistband of his jeans. To prevent spread of the rabies virus, it was necessary to bag the coyote and put it in a protected place until he could return in the morning with a shovel and bury the dead body.

Quickly, he attended to the last rites. *You were brave. A fighter to the end. May you join a ghostly pack in happy hunting grounds.* Satisfied with the work, he retraced his path. The air was a shade darker than when he'd first set out. At a fork on the dirt trail he hesitated. Better check on the old man. Grandfather had missed dinner and the thought of his eighty-two-year-old grandfather being unaccounted for left Nash uneasy. Instead of continuing home, Nash set off for the marsh. Sam often fished all day out there.

Sure enough, he found his grandfather sitting in a chair, fishing pole in hand. The tip of his cigar glowed in the gathering twilight. Nash walked up behind him.

Without turning around, Sam spoke. "Heard the shot. You get that coyote?"

"I did." Nash settled on the ground close by after making sure he was clear of fire-ant mounds. Their sting was like being poked by flaming hypodermic needles. "Sorry I haven't been to see you in a couple days."

"You're busy. Besides, I went years without seeing you. Two days is nothing."

Guilt made him defensive. "You were always welcome to visit *me*. Why do you stay here all the time? There's a big, wide world outside this backwoods."

Sam stared ahead at the black water. "True. But there's also a whole world here you're missing."

"Hardly. I've hiked every inch of this area over the years."

"Ah, but you haven't swam all over it."

Nash gave him a sideways glance. "And if I did, what would it matter? I've swam in all the seven seas."

The tip of Sam's cigar glowed brighter as he took a draw.

"Should you really be smoking with your heart trouble?"

"I'm not forsaking my little pleasures. I've lived over eight decades, you know."

"Yeah, but if you want to make another decade, you need to give up those things." He pointed to the cigar with a jab of his finger.

Sam tipped his head back and exhaled a smoke ring within a smoke ring.

"When do you go back for another doctor's visit? I want to go with you." Guilt lashed him; months ago when Sam had undergone a triple bypass operation, Nash had been on an African safari assignment. His grandfather had recouped alone until he'd finagled an assignment nearby. Nash had sent a paid home health care assistant, but his grandfather had dismissed her before two weeks were up, claiming he could take care of himself.

"At least think about giving up frying everything in bacon grease," Nash urged.

Sam didn't respond and Nash frowned at the grey tinge that underlaid Sam's olive skin. The fishing pole trembled slightly in his grandfather's unsteady hand.

A rush of nostalgia overcame Nash. As a child, his grandfather's cabin had been a haven of peace from his parents' tumultuous marriage. He'd missed the summer visits after Mom had whisked him away to her home state of Massachusetts. His grandfather could have visited them, but he refused to leave the bayou. Nash doubted he'd ever been north of the Mason-Dixon line his entire life.

The pole jerked and Sam smiled, face crinkling. He detached a good-sized brim and placed it in a rolling ice chest with several others. "Fried fish dinner tonight."

Nash shook his head. He'd suggest baking the fish but knew his grandfather wouldn't go for the healthier option. "Ready to get home and eat? It's getting dark."

"I can see well enough, plus I have my flashlight."

A knowing look passed between them. They could each sense their way in darkness. His grandfather had some of the same supernatural senses that he did, although not as strong. By agreement, they seldom spoke of it.

Sam closed the lid of the small cooler. "Let's sit a spell afore we go. Have I ever told you the story—"

Nash almost groaned. Not another story.

"—of the Okwa Nahollo?"

"No," he said, surprised. He thought he'd heard every Choctaw tale a thousand times, but this was new. "Does that translate to 'pale water people'?"

"White people of the water," Sam corrected. "Extremely white."

An image of Lily's soft-hued face flashed through him. He hated admitting it, but he'd missed her the past two days he'd stayed on the island.

"With skin the color of trout because they lived undersea," his grandfather continued.

Talk about a tall fish tale. Nash refrained from grinning. "Like mermaids?"

Sam shook his head. "No. They aren't half fish and half human. They have human form except their legs are almost twice as long as ours. Their fingers and toes are webbed and their eyes glow like some deep-sea fishes do."

"Of course, so they can see better in dark water."

Sam narrowed his eyes, as if suspicious Nash was amused. "Exactly."

Nash wrapped his arms around his bent knees and stared out over the marsh. "Go on."

"Whenever you find patches of light-colored water in the bayou, that is where they live. If you swim near them or fish near them, they'll grab your ankles and pull you under."

The theme from *Jaws* played in his mind. "So don't

worry about sharks. People should fear capture by mermaids." *Death by mermaid.*

Not even a ghost of amusement lit Sam's eyes. "Yes. Except, like I said, they aren't exactly mermaids, although they must be closely related."

"C'mon. I'm not a kid anymore. You don't really expect me to believe that tale. Surely you don't either, do you?"

"It's passed down from our ancestors." Sam's eyes flashed and his spine stiffened. "Every word is true."

Nash kept his face blank and his tone neutral. "I mean no disrespect."

"Of course you do. You think I am a foolish old man." Sam eased up out of the chair and stood, looking out to sea.

Nash reached up his hand and touched his grandfather's knee. He might be a skeptic and occasionally amused at his grandfather's ways, but he would never think him foolish. "Not foolish. Please sit."

Sam stayed rooted, as if debating. Finally, he sat. "I'm an old man. I've kept in shape by walking these woods for years, but my time's short. So while you're here I need to explain more of your heritage."

"I'm listening." He felt chastened like a small child. "I respect my people and their ways. Nothing will ever change that."

"I know it makes you uncomfortable when I speak of the spirit world. But it's there. It's real. Just as you are sensitive to nature and its creatures, my gift is seeing the spirits around people. They can be human, animal or plant spirits, sometimes all three."

"Father said you chose my name because you saw a wolf spirit near me."

Sam nodded. His serious, deeply lined face rearranged

to an unexpected, wistful smile. "When you were born, I fasted three days and went on long walks, seeking guidance. The first time I held you in my arms I heard a wolf howl. I envisioned a pack of wolves celebrating your birth, tails wagging, the males wrestling one another in a show of affection."

"So you named me Nashoba—Choctaw for *wolf*." He'd heard this before, remembered Mom rolling her eyes at Dad's insistence on naming their children with traditional names. "So how did you end up with a name like Sam?"

"My parents did it to honor a gentleman named Samuel who was good to them. He hired my father as a laborer and paid him a decent wage for the times. But my middle name is Chula."

"*Chula* means *fox*," Nash said, combing through his memory of their native language.

Sam fixed his gaze back to the water's expanse with an absorbed look Nash remembered from childhood. He would stay in this same spot for hours in deep contemplation, the fishing pole loose in his hand like an afterthought.

"Do you think about grandmother out here?"

She'd died decades ago from a boating accident. The one memory of his grandmother was of her shucking corn in the kitchen. The room was cozy and warm, smelling of fried goodness, fresh vegetables and herbs. When he'd entered, her dark eyes sparkled in greeting. She'd dropped to a knee and held out her arms and he'd run into them. The safest, most loving, secure spot in the universe. And it was but a thirty-second memory.

"Yes. And all the others that have passed before and since."

It was a shame he'd never remarried. Nash struggled for words to convey sympathy while not sounding like a condescending jerk. "I wish you would leave this place. At least for a few vacations. You should see new things, meet new people."

"I can't leave."

More like don't want to leave. Sam was old and stubborn as barnacles clinging to a ship hull. No changing him at this late date.

The silence stretched between them as the sun had completed its day's journey and disappeared. All that remained was the water's memory of it in coral-and-purple sheens that rippled in the Gulf breeze. Grandfather turned to him. "The spirits say it is time."

"Time for what?" So that's what he did alone out here—communed with spirits. He should have guessed.

"One last story."

Alarm brushed the back of his neck like a nest of crawling spiders. He half rose. "Do you have chest pains? Should I call a doctor?"

"It's not my time tonight. Although it draws near."

"Don't say that. There must be something the doctors can do." A suspicion gurgled up. "Are you taking your medicine? You can't depend only on the spirits and herbs for healing."

"There's more to tell you of the Okwa Nahollo," Sam continued, ignoring Nash's question. He fixed him with sharp, dark eyes. "You are a descendant."

"Of the mermaids?" Nash scoffed. Really, Grandfather had gone too far this time.

Sam's jaw clenched and his mouth set in a determined line. "It is in your blood."

"I want purple or pink highlights. Something striking." Opal fingered a lock of lavender in Lily's hair. "Something deeper than this."

No point mentioning the subtle pastels in her hair were entirely natural. Fortunately, Lily kept a rainbow of hair-dye colors stocked because so many requested some version of her unusual hair hues. The beauty shop, Mermaid's Lair, was officially closed, but Lily did the odd job for customers who begged for her service. Plus, it was convenient for Jet and Shelly to come in for weekly hair-and-nail maintenance—important because both grew at three times the normal human rate.

Jet winked at Lily from behind the desk where she sat running the numbers for their various family businesses: a maritime and antiquities shop, aquatic therapy and the small income from the beauty shop that kept the rent and utilities paid.

"You made a grand total of fifty dollars in profit last quarter," Jet said, frowning.

Lily laughed, expertly assembling mixing bowls and chemicals. "Ah, but it was double that amount if you included tips."

"I'll tip handsomely," Opal promised, an earnest look on her face.

Probably thought she was broke. As if. Lily styled hair because she enjoyed it and was good at it. "This is on me."

"Maybe you should reopen full-time," Jet persisted. "It would give you something to do."

Hell, no. She'd had enough of the town women's snotty, superior behavior and the men ogling her breasts as she stood close by to trim their hair. Besides, shop hours would interfere with her painting.

"Don't need to." They were stinking rich.

"But you're home alone. What do you do all day?"

Lily shrugged. "Paint."

"She's really good," Opal cut in. "I saw her sketchbook."

"Sure, I know that." Jet waved a hand around the room. "She did this, after all."

Opal surveyed the varying shades of coral, rose and ivory on the walls. Lily had painted pearly tones that gave the effect of being enveloped in the shelter of a giant conch shell.

"Remarkable," Opal said in a hushed tone.

Lily felt a tiny glow of satisfaction at the praise. She'd spent lots of time with Opal the past couple of days, enjoying the novelty of shopping with a girlfriend and showing her around the bayou.

"But I don't see art as a career path."

Jet's acerbic observation squashed the flicker of warmth. Her sis was in a lousy mood today. Must be some hormonal pregnancy thing.

Lily absentmindedly brushed Opal's red hair. She'd been thinking of entering the prestigious Garrison Hendricks art contest. All finalists would be invited to showcase their work at a premiere gallery in New York City. The chances of placing were slim, but the rewards could launch her fledgling dreams.

The click of Jet's fingers on the adding machine resumed.

"How's Nash's work going?" Lily asked Opal casually.

"It's been a challenge, but he enjoys it. Doesn't he talk to you about it?"

"I haven't talked to him in a couple days. Maybe I'll run out there tomorrow."

Opal winked. "Bet he'd love to see you. You two can pick up with the passionate kiss I interrupted at the picnic."

The clicking stopped. "Passionate kiss? I thought you were seeing Gary Ludlow," Jet said.

"I cut him loose last week." Lily sharpened her scissors, ignoring Jet's exasperated sigh.

"One day you're going to run out of men to date around here," her sister warned.

Lily placed chunks of Opal's hair between her left index finger and thumb and made the first cut. She didn't defend herself against Jet's remark. It wasn't that she deliberately set out to hurt anyone. When she saw it couldn't work, she ended it quickly, figuring that was the kindest thing in the end.

A ping sent Opal scurrying through her purse. "Gotta take this," she apologized, scooting out of the chair. "Is there somewhere I can talk privately?"

Lily pointed to the break room in back.

"Be back in a minute." Opal hurried away, the black vinyl cape flapping behind her like a bat.

Jet arched a dark eyebrow. "Kind of secretive, isn't she?"

"A little." She wondered if Opal's boyfriend might be married.

Jet sipped from her water bottle, then set it down slowly and deliberately. Her gaze drifted to the shop window. "I went for a swim last night and the current brought interesting news."

"Let me guess. Mom's coming."

Jet nodded. "Judging from the sound-wave strength and pattern, I'd say to expect her in about two days."

Mother was the last person Lily wanted to see right now.

"Maybe she wants to check on you. Make sure everything's okay with the pregnancy," Lily said hopefully.

"Nah. It's you she's concerned with."

Lily swept up snippets of Opal's hair on the floor,

aware of Jet's scrutiny. Damn, she didn't want maternal pressure to leave the bayou for good and "resume her rightful position as the best siren of the sea"—words her mother eschewed with increasing regularity. Mom had gone from baffled to miffed to frustrated over the past few visits.

A few minutes of silence descended before Jet spoke up. "You okay?"

"Nothing I can't handle. She'll just pester me to take my rightful place with other merfolk."

Jet regarded her, eyes direct, brows knitted and chin down. A fierce look that Lily knew masked concern. "Not such a bad idea. Especially with this Twyla business."

"Twyla still bothering you?"

Lily jumped at Opal's voice and cast a furtive look at Jet, wondering how much Opal had overheard. She patted the seat for Opal to sit down. "Maybe."

She stirred the color and developer together and brushed streaks of color on Opal's hair. The bright colors should perk up the rather plain face with its scattering of freckles and a slight scar that spread across one cheek. "This is a temporary dye," she explained. "You can try out the effect and see how you like it."

Jet persisted with her questioning. "What does *maybe* mean? Either she is or isn't bugging you."

"I got several hang-up calls last night. They never spoke. After the third one, I turned off my ringer." The scissors trembled slightly in Lily's hands as she trimmed a few uneven locks of Opal's hair. "When I checked this morning there were seven missed calls and no voicemail messages."

"Ouch!" Opal swiped the side of her neck and stared at a blood splash on her fingers.

"I am *so* sorry." Lily grabbed a towel and wiped the nick. "That's never happened before." Geez, how embarrassing.

"No problem, I'll live," Opal assured her.

Jet cut in, still focused on the phone calls. "Did you call back the number on the screen?"

"Of course. But I got a recording saying the number was no longer in service. Must have used a throwaway phone."

Opal circled her index finger around her right temple. "Somebody's cra-*zee*."

"Say the word and I'll have Landry talk to Twyla," Jet said.

"No need to drag him into it." Lily didn't want her brother-in-law knowing her business.

A collective mewling of cats turned their attention to the shop front. More than half a dozen felines in various colors and sizes perched along the window ledge, motionless and unblinking except for licking their mouths. As if they observed a delectable treat fit for a feast.

Jet frowned. "We ought to bring Rebel to chase them away."

"Dog's so ugly he wouldn't even have to bite or bark to scare them," Lily said drily, returning to the familiar routine of coloring and styling hair.

The three settled into a comfortable silence as Jet continued crunching numbers and Opal observed Lily at work.

A loud rap on the front window scared off their cat stalkers. A husky guy wearing a camouflage shirt waved and motioned for someone to open the locked door.

"Who's that?" Opal asked.

Lily unfastened her apron with a sigh. "Gary."

"Thought you broke it off with him," Jet said.

"I did."

Jet scowled at Gary and motioned him to go away.

Gary rapped harder on the glass. "Open up," he yelled. "I need to talk to you, Lily."

People passing by on the street stopped and stared.

"He's making a scene," Opal noted, tapping her lips.

Jet stalked to the front door in brisk strides. "I'll get rid of him."

"No. Let him in before he breaks the glass," Lily said. She picked up a pink chiffon scarf from the counter and knotted it at her throat, hiding the faint line of scars where gill slits aligned both sides of her neck. She didn't bother with it around Nash because he'd seen the marks when they were children and she'd made up a story about an accident. And she hadn't bother to cover it up around Opal. Seeing as she had her own scar to deal with, they figured she wouldn't ask prying questions.

"You sure?" Jet hesitated, hand on the doorknob.

Lily touched her scarf in a silent reminder.

Jet turned up her collar, covering the gills that were also three inches in length on either side of the neck, extending from the top of the collarbone to her windpipe.

At Lily's nod, Jet unlocked the door. The smell of whiskey preceded Gary as he staggered straight to Lily.

"Whatever I done wrong before, Lily, I'm sorry." His eyes were weepy and red-rimmed, yet also held an odd glimmer of hope.

"You didn't do anything wrong," Lily said, sweeping up her station. "I wasn't feeling it anymore."

"But why? I must have done something."

She almost winced at the pleading note in his voice. Best to cut him off quickly.

"I promise whatever it was, it'll never happen again."

He stumbled closer and drew his face next to hers, trying to kiss her cheek.

Lily stepped back, eyes watering from the whiskey fumes on his breath. She hated these kinds of scenes.

He straightened, took off his baseball cap and began twisting it between his hands. "I couldn't believe it when I got your message. Thanks for giving me a second chance."

"Message? I didn't send you any message." Her sympathy vanished. Stupid drunk. What a lame pretext to make a play at her again. "For the last time, Gary, I'm not interested anymore. Let's leave it at that."

He flushed. "I can't believe this. I thought you wanted to get back together but you're so…" he waved a hand in the air "…so cold-acting."

Lily shrugged. "Move on. I have."

Gary rocked unsteadily on his heels, as if she had struck him. "But…I broke up with Wanda to see you."

Jet stepped in front of him. "You heard her. Time to move on." She laid a hand on his arm and pulled him forward.

"I'm not going anywhere." Gary jerked his arm back and glared at Lily. "Not until she explains why she's playing games."

Lily crossed her arms. "I'm not playing and I don't like *your* game." Despite the show of bravado, Lily's stomach fluttered. Had someone—Twyla—set this up to cause trouble?

Opal stood and placed a hand on Gary's arm, trying to ease the confrontation. "This is obviously not working out. Maybe you and Wanda can get back together."

"But I want Lily," he insisted like a two-year-old denied his favorite toy. He advanced toward the object of his desire.

"Oh, no, you don't." Jet clamped an arm on him and yanked. "Time to go."

"No, I don't want— Hey, you're strong."

Lily almost laughed at his stunned expression. Jet, with her rare blue mer-clan bloodline, had the strength of two men. Too bad they didn't share a paternal parentage. The physicality could come in handy.

Jet pushed him out the door hard enough that he fell on his ass. Gary shook his head as if to clear his mind, obviously stunned he'd been manhandled by a woman. Jet locked the door behind him and pulled down the shades.

"Wow." Opal pressed her fingers into Jet's biceps. "You've got muscles."

"Um…yeah. I work out a lot." Jet went back to the desk and resumed working, head bent over the figures.

"Do you get that a lot from old boyfriends?" Opal asked. "Must be scary."

"Sometimes. He was more forceful than most."

Opal clutched the plastic cape closer to her body. "Twyla might have done it to piss you off."

"Maybe. You think so?"

"Sure. Could be a warning for you to cool it with the men awhile."

Lily studied Opal's blue eyes. They were shot through with alarm. Nice to have someone outside of family actually give a damn.

"You could be right." Lily lifted her chin. "But my interest isn't with a local man right now. That should keep me safe."

"Really? I wouldn't be so sure." Opal absently ran an index finger over the scar on her cheek. "If I were you, I wouldn't see anyone for a few weeks. Let everything cool down a bit."

Lily lifted her chin. "No way. Nash will be gone by then."

"Okay, ignore the warning signs. I just don't want to see you get hurt." She crossed her legs and folded her hands in her lap. "Your decision."

Chapter 6

The red moon of August lay low and full, as if scorched and swollen from summer's heat. Lily's step skipped in time to the rhythm of her rapid pulse. It seemed like it'd been three weeks instead of three days since she'd seen Nash. She grinned at the sight of his truck and the light in the cabin. Even better, Sam Bowman's vehicle was gone. She rapped at the door, feeling like the wolf descending on the innocent Little Red Riding Hood.

The door flung open and she was eye level to Nash's bare chest. She looked up and stared into verdant green. He registered no surprise at finding her on his doorstep. Casually, he leaned an arm against the doorframe.

"You again," he said, voice tinged with smoke and velvet.

The low, deep timbre of sound vibration made her gut clench. Is that what her voice did to men? It was wonderfully disturbing.

"What kind of welcome is that?" she purred, reaching up and laying a hand on the curve of his jaw.

Nash stepped away from the heat of their touch and waved her inside. He shut the door behind her, and Lily was struck by the fact they were alone and sheltered from the world. A cozy company of two. Without a word, Nash walked into the den, snatched a T-shirt from the back of a chair and pulled it over his head.

Darn it.

"Why are you here, Lily?" he asked, plopping down on the sofa.

She sat across from him and crossed her legs demurely. "To see you, of course."

"What do you want from me? I get the feeling it's not to resume a childhood friendship."

She leaned into him, resting her hands on his bare knees. "Don't you find me attractive?" Her lips curled upward, certain of his answer.

"You'll do, I suppose," he said drily.

Lily straightened. "Why are you so hostile? I thought after our kiss we were on more…friendly terms."

He frowned. "You know I'll be leaving in a few weeks. I'm not the settling-down type."

But that's because you haven't known me. "So you say."

He crossed his arms, studying her. "I'm not in the market for a permanent relationship."

"Don't flatter yourself, Nashoba Bowman. You haven't heard me say I want anything of the kind."

"Then that leads back to my original question. What do you want?"

You. I want you. "While you're here, let's see what happens," she answered carefully. After what had happened with his past two girlfriends, she didn't want to push too hard and scare him away. "Look, you used to be my best friend. Can't we at least be friends now and explore if something else is there for however long you're here?"

His mouth twisted. "Friends with benefits?"

"Ouch. Sounds crude when you put it like that." That hurt, although given her reputation, most would doubt she'd be insulted by such an offer.

"Do you think so little of yourself you're willing to do that?"

Lily jumped up. "According to you, my problem is that I think too highly of myself, not too little. Maybe the problem here is that you're a coward. You think because of what happened in the past—"

"What do you know of my past?" He rose and glared down at her, body crackling with tension.

Oops. Best to let him tell it in his own way and in his own time. "I'm assuming something traumatic happened because of the way you act." She paused expectantly. There—she'd provided him the perfect opening.

He said nothing.

"And also because you once told me you were poison."

"The past is dead and buried."

Lily shook her head. "No, it's not. It haunts you like a ghost. Might as well have a white veil over your eyes. It clouds everything you see—and don't see."

Nash walked to the back window and looked outside. "The things I don't see," he muttered, stuffing his hands into his pockets. "Ghosts, huh?" He rubbed his chin. "Ghosts and mermaids."

Lily's stomach flopped like a fish at the conversation switch. "Mermaids?"

"According to my grandfather, there's an old Choctaw

legend that people live undersea in the bayou swamps. He believes it, of course."

"Why?" Her voice was so faint, Nash didn't hear. Lily cleared her throat and spoke louder. "Has he ever seen one?"

Nash snorted and strolled back toward her, most of the former tension gone. "I can do you one better than that. He claims I *am* one. A distant relative of the undersea white people."

Lily gripped the sofa arm. All went dark and her peripheral vision narrowed. The only light in the opaque pitch was the green rim of Nash's eyes; otherwise she was immersed in the black hole of his pupils. The leaf-green grew darker and all that remained was an awareness of being anchored by a sudden, strong grasp on both sides of her waist.

"Lily?"

The sound echoed around her brain, as if it came from some deep-sea abyss.

"Come back to me."

Oxygen and lightness whooshed back into her body, as if diving upward to the sun, breeching the surface with the speed of a dolphin.

Nash held her. Lily laid her head against his chest, closed her eyes and breathed in his scent of clean earth. The steady, strong pound of his heart hammered like a sonic boom against her ear. *Thump thump. Thump thump. I am here. I am here.*

Lily's arms folded to his back, palms pressed into the ridge of his spinal column. Sanctuary. Haven. Home.

Time warped to snail speed like an alternate dimension or a dream where every motion, every inhalation slowed enough that every detail heightened. The warmth of his skin through the cotton fabric, the scent of musk and sandalwood, the ridge of one of his nipples against her cheek. She wanted to feel the fire of his lips, explore his mouth and lick the salty taste of his skin. Lily lifted her head, half opened her eyes, then swiftly closed them again as his head bent toward her.

His lips kissed her forehead. Even with that chaste contact, his mouth imprinted heat.

Nash inched away and moved his arms from her waist to her elbows. "What happened to you there? I was afraid you would fall off the couch before I reached you."

For once, a quick lie didn't present itself to Lily. "I'm not sure."

"How long since you've eaten anything?"

She scrunched her forehead. "I skipped lunch today, so it's been hours."

"I'd offer you something here, but I'm a lousy cook. Traveling like I do means eating out most meals. So let's go grab a bite somewhere. If you're up to it."

"What about your grandfather? Shouldn't we invite him?"

"He's in Mobile at a pow-wow. Goes at least four times a year and meets up with his old cronies."

Lily smiled as her strength returned. "So just the two of us. Like a real date?"

"You never give up, woman." His tone was mock-severe, lips twitching at the corners.

"Not when I see something I want," she agreed, dead serious.

The concern and camaraderie in his eyes shuttered. "Friends," he said harshly. "That's all I have to offer."

"It's a start. I'll take it."

Thirty minutes later, they were seated at a local diner. On the way over, she'd dropped her car off at home and continued to the restaurant with Nash. Lily ordered her usual shrimp cocktail and delicately nibbled on it as he cut into a huge porterhouse steak. She'd tried her best to coax Nash into going to Mobile for dinner, but he'd insisted she needed food in her system fast.

Lily glanced uneasily at a pack of men at the bar. Gary was there, slinging back whiskey with his buds. Her ex kept looking over and muttering something to his friends. They all stared at her, smirking. And, damn, looked like most were former boyfriends.

Between the guys at the bar and every woman making eyes at Nash, it felt as if a giant spotlight shone on the two of them. Too late, she wished they'd made do with a sandwich at the cabin.

Lily pretended not to notice the attention. "Tell me more about the Okwa Nahollo," she said, determined to learn more about the Choctaw legend. She'd have to ask Mom if she'd ever heard of it, too.

"Not that much more to tell. Grandfather said if you swam near their home, they'd grab you by the ankles and pull you under. If you stayed underwater with them more than three days, you could never return to land."

Fascinating. "So you would become one of the undersea people?"

"He didn't say. I suspect the story was told to keep children from swimming too far from home, unsupervised by their elders."

"Maybe." Lily hesitated on how to proceed, recalling how touchy Nash had become in the grocery store when she'd mentioned his unusual affinity with animals. But curiosity won out. If she wanted to know more about Nash and pursue his ability to resist her siren's call, this could be important. "Don't get hypersensitive on me, but I wonder if you're discounting the story too easily.

There are plenty of unexplainable things in the world. We both know you have some kind of unearthly connection to animals."

Nash set down his fork and knife. "I don't know what you're talking about."

"Sure you do," Lily said brightly, ignoring his denial. "When we were young, you could summon birds and foxes and raccoons."

"I never told you I could do that."

"You didn't have to. I saw it for myself. Whenever we walked together, you'd tell me some Choctaw lore about an animal and within minutes one would appear. And they didn't display the normal wariness of a wild creature. They were as tame and domesticated as a dog."

"Coincidence."

"No."

His eyes were malachite-dark and hard as the stone, but Lily steeled her own sea-blue eyes and didn't back down.

Nash took a swallow of whiskey and Coke and set it down so sharply the liquid precariously sloshed near the rim, like a tidal wave about to engulf a beach. "What is it about this bayou? Do you all believe there's something supernatural happening here? That it's perfectly acceptable?"

"Yes," she answered immediately.

Nash picked up the knife and fork and resumed cutting his steak. "Okay, tell me some local legends."

Lily twisted a lock of hair, frustrated at his refusal to open up. Maybe later, in a not-so-public place, she could coax some revelations. For now, she'd play along with his conversational detour. "Well, there's your usual assortment of haints and—"

"Haints?"

"Ghosts. I can't believe you haven't heard that word before. Anyway, there's also the requisite voodoo priestess, or witch, named Tia Henrietta. People seek her all the time to read their fortune, concoct a love potion—stuff like that." She really should make time to visit Henrietta and tell her about the coyote and the phone calls.

Nash grinned. "Have you had this witch make you a love potion?"

Lily bit back a snort. "Never needed it." She waited a heartbeat. "Until now."

Nash ignored the jibe. "What about mermaids? Are there other tales about them down here?"

If you only knew. "Oh, there are plenty of legends. The town was even named after them. Bayou La Siryna—*Siryna* meaning *siren*."

"I assumed *Siryna* was a woman's name."

Lily considered her words. Should she tell him more? Give credence to the Choctaw lore? Shelly and Jet had both found human males who accepted their mer-nature. Maybe Nash could as well one day. And if there was a possibility, she could prepare the way now.

"I wouldn't say mermaids don't exist," she began. "Earth is ninety-five percent covered in water and humans have yet to explore its deepest depths. Who are we to say what lives in its depths? Our ancestors used to believe in them—as much as modern people speculate on UFOs and alien life from other planets."

Nash wasn't buying it. "I'm more prone to believe in aliens than mermaids myself."

"Mermaids are as plausible as other things, like the Choctaw legends of little people or shamans who see spirits," she argued.

He drummed his fingers along the tabletop and regarded her thoughtfully. "Grandfather is a shaman."

"He is? I never knew." Lily's respect for Sam Bowman rose even higher.

"He mostly keeps it to himself. But there were several occasions when I saw others come to the cabin for a cure."

"How does it work?" Lily made a mental note to mention this to Jet in case there was any trouble with her pregnancy or childbirth. "What does he do exactly?"

"He asks the spirits to restore a person's spiritual power for healing. He merely serves as a link between the seen and the unseen."

"That's so cool. Do the spirits always help?"

"As far as I know. He says every person is surrounded by animated human, plant and animal spirits. But some are easier to contact than others. If he's having difficulty connecting, he'll drum and chant. Sometimes the cure is instant, and sometimes it takes days—but I've never known him to fail."

"You've seen him do it?"

"Many times." He gave a sheepish grin. "He's even used it with me. Anytime I came down with a cold or virus, grandfather would zap it right out of me."

She tried to imagine what that would feel like. "Does it hurt, or is it an immediate kind of relief?"

Nash shrugged. "It doesn't hurt. But immediate relief? I'm not sure. Grandfather always did it at night, right before bedtime. The process relaxed me so much I'd fall asleep almost at once. When I woke up the next day, I wouldn't be sick."

"There you go," Lily said triumphantly. "With a grandfather like that, you should keep an open mind about *everything*."

"I try to. But some things are too preposterous." He shook his head and dug into his steak.

"Doesn't make it any less real." Lily set aside what remained of the shrimp cocktail. "How can you draw a line once you've admitted there are spirits and circumstances beyond what the rational mind can see?"

He took another slug of his drink. "You're probably right. I was disrespectful when he told me of the Okwa Nahollo. I'm arrogant at times, but not so arrogant as to think I know everything."

Lily took heart at his words. "Keep an open mind," she urged. Despite all his warnings about not being in the bayou long, Lily couldn't help feeling encouraged that he might one day accept her shape-shifting. Besides, there was mystery about him as well. "Can't help noticing you neatly sidestepped the issue of your own powers. That stuff must run in your family."

Nash said nothing and ate his steak in silence. She'd pushed him enough for one night. Once he got to know her better, maybe she'd gain his trust and he'd open up about his gifts and his past.

"By the way, I buried that coyote. It did have rabies."

Lily shuddered, remembering the yellow-brown predatory eyes. If besieged undersea, she had the advantage of speed over most other creatures, except dolphins, which were friends anyway. But with human legs, the coyote could have easily overtaken her. "That reminds me of Sam's warning. Since your grandfather sees things, should I be worried someone's deceiving me?"

"Maybe. You had any more trouble with Twyla?"

She debated telling him about the hang-up calls, reluctant to sound like an alarmist. But if she hoped to gain his trust, she'd have to be a little more forthright herself.

"For several days I've had a string of phone calls where the person hangs up as soon as I answer."

Knife and fork slipped from his hands and clattered

on the plate. "Harassing calls," he said slowly. His lips pursed to a fine line.

Lily wondered at his extreme reaction. "Could be kids making prank calls." Out of the corner of her eye, she saw Gary teetering off the bar stool. His posse stared straight at her, smirking.

"Coincidence," Nash muttered. "Has to be."

All her attention was on Gary. A trickle of sweat ran down her cleavage. Holy smokes, the guy was going to make another scene. Lily licked her dry lips. Should she make a mad dash to the ladies' room?

Fight or flight. Sink or swim.

She felt trapped like a caged rabbit. Gary headed over to where they were sitting. Nash scowled, deep in his own thoughts, unaware of the oncoming disaster.

No way to avoid trouble. Lily desperately sought a way to minimize the damage. Too late—or early, as it were—to call the waitress for their ticket and make a quick exit. Only one thing left to do. Lily lurched to her feet, hoping to head Gary off at the pass. She'd put her hand on his arm and talk sweet nothings to calm him until she and Nash could exit the restaurant. She'd even beg, promise Gary a date later to prevent him from ruining everything with Nash.

"Hey there, Lily-Gily girl," he slurred. "Who you with this time?" He stopped at their table and sniggered at Nash. "Well, hello there, Chief."

Lily gasped at the insult.

Nash rose slowly. "Go away," he said in a low, calm voice.

Knowing it was too late to stop the inevitable, Lily sat.

Gary pointed at Nash's whiskey glass. "Shouldn't be drinking that there firewater, Chief. Will make you a Heap Big Drunk."

Much snickering erupted from his friends at the bar and Lily glared their way. She'd expected to be the one insulted, not Nash.

Nash raised an eyebrow at Gary. "I can handle my liquor. Unlike you and your friends." He raised his glass and took a long swallow with a steady hand.

Gary switched tactics. "Got me there, Chief. Word to the wise, though, about your *date*." He spit out the word as if he'd swallowed tainted moonshine. "She's used goods. Probably every guy in this town has had Lily. And I do mean in the biblical sense."

Nash rose slowly to his feet and spoke in a low, deep voice. "Please go."

Gary opened and closed his mouth as if to speak again, but thought better of it. Something in Nash's eyes and still posture must have penetrated his beer-sodden brain. He held up both hands. "No problem, Chief." With an exaggerated swagger, Gary made his way back to the bar.

Lily stiffened in her chair and snuck a peak at the other restaurant patrons. Most were busy eating, but she caught a glimpse of Twyla at a back table. Her arm rested on the shoulder of her toddler and J.P. was by her side. Twyla stared at her intently. Lily had expected a smirk, but Twyla's face was tight and her eyes sharp with pity.

But that couldn't be right. To hell with anyone's pity. She was Lily Bosarge, the great siren of the seas.

Nash sat down and she studied his stoic face.

"Sorry about that," she mumbled, fiddling with her napkin.

"No need to apologize. You've done nothing wrong." Nash calmly picked up his knife and fork and resumed eating his steak.

Respect and gratitude swept through Lily like a wave. Nash's dignity had been a powerful weapon against

Gary's mean stupidity. She wanted to signal the waitress and escape, but she followed his lead. No sense giving Gary or anyone else the satisfaction of believing such lowness had disturbed their date. Lily took a bite of shrimp, digging in with gusto.

They spoke little, as if by mutual pact. At long last, they finished and exited the diner with a deliberate grace. The ride home was also quiet and Lily's stomach churned, wondering what he thought of her in light of Gary's insults.

He pulled into her driveway and turned off the motor. The ping of the heated engine clattered in the dark night.

"Gary's an asshole," she blurted out. "I have *not* been with every man in the bayou."

Nash shrugged. "Wouldn't matter to me if you had. I've had more than my share of women. Way more."

An unexpected tightening in her chest surprised Lily. So this was how jealousy felt. Best not to let Nash see it mattered.

"Rumors of my promiscuity are greatly exaggerated," she continued. "I don't want you to get the wrong idea about me."

"Like I said, it doesn't matter."

Lily cleared her dry throat. "Okay, then. Want to come in for a drink?"

Nash strummed his fingers on the dashboard, as if debating. "Why not?" he answered in a rush. "Been some kind of evening."

They walked to the darkened house. Strange, she usually kept the porch light on because returning to an empty, dark home was depressing. She missed Jet and Shelly more than she'd ever anticipated. Lily fished out her keys and opened the door. In the entry, she flicked on the light switch and frowned.

"Something wrong?" Nash asked.

"I'm not sure." Nothing appeared out of place, but the energy in the house felt...altered. That brush Shelly had had with a serial killer last year was making her paranoid, that's all. And that coyote stalking hadn't helped her peace of mind either. *Nothing's wrong.*

Yet Lily couldn't shake off the feeling someone had been in the house. She turned on the kitchen chandelier. Everything was as she'd left it earlier this afternoon. Lily hugged her chilled arms.

Nash pulled her to him. "What is it?"

She shook her head. "Nothing." Telling the truth would make him think she was nuts. Bad enough Gary had planted the notion in his head she was slutty. "How about a glass of Moscato? Or would you prefer a beer?"

"Whatever you're drinking is fine."

Lily pointed to the den. "Go have a seat and I'll bring it to you."

She found the wine bottle in the refrigerator and poured some into two antique crystal glasses as she admired the dancing of light in the pale citrine liquid. The fruity aroma tantalized, and she took a sip and closed her eyes, savoring the shot of jeweled ambrosia as it warmed her stomach. Another sip and the unease evaporated like fog in daylight. Nash waited in the den and she intended to get to know him better—in every way.

"It's as I remembered," Nash commented as she entered the den. He stood before an opened curio cabinet, running his fingers along a rare pottery vase. "Enough collectibles here to fill a small museum. As a kid, I imagined this place as a pirate's secret cache for his stash of treasures."

A fitting description. "Is that so?"

Nash closed the cabinet door and moved to the mantel, festooned with marine astrolabes positioned below a collection of antique swords. "Very cool." He examined one of the brass instruments and set it back on the mantel. "Your home's a stark contrast to my grandfather's cabin."

"But his is charming in its own way. Minimalistic without being stark." She hadn't considered the differences before. The ornate style of the Bosarge Victorian home, with its plethora of plundered goodies, jasmine scent and overall feminine vibe, was a counterpoint to the Bowman utilitarian aesthetic. The cabin was woodsy, everything in it had a purpose, and it held the faint, unique smell of burnt sage from smudging rituals to ward off sickness and negative energy.

Yin and yang.

Lily held out the wineglass. Their fingers touched against the delicate stemware as he took the drink, sending Lily longing for more intimacy.

Nash raised his glass for a toast. "To friendship." Green eyes bore into her, his expression intense but unfathomable.

"I want…" Her voice trailed off, afraid to give voice to her wish only to have it rebuffed once more. She took a deep breath. "I want more."

"More of what? This?" He leaned into her and kissed her, his lips hot and pressing, full of passion and promise.

Anxiety fisted through desire and Lily pulled away. "Did you reconsider seeing me because of what Gary said tonight?"

Nash cocked his head to the side. "I'm not following you."

Geez, he was going to make her say it. "You figured I would be…you know, easy. Easy to have and easy to leave." Not that her bold overtures to Nash contradicted anything Gary had said, but her former boyfriend's words made everything appear cheap and ugly.

With Nash it will be special, she vowed.

"Hell, no. I don't think you're easy," he growled. "I can't believe you'd say that." His face softened. "C'mon, Lily. You were the first girl I ever kissed, my childhood friend. I would never think badly of you."

The tight tangle of her heart loosened. "Really?" she whispered.

"Really." Very deliberately, Nash took the wineglass out of her hand and set his and hers both down on the coffee table. Time thickened, grew heavy, as if the weight of air pressed down, making every movement languid and deliberate. Nash faced her and pulled her body alongside his own. His eyes lowered to her mouth and he cupped her cheeks with calloused hands. Ever so slowly, he leaned down to join their lips.

The kiss was sensuous and steamy with a touch of gentle wonder. Lily twined her arms around his neck, reveling in his closeness. Nash's mouth opened and she tasted a combination of citrus, peach and apricots from the Moscato. Her body felt as liquid and weightless as if she were afloat at sea. His arms wrapped around the small of her back, pressing—an anchor in the maelstrom of desire.

Nash withdrew and leaned his forehead against hers. Their deep breaths mingled and merged as one. Passion ebbed, replaced by an undertow of tenderness, like an unspoken prayer.

She'd never come close to a kiss such as this, although with each new man she'd been searching, always hopeful.

Nash straightened. "I should go."

Lily opened her mouth to tell him to stay, but thought better of it. He liked and respected her—why ruin it tonight with sex? The timing was wrong. It might reinforce Gary's accusations, despite Nash's claim to the contrary. She wanted his respect, wanted his opinion of her to be different from everyone else's in the bayou.

She squeezed his hand. "Yes. It might be for the best." They strolled to the entrance, holding hands. If Nash was disappointed at her quick agreement, he didn't show it.

At the door, he placed a quick kiss on her mouth.

"Soon," he whispered, his tone as hot and dusty as the bayou breeze.

Oh, I hope so.

He stepped into the night, olive skin and black hair blending to near invisibility. Lily hugged her arms and shivered, bereft with loneliness. The empty house mocked with a sullen silence. She craved the sea and its teeming life, from the smallest plankton to the great white whale; it afforded a measure of companionship. As a remedy for the loneliness and thwarted physical release, Lily had an even better coping strategy than a cold shower.

Time for a swim.

Chapter 7

Water swaddled Lily's body like liquid silk, a lush weight of peaceful suspension to douse the fevered need of desire Nash left behind. More than physical, the aching need inside sought communion with him on every plane, a complete opening, an illuminating light on all her secrets. A plunge together through a dark labyrinth where she hid unvoiced wishes and insecurities in secret passageways.

The idea of such intimacy both terrified and excited.

Lily navigated through an undersea field of sea-grass roots whose long tendrils swirled like locks of curly hair in the wind. The roots stroked her body in a passing caress, unbidden but welcome. She swam deeper, eyes accommodating to the velvet darkness. Nictating membranes, that useless pink clump in the corner of human eyes, spread over Lily's delicate exposed eye tissue. What was merely an unused, evolutionary holdover in humans served as protection against salt and debris while undersea.

She flipped and rolled in the water—mermaid dancing—a spontaneous celebration after shape-shifting from land to sea. Hope kicked in, an unexpected guest in Lily's heart. She could fall in love with Nash. Really, *really* give herself over to another person. If Shelly and Jet could do it, why not her?

Love happened. Even for mermaids.

She hadn't known how lonely she was. Solitary swims, days and nights at a time with nothing but canvas and acrylics for company.

She hadn't known her childhood friend would return in a grown-man version that would quicken her heart with hope.

She hadn't known what it felt like to have no control of her emotions with a man. She'd always been the one that set the parameters in every affair.

Until Nash.

Bubbling joy could no longer be contained and her lungs opened. Lily sang. Glorious, magical notes that carried for miles in the currents. The reverberating vibrations of harmony attracted swarms of silver fish that encircled her body like a living metal gyroscope. Lily reveled in the kinship. She'd devoted so much time lately to painting that undersea time had suffered. So she danced, tail fin glittering like emeralds and diamonds and sapphires afire. And she kept singing—deeply, freely, uninhibited.

Tired at length, Lily relaxed and let the undertow pull her where it willed. Half-awake, half-asleep, she drifted like flotsam atop a wave. Healing salt water swished an eternal echo in her ears like a lullaby.

A disturbance in vibrational pattern put Lily on alert

and she cupped a hand to an ear. Something large would be in range momentarily. A curious dolphin, or hungry shark? Friend or foe?

Faint humming notes wavered through sea static. Was it— Could it be? Yes, she recognized the sound pattern. Lily began singing an old haunting melody that was one of her mother's favorites.

Adriana Bosarge cut in at once. "Lily! Over here," she called.

Lily homed in on the location and swam toward her mother, tail fin swishing eagerly. Mom was a pain at times, but she still loved her. Thanks to Jet's heads-up on the impending visit, she'd mentally prepared herself as much as possible. Through a series of hums and whistles mixed with her bio-sonar ability, Lily altered her course in a mermaid version of Marco Polo.

At last she caught site of her swimming alongside a school of speckled trout. Mom's multicolored hair streamed behind her like a paler version of her sparkling tail fin. Lily had inherited similar coloring, but Adriana was bolder, more striking. Where Lily was ethereal and angelic with delicate facial features, Adriana's cheekbones were prominent, displaying a larger nose and a more squared jawline that hinted at her formidable personality. A kind of beauty most often described as "handsome" or "arresting."

Lily mentally catalogued the image of her mom for a future painting. Of course, that particular piece would forever remain in her own private collection. But art wasn't always about public selling or trading; it was about private satisfaction and creative expression.

Adriana swam closer and rubbed her tail fin against Lily's in an affectionate mer-greeting. "You look bewitching as usual," she stated in a prideful tone, as if taking credit for the fact. "And that bewitching siren voice is absolutely wasted out here in the bayou."

A new record. Less than thirty seconds, and Mom had delivered the first jab in her ongoing campaign for Lily's return to sea.

"Not wasted. I've snagged my fair share of men."

Adriana snorted, sending a bubbling stream upward. "Human men. You need to mate with your own kind. Do your duty."

Annoyance, along with a smidgeon of guilt, rippled through Lily. Their race was dwindling, in no small part because of past inbreeding with humans. Increasingly, the merfolk frowned on mating with humans, and those who did were partially ostracized for not procreating the mer population. Shelly and Jet had both experienced that alienation.

"Mom, please. Can you give it a rest? At least for one day?"

"Humph." Adriana swept past her, chin lifted.

Lily sighed and darted ahead. "C'mon, Mom. I'm not ready to have children and stay at sea forever."

"You're almost thirty."

"Give me some more time."

"You say that every visit."

"It's different now." Lily laid a hand on her arm. "I've met someone special."

"Heard that before, too."

Lily winced. "I mean it this time. It's Nashoba Bowman. You remember him, don't you?"

Adriana tapped her lips. "Ah, yes, the little Indian boy."

"Native American." Lily barely refrained an eye roll. At her mom's questioning look, she added, "We don't say *Indian* these days. And Nash is no longer a little boy."

She couldn't hide a smile, recalling the taste of his kiss and the heat of his body pressed against hers.

Adriana resumed swimming, and Lily fell in beside her. Why couldn't her mother understand her longing for true love? True, her boyfriend track record was lousy, but she wasn't ready to give up on human males and settle for the male mermen with their wanderlust and a limited interest in monogamy.

They passed a rock outcropping, a familiar landmark signaling they were close to home. She glanced at her mom's face but couldn't judge her mood. "You always liked Nash when we were children," Lily ventured. She'd rather hash this out now, and talking undersea was easier—freer somehow.

"That doesn't mean he's suitable for pair-bonding. You'll tire of him like you have all the other human males."

"Not this time. He doesn't care for my singing and he hasn't stumbled all over his land-legger feet to date me. I've been the one chasing him."

Adriana stopped swimming and her long locks of silver-blond hair floated around her torso like a cluster of glowing stars. "Impossible."

"It's true. I can't figure it out. Do you have any ideas?"

"The degree of a human male's response to your voice varies depending on how much merblood runs through his veins. The more distant, the greater the attraction."

"His grandfather claims they're related to the undersea pale people. Have you ever met Sam Bowman?"

"I don't think so." She tilted her head to the side. "I was aware the Choctaws had a legend about our kind. Although that's hardly surprising. Most countries and cultures do."

"But how much merblood could be in Nash? If his parents or grandparents were mer, we'd have surely seen or heard them undersea."

Adriana tapped a forefinger on her chin, musing. "There's only one explanation for a human male not being entranced by your singing. I've only heard tell of this happening once before to a siren." She looked into the distance, silent and absorbed.

"Come on, tell me," Lily urged.

"Nash doesn't just have merblood. He's a descendent of a male siren. As such, he's immune to the siren's lure himself."

Lily's nictating membrane blinked for several heartbeats. She recalled all the women vying for his attention wherever they went, Opal's hints that Nash had tossed aside many lovers, the deep timbre of his voice. Of course. "And he doesn't even know what he is," she murmured.

"No reason he should ever suspect," Adriana said. She eyed Lily sharply. "Forget him. Mate with a pure merman and spawn me grandchildren." She resumed swimming, signaling she was done with the subject.

Grandchildren. Is that what this was really about? Lily swam alongside her. "Jet's about to have a baby. Shelly plans on having children, too, eventually. You'll have plenty of grandchildren."

"And not a pure-blooded one will be among them."

Lily's tail twitched. "Kinda harsh, Mom."

"I don't mean to be. You know I love Jet and Shelly. But *you're* my only biological daughter, and the pure merblood numbers drop every year."

"You're becoming a zealot in your old age." Lily said it with a smile that contrasted with her stiff spine and fisted hands. No sense bumping tail fins tonight. Maybe when her mother met Nash again she'd mellow on the issue and yield to allow her daughter happiness.

Adriana fiddled with her pearl bracelets, which Lily recognized as a sure sign of her annoyance. "You've spent so much time in Bayou La Siryna you forget how rigid mer society has become on interspecies mating."

Ugh, interspecies mating. Her Mom made it sound vulgar and clinical at the same time. Lily's smile strained at the edges. "How long are you planning on staying?"

"Oh, I don't know. Perhaps until Jet's baby arrives."

Holy Neptune, this was going to be a long visit.

Nash's senses opened in a way they never had before. He felt summer down deep in his bones. So deep, the marrow tingled and pulsated with heat and light, a contrast from the winter's dead darkness. It had never been this intense before. Each day in the bayou he drew closer to the land and wildlife.

Today was well-earned time off from work at the island and he'd invited Lily to his grandfather's cabin for a hike. The three days he hadn't seen Lily seemed like forever.

Nash held back a low branch for Lily. Desire as rabid as a stag in heat fevered his skin where she brushed against his forearm. They had hiked this trail hundreds of times as kids, but this heightened awareness between them was an entirely different sensation.

Each time he saw Lily, she appeared more beautiful, more irresistible. He feared she would end up hurt when this assignment was over and he left, but being apart was unbearable. The island lodge was lonely and too quiet, especially now that Opal had left for another assignment.

Lily caught his gaze, eyes widening at the desire that

must be written all over his face. They leaned in for the day's first kiss.

Caw, caw, kow-caw. The sudden shrill bark of a crow, accompanied by the flapping of feathers, swooped overhead.

Lily laughed. "It's as if he disapproves. I feel chided, like I was caught pulling down my pants in town square."

The image of her naked had Nash pulling her roughly against his body. He planted a hard, quick kiss against Lily's lips, a promise of more to come. They continued onward until they came to a clearing. In the center was "their" place from old times—the base of a felled oak whose surface provided enough space for them to both sit on it cross-legged.

He used to bring Lily here and retell his grandfather's wilder stories—tales of the tiny forest dwellers and the dark spirit of Nalusa Falaya, which crept into a person's soul, causing misery or even death. Lily had been a good audience, wide-eyed and just younger enough that she regarded him in higher esteem than warranted. She rarely had stories of her own. Instead, she would sing silly songs and old-fashioned ballads that he'd found dull. Twelve-year-old boys cared little for nonsense love songs.

Nash sat first and offered a hand, a gallantry that had never occurred to him as a boy. Lily placed her hand in his and he drew her to him as easily as pulling a minnow out of water.

Caw-caw. A sweep of metallic violet swooshed within a few feet of their bodies. The crow perched on a nearby oak branch and cocked his head to the side, studying them. It raised its bill and cried again, louder.

Caw, caw, caw. You again. You're back.

The crow's words sprouted in the pith of Nash's core; he could feel the language resonate in his solar plexus like the echo of a pealing bell. Or as if a long-dormant seed sprouted in a burst of DNA fusion, a blade of green energy emerging beneath the soil.

Nash stared into the dark brown eyes of the old crow. "Yes, I'm back."

"Um, yes. I'm glad you're back." Lily cocked her head in much the same manner of a bird, studying him with a quizzical gleam in her eyes.

A rush of flapping erupted from across the field and a murder of crows flew in, landing on the branches beside the lone crow.

Caw caw. Long and short chirrups erupted in a cacophony. Nash picked up on the gist of their conversation—*he's back, the girl with him.*

This was new territory. He'd always sensed things, guessed at what creatures thought, but this was downright eerie.

Stay in the bayou. Bayou stay, they each shrilled in a thunder of sound.

Could they understand his speech as well? "I'm only here for a visit," he said aloud.

Lily sighed. "I know, I know. You've made that clear. As soon as your latest project is finished, you'll be jet-setting to some other corner of the world." She settled gracefully on the oak stump, tucking her long, pale legs beneath her. "How are the bird photos going?"

Nash eyed the crows warily. "Fine. I'm homing in on their secret mating and nesting sites. Those clappers are surprisingly cagey."

"Can't blame them for seeking privacy. If I were them—" She raised a hand over her forehead, squinting. "What are those crows squawking about?"

"How should I know?" Nash snapped. "Sorry," he said at the startled hurt in her eyes.

Lily's hair billowed in the breeze and he brushed back a stray lock from her face. The midday sun emphasized subtle highlights of pink and lavender blended among the blond waves. Nash caressed a handful, admiring the softness against his calloused palms. "It's like cotton candy."

She laughed. "Are you saying it's dried out?"

"No. I'm talking about the colors."

"Oh, that's the miracle of hair dye."

The crows kicked up again. *Caw—ca-caw. She's not of us. Not of us.*

Nash looked up at the tree. "What do you mean?"

Lily tugged his shirt. "What's wrong with you today? You're acting strange."

"Just distracted." If she only knew. He could hardly believe it himself. What would happen if he stayed in the bayou more than a couple of months? How much more attuned to nature could he become? Nash forced himself to ignore the crows' clatter.

"A man's attention has never been a problem for me before." The petulant words were delivered with a grin and held no rancor. She laid a warm hand on his bare knee and beads from her bracelet rubbed his skin.

The bracelet jolted a memory. "I can't believe you wear that old thing." He ran a finger along the beads that had faded over the years. A few of them were missing. The frayed fringe ties were knotted at her slender wrist. It was out of place next to her jeweled, expensive rings and thin gold bangles.

A rose glow lit her face. "It's special, a memory of our last summer."

"I remember." They'd been here, at this very spot. Grandfather had helped him string the beads, although the workmanship on his part was still clumsy.

"You said we'd be friends forever," Lily whispered.

She touched the beads. "Sad to say, you're the only true friend I've ever had. Outside of family."

"Oh, come on. That can't be true." Their fingers entwined above the bracelet.

"It is true. You've seen the way women act around me. And the men..." Her voice trailed off in an unhappy sigh.

"Jealous bitches, every last one," he said quickly. "As far as the men, well, understandable that you make them a little crazy." He shifted uncomfortably, guilt arrowing him in the gut. He was as bad as the rest of them. Over the years, he'd been careless and selfish in his affections. Until the deaths of Rebecca and Connie had filled him with shame and regret.

Nash looked up at the crows that stared back with dark, otherworldly eyes. Silent at last, he imagined they judged him for past sins.

"I don't mean to make the men crazy," Lily said. "It... just happens."

One crow flew closer and perched on a nearby limb. Its eyes were blue, indicating youth. *Caw-caw-caw-caw. She is not like us. She is of two spirits.*

Nash leapt to his feet and waved his arms. "Get out of here!"

The crow flapped its wings. *Caw. Ask her.*

"I said get out. Now."

The crow dipped its head, revealing faint blue speckles on its crown. Suddenly, it took flight, the rest of the murder following in its lead.

Two spirits. Not of us, they cawed.

"Weird," Lily said. "It was as if that crow was trying to tell you something."

He turned slowly to face her. What would she think if...

"Was it?"

"Was it what?" he repeated stupidly.

"That crow. It spoke to you. When you were little, you seemed to sense an animal's feelings. Appears it might even go beyond sensing now, like your telepathy with them has grown."

His mind whirled, as if taking flight with the crows and circling from above. She'd guessed correctly. Did this telepathy expand as he matured, or was it something weird about this bayou? Could be a combination of both.

Lily rose slowly and stepped close, one hand cradling the right side of his neck. "Never mind. You don't have to tell me anything you aren't comfortable sharing. I'll understand."

Nash wavered; the need to talk about his gift was strong, but doing so would be another bond with Lily and she would be hurt even more when he left. Rebecca's and Connie's faces appeared in his mind. He was toxic to women. It never ended well. He couldn't, wouldn't contaminate her with a lengthy relationship. She might already be infected. Nash removed her hand. "Have you gotten any more harassing phone calls?"

"No. What made you think of that?"

"I need to tell you about the last two women I was involved with."

"Okay." No surprise registered on her face.

"Something tells me you already know the whole story."

"I did hear some talk," she admitted.

So word of his past had followed him even here. "From Opal?" he guessed.

Lily kept silent.

He took a deep breath. "Rebecca and I saw each other whenever I returned from a trip. It was pretty casual on my part, and I thought it was on hers, too. But when she asked for a commitment I balked. She left that night, angry and hurt. The next morning I found out that she'd returned to her apartment and started drinking. A lot." He swallowed. "Then Rebecca got back in her car, drove off the road and hit a tree. Doctors pronounced her DOA."

Lily's lips tightened. "Not your fault. Damn it, Nash, don't you dare blame yourself for her death. It was a tragedy—"

"And then, a year later, there was Connie." Now that he was actually talking about it, he couldn't stop the flow of words. "We'd been dating a few months and I mistakenly thought I'd found a woman who could accept my long trips. But she wanted more and I didn't. Connie ended her own life." His throat felt dry, parched. "Overdose of pills," he ground out past the lump in his throat.

"Oh, Nash. I am so, so sorry." She circled her arms around his waist.

Her body felt smooth, cool, a balm to the burning hurt. But he stood stiffly, fists clenched at his sides. He didn't deserve comfort. If he'd been a better man, more selfless, more cued into another's feelings... But no. His career had always come first and there'd been some part of him that held back, that couldn't see another's needs.

"Don't," Lily whispered fiercely into his chest. "You can't accept responsibility for others' mistakes."

Couldn't he, though? Shouldn't he? He stepped back and held Lily at arm's length. "About those phone calls," he said sternly. "Are you in some kind of danger?"

"Not that I'm aware of. And if someone was upset with me, you can hardly think it has anything to do with you."

"There's more. Before Rebecca died, she had a few hang-up calls. And Connie once said that she felt like someone was following her, although she never saw anyone or had evidence."

"Coincidence," Lily insisted. "Prank calls are common and everyone thinks they've been followed at one time or another." Her tone gentled. "You can't scare me away, Nash. I'm a strong woman."

He wanted to believe Lily. The past few years had been a lonely, hard existence. An affair, however brief, would be a welcome return to some normalcy. Lily seemed lonely herself, a bit of an outcast. But the shrill cry of the crows replayed like an echo of a dream. *Not of us. Two spirits.* What was that about?

Lily made him uneasy. He wanted a nice, normal woman who didn't probe too deep or demand too much.

Nash focused on the problem at hand. First hint of danger and he would leave, whether or not the assignment was finished. To linger might place her in jeopardy. But maybe this time would be safe, a kind of healing for both of them. "You'll tell me if anything weird happens, right? And I mean immediately."

"You'll be the first to know." Lily smiled and took his hand, and Nash clasped it tightly—as if they were taking a high dive off a rocky cliff together.

Another crow flew close by. It didn't utter a sound, but the flapping of its wings and the glisten of its coal-black eyes were like a warning. Abruptly, Nash dropped Lily's hand. "I'm not ready for this. Something's…not right."

Chapter 8

The warped voice crackled over a phone line so full of static Lily had trouble deciphering the words.

"Stay away from Nash," came the disembodied voice again. It sounded like a recording, the voice so robotic she couldn't determine if it belonged to a male or female.

"How did you get my cell phone number?"

The connection terminated and a buzzing noise filled her ears. Lily sank onto the couch and frowned. She'd had her share of such calls from irate girls while in high school, and even some more sophisticated versions of the same message later in life, but none had rattled her like this.

Nash's former women... What if they hadn't died by accident? Her skin crawled imagining a psycho, an unknown enemy intent on destroying Nash's happiness. *But why?*

"Stay away." Ha! Just as they were so close, about

to take their attraction to the next level, Nash had been spooked by a bunch of birds. Birds, damn it. And how was he resisting her siren's voice? She was no closer now than when she'd first seen him at the grocery store. He drove her crazy—why not the other way around?

Lily drummed her long, pointed fingernails on the end table, the sharp clicks a loud staccato in the old Victorian house. For the first time, she wished her mother had stayed here instead of with Jet. Adriana was still in a bit of a snit over her refusal to return to sea and was giving her the old silent treatment.

She remembered how odd the house had felt a few nights ago—as if a lingering smell had been left behind by a stranger. But she'd never found anything out of place and had dismissed the feeling. Now she wasn't so sure. Lily debated how to proceed.

She had two brothers-in-law, one a sheriff and the other a deputy sheriff, but she hated the idea of getting them involved. They'd make a big stink over it and question Nash. And if there was one thing she knew, it was that Nash couldn't know the phone calls were back. He'd leave Bayou La Siryna and she'd never hear from him again.

Which left only one option.

Lily grabbed her purse and, twenty minutes later, arrived at the ramshackle cottage of Tia Henrietta. It was still decrepit but much neater than she remembered from her last visit a couple of years ago. A fresh coat of salmon-pink paint had been slapped on the exterior, complemented with vibrant turquoise shutters at the windows. Bright colored bottles hung from every low-lying branch near the house. A maze of large knickknacks remained at the entrance—conch shells, bowling balls, plastic pink flamingos—but there were less of them and they were arranged with a certain precision that suggested loving care and not random neglect.

She got out of the car, determined to tie Tia down to specifics on who was behind the calls. The woman liked to play it loose and cagey if you let her get away with it. The screen door creaked open and Tia waved her inside, as if she'd been expecting her visit.

"Got everything already set up for yer questions." Tia's face was solemn and set. No hint of her usual mischievous smile, as if she knew a great secret but couldn't share it.

White candles flickered throughout the small den and old framed pictures of Jesus and various saints aligned the walls, shelves and tables. Dark scents of nutmeg, cloves and cedar wood permeated the air instead of the green herbal smell she remembered from long ago. A card table and two chairs were set up.

"Sit," Tia said, folding her purple sarong underneath as she sat down and shuffled the tarot cards. Bold rings and wooden bangle bracelets clinked as she manipulated the deck. Instead of her usual turban, Tia's hair was covered with a scarf. Deep lines in her face and neck were highlighted by the striated candle glow.

Did the old woman really know why she'd come? Tia had helped her decide to go for her painting dream last time she'd visited, had intuited or pulled out the artistic dreams. She'd even guessed at Lily's hurt over the way people of Bayou La Siryna treated her.

"How did you know to expect me today?" Lily asked, secretly impressed.

Tia frowned, never responding or looking up from the cards. "This time be serious," she said in her accent, a strange mixture that Lily couldn't decide if it was Creole or Gullah or something else all together. She handed the cards to Lily. "Cut the deck."

Lily moved a stack of the colorful cards from the top to the bottom and Tia asked her to select cards as she felt drawn. Lily selected a few and Tia spread them in a Celtic cross design. She flipped the cards over one by one, not commenting.

A humming sounded on the porch, a familiar, soothing rift, followed by the creak of the screen door. A dark waif of a girl slipped into the room with a wicker basket of herbs. She scurried past them singing softly, beguilingly, from the kitchen:

"Sweet little darling, adrift undersea

Float with the current, mamma's with thee

Listen to the echo of the waves

Sleepy, sleepy, all is saved"

A jolt of recognition stirred Lily's memory, turning her skin prickly with surprise. It was a song every mermaid learned at her mother's tail fin. She joined in the mermaid lullaby:

"And when the moon shines way down deep

Baby should sigh and dream, not weep."

The girl stuck her head into the den, mouth agape. "You have the voice of an angel," she said in awe.

Lily stood. "Who are you? How do you know this song?"

The girl paled underneath her olive skin and quickly scurried to the kitchen.

"Don't be so dang bashful, Annie," Tia called out. "Mind yer manners and come back and say hello to company."

Annie entered with slow steps, head down, her long black hair a veil.

"This is my granddaughter, Annie. She's come to stay

with me a spell, helpin' with chores and studyin' the ways. Annie, this is Miss Lily Bosarge."

So that explained the spruced-up exterior.

"Hello," Annie mumbled in a soft voice, face still hidden beneath her hair.

"Git you a chair from the kitchen and join us. You need to be learnin' the tarot." Tia leaned toward Lily. "She'll be takin' my place one day. Gotta get her trained."

Clever old lady. Lily sat back down on the metal folding chair. "Don't try to distract me. Tell me how Annie knows that song."

Tia stared back with rheumy eyes; a mysterious smile tugged the edges of her lips.

"Of course," Lily said, snapping her fingers. Those cloudy eyes were from a descending nictating membrane, a common occurrence with elderly merfolk. "You and your granddaughter are one of us. Maybe fifth or sixth generation removed."

Tia didn't ask what she meant by "one of us." "All people, all creatures are the Good Lord's doing. Each of us goes back to the Garden of Eden."

Lily was familiar with the myth that merfolk were cast-off angels that had fallen into the sea during Lucifer's revolt from heaven. But if Tia didn't openly admit or say the word *mermaid*, then she refused to be the first to say the word aloud.

Annie dragged a chair across the wooden floor and primly crossed her ankles and folded her hands in her lap. She kept her eyes on the floor.

"I'm not cross with you," Lily said. "You just surprised me singing that song."

Annie took a quick peek from behind her long wave of hair and Lily was taken aback by her exotic beauty. Annie had dark brown eyes shot through with orange rays that made her irises appear a unique cinnamon color. They weren't the innocent eyes of a child, either. Lily noticed the ample breasts and the slight curve of her hips, whereas before she'd only caught the impression of a short, thin body.

"I can't help singing," the girl mumbled. "The songs play in my head and I have to sing."

Lily turned questioning eyes to Tia.

"It's true. An unusual gift my Annie's received from the spirit world. Never heard of no one else pick up music from a person's aura."

And the girl sang so beautifully, not as well as herself, but the notes were pure, haunting even. Lily shook her head to clear it. Fascinating, but not why she'd come. "Let's return to business. I need information."

Tia didn't respond. The only sound in the room was the slight jangle of her arm bangles as she flipped cards.

"Well?" Lily broke in, impatient with the silence.

"Not good." Tia shook her head. "Danger surrounds you on two sides."

"What danger?" Lily asked, not volunteering any information.

"There are two people who wish you harm. One is much more evil than the other. One is motivated by money, the other love."

Two? Her scalp prickled. "I need names."

Tia clucked in disapproval, as if she were a recalcitrant student. "The spirits are never that open."

"Can you at least give me some clues?"

Tia's brow wrinkled and her words dribbled out slow as honey. "It's a different person than who's troubled you in the past."

"Maybe Twyla Fae. I confronted her yesterday but she swore she's not behind my current problem." Surprisingly, Lily had believed her. Twyla had appeared tired and anxious, fretting over her sickly child. She'd even expressed sympathy for the way Gary had created a scene at the restaurant and apologized for the way she'd acted in the grocery store. A minor miracle.

Tia shook her head. "It's not Twyla."

"If you can't give me names, can you at least tell me *why* these people want to hurt me?"

Tia scooped up the cards with a deft hand and reshuffled. She laid out two more cards. "The one motivated by greed and revenge is a male. His anger is directed more at your family, but you could be hurt in the cross fire." She took a deep breath, nostrils crinkling. "I'm picking up the scent of fresh-cut wood. Like wood chips."

Carl Dismukes. Her brother-in-law's ex-deputy who'd once blackmailed Jet over her illegal maritime excavations. His image arose, sitting at the sheriff's headquarters whittling one of his many wood carvings.

"Tillman fired him months ago. He's still angry? Why can't that old man just enjoy retirement?" He'd served so many years on the force that he'd been allowed to collect his pension. "Dismukes I can handle. What about the other person?"

Tia tapped her finger on the Tower card. "This one is murkier. The Tower represents death and destruction." She frowned, as if peering into a shadowed realm.

Lily found herself holding her breath, afraid to break Tia's concentration by even the tiniest of movements.

"This person has murdered two persons, yet harbors no guilt."

Lily's heart thundered like a herd of wild stallions. Rebecca and Connie?

Tia looked up, regarding her with anthracite-black eyes. "You may be next."

The air pressed around her, thick and dense. "What should I do?" she whispered.

"Talk to your family. Report the phone calls."

An electric tingle buzzed through her body. No! Nothing would send Nash packing as quickly as believing his presence put her in danger. "There's got to be another way. Can't you tell me anything else to pinpoint who it is?"

Tia closed her eyes and laid large wrinkled hands on the table. Lily was surprised how vulnerable and frail the hands appeared. Tia was well-known in the bayou as a combination voodoo priestess/witch or gypsy fortune-teller/hustler—depending on who you asked. The woman had always seemed large and powerful and more than a little scary when Lily was younger. Lily had been afraid she'd direct those black eyes on her and pronounce her some kind of swamp monster.

Now she knew better. Tia was one of her own kind—however distant. And she was an old lady who needed her granddaughter to get by.

Tia threw her head back and began a guttural hum that sounded almost inhuman. Her chin snapped forward and the humming ceased. The rolling white of her eyeballs flickered before the black irises descended. "That's one of the most evil spirits I've ever encountered."

"What can you tell me?"

"It's a female."

Well, that cut the field by half. Lily restrained from rolling her own eyes. "What else?"

"The more evil the spirit, the more darkness surrounds 'em. Makes it hard to identify. Night and shadows stick to 'em like fly paper 'cause they don't want to be seen for what they truly are. They cower behind fog and veils and any trickery they can nab."

A loud, dissonant humming erupted. Lily jumped and stared at Annie. The girl's eyes were wide and their cinnamon rays glowed like jack-o-lanterns around the black pupils. Her lips moved as if she had no control over the jerky rhythm and nonsense words coming out. Tia placed an arm over her granddaughter's shoulder and the wildly pitched chanting slowed, giving way to a mournful parody of a children's song.

"Ring around the rosie
Pocket full of posies
Ashes, ashes
We all fall down."

Ice spurted through Lily's veins. The happy, nonsensical ditty had morphed to a low, funereal dirge like a devil's hymn, sinister as a baroque fugue.

"Ring around the rosie
Darkness befalls thee
Ashes, ashes
They all must drown."

Annie's mouth clamped shut and in the abrupt silence, the candle flames sizzled, their thin columns of fire doubling in height liked an amped-up Bunsen burner. Tia snuffed them with a brass candle snifter and they hissed like an angry cat. Sickly gray smoke perfumed the air with an acrid stench.

"Got to give this place a good sage smudgin' when you leave," Tia mumbled.

Lily coughed and waved the smoke from her face. "What's the significance of that song?"

"I d-don't know," Annie said in a thin voice. "It came to me." She fidgeted with the hem of her shirtsleeve. "Maybe it's somehow connected with the killer."

"Impressive. But I don't see how it can help me nail the woman unless I take you everywhere I go."

Tia gave a reassuring squeeze to Annie's shoulder before gathering up the tarot deck. "Oh, she's much too valuable for me to let her go traipsin' off with folks. Besides, the spirits have revealed all they want on the matter."

Lily couldn't complain, had found out more than she'd expected from the visit. She'd learned that Nash definitely had an enemy, one that had killed before and now sought her out. And that the killer was a female who enjoyed distorting children's songs into creepy messages of doom and death. Lily dug into her purse for the love offering.

A soft knock sounded at the door—so soft they each paused and eyed the door, as if unsure someone was on the other side. Another rap sounded, a bit firmer.

'Wasn't expectin' nobody but you," Tia said.

Lily arched a brow. "Your psychic powers slipping?"

Tia ignored the barb. "Get that for me, Annie."

But her granddaughter was already at the door, eager to slip away.

"I'd like to see Miss Tia, please."

Lily tensed at the familiar drawl, a habitual response to Twyla Fae's voice. She slapped a couple of twenties on the table for Tia and scrambled for the entrance.

Annie silently opened the door and Twyla and her son crossed the threshold, pausing when she saw Lily. Her child's eyes were a dull blue and he hiccupped, the kind you got from crying hard and long. His thin arms and legs dangled listlessly.

Twyla looked like she'd been sucked dry by a pack of rabid vampires. What should have been the whites of her eyes was so threaded with broken capillaries they appeared pink. Her arms were pasty and limp, as if she'd undergone rapid weight loss and lost muscle tone.

"Oh, hello again, Lily." She jostled the child on her hips and shifted her feet.

Tia stood slowly, knees creaking. "What's wrong with that poor young'un?"

"I don't know." Twyla slid a glance at Lily, clearly not wanting to speak her business in front of her.

Lily perversely crossed her arms and planted her feet. The ceasefire of hostility from Twyla was still too new, too fragile for her to feel comfortable in her presence. But a reluctant sympathy cut through her unease. She nodded at the boy. "You feeding this child enough? He's too skinny."

"That's why I'm here." Twyla looked hopefully, desperately at Tia Henrietta. "Please, is there anything you can do?"

"May I hold him?" Annie held out her arms.

So she wasn't shy when it came to children, Lily noted.

Twyla handed him over with pitiful haste and sank onto the sofa, deflating as quickly as a punctured balloon. Annie went to the rocker in the far corner of the room, humming softly and running fingers lightly against the boy's face. He stopped crying, fascinated by the stranger cradling his body.

"That boy need a doctor," Tia pronounced. "Can't be using no herbs on a child. Too risky."

"Can't you say a prayer or do a chant or something?" Twyla asked in a whoosh of breath. "Please?" Teardrops spangled her pale eyelashes.

"If you can't afford a doctor, I'll pay for one," Lily offered. She pulled two one-hundred-dollar bills from her wallet and regarded them thoughtfully. "Is this enough for a doctor's visit and some medicine?" she asked doubtfully. She'd never set foot in a doctor's office.

Twyla stiffened. "I *have* taken him to the doctor in

town. He don't know what's wrong. Said he had some sorta failure to thrive. He made an appointment for us at the Children's Hospital in Birmingham next month for more testing and evaluation."

Tia handed Twyla a tissue and patted her back. "I'll light a candle and say a prayer for him every night. What's his name?"

"Kevin. Kevin Leroy."

"That's it?" Lily asked Tia. "There must be something else you can do."

Tia's chin rose an inch. "Prayer can be powerful."

There had to be a way to help. Lily tapped her foot, thinking. "I've got an idea," she said suddenly.

Everyone in the room regarded her expectantly, making her instantly sorry she'd thought aloud. "I'll have to check with someone first," she said hastily. "It's kind of a long shot." Twyla might even laugh at the idea.

"I'd do anything," Twyla said. "As long as it doesn't hurt Kevin, of course."

Lily nodded. "All right, then. I'll check on it and let you know."

Twyla scribbled on a piece of torn paper and handed it over. "Call me anytime. And...thank you, Lily. I know I've been mean and petty in the past and I'm sorry."

"Nothing like a sick child to change a hard heart," Tia said with a cluck.

Lily accepted the apology silently. Twyla needed her help, that was all. Once the crisis with the child was over, she'd probably revert back to her mean old self. "I'll be in touch," she said, heading out. She had her own problems to take care of.

"Hurry!" Twyla called to her back.

Lily strode through a thick wall of humidity and eased into the Audi, blasting on the AC, mentally mapping out her errands and priorities. Concern for Twyla and Kevin added an unexpected mix to the day's errands. Her visit to Tia's hadn't yielded a name, but the clues all pointed to a spurned lover. Given Nash's past, that didn't exactly limit the suspects to one or two women. Lily considered questioning Opal about his past lovers, but decided it would put Opal in the unfair position of tattling on her boss.

She eased onto the sandy lane, making her way toward town. There was no hope for it. She had to talk to Tillman and Landry. With their training and contacts, they could help solve the mystery. And then Nash would be free from the guilt and burden of his past, clearing a path for their own relationship to progress. Right now, she sensed he held back, unwilling to draw her into his mess.

And they didn't have all the time in the world. When Nash finished this current assignment, he'd set off again, working a job that would keep him from the bayou. And her mother couldn't be put off forever. She knew her duty. It was time to stop fooling herself. If she couldn't find true love with a human male, she might as well return to sea and be with her own kind.

"What do you mean, 'keep this under our hats'?" Landry bellowed from behind the desk. "Didn't it ever occur to you that this Nash Bowman might be responsible for the deaths of his former lovers?"

"No freaking way," Lily said stiffly. "Tia Henrietta said the killer was female and motivated—"

Landry snorted. "You can't expect us to take the word of a psychic."

Tillman slashed his hand at Landry, indicating silence. "Lily," he began reasonably. "Of course we're going to look into this right away, but we can't promise not to contact Nash if we need more information. Your safety is our main concern."

Lily did battle with her pride. "Please," she said, hating to beg. "It will ruin everything if you tell him."

"Why don't you want him to know about the latest call? If he cares about you, he'll want to protect you," Tillman said.

"Unless he's the one behind these deaths," Landry added quickly.

"He's not behind them. I've known him for years."

Landry glowered. "Jet told me about him. You used to see him summers when you were kids. But people change."

"He's not a killer," she said, hot anger burning her cheeks. Tillman and Landry were each cut of the same cloth—typical law enforcement types, suspicious of everyone. She regarded their tense expressions and crisp brown uniforms with the polished silver sheriff's badges over their left front pockets. Landry was a bit more hard-edged, probably because of the violence in his family's past.

At least they'd never hit on her like most every other man in Bayou La Siryna. Lily stood and grabbed her purse. "I know neither of you has ever cared for me. You tolerate me because of Shelly and Jet. But I'm begging you for this one favor. Say nothing to Nash."

They exchanged glances and shuffled to their feet.

"I can't promise, Lily," Tillman said. "If I see something suspicious about Bowman, all bets are off."

She considered turning up the volume on her siren charm, but the thought of it made her squirm. These men were off-limits. She might be a lot of things, but she'd never betray her own sister and cousin that way. And these two were strong and decent enough men that they wouldn't let the sexual pull deter them from doing their jobs.

Landry extended a hand. "Be careful," he warned. "Let us know if anything else happens."

She shook his hand and turned away until she remembered there were two people that were dangerous. Lily whirled around. "I almost forgot. Tia mentioned to be on the lookout for Carl Dismukes. Y'all ever hear from your old deputy sheriff?"

Landry shrugged. "I've never met the man."

"Yeah, every now and then I run into him." Tillman ran a hand through his short brown hair. "He hasn't come right out and threatened me, but he insinuates that he'll bring up my father's crooked dealings when he was sheriff. Guess he's saving that news-media bombshell for the upcoming sheriff's election."

"This fall?" she asked.

He nodded.

"So what are you going to do about it?"

He raised both hands palms-up. "Nothing I can do. He knows he can't blackmail me like he did your sister. I'll have to ride out the storm if it comes."

It was no less than what she expected of Tillman. He was as honest as his dad had been corrupt. No wonder Shelly had fallen for the guy.

"What specifically did Tia Henrietta say about Dismukes?" Landry asked, voice roughened around the edges and arctic-blue eyes narrowed. He wasn't as fatalistic as Tillman, and Lily bet he wanted to confront Dismukes head-on. Somebody had to. If not, that was another item to put on her to-do list.

"Oh, so *now* you're interested in what Tia had to say?"

The jibe hit home and Landry's lips tightened.

"Typical psychic revelations," Lily mocked. "Nothing specific, other than he was a danger to all of us."

"Forget Dismukes," Tillman cut in. "We're going to check out this Nashoba Bowman. In the meantime, why don't you stay with me and Shelly until we know you're safe?"

"You have enough to worry about with Eddie," she cut in quickly. Even though Tillman's mother was several months sober, he still spent lots of time with his autistic younger brother. "And Shelly's busy with her job. It's not like either of you would be around for protection."

"You could stay with us."

Lily stared at Landry in surprise. A muscle in his jaw twitched. "Your mother's already staying with us. You might as well, too."

She laughed, guessing at the effort it took for him to extend the invitation. "No, thanks."

"You shouldn't be alone," Tillman insisted.

"I only want you to look into the records of Rebecca and Connie's deaths. I'll get their last names from Nash's assistant." Lily opened the door and the noisy hubbub of the sheriff's office filtered in—ringing phones, citizens shuffling about in the waiting room, a line of people at a desk paying tickets.

She stepped into the fray and heard Tillman call out a warning.

"Be careful."

Chapter 9

Nash threw another dried oak limb on the bonfire.

"Thank you," Lily whispered in his ear, shooting sparks of hot desire to his groin. She'd come to him yesterday, asking for his help in arranging a healing. She was acting as if his rejection on the hike hadn't happened, as if they were only two old friends.

Nash didn't know what to make of that. He should be pleased she accepted they weren't going to become lovers, but his body and heart weren't happy. Not in the least.

He forced his attention on the fire. First things first. It had been years since he'd attended one of his grandfather's healings, and Nash was curious to see if it affected him as deeply now that he was a grown man and long removed from his tribe's customs.

His grandfather had agreed to perform the healing ritual today despite the toll it would take. Physically, it exhausted Sam to do the twenty-four-hour fasting necessary to prepare. And then, once begun, the ceremony itself drained his energy. Also, he didn't like exposing his practice to those outside his tribe. Even within the tribe, a few grumbled that his work wasn't strictly according to Choctaw customs, which really ticked Nash off. Their particular band of Choctaws was a blending of many tribes anyway—Choctaw, Chickasaw, Creek, Apache, Cherokee—and Sam Bowman combined techniques from various tribes within and outside of their mixed band.

It usually worked.

"I can only honor what my spirit guides have taught me," his grandfather always said. "If someone doesn't like that, they shouldn't join the healing circle."

Sam emerged from the back door of the cabin and nodded briefly at the small group standing outside the medicine-wheel circle. The outer edge was lined with conch shells and gay granite rocks. In its center, the small fire lit the late afternoon shadows and contributed to the humid, muggy air. Nash had everything prepared according to his grandfather's instructions. By a large chair, he'd placed a mortar and pestle, several glass vials and a small empty mason jar.

Sweat and smoke stung his eyes, but Nash knew better than to complain. The sweat provided purification for the ceremony. Through the heat glaze, Lily, Twyla, J.P. and Kevin appeared distorted and fuzzy. His gaze lingered on the husband, surprised the guy had shown up given his history with Lily. Hell, it had shocked *him* when Lily had told him the healing was for Twyla's son. But J.P. had acted civil, although he was clearly on the skeptical side and careful to avoid giving Lily much attention.

Smart husband.

Sam entered through a small gap in the circle border

on the south side. He cupped a golden bowl half-filled with dried ground corn. Close to the fire, he raised it above his head. "Great Spirit, hear the prayers of your children. We stand before you humble and grateful for your many blessings. We ask a healing for Kevin." He walked a few steps to the north and lifted a handful of the dried grain, letting it slip through his fingers. His head tilted back and he closed his eyes, gathering the wisdom offered from the north. Satisfied, he repeated the same process three more times—east for gathering birth, south for growth and west for healing.

Nash fought the impulse to stand at his grandfather's side and hold his arm. Sam's face was haggard, his movements slow and slightly unsteady. He was too old and sick to fast and then endure the outside heat coupled with the mental intensity of the ceremony. He shouldn't have asked his grandfather to do this, but Lily's plea had overcome his misgivings.

At least Sam had agreed to the chair inside the sacred circle. With the supplication finished, he sank into it. His gnarled, wrinkled hands gripped the wicker arms so tightly that Nash knew its pattern would be imbedded in his palms. His back was straight as an arrow, tensed and poised for action, and his eyes were closed.

No one dared speak. Nash imagined his own face was as still and intense as the rest of the party. Even Kevin was silent. The wind carried off his feeble whimpers as if to clear the circle for the needed silence. Nash closed his eyes, too, in a long-shot attempt to help his grandfather in the shadowy spirit realm. If such a thing existed. And if he had any power to lend.

The fire popped and crackled, the sound unnaturally loud above the faint ocean waves and the more immediate rustle of birds finding their roosting spot before night settled in. The sweet smell of maize mixed with the scent of the burning sage his grandfather had asked him to place on the fire, a protection from any evil seeking mischief.

Nash's body felt light and barely rooted to the ground. The sky darkened and a hot breeze lifted hair at his nape. Muffled voices carried in the wind.

Had the heat caused his mind to play tricks? Nash opened his eyes and caught his grandfather's eyes fixed on him. Sam nodded, the movement barely perceptible. His grandfather cocked his head to the side, as if listening to the voices. Nash couldn't make out what they were saying; it was as if they were speaking some ancient language.

A piece of burning oak fell off the woodpile, sending embers spiraling upward. The sparks coalesced for a moment in the form of a starfish before melding into the shadows and losing their glow.

This was no trick, no mind game, no simple prayer request, no empty symbolic gathering. The starfish represented rejuvenation ability and lent its essence for healing the child. Nash couldn't explain how he knew this. He just did. His grandfather truly connected to actual spirits. Nash let that truth seep into his soul, obliterating his skepticism. He believed in it again as purely as he'd done in his youth.

Sam nodded, as if understanding and accepting otherworldly guidance. His hands eased their grip on the chair and he unfastened the small medicine pouch looped at the waistband of his pants. He withdrew a couple pinches of a green herb. He picked up the empty offering bowl and dropped in the herbs. Next, he opened the larger medicine bag strapped across his waist and pulled out the head of a dried cattail, a withered root, fresh silvery-green sage and a single, sharp leaf from a saw palmetto.

In the mortar and pestle he emptied a vial of liquid and slowly added snippets of the herbs and roots, crushing them to form a paste.

"What's he making?" Lily whispered by his side.

Nash laid a finger against his lips, not wanting anything to disturb his grandfather's concentration.

Sam ladled out the paste with an index finger and scooped it into the mason jar. He screwed on the lid and signaled Nash it was time for his part in the ceremony.

Nash stood and felt heat rise at the back of his neck when everyone stared. *Buck up. This is for Grandfather. For a sick child.* He undid his own medicine pouch from the waistband of his jeans and opened it, conscious he'd never done so in front of another person before. His grandfather had insisted he be a part of this healing. Had told him that when the time was right, he would be called upon to use an item from his own pouch and he would know what to do.

But what if he failed? What if *he* was the reason Kevin didn't heal? The soft brush of feather against his fingers stilled his hand. A whooshing came from above, with all the force produced by an eight-foot wingspan. Nash looked up but could barely discern a solid shape in the shadows. Citron-colored eyes surrounded by white feathers pierced through the shadow realm. The large chocolate-brown body of the bald eagle blended into the deep purple sky. A shrill piping escaped its golden beak.

Kuk-kuk-kuk. I will help you.

Nash grasped the tip of the eagle feather he'd found as a child, never realizing its discovery had been planted for this future moment. He withdrew it from his pouch, meeting Lily's curious eyes. Twyla, J.P. and their child focused on him, as well. No one looked above. No one else saw or heard what he did.

Except his grandfather.

Sam cocked his head toward the child and Nash knew what to do. He went to Kevin and the child reached out a hand, grabbed the feather and clutched it to his chest.

Nash returned to Lily's side and Sam rose from the chair, opened a sealed plastic pouch and sprinkled the brown leafy contents at each circle direction. Nash knew from times past this was tobacco, a sacred herb offered in gratitude to the spirits for their assistance.

Sam exited the circle holding the lidded jar. He ambled over to Twyla, who held her son against her right hip and arm, and placed it in her left hand. "Rub a pinch of this on his stomach every night for the next week."

J.P. eyed the green mixture with narrowed eyes. "What all is in that?"

"Nothing that will harm your son. A mixture of cattail, galangal, fresh sage and saw palmetto. His stomach ails him," Sam explained. "This will balance his digestion."

"Couldn't hurt, I guess." J.P. reached for his back pocket. "How much we owe ya?"

Sam stiffened. "I take no money for spirit work."

Twyla shot her husband a warning look. "I've already got it covered." She dug in her purse and pulled out a sealed pouch. "Will you accept this gift of tobacco?"

Sam nodded and stuffed it in his large medicine bag. "And this is for you." He produced a small dream catcher, the size of a salad plate. Feathers were attached to its wooden hoop with leather strips. "Place this by his bed at night. It will help his guardian spirits keep away those spirits who would steal your son's energy."

Kevin grabbed the dream catcher and tugged it to him, giggling as feathers tickled his face.

A look of mutual admiration passed between Sam and the child. A ping of understanding hit Nash. Little Kevin was going to be okay. The sallow skin looked pinker and the listless eyes held a newfound spark.

"You think he's cured?" Twyla asked in a rush, her voice a mixture of hope and desperation.

"The spirits have confirmed your son is fine. But I always recommend people follow up with their doctors to be safe."

Nash shook his head. Even mystical healing these days required a "cover your ass" disclaimer.

"Would save us a boatload of cash if we didn't have to travel to Birmingham," J.P. observed. He hung his head and shoved his hands into his pockets. "Not that we wouldn't do everything possible for Kevin."

"Of course," Lily agreed. She shot Nash a look of such awe and gratitude it made him squirm.

He'd done nothing to earn this respect. For years he'd barely acknowledged Sam's or his own abilities. Nash saw how selfish he'd been, even if he still wanted no part of shamanism or further development of his own earth magic.

Perhaps Sam had agreed to the healing partly to show Nash why he should respect and honor his heritage.

He moved to his grandfather's side and addressed everyone. "I think my grandfather needs a good meal and rest now. This kind of work is tiring."

Twyla and her family offered profuse thanks and hurried away. Twyla clutched the jar of green salve as if her son's life depended on it. Perhaps it did.

Lily hesitated. "Can I fix a meal for y'all before I leave?"

"Not necessary," Sam objected. "I have a pot of stew on the stove. I'll eat and then head off to bed. You two can go about the rest of your evening."

"You sure?" Nash asked. "Today's been tiring and with your—"

Sam cut him off. "What are you going to do? Hold my hand while I sleep? I'll be fine."

Nash grasped his grandfather's hand and gave it a firm shake, hoping it conveyed his love and respect. He'd been away from the bayou too long, had neglected the person who best understood him. Somehow, he had to atone for the thoughtlessness.

Sam squeezed his hand. "I am well pleased with you, Nashoba. Always knew you'd return when the time was right."

Nash covertly watched his grandfather as they made their way back to the cottage. Sam's steps were slow but sure. He'd make it up to him, would arrange to stay in Bayou La Siryna until his grandfather's heart beat for the last time.

"What did he mean about returning when the time was right?" Lily asked in a low voice.

"I'm not sure," he admitted. "Sam often speaks in riddles."

They waved goodbye to Sam and climbed into Nash's truck. Lily snuggled against Nash as best she could, considering the truck's bucket seats that separated them.

"Thanks again for talking Sam into helping them." She shot him a sideways glance. "Think it worked?"

"My grandfather says it's up to the spirits to decide if there's to be a healing, especially with babies and young children. But I believe Kevin will be fine."

"You sensed the spirits, didn't you? That's how you knew what Kevin needed from your medicine bag."

"It's not easy to explain," he hedged.

Lily tapped her fingers against her lips. "Will you take Sam's place one day as a healer?"

"Hell, no."

His answer surprised her. Nash had acted like a natural at the ceremony. She stared out the window at the dense clumps of saw palmettos and the occasional one-story cottage. After spending months at a time undersea, this was the one constant place in her life—this bayou where generations of Bosarge women had shape-shifted and found a second home of sorts. In Jet and Shelly's case, it was their primary home.

Nash turned sharply onto Main Street and drove past the drawbridge where large shrimping vessels returned with the day's harvest. "The healing art will probably die with my grandfather. Speaking of which—" Nash hesitated.

"Go on."

The sharp planes of his face grew sharper. "Sam suspects he won't make it to the Green Corn ceremony later this month."

Damn. "Can't he call on the spirits to help himself?"

"He says it's his time and he's ready."

"Surely the doctors can do something. He doesn't look so bad for his age."

"He's already had one bypass surgery and refuses another. At first, I thought he looked fine myself, but after spending time here, I see how easily he tires."

"Is that why you really came home? To help him and to say…goodbye?"

"Pretty much. Finding this assignment was easy. Gave me an excuse to hang around indefinitely."

Lily guided a hand underneath the leather cord that pulled back his long black hair and rubbed the stiff muscles at the nape. "Bet he's glad for the company."

"Mmm." He softened under her touch. "That feels incredible."

Lily reached up with her other hand and kneaded the top of his shoulder blades. "How about a full-body massage when we get to my house?" she whispered.

Nash moaned. "You do that and I might never leave."

The words lay between them, heavy and tantalizing.

"My plan is working," Lily said hoarsely.

"Sweetheart, if that's an invitation, I'm in." He laid a large palm on her bare thigh.

Her flesh burned and rippled, heat spreading upward like a current to her core. Nash slid her a molten look and shifted uncomfortably in his seat.

She cast a feverish glance out the window at the tree-lined street. Another mile. She groaned and nestled her head into his chest. Nash threaded the fingers of one hand through her hair, while the other hand gripped the steering wheel like a lifeline.

He wanted her. Really wanted her like she wanted him. It was time. She wanted to be with him as much as possible, in every way possible. The thought of him eventually leaving the bayou pinched her heart. She wouldn't think of it now. Anything could happen in the next few weeks. Tonight was for exploration, and she intended to make love to every inch of his body.

Nash hit the accelerator and she grinned into the soft cotton of his T-shirt. Soon. She sniffed, heady with the earthy male scent that belonged to him alone. "Nashoba." She whispered his name, a muffled sound that warmed his shirt against her lips.

"We're here." Truck tires crunched against the ground shells of the driveway.

Lily raised her head. Through a haze of lust, something tickled in her consciousness, a feather prickling warning sensors in the deep, primitive cerebellum. A distant warning that the world had shifted in a minor, yet important way. She cocked her head to one side, considering. No unusual sounds or smells or out-of-place objects. She scanned the yard, but nothing ominous hovered in the gathering twilight.

Ring around the rosie...

Annie's voice flashed in her memory, singing in that high-pitched creepy cadence.

Pocket full of posies...

Da duh da duh da, it chimed in a familiar singsong pace as Lily searched the shadows.

Evil surrounds me...

The evil had something to do with shadows. It was too dark—

We all fall DOWN.

Down.

Down.

At the crescendo of *down*, Lily's mind heaved like the turbulence of a strong undertow, pulling her down into its dark depths. Darkness—that's what was wrong—the house was too dark. The porch floodlight was off again.

Nash stopped the car and shot her a wary glance. "Is something wrong?"

"Looks like the porch light must have burned out." No sense alarming him until she ran out of options. Damn it, they'd been minutes away from the ultimate intimacy, and now this.

"I'll check it out."

Nash got out of the truck with the silent, fluid motion of a cat. Hands on hips, he surveyed the yard and house. Lily was certain he could sniff out danger, see and sense what she could not. Undersea, she had the same ability. Echolocation allowed her to perceive the shapes and natures of moving creatures at far distances.

Lily climbed out the passenger side and quietly approached, not wanting to disturb his concentration.

Without looking at her he raised an arm and drew her into his side.

"Go back in the truck and lock the doors." He pressed a set of keys into her hand. "I'm going to take a look at the porch light."

"I'll go with you."

He leveled her with a stern gaze. "As stubborn as you ever were." But he held her hand and proceeded forward.

"The porch light's in that corner." Lily pointed to the far right wall, and Nash picked his way through the white wicker rockers and potted ferns.

He reached up and turned the bulb, which fell immediately into his hand.

"Must have come loose?" she asked, relieved to see it hadn't been smashed.

"Must have been deliberately unscrewed."

He returned the bulb to its socket and light burst upon them with shocking intensity.

"Hand me your keys," he commanded.

Lily turned them over, thankful she wasn't alone.

"Stay behind me. And this time do as I say."

Lily snapped him a salute. "Aye, aye, sir."

He scowled, not amused. "And keep quiet."

A familiar click of the lock and he eased open the door, stepping cautiously over the threshold. Lily placed her hands on either side of his waist, face almost pressed into his back. She inhaled the earthy sandalwood scent that made her feel protected and safe. Once inside, she let go and took two steps toward the kitchen.

The iron band of his forearm blocked her path.

"Behind me," he hissed. "Light switch?"

She pointed to the left interior wall of the kitchen.

Nash flipped it on and a massive chandelier cast brilliant prisms of amber, coral and teal light into the kitchen.

Lily exhaled and spoke without bothering to keep her voice low. "I must have forgotten to turn it on when I left earlier."

"There's still the matter of the front porch light. I don't like it. Not after you told me about the phone calls."

"I'm sure it's nothing." Yet she glanced around the pristine room where everything appeared in place.

"Let's check the rest of the house to be sure," Nash said with a frown.

Lily led him through the downstairs rooms, which showed no signs of disturbance. She was beginning to feel foolish. Maybe that trip to see Tia Henrietta had done more harm than good, had put unwarranted suspicions in her mind. They proceeded upstairs and did a walk-through of the bedrooms, saving hers for last.

The closed door to her bedroom gave her pause. The only time she'd ever kept this room shut was after Jet's dog, Rebel, had chewed on a pair of her designer shoes. Now that her sister and the dog were gone, there was no reason to shut it. Lily halted, hand on the knob, a faint echo of a child's song bouncing in her mind. *It's okay. Nash is here.*

Nash laid a hand over her own. "I'll go in first."

She stepped back. "No argument from me this time."

He snapped on the light and a fusillade of color bombarded Lily. The worst damage was at the back wall where her easels and paintings were stored.

Slashing X tears ripped through her latest watercolor. An explosion of acrylics had been smeared across her other works mounted on a drafting table in the far right corner. Angry rainbows of blues, greens and purples marred her delicate artwork. Paint tubes lay scattered on the floor, twisted and empty. In the middle of her lavender-flowered bedspread was a huge blob of red paint in the shape of a severed heart.

Her ears buzzed as if a cacophony of ricocheting bullets had been fired.

Someone hated her. Hated her with a primal fury that wouldn't be sated until her own heart was gutted and bared like the painted one on the bedspread. *Why?* She stepped forward, dazed, fingers outstretched and trembling, wanting to touch the red acrylic, wanting to prove this was real.

"Don't touch anything," Nash said harshly. "The police will want everything undisturbed. I'm calling them now."

"What if someone's still here?" She glanced at the frilly lace bed skirt, wondering if the childhood bogeyman she imagined living underneath might have morphed into the real thing—ready to snake out a hand and grab her ankles if she neared its lair. Her gaze shifted to the open closet door and then the attached bathroom.

Nash stopped mid-dial, fingers poised above his cell phone. "Right. Better check first." He stuffed the phone into his back pocket, grabbed a broom that leaned against a wall and strode to the closet. He ran it through the rows of clothing as if he were wielding a weapon, ready to impale anyone hiding among the clothes. "Nothing there."

Lily jumped out of his way as he headed to the bed; the fury on his face was wild and primitive. She wouldn't want to be on the receiving end of such raw anger.

Nash lifted the bed skirt and slashed through the underbelly of her bed with the broom. "All clear there."

He straightened, eyes unfocused, as if sensing something beyond the immediate.

"Let's get out of here," Lily urged. "What if there's someone here? Someone armed?"

He was past reason, intent on finding the culprit. Nash acted as if he didn't even hear her.

"There's something here," he murmured. "Something alive and deadly." Ever so slowly his neck swiveled toward the bathroom door. "There."

Lily raised a hand and laid it over the vulnerable, exposed carotid artery and windpipe beneath her neck. "Don't go in there," she rasped.

But Nash lifted the broom in his right hand and didn't turn. "Stay where you are."

As if. This was her house, after all, and she needed to know how far this violation of her space extended. Lily followed.

He jerked open the shower curtain and the top rings screeched and clanged against the metal rail. At eye level, the baby-pink tile was visible and she uncurled her fists, relieved not to find…someone…a monster in hiding. A loud machine-gun rattle erupted and bounced around the tiled room. She'd never heard a rattlesnake, but its dry buzz of warning sent an instinctual chill down her spine. Her scalp prickled with awareness. Despite the heavy dread thickening her threat, Lily inched closer.

A diamondback rattler wriggled inside a large black mesh bag attached to the faucet head. Coiled into an S shape and fangs bared, it signaled attack mode. She bit back the high-pitched scream burning inside her lungs. "That's one pissed-off snake," she said, voice thin and reedy.

"More terrified of us than we are of him."

"I doubt that," Lily muttered.

Nash leaned in closer to the tub and she tugged the back of his T-shirt. "Don't get in striking range."

"I'm not stupid. What's it doing in that bag?"

"Whoever left it didn't want it crawling off. They wanted to make sure you saw it."

Nash chanted words unintelligible to her. Probably Choctaw, she guessed. His deep baritone underpinned the snake rattle like a bass in a macabre war song. The rattler retracted its fangs and the striped tail lowered fractionally.

Lily gave a shaky laugh. "What are you—a snake charmer?"

He didn't bother answering but continued chanting until the snake uncoiled and lay flat. Lily didn't let go of her grip on his T-shirt. Nash would keep her safe. He was solid as the earth itself. Dependable. Even at age twelve when he'd found her in the woods. She'd heard his voice first, calling her name, and had known immediately that all was well. As long as she held on to him, no striking snake could sink its fangs into her, no evil could befall her. Nash wouldn't allow it. She let the knowledge sink in deep, let it warm her chilled body and stay the shivering and chattering teeth.

"Get me a bedsheet," Nash said, eyes never leaving the snake.

Reluctantly, Lily released her hold on his shirt and raced to her bed. She hesitated. What if another snake was coiled beneath the bedspread? She kept her body as far from the mattress as possible, leaned over and yanked off the bedspread. So much for not touching anything. Thankfully, there was no nasty hidden surprise. An exterminator would have to do a thorough sweep of the house before she ever set foot in it again. She quickly stripped off the cover linen and rushed back to the adjoining bathroom.

Nash grabbed the sheet and spread it on the tile floor. He resumed chanting, lifted the mesh bag with its deadly bundle and placed it in the middle of the sheet. He gathered the cloth and tied it at the ends. "This is only for a little while," Nash said, addressing the bagged snake. "You'll be released in the woods later." He set the bag by the door and Lily backed away, giving the wriggling bundle a wide berth.

She went to the bedroom and stared again at the ruined paintings. All that work, all that painstaking detail she'd created with such hope and pride—gone. She barely listened as Nash placed the emergency call.

Nash came by her side and placed the heavy weight of an arm across her shoulders. "All your beautiful paintings," he whispered.

Her chances of entering and winning the prestigious art competition lay destroyed among the slashed watercolors. Her hopes and dreams were destroyed, too, detonated by some anonymous bomb of fury. A few more days and she'd have had them packaged and in the mail. The sharp edges and harsh lines of ripped paintings blurred.

"I'll never win that competition now." She raised her hands to her eyes, trying to staunch the ridiculous tears. Her nonexistent art career should be the least of her worries.

"What competition?"

"Some dumb event that I hoped would get my art noticed." No doubt he'd think her twice as vain as when he'd first come back to the bayou. "It's not like I had a real chance of winning anyway."

Nash studied what remained of her work. "Sure, you had a shot at winning. These are amazing."

"*Were* amazing."

He enveloped her in his strong arms.

It undid her. Lily sobbed into his chest, mourning the loss of her dream.

"There'll be other contests," he whispered into the top of her scalp, his breath warm and comforting. "Other paintings."

"I know," she agreed, crying all the harder. Stupid to let the paintings matter more than the threat to her life. More than Nash's feelings. She swallowed hard and gazed up. "You're right. We need to focus on what's really wrong, on discovering this enemy."

He disentangled from her arms and lifted her chin. "*I* need to figure it out. Not you."

"No." She couldn't let him pull away from her now. Not when they'd drawn so close. "We'll do it together."

"I should have known this would follow me." Nash slammed a fisted hand into the palm of the other. "The past hounds me. I'll never be free."

His wounded fury hurt worse than anything else that had happened. He'd suffered more than anyone should have to endure. Regret and guilt pricked her conscience. She hadn't used Sam's sage for days. If she'd smudged the house like he'd instructed, maybe none of this would have happened. "It isn't your fault. Some crazy, obsessed woman is to blame."

"Why the hell would you say that?"

"I went to see a woman who...sees things, *knows* things. You met her a few times when you were little. Tia Henrietta?" she questioned.

Nash folded his arms, unresponsive and withdrawn.

"Tia told me I'm being harassed by a woman motivated by love and that she's killed more than once."

He paced the bedroom, consumed with his own thoughts, working out the facts.

"Don't shut me out, Nash," Lily implored. "I know this

is hard for you to accept. But deep down, haven't you always suspected Rebecca's and Connie's deaths weren't accidents? Even without evidence?"

He stopped pacing and faced her. "Of course I have. Makes the guilt a million times worse."

She moved to him, wanting to cross the distance between them, to comfort him. "There's no reason for you—"

Nash held up his hands, blocking her advance, stopping her words. "Tia give you a name?"

"No."

A siren blared in the distance. Lily glanced out the lace-curtained window, where flashing red-and-blue lights strobed through oak and cypress limbs. "I should probably warn you about my brothers-in-law. They're the sheriff and deputy sheriff in this county. I spoke with them this morning about my...situation."

Nash nodded. "Good."

"I told them because there've been more calls."

His eyes hardened. "And you had no intention of telling me, did you?"

She'd promised him and now he took her omission as a betrayal. "I didn't want you to worry. I—I was afraid you'd leave me."

Headlights beamed through the window, casting his face in sharp focus, luminous against the darkness.

He was in no mood for apologies.

But she at least had to warn him of what was about to burst upon them. "There's something you should know," Lily continued miserably. "Tillman and Landry—my brothers-in-law—immediately jumped to the wrong conclusions. You know how suspicious and jaded cops are."

"They think I'm responsible for Rebecca's and Connie's deaths and whatever befalls you now." His words were hard and scratchy, like two granite rocks scraping against one another.

Reluctantly, she nodded.

"It won't be the first time I've been under suspicion. And here we go again."

The empty resignation in his voice, the flatness of his eyes, bruised her heart. "I know you've done nothing wrong. I'll make them listen."

The trill of her recently purchased cell phone made her jump. Probably the cops wanting the front door unlocked. The text on the flat screen glowed with two words.

He's mine.

Chapter 10

It was happening again, Nash realized. Past and present merged into a maelstrom of despair, anger, regret, frustration. Who was behind this? Why?

He rubbed his temples, trying to stamp out what felt like a swarm of stinging bees beneath the sensitive flesh.

"You must have some guess as to what's going on here." The sheriff cut him a hard stare and gestured at the slashed paintings. "This is the third woman who's been harassed after being involved with you."

"If I had a clue, I'd tell you. For the last time, I don't know." He kept his tone as flat and neutral as his interrogator. Sheriff Tillman Angier and his deputy, Landry Fields—or the BILs, as Lily liked to call them—did nothing to conceal their distrust of Nash.

The sheriff held up an index finger. "First, it's Rebecca Anders. She crashes her car weeks after a string of harassing phone calls with a message to break it off with you." He held up a second finger. "Then, two years later, Connie Enstep has a drug overdose. Again, after receiving a mysterious phone call warning her away from you. And now—" he waved a hand at the vandalism "—this."

Damn. It sounded incriminating as hell. He'd tried to convince himself with the first two that it was coincidence, even when his instincts had rejected the notion. But with a third occurrence, there was no denying it any longer. An unknown evil was wreaking havoc in his affairs, crushing out any woman he'd tried—however casually—to let into his life. "You're not telling me anything I don't already know."

"Leave him alone." Lily spoke up from behind. "I wish I'd never told you about the calls."

"You did the right thing," Fields admonished. "We looked into the records today and I don't like what we found." He leveled glacial blue eyes on Nash. "You have quite the reputation as a ladies' man."

"And I have my own reputation in Bayou La Siryna," Lily cut in. "Doesn't mean I'm a killer. Besides, he has the perfect alibi. We were together when someone crept in and destroyed my bedroom."

Nash's lips curled up involuntarily. Lily's swift defense was a relief. She understood him and didn't judge, a rare occurrence in his experience. Her belief in his character and innocence was absolute. All anger at the broken promise evaporated.

"No one's accusing Mr. Bowman of murder or even conspiracy to commit murder," said Angier. "We're trying to protect you and find out who's behind this."

"Then get your fingerprints from my room and trace the calls or whatever it is you do to find the bad guys."

A look passed between the BILs and, as if in unspoken

agreement, Fields took Lily by the hand, subtly guiding her to the opposite side of the large bedroom.

"Now, look here," Sheriff Angier said in a hushed voice. "Lily is family. I can't let anything happen to her like the others. If you have any ideas who the culprit might be, spit it out."

"For the hundredth time, I don't know."

Angier studied him. "Tell me about these two other women. Were they serious relationships?"

Nash gritted his teeth. No matter how he answered, he was damned. If he said they were serious, the sheriff would think he had arranged for them to be killed because he got cold feet. If he said they weren't serious, the sheriff would think he didn't care they'd been killed or, worse, that he had tried to get rid of them permanently. Might as well tell the truth.

"More serious on their part than mine," he admitted. A familiar twist in the gut tugged at Nash. They'd deserved love and commitment. Instead, his job had always been the top priority. "But it was devastating. Especially wondering if their deaths were connected to me in some way."

"No doubt about the connection now. Not with a third person threatened."

"I won't let anything happen to Lily," Nash vowed, mind racing on the best way to keep her from harm. It needed to be someplace remote, somewhere that allowed him to use his gifts to advantage.

Angier's lips pressed to a grim line. "And how are you going to do that?"

How, indeed. He should never have gotten involved in another relationship. But since he had, it was too late to end it now and still keep Lily safe. An image of swaying sea oats and a knell of cypress trees arose. "I'll take her to Herb Island with me."

A sharp gasp came from behind.

"You will?" Lily's face suffused with a glow, as if he'd presented her with an unexpected present. She was the one beautiful, perfect thing in this nightmare of an evening. The thought of her meeting one of those mysterious, unfortunate accidents twisted his guts. A pressing urge screamed inside him to whisk Lily up and instantly escape to the island.

"Is there anything else?" he asked the sheriff. "We'd like to be on our way."

Sheriff Angier addressed Lily. "You don't have to go with him. Shelly would love to have you stay with us until the investigation ends."

"Or you could stay with me and Jet," the deputy offered. "Your mom wants to spend more time with you, anyway, during her visit."

"I'm going with Nash. I'll pack while you finish up in here." She turned and looked over her shoulder. "How long do you think we'll be gone? Oh, never mind. I'll pack a bunch and come back later if I need to."

"Impulsive," said Deputy Fields. "Just like her sister."

"Stubborn as Shelly," Angier said with a rueful shake of his head.

Nash raised a brow. "Runs in the family, I see?"

Angier snickered. "Better get used to it."

Nash couldn't blame them for their concern. If he were in their shoes, he'd have the same misgivings. "I'll protect her," he vowed again.

Angier held out a hand. "I'm holding you to it. Your grandfather is one of the finest men I've ever known. And Lily obviously trusts you."

Nash shook the proffered hand, humbled and relieved at the overture. "The island should be safe. I'm the only one out there at night. Even during the day, there are few tourists. If any woman from my past shows up, I'll know it right away."

"I approve," Angier said with a nod. "And Ned Brock, who operates the ferry, can keep a log of everyone that boards for the island."

Deputy Fields opened a notebook and scribbled. "Here's our cell phone numbers if you need us. The ferry's closed for the day. Where will you spend tonight?"

"We can stay with my grandfather." But the idea stirred a qualm of unease in his gut at placing the old man in jeopardy. If he and Lily avoided his grandfather's place, Sam would be safer.

Angier was already pressing buttons on his cell. "No point drawing Sam into this mess. I'll have Ned make a special run tonight. He's made them before for emergencies."

Lily dragged over two suitcases. "We can grab some provisions from my pantry. Should I bring linens, too?"

"No. There's plenty at the lodge," Nash said. "Opal arranged everything before we arrived."

"Who's Opal?" Angier asked.

"Opal Wallace, my photographic assistant. She was here a week or so when I first arrived, but she left on another assignment."

Deputy Fields wrote down the name in a small notebook. "Opal Wallace. Tell me about this woman." He snapped the book shut.

Nash shrugged. "What do you want to know? I've worked with her on and off over the past several years on various projects. She's an excellent photographer in her own right, but works with me as an assistant between her jobs."

"Opal's my friend," Lily said quickly. "She's been

gone for days, so she couldn't have anything to do with this break-in."

"Better safe—" Angier began.

"—than sorry. Yeah, yeah. We get it." Lily waved a hand dismissively and faced Nash. "I'm ready."

The sun called him. Fire rays of warmth that beckoned Nash to arise and greet the new morn. Even lying in bed, eyes closed and head cradled in clean-smelling cotton linen, he divined the sun's energy had risen.

He'd lain in bed awake most of the night, stiff and tense, unable to relax after the evening's hellish events. But sleep had briefly claimed him unawares in the darkness. Nash pushed aside the sheet, untangling his long legs, and walked to the window. Drawing the curtain, he took in the dawn's ascension over the brackish water, its light shimmering in bits of silver, as if the Great Spirit had tossed chips of clear quartz crystal across the sea. Clouds of violet and magenta danced in the sky. It felt like a sign, hope for a new beginning.

Time to confront the past and stop the killer. Time to seek help from any source. Time to accept any comfort offered and mentally prepare for what was to come.

He'd traveled the world and seen thousands of majestic sites, but nothing sang to Nash's soul like his homeland. Like this moment of peace and promise in the land of his ancestors.

Don't fight it, his grandfather had said. *Listen to the land and its creatures and the spirits of your ancestors in the piney woods and the Gulf breeze.* Sun heat invigorated his body with a glow of energy. For the Choctaw, his tribe and nation, the sun endowed life, was the epicenter of the world that illuminated Mother Earth and Father Sky.

I will fight no more. For the first time in two decades, calm washed his mind, cleansed his quibbling and unease with his extraordinary connection to nature and earth's creatures. Accepting the gifts didn't mean he'd have to end up like his grandfather, stuck in the bayou and serving as some ad hoc medicine man. No matter where the next assignment led, he'd keep a piece of home in his heart. His talents were a gift and, if possible, he intended to use them to help keep Lily safe.

The need to be outside and greet the sun gripped him with a passion as fervent as the animalistic urge to mate in spring. Quietly, so as not to awaken Lily in the adjoining room, he pulled on a pair of loose drawstring pants and gathered the needed tools to bless the morning—a ritual he and his grandfather had shared in days past. Arms laden with a woolen blanket and totems, Nash tread barefoot across the sun-warmed oak floor and opened the screen door, pausing at the rusty screech of its hinges.

He stilled, ears attuned to the slightest sound from the next room, but Lily didn't stir. Still barefoot, Nash walked down the porch steps until his calloused feet sank into the white sand that held the warmth of yesterday's sunlight. Cerulean warblers chirped a welcome that seemed a personal greeting for him. *Chirrup. Chirrup. Come into the light.* As if he had done it all his life, had walked this path before. Nash picked his way to shore until he arrived at a mound of sand dunes. In between the dunes he spotted a level middlemost point where the sand mounds surrounded him on all sides like a private oasis.

Here.

He climbed a dune plumaged with sea oats and arrived at a consummate ceremonial spot. At once, he spread out the turquoise, red and yellow blanket with a woven symbol of the sun and the crossed kabocca sticks. Carefully, he arranged the materials—his ever-present medicine pouch, a leather-sheathed hunting knife, a bag of cornmeal and bald-eagle and turkey feathers. He grasped the waistband of his pants and tugged, shedding the cloth that separated his body from all that was natural and free.

Unencumbered, Nash stretched his arms toward the sky. An ocean breeze lifted his long hair to the winds; the salty air swooshed every inch of his skin in blessing. He lifted his head, closed his eyes and fully experienced creation. The eternal crash of the tides pulsed through blood and bone and sinew, the sun caressed his naked body and, through the blanket, the soles of his feet yoked to the earth's core, grounding and centering. He inhaled the clean scent of water and salt as savory as a bountiful feast to a starving man.

This was what he'd been missing for years, what he'd unknowingly sought in wild African safaris, in the chill, lonely splendor of the Arctic, the high mountains of Nepal and the valley of the Grand Canyon. Ancestral land held a sacred belonging unparalleled anywhere else one roamed. To walk among one's forefathers and behold the place where they'd once breathed and loved and struggled and eventually died and returned to dust.

Incredible. Nash dropped his hands and opened his eyes, eager to express his gratitude, his blessings, all the more precious from the guilt and regret he'd suffered the past three years. He dropped to the blanket and sat crosslegged, the totems within arm's reach. He opened the suede medicine pouch and emptied its treasures: the tip of an eagle's feather, a vial of dirt from the backyard of his grandfather's cottage, tiny perfect shells he'd collected as a boy, a sand dollar, a smooth carnelian pebble and a narrow beaded bracelet crafted and handed down from some unknown female relation. He let the sunlight bathe and bless the relics, renewing their energy and spirit.

Nash held up the turkey and eagle feathers to the light before braiding them into his hair, framing both sides of his face. And this might be what helped him heal and find answers. After bubbling burst from deep in his throat, he chanted, *I seek and accept all that is offered.*

This was good. This was right. This was his heritage. No more would he shut out the gift or resist what was so freely offered. Nash again stood, lifting the bag of cornmeal. He opened it and grabbed a fistful of the golden maize that had been the sustenance of his people over the ages. With a powerful thrust, he released the ground corn, scattering it in the Gulf wind. Turning in all directions, he tossed more cornmeal in private thanksgiving. An offering to the earth in thanks for its power and bounty. Grains of yellow corn mixed with the pristine white sand. In a final movement, he emptied the bag in one fell swoop, watching the swirl of it rise upward and then fall to the ground.

Over and beyond the dunes, a woman with silver-blond hair stood and waved. Her blue nightgown fluttered in the breeze like an errant pool of water, and then it pressed against the feminine curves of her body.

Lily.

She approached with a dignity and purpose he admired. He wouldn't let anyone hurt her. She possessed an inner strength and beauty that called to him as strongly as any ancient spirit. He'd never experienced this call with anyone else. Never been drawn to want to completely possess a woman. This longing to be with Lily felt as natural and as deep as his connection to earth and sun. As before, an otherworldly message heralded her presence. A lone seagull screeched. *Two spirits.* Another squalled, *but your destiny.*

She wasn't what he'd thought he wanted in a woman. Nothing about her was normal. Lily was as mysteriously tied to the bayou as his spirit was bound and connected. Lily accepted and believed in his Choctaw roots, his connection to the land and its creatures. And he wanted her with all his heart. Mind, soul and body yearned to be one with Lily and discover all her secrets.

And so he stood, naked and unashamed and open.

Unbounded black hair fluttered wildly in the wind like a constable of ravens, alerting Lily to where Nash had disappeared. The screeching of the screen door had awakened her from restless dreams of exploding cars, empty pill bottles and a dark menace hovering in the mist.

She walked closer until she was near enough to see past the dunes and view his body.

His naked body.

Bronzed and muscled, Nash stood as proud and powerful as a warrior. *Her* warrior. For as long as he stayed and wanted her in return. Anticipation quickened her pace. She ached to be one with him.

The first ferry ride to the island was hours away. They were alone on this paradise and Lily intended to make the most of it. They'd arrived late last night, somber and weary. Nash had matter-of-factly showed her around the small wooden lodge, pointing out where supplies and toiletries were kept. He'd immediately retired to a separate bedroom, obviously wishing solitude after the grueling realization that the past's evils had followed him all the way to this remote bayou.

Two seagulls screeched as they dove down and flew between her and Nash.

As before, Lily fancied their arrival was intentional and that they mysteriously communicated with Nash. Not that any of that mattered at the moment.

She would greet him as unafraid and bold as he stood before her. Lily slipped off her nightdress and held it casually bunched in one hand. Nash was still as a sturdy oak, but his eyes darkened with a need that matched her own. She stumbled in the sand but regained her balance and kept walking, undeterred. Nothing could stop her from joining with Nashoba. Nothing. Even if he broke her heart when he left. If she returned to sea with her mother and rejoined the merfolk, she'd do so knowing her heart would forever stay with Nash no matter where he wandered the earth.

No. She wouldn't think of it now. Wouldn't allow the unforeseeable future, or last night's events, to rob the present.

She was so close. A few more feet. Nash held out his arms and she stepped into his embrace, his strength. They clung to each other, the breeze whipping around their bodies. She buried her head in his smooth, broad chest as her hands explored the hard, silky skin of his back, stretched taut over lean muscles coiled tight as a loaded spring. She didn't want to move. Ever. Not even for a millisecond to let go and raise her face for a kiss.

Nash's hands entangled in her hair and cupped the base of her neck. He lifted her face as he lowered his own. Lily closed her eyes, her last sight the full lips coming to press against her mouth. A whimpering rumbled in her throat until Nash's tongue invaded and quieted her cries.

Oh, he was skilled. A master kisser. Just the right pressure, just the right amount of teasing and claiming. The press of his need against her stomach fevered her core and she rocked her hips against him. She didn't know how it happened—there was a sensation of falling—and then she lay on a blanket, Nash's body covering her own. The delicious heaviness of his weight anchored her so there was no escape. Not that she ever wanted to be anywhere but here, making love with Nash.

His erection pressed against her womanhood and she lifted her hips, aching for him to fill her as she signaled her readiness.

Nash rose up on his elbows and stared down, eyes harsh and stern with desire. "Are you sure about this?" he asked, his voice as hoarse as the screeching seagulls that had flown between them earlier.

Lily marveled at the contrast of her voice compared to Nash's. Where hers flowed, liquid and beguiling, his rumbled in a deep baritone, as powerful as an earthquake, the low notes vibrating deep in her core. "I want you," she moaned. "So much."

Nash sank and lowered his head until their foreheads touched. "I'm nothing but trouble. I've brought pain to anyone I've been close with."

"Even if that were true, I don't care." Lily ran her fingers through his long hair, which was smooth and fluid as water.

"I won't let anything happen to you, Lily," he said, his breath fierce and hot upon her face. "I promise."

She'd never felt so protected, so safe. *Everything will be fine.* "I know you won't." She kissed him and again rocked her hips against his stiff manhood, ready for him to claim her as his own, to be as one.

Nash planted a series of featherlight kisses down her neck and shifted his body back as he edged lower. He cupped a breast in his large, calloused hand and Lily sucked in her breath. His mouth came down and suckled one nipple, then another. Wet heat flicked her sensitive buds until she pushed at his shoulders. "Let's do it," she said raggedly.

"No way."

He shook his head, obsidian hair falling over the sides of her face, neck and shoulders, a velvet veil that obscured everything, as if they formed their own private island that excluded the world. There was only this moment, this passion, the exquisite sensations that left them both trembling and consumed. Lily could see nothing but the harsh planes of his jaw and high cheekbones and burning stare. The green of his irises darkened, lasered through her defenses until she was stripped clean—raw and trembling and desperate for Nash to claim her body. To be so filled deep inside that the soft curves of her body melded into his muscled strength and hardness.

"Now," she insisted.

He grinned, a pure male smile of pride. "No. Not for all the pirate treasure supposedly hidden in Bayou La Siryna."

Lily would have laughed if she hadn't been so frustrated. She was used to calling the shots in everything. *Everything.* But this time, Nash wielded control.

It pissed her off. And excited her.

Nash shifted his weight until he lay alongside her and cupped her breasts, fingers kneading the soft flesh. Eyes still on her, he rolled a nipple between his thumb and index finger.

And squeezed.

Lily moaned as her core tightened and inner thighs pressed together. Nash lowered his hand past her rib cage until it rested over her belly. The warmth of his fingers and hand splayed over her stomach was tender—and a pregnant pause that foretold more to come.

She'd waited long enough. Lily shifted in the sand

until she also lay on one side. Gently, teasingly, she ran a finger down his hard shaft and cupped the tight, hard sacks at its base.

And squeezed.

This time, it was Nash who groaned with need.

"Now, please," Lily breathed, face pressed into his wide chest.

In one fluid motion, Nash lay on his back and pulled her so that she straddled his midsection. Lily threw back her head and closed her eyes. The sun shone down on her exposed skin, seeping into every pore like a blessing. The tide surged, crested, broke and then surged again, timeless and powerful.

I'll never be the same. Another moment, and my life changes. Lily knew it, as if the universe sang the message in her ear.

No more begging. Nash seemed to want her as badly as she wanted him. He guided her over his shaft and entered, filling her, claiming her in a way she'd never experienced.

They moved, slowly at first and then faster. Harder. She locked eyes with his, studying the awed, determined darkening of his dilated pupils. The blue of her irises was reflected in his like round orbs of water in a pool of blackness. Mind, body and soul joined and bound together until they melded in a fire as bright and hot as the risen sun.

Talk about backfire. *Stupid, stupid, stupid.* Opal clawed the right side of her face, her sharpened fingernails abrading the skin around the scar. She'd driven that bitch right into his bed, his heart.

Lordy, she hated this stinking bayou that reeked like rotten fish. And the heat! It was smothering and thick as sickly sweet syrup that coated your skin until you were constantly sticky and nasty-feeling.

The cheap motel room was as tiny and constricting as a jail cell. She'd suffered it for days now, venturing out only at night—scurrying about like a rat searching for a bite to eat. The only daylight she'd been out in was when she'd gone to Lily's house to execute the final warning. Sneaking in had been as easy as leaving a utility room window cracked when Lily had invited her over for dinner before she supposedly left the bayou.

Easy entrance, but no fun. There was a faint herbal scent that was off-putting, yet not strong enough to keep her away. She'd spent hours rambling about the house, seething at the opulence. Rich bitch.

Opal held out her hand—the blue sapphire mounted on the gold ring gleamed mockingly under the fluorescent light. Lily would never miss it. She had dozens of jewelry boxes stuffed with such baubles. Opal had opened each one, fuming at the pearl bracelets, ruby necklaces, emerald brooches and precious stones in every rainbow color, every shade and hue of expensive stone.

And that closet, row upon row of expensive, lacy and satiny concoctions. Opal ran a hand down the bubble-gum-pink nightgown she'd lifted. Lily would be breathtaking in it. But on her, the ultra-feminine gown was a mockery.

This was supposed to be *her* time with Nash on Herb Island. She'd undergone three plastic surgeries until the idiot doctors claimed the scar was barely noticeable and was as good as it was going to get. Damn liars. She was a Frankenstein. She'd wanted perfection before telling Nash she loved him, but now would have to do.

Lily was ruining everything. That woman could have

any man she wanted in the bayou, yet she selfishly had to claim Nash.

It was so unfair.

Why didn't they ever listen to her warnings? Lily was as daft as Rebecca and Connie had been. You tried to play fair with people, you gave them a warning, and they continued to go their own selfish way. Just once, Opal wished she'd been given more warnings growing up. But no, she was never given advance notice of when the next move would take place. One day a social worker would pull up in a government-issued sedan, tell her to pack her bag of belongings and that would be that. On to a new foster home.

At first, Opal had been terrified of a new family and new school but always hoped *this* time would be better. That *this* time they would love her. *This* time they wouldn't find her strange. This time she'd be well-fed. This time she wouldn't be beaten.

The memory of the last family haunted her. They'd been kind initially; the foster parents were gentle and their son had…liked her. Liked her *lots*. Tommy would sneak into her bedroom in the dead of night and show his love. It had been glorious up until the moment his mother had caught them. She'd shrieked and shaken Opal so hard she'd wondered if it was possible to die of adolescent-shaking syndrome. Her head had whipped back and forth so forcefully Opal had been sure her neck would break.

The shrieking had stopped, followed by a venomous hiss. *Don't you ever come near my son again, you filthy slut. What would the neighbors say?*

That had been the first and last warning.

She and Tommy had been oh-so-careful after that, knowing their time together was limited since his mom had told the social worker to take her away at the end of the month. But there wouldn't even be that if they were caught again; she'd be out on the streets immediately.

Opal had learned to school her features, to give the appearance of calm and nonchalance, even when her inner world roiled with self-loathing and despair. The external could be controlled if she was very, very careful to mask her pain.

On the last night with them, the foster mom had evidently been lying in wait for the creak in the hallway. Again, Opal was jerked up in the woman's vise and the shaking and shrieking had started again. *I warned you! I warned you!* Opal was disoriented, the room blurry and spinning. Why didn't Tommy help her?

With a mighty thrust Opal never would have guessed the petite foster mom had in her, the pinching, bruising hold on her arms was gone and she fell forward, toppling into a dresser. Her face smashed against a mirror. An explosion of glass shards pricked her face and wet goo inched down her neck. She sank to the floor, palming the shredded flesh of her right cheek, her screams mingling with the foster mother's.

She'd escaped the system at age eighteen. It had been rough but better. The thing was to keep moving, keep on the run, keep to yourself. And always, always maintain.

She'd survived. Opal hated the platitude "What doesn't break you makes you stronger."

No. Her life was nothing but brokenness, even if the only evidence was the scar on her cheek and the ones on her forearms from the self-induced cutting. The blessed cutting that allowed a small portion of the pain to seep out with the blood. A minidetox for the soul.

Opal rushed inside the motel bathroom and unwrapped a new razor. The thin edge of the blade flashed like quicksilver in the afternoon rays before sinking into her skin. The sharp bite of pain was so bittersweet, pain and pleasure intermingled like animal sex. Hurting so good she moaned. A ruby rush of liquid ran down her arm, sticky and hot. With the letting came clarity.

She'd handle Lily. Take her rightful place in Nash's arms. He loved her, she knew it. If he didn't realize it, he'd learn to. Rebecca, Connie and Lily bound them together. He'd know he was at fault for their deaths as much as she was—and that death and secrets yoked an unbreakable tie.

He'd be her forever love. Her forever home. And if he left, she would follow him to every square inch of the globe and poison any other woman he ever looked at. She would warn him of her intention, too.

Because you had to be fair about it. If you didn't play fair, you were as bad as the rest of them, deserving of hell and vengeance and death. Those filthy sluts deserved to die.

As did Lily.

Chapter 11

Nash stroked the curve of Lily's hip as she lay on her side, one arm stretching out, head cradled on her forearm, eyes closed. He wished he had his camera to capture the image of his dark, rough hand as his fingers rested on the fair plane of her hip. Lily's skin wasn't a pure vanilla-white. Pinpricks of pink and silver and green and blue pastels shimmered, as if she'd been dipped in crushed mica. A black-and-white photo alone couldn't capture the nuances of Lily's beauty.

One day he'd have to ask her permission to photograph her nude. Not for public view, but for his own nostalgic remembrance when he was alone again far from his bayou home.

Home. Nash eased up on an elbow, determined to move past such sentimental musings. Special as it was, the bayou was not home. The world was his home. He'd achieved a slice of fame, and a milder portion of fortune, but he was in his prime, beginning what could be a long, profitable career. He could maybe even become the best wildlife photographer ever.

Better yet, he would leave Bayou La Siryna with the issue of the mysterious stalker resolved and be here for his grandfather in his dying days.

If this morning was no hallucination—no trick of the mind—if Lily was truly his destiny, then she would have to follow him. But he couldn't imagine her uprooting from this place and her family.

Nash ran his hand up and down Lily's right thigh. "Hey, sleepyhead, you'll burn up if you stay naked out here with no sunscreen."

Blue eyes popped open. "True. My skin burns in no time."

"I remember."

Even as a kid, Lily had been fastidious about applying sunscreen and avoiding direct sun at midday. Nash grinned as Lily retrieved and shook out the now-wrinkled nightgown. She pulled it on and began braiding her long hair, the colorful beads of her friendship bracelet highlighting the graceful bend of her wrist.

"Allow me." He took hold of her hair, gently teased it into three parts and weaved them into a thick plait, enjoying the feel of shifting satin in the roughened skin of his palms and fingers. He tugged gently at the end. "You have anything to fasten it with?"

"No, but this will do to keep the wind from whipping my face until we reach the lodge."

Nash kissed the exposed nape of her neck and an unexpected tenderness twisted inside. It would be hard to leave Lily. And he wouldn't until the killer was found and she was safe.

With effort, Nash brushed aside the worry that invaded his peace. This morning was for exploration and he wanted to prolong the lightness from his burdens. He couldn't recall the last time he'd felt so free, so light and open.

Inspiration struck. "How about a morning swim?"

"You know I can't swim." She stood and stretched, the thin nightgown so transparent he could trace the rosy nipples and thatch of hair between her legs. He imagined the gown wet and plastered against her skin.

"C'mon, I'll teach you," he said past the thickness of his tongue. "It'll be fun."

"I don't want to learn."

Lily stepped off the blanket and dug her pretty pedicured toes in the sand. "Shouldn't we head back to the lodge for breakfast?" she asked.

Nash rose. "We're on an island. Now's the perfect time to learn to swim."

Impatience swept across her face. "Maybe later."

"Okay." He dropped a kiss on her forehead. "No swim lessons. But let's bathe in the ocean. You don't have to go farther than waist-deep. I'll hold you."

Lily turned up her exquisite nose and he laughed, feeling as playful as he had in childhood. On impulse, he scooped her into his arms and twirled her around. Lily threw back her head and giggled. The sound enchanted him.

"You trust me, right?" he asked.

She lightly brushed her fingers along the side of his neck. "With my life. After all, you saved me once before." She grew serious. "I never thanked you properly."

"No need," he assured her. "I think you just did."

Lily kissed him on the mouth, a hard press of lips that left him wanting a repeat performance of the morning's activities. But if he did, he'd lose all track of time. Nash strode to the water. A quick skinny-dip, and then they needed to get dressed before the ferry arrived.

"What are you doing?" Lily shrieked, craning her neck toward the sea. "Put me down."

Nash hesitated. Did the water scare her that badly?

She leveled him a gaze that meant business. "Now."

Wordlessly, he released her. Lily hit the sand running, bits of white sand puffing at her heels. Near the dunes she turned and waved, face sunny again.

"Beat you to the lodge," she shouted.

Would he ever understand her? The woman was even more of an enigma than most. But he liked that she stood up to him, not afraid to express her feelings. He was used to women fawning over him, seemingly grateful for his attention.

It wasn't as fun as you'd think. Not after a few years, anyway.

Nash gathered his treasures, placed them in the medicine bag and sheathed the knife, everything now blessed and cleansed by the sun. He shook sand from the blanket and made his way back to the lodge, wondering at Lily's changing mood.

A hiss of pipes sounded as he climbed the front steps, announcing she was in the shower. He debated joining her but decided it'd be best to wait for Lily to offer such invitations. Their rustic accommodations didn't include a large supply of hot water and he doubted there would be any left when Lily finished. With a sigh, Nash set his things on the porch and headed back to shore. He'd bathe in the ocean alone.

Cleansed, he returned to the lodge and was greeted by the smell of bacon. Sex had kicked his appetite in gear and he followed his nose to the kitchen. A pot of cheese grits bubbled on the stove and three crisp bacon slices lay on a paper towel.

Nash opened a pine cupboard and got a bowl. "Lily?" He ladled the gooey orange goodness into the bowl and rattled around the drawers for a spoon. "Lily?" he called again.

No answer, but he was too hungry to wait. He spooned up a mouthful of the grits, and the melted cheddar and butter was hot, creamy heaven. He looked out the kitchen window, eating grits and taking bites of crisp, salty bacon. Where had she gone? He was used to the solitary life, but an unexpected pang of disappointment hit him, as well as worry for her safety. Would have been nice to share breakfast. She must already be out with her watercolors, searching for a subject to paint.

At least he wouldn't have to worry about keeping her amused while he worked. But he'd caution her from now on to let him know where she was before other people arrived on the island. He wanted to keep a close watch.

Nash's fingers tightened on the counter. In the excitement of the morning, last night's events had slipped to the background of his mind. Now they burst forth again, the ripped canvases, angry slashes of paint and, worse, the hissing snake.

Who?

Nash circled around the long list of women he'd ever been involved with, inwardly wincing. Sex had been too quick, too easy for him in his youth, and he'd done little to resist the women who'd made advances. Eventually, he'd grown bored with the easy pickups and ashamed of the casual flings. Both Rebecca and Connie had been longer-term relationships; they hadn't seemed to mind his frequent trips and lack of exclusive affection.

Nash mentally shook off the painful reveries. This

didn't do anybody any good. He stretched, stiff muscles alerting him he'd been reminiscing more than a few minutes. He went to the fridge, poured a glass of orange juice and took a sip, the sugar hitting his veins with a pop of instant energy.

Faint splashes and voices drifted through the open window. Nash checked the stove clock and frowned at the time—almost 7:30 a.m. Ned was usually predictable in his scheduled ferry arrivals: 8:00 a.m., noon, 3:00 p.m. and 5:00 p.m. People had arrived and he didn't know where Lily had run off to. Nash set the glass of OJ down on the cheap laminate countertop so hard he was surprised the glass didn't shatter.

He started to run out the front door in his underwear. "Damn it," he muttered, hand paused on the door handle. He snagged a pair of jeans hanging on the back of a chair in his bedroom. Zipping and buttoning the waistband, he took off in the direction of the voices, somewhat mollified that there only seemed to be a few voices and the tone was light. No screams or angry words signaling danger.

Past a bend in the curve of a shallow inlet, he found an older woman with hair the color and length of Lily's slipping on a pair of jeweled sandals. She wore a long coral sundress and her eyes widened when she caught his glance, then cut quickly out to sea.

Nash followed her gaze and saw two clones of the woman as well as another with short, dark hair. Was that—? His eyes narrowed and he shaded them with one hand until he made out the delicate planes of Lily's face.

Lily—who repeatedly claimed she couldn't swim and had refused to even get her toes wet with him this morning. She was too far out in the ocean for her not to be swimming or doing some sort of dog paddle that kept her torso above water.

She lied to me. Disappointment warred with anger and confusion. Why lie about such a trivial thing? More important, what else had Lily lied about? Even after the morning's intimacy, he noticed a secrecy, a holding back on her part.

The older woman on shore let out a shrill whistle and three startled faces turned as one in his direction.

A seagull shrieked overhead. *They all are of two spirits.*

Whatever the hell that meant.

"Hello," said the woman, walking toward him with a confident smile. "You must be Nashoba Bowman. I'm Adriana Bosarge, Lily's mother. We've met before when you were a little tyke."

She took his arm and started leading him back to the lodge. He glanced over his shoulder, but Lily and the others had vanished.

"You've placed my daughter in danger," Adriana admonished, drawing his attention to her once again.

The tone was light but the reprimand was there, sharp steel wrapped in delicate silk.

"Yes, ma'am, but I'm watching her and won't let anyone hurt her."

She cocked a brow. "Watching her so well that her family arrived and you didn't even realize it for several minutes."

Nash's face burned, but not from the summer heat. "What did you do—bribe Ned to ride out early?"

"Ned's an old friend," she answered, sweeping past him and up the porch steps.

Which didn't really answer his question.

He followed her inside, where she settled in on the old, faded sofa. Her dress billowed out with a coral glow that attracted the room's light and energy. What an arresting photographic subject she'd make. He'd develop the photograph in black-and-white; the only spot of color would be the dress. Nash shook off his professional wanderings. This moment could be an opportunity. Lily and the others might traipse in at any moment.

"Great to see Lily in the water this morning," he said, settling in a chair opposite Adriana. "Considering her childhood trauma."

"What?" She straightened, alarm flickering across her placid face. "Oh, that." She jiggled a set of thin gold bangles on her right arm. "Lily told you about it, then."

"Yes. Must have been a difficult time. How did she escape?"

"Escape from what?" Adriana's smooth brow furrowed and her jaw dropped a fraction until she regained her composure. "I really don't like to talk about it. You understand."

"Escape her fear of the water," he insisted. He understood he was being fed a load of bullshit. Secrecy must be a Bosarge family trait. Privacy and reticence Nash understood from his own childhood warnings not to broadcast his grandfather's healing abilities outside their tribe. But outright deception was an altogether different kettle.

"No. I really don't understand."

Adrianne crossed her legs and smiled. "That's because you don't have children and understand how hard it is to talk about their problems. Be a dear and fix me a glass of cold water or iced tea. Whatever's easiest."

He rose reluctantly, but Southern manners had been drilled into him too deeply to refuse her request or to continue challenging an elder. And this was Lily's mother, after all. No point in antagonizing her family.

Nash entered the kitchen, poured a glass of iced tea and returned.

Adriana thanked him demurely and nodded at the chair opposite the sofa.

"I'll be direct with you, Nashoba. I am not thrilled about your relationship with my Lily."

I bet you aren't. His fingers dug into the soft, worn leather of the armchair. Bitterness peppered his mouth and stomach, but he kept his tone civil. "Because we're so *different*, right? Our backgrounds and heritage are too far apart." Which was the polite way of saying he was the wrong color, the wrong ethnicity for her lily-white daughter. Like he hadn't heard that before.

"Oh, not that." Adriana shrugged and gave an I-know-something-you-don't smile. "Although the two of you are monumentally mismatched in every way. But that's not my greatest concern. I've spoken with Tillman and Landry. Your last two girlfriends didn't fare too well."

"I would do anything to change what happened."

"I'm not blaming you. But of all humans, I would have wanted someone at least safe for my daughter."

Humans? What an odd choice of words.

At the creak of the porch steps he turned to look out the front window. Lily and the other blonde looked so alike it was startling. Jet was the odd duck with the black hair and eyes. All had damp hair and T-shirts that clung to their sea-slick skin. They laughed and chattered like tourists on a vacay.

Lily entered first, wearing an insouciant smile like armor. "Mom's not giving you the third degree, I hope." Her tone sounded deliberately chirpy. She sank into the chair next to him and began twirling fistfuls of hair.

"She's your mom. She has the right to speak her mind," he said flatly.

The other two scampered in, sat on either side of the sofa by Adriana and began chattering away in earnest.

"I'm Lily's cousin, Shelly," the blond said, introducing herself. She turned to Adriana. "How long are we staying this morning?" she asked. "I'm teaching a water aerobics class at noon."

"And don't forget you're supposed to take me shopping today in Mobile for nursery stuff," Jet piped in.

It dawned on Nash that they wanted to spare him the mother-dragon act by engaging Adriana's attention on them. He faced Lily.

"Have a nice swim?"

"I don't know what you mean." She crossed her legs and her right knee jittered back and forth.

He pointed to her damp hair. "You're all wet. Besides, I saw you out there swimming."

"No, you didn't." Lily's eyes were steady, her gaze steadfast and true. "I only stepped into the water a few feet, and my hair's wet because Jet splashed me."

Jet nodded their way. "That's right. Sorry, Lily. I do still like to tease my little sis."

"Lily's afraid of the water," Shelly said. "Ever since that time she almost drowned."

The girls had evidently concocted a story on the way in. "Of course," he agreed, folding his arms across his chest. Unbelievable. Nash frowned, but he wouldn't call Lily out in front of her family. A frisson of disappointment gnawed his gut. After the earlier intimacy, a chasm now separated them and he felt further from Lily than the day he'd bumped into her at Winn Dixie.

"Excuse me a moment," he said, walking out of the room. He'd had enough of their chatter. The minute he and Lily were alone, he'd get some answers.

Adriana's long hair tossed wildly in the sea breeze as they stood on the shore, saying their goodbyes.

"Sweet seven seas, Mom. What did you say to him?"

Adriana lifted her chin. "That the two of you are totally unsuitable."

Jet stood behind Adriana and rolled her eyes. "No one's good enough for Lily."

Lily inwardly winced at the slight bitterness in Jet's voice. Having their mother's favoritism growing up had complicated their sibling bond. Things were better between them these days, but Lily realized she'd often been insensitive in the past, especially last year when Jet had won her event in the annual Poseidon Games. Her sister had trained relentlessly for months, yet when Lily had entered and won the Siren's Call event, as she effortlessly did every year, the family and merfolk had excessively lauded her instead of Jet. Yet she'd only done what came naturally.

Lily made a mental note to have a private talk with Jet to apologize and try to set things right. She couldn't change her mother's behavior, but she didn't have to encourage it.

Shelly, ever the peacekeeper, hugged Lily's neck. "We need to get a move on. If Ned sees us, he'll wonder how we got here without his ship."

Adriana didn't budge. "Leave, Lily. You don't have to stay here and put yourself in danger. Come out to sea and take your place where you belong." She stepped forward, face softening. "You can have your pick of any merman."

Her mother would never understand. She wanted to be joined heart and soul with a man, wanted someone to share her life with. With mermen, sex was enjoyed and encouraged for the propagation of the species. That held little appeal to Lily. She saw what Shelly and Jet had and it was far superior to pair bonding with a merman for an occasional mating, the spawning of merbabies and then raising the increasing fry of merbabies alone.

If Adriana hadn't wanted her to live in the bayou, she should have kept her daughters at sea more growing up. Although, to be fair, her mother had done it to try to protect Jet from discovering some ugly truths about her true biological parentage.

It had almost worked. Lily hadn't known that Jet was actually her cousin, not her sister, until last year. Even though the tragic past had been dredged up, Lily would always consider Jet a true sister in every way.

"Maybe later I'll return and find a suitable merman." Lily drew a circle in the sand with the tip of her big toe. She was too emotionally on edge to have this confrontation with her mom right now. If things didn't work out with Nash…life at sea was a possibility. No sense in drawing a line in the sand over a man who probably was going to leave her by summer's end. "Give me a few more weeks. You want to stay until Jet's baby is born anyway."

Adriana placed her hands on Lily's shoulders. "I can't make you go with me like I did when you were a child. But at least promise me you'll be careful."

"At the first hint of danger I'll head out to sea," Lily promised, fingers crossed behind her back. "Now y'all need to scoot before Nash comes searching for me. I'll hide more clothes for you again in the same hidey-hole in case you return underwater."

One by one, they each disappeared behind a rock, disrobed and dove underwater. Lily cast anxious backward glances, sure Nash would pop up at any moment.

"I'll come back later with your paint supplies," Shelly called out from behind the rock. Three distinct splashes and the island was a party of two again—just her and Nash.

Everything was so much simpler with the outside

world held at bay. No murders, no meddling family, no job assignments to foreign lands. Lily picked her way back to the lodge to fetch the sketchpad and pencils she'd brought last night. Being caught lying unsettled her in a way it never had before. She was used to lying about everything to the land dwellers and even kept a tiny part of herself hidden from her family. For all they knew, she reveled in her siren powers, enjoyed the adoration of the merfolk and was amused by her dalliances with the local bayou men.

None of that was true now that Nashoba Bowman had returned.

Lily quickened her pace, eager to draw. She'd immerse herself in art and forget Nash's condemning stare when she'd entered the lodge. She'd been having such fun, too, until she'd spotted him on shore. Splashing, diving, the water invigorating and salty, her mer fin whipping in the Gulf current.

Impossible to live on the island for days or weeks without swimming. Lily resolved to be very, very careful until she could tell him the truth. When Nash fell asleep in the evenings, she'd slip out in the moonlight and swim under its silver orb, connected even deeper to the tide by the pull of the moon. In some ways, Mom was right. She and Nash were opposites. He was of the sun, dark golden and grounded to the earth, whereas she was of the moon, moored to the fluid sea and bewitched by moonbeams.

In no time, Lily gathered the needed supplies and one of the rolled woolen blankets Nash kept on the porch. She meandered down narrow trails with blizzards of cypress, pine and saw palmetto. That was one of the things she loved about the bayou—the varied landscape. You had the white sandy shore and the sea, but you also had green woodland heavily scented with pine that mixed with sea brine in the breeze.

The millions of mosquitoes and gnats were the only undesirable trade-off for such paradise.

Lily found a patch of Southern seashore mallow in full bloom cheerfully waving their delicate pink petals surrounding a sunshine-yellow corolla. She spread out the blanket and opened the sketchpad. Such a shame she hadn't packed colored pencils last night, but she'd make do with her pencils and paint a watercolor of the flowers later.

"What you got there?"

Her heart exploded, pulsing and pounding *danger danger danger* to her brain and limbs. The instinctual command to flee was immediate and she lurched forward, scrambling to her feet.

A strong hand gripped her right forearm, preventing escape.

"It's me, Lily. Nash."

She drew ragged, painful breaths. She was safe. Last night had rattled her more than she'd realized.

"Hey, I'm sorry." Nash wrapped his arms around her waist from behind and she melted against him, wilting like an uprooted flower needing to bury into soil.

"I've got you," he whispered into her hair.

"I thought you were angry with me."

"I am. But I'd never scare you on purpose. What kind of man do you think I am?"

"A good one. The best," she said softly. Lily closed her eyes and enjoyed the heat of his skin pressed against her back, the comfort of his arms circling her waist.

"So why did you lie about swimming?"

Nash wasn't going to let this go. Lily swallowed hard. Normally, lying was no problem, something necessary to keep hidden in the bayou and protect her family and all the other merfolk—what remained of her kind. But now the unspoken lies soured on her tongue and she struggled to explain with at least a modicum of truth.

"I only swim with my family," she offered lamely.

"Why?"

Damn. As if she didn't know that would be the next question. "I'm a terrible swimmer—all leg kicks and thrashing arms. It's embarrassing."

"Hmm."

The vibration of his voice rumbled deep in his chest and radiated the length of her spine.

"But you didn't have to go in deep. I only wanted—"

"Sorry," she interrupted, turning in to him and kissing the hollow of his throat. "What were you doing naked out there this morning? Not that I'm complaining."

Nash studied her and a muscle in his jaw twitched. Lily's breath stilled. Would he let the matter go for now?

"I know what you're doing." His voice was husky, thick with either anger or desire. Possibly both, Lily wasn't sure.

"Did it work?" She gave him her most dazzling smile.

He didn't return her smile. "I'll let it go for a moment." Nash guided her shoulders forward and dipped his chin onto the top of her scalp. "To answer your question, when I was young, my grandfather and I had this dawn ritual where we greeted the sun and thanked the earth for its blessings."

"Naked?"

"No." He chuckled. "I'm not sure why I took off my pants. It seemed the right thing to do at the moment. When Grandfather and I used to do this, we'd open our medicine bags for the sun to bless the contents and sometimes we'd chant or dance to the beat of his drumming."

"Like a moving prayer," she whispered. Exactly how she felt during moonlit swims. "I know what you mean."

A comfortable silence descended, and, emboldened, Lily ventured another question. "Sometimes, like today with the seagull, I imagine birds are talking to you. Really talking."

His hands, which had been stroking her forearms, stilled. She hardly dared breathed while she awaited his response.

"And if I told you they were?"

"I'd believe you."

His heart thudded against her back and his muscles tensed. "They do."

The admission hadn't been easy for him. "Thank you," she said, encouraged he felt safe to open up. "One last question. What do they say?"

"I knew that was coming," he said ruefully. "Actually, this is new to me and it's only happened twice. Both times while I was with you."

"Go on," she breathed.

"They say you are of two spirits."

Chapter 12

Two spirits.

Lily pondered the mysterious words, her spine tingling with wonder. Two spirits—as in she was two-faced? A liar? That she was, and so much more. And to think all this time she'd never suspected her secret would be betrayed while she walked on land, least of all by one of earth's creatures. Instead, she'd always feared being spotted at sea by human eyes.

"What does it mean?" Nash asked. "Assuming, of course, you don't think I'm crazy and hearing imaginary voices."

"No!" Lily moved out of his arms, sat cross-legged on the blanket, took hold of his hands and drew him down with her. "You're the sanest person I've ever met."

He ran a hand through his long hair. "Have to admit, I've doubted myself at times, especially since coming here. Everything's intensified."

"Your connection to the land and animals?" she guessed.

Nash stared. "You've always intuited it, haven't you?"

"I sensed it when we were kids. The way you would grow still and cock your head, as if listening to whispers in the wind. I knew it for sure the time you found me when I was lost. How did you do it?" She shuddered, remembering the horror of the day and night she'd spent alone in the woods.

She'd gone looking for Nash and, not finding him in their usual hangouts, had meandered down obscure trails until she'd realized nothing was familiar, or rather everything was the same in all directions. Merely clumps of pine trees and knotty dirt trails with no distinguishing marks. She'd tried to imagine what Nash would do if he were lost. Inspired, she'd ripped one of her socks with a sharp rock and unraveled the threads, deciding the best course was to pick a direction and stay with it. She'd walked along and, every few feet, tied a string on a low-lying branch to mark her progress.

Hours later, exhausted, thirsty and increasingly panicked, Lily spotted one of the knotted cotton strings and realized she'd been walking in circles. Defeated, she strategized that the next best course of action was to stay put. She built a bed of pine needles and sat to wait for help.

And waited, waited, waited. Until the sun had sunk below the horizon and complete darkness had shrouded the woods. The only flicker of light came from fireflies randomly darting above dense shrubbery. If only she'd had a jar, she could have collected the fireflies and kept them encased by her side like a lantern in the gloomy pitch. She'd imagined the woods would be a quiet place, but she'd been wrong. Owls hooted and insects buzzed.

Unseen animals scrambled about. Lily had forgotten her hunger and thirst as fear filled her stomach and lungs.

The worst had been an eerie high-pitched caterwauling. Bobcats weren't unheard of in those parts. What if one stalked in the trees above, ready to pounce the instant she drifted to sleep? Lily had hoped the wail was from the ginger-colored feral cats that peppered the bayou. Nevertheless, she'd resolved to stay awake.

She fought sleep, remembering Sam and Nash's Choctaw tales of mysterious beings in the bayou. If there were supernatural creatures roaming the forest, she hoped it was only the Little People—Kowi Anukasha—known for their mischievous pranks, like throwing sticks to try to scare humans. They meant no real harm. Unlike the Hoklonote, an evil spirit who could assume any shape and read people's thoughts. If so, he'd know she was alone and frightened. Even worse, there was Nalusa Falaya, the dark being who could eat your soul.

Eventually, her eyes had ached and her mind had fallen into sleep's blankness.

Twigs snapped and pebbles crunched, jerking her awake. An oval of light beamed on her face, blinding in the sudden brightness.

Lily?

Nash's voice had slashed through the haze of alarm, and relief washed over her. She was safe.

A gentle squeeze of her hand jolted Lily from the memories.

"You were a pitiful sight, but a welcome one," Nash said.

"So how did you find me when no one else could?" She tilted her head, wistful. "Let me guess. A little birdie told you."

"Nothing that dramatic." His lips twitched at the corners and then he sobered. "I figured you'd gone out looking for me at the usual places. When you weren't there, I retraced my steps until I neared the felled oak seat." A heartbeat's pause. "It's hard to explain, but something in the air's energy shimmered...as if it had been recently disturbed. The soles of my feet tingled and a *knowing* slammed my gut that you'd walked the path behind the rock. I plunged ahead and found the bits of string you'd tied on the trees and shrubs. After that, it was easy."

"My hero," she said simply, with no trace of irony.

Nash snorted. "Some hero. I've brought you nothing but trouble and danger this time around."

Nothing but love. Instead of bursting fireworks, the realization settled on her soul with the tranquility of still waters—deep and pure and abiding. It had always been there and would always remain.

"Nash, I..." She hesitated. The time for confessions could come later. He was consumed with guilt and anger over the stalker who hurt any woman he'd had a relationship with. The last thing he wanted to hear right now was that she loved him. She wouldn't add to his burdens.

He released a hand and stroked a finger along the curve of her jaw. "What?" he prodded.

"Just... None of this is your fault."

His face darkened and he dropped his hand into his lap. "Maybe it is. Maybe I've played fast and loose once too often with a woman's affection. Now I must suffer for past wrongs."

"Look who you're talking to." She thought of Gary, of all the men she'd dated and dumped. What would it do to her if Nash didn't return her love? She hadn't meant to hurt anyone, had been seeking love in her own way and breaking it off before they fell too deep—at least that was how she'd justified it. Shame burned her cheeks. If there was such a thing as karma, she was doomed. Lily ducked her head.

"Hey," he said, gently brushing back her hair. "I don't care about your past. All that matters is the future."

"Then cut yourself a break, too. Goes both ways."

A muscle worked the side of his jaw. "At least none of your boyfriends died."

"It's not your fault," she repeated.

"If I'd been more careful, if I'd even loved them a little in return..." He closed his eyes.

"There was nothing you could have done. You aren't responsible for the actions of a crazy person."

Dark eyes snapped open. "Don't you get it? It's probably some ex-lover I disposed of as casually as a used paper plate."

"Stop it." She gave his hands a shake. "Tillman and Landry are good cops. They'll find who's responsible. And when they do, you're going to have to find a way to let it all go."

"Yes, ma'am." He gave a mock salute.

Garbled voices drifted over. "Seems we have some bird-watchers about. Why don't we grab lunch? I'm starving."

"Good deal." He arose, seemingly as relieved as she was to drop the self-flagellation over ex-lovers. He pulled her up and planted a quick, fierce kiss on her mouth.

"You're all right, Lily Bosarge."

Lily beamed as if he'd bestowed a grand compliment. "You, too. Now let's get out of here."

She bent down to retrieve her sketchpad.

"Whoa, let me see this." Nash took it from her and stared at the drawing. "This is really good."

"You think so? You're not saying that to be nice?"

Nash whipped a sharp glance. "How can you be so self-assured in everything except your art?"

"Because it wasn't handed to me at birth." Unlike her looks and her voice. "Plus…" She hesitated, but if Nash could open up about his gift, she should in return. "It's important to me that it's worthy. I want to be noticed for something other than my looks. Everybody in Bayou La Siryna thinks of me as the slutty blonde whose only talent is styling hair."

His brows screwed together. "Styling hair?"

Lily picked up the blanket and rolled it, tucking it under an arm. "I used to own a beauty shop in town. I closed it down a few months ago to paint more."

"To hell with what others think."

"Easier said for a guy, especially one that doesn't live in a small town."

"I suppose," he agreed with a slight shrug.

She shot him a sideways glance. "Aren't you curious about my past? My reputation?"

"No," he answered shortly. "You're not guilty of anything that I haven't done. I don't believe in double standards for men and women."

They returned to the lodge, holding hands in companionable silence.

"You made breakfast, so I'll make lunch," Nash said. "Just going to wash up first."

Lily stretched out on the sofa, absorbed with a rare feeling of lazy contentment. What a perfect day. If only they could share every day together. She tucked a pillow under her head and closed her eyes. She'd worry about the future later. Her mind drifted to slumber. A little nap while Nash made lunch…

"What's this?"

Lily jerked awake at the loud voice and sat upright.

Nash carried in the straw basket she'd carelessly laid in the bathroom. Her mom's coral dress was bunched in his right hand, the basket with the rest of the clothes in the other.

Lily blinked, mind momentarily fuzzy from sleep. "It's, um, Mom's dress."

"I recognized it. Shelly and Jet's clothes are in here, too. What'd they do? Board the ferry naked?"

"Don't be silly. They brought a change of clothes with them."

He frowned. "That doesn't make sense. This is what they wore after they finished swimming."

She shrugged and faked a yawn. "They decided to change again." She had to get his mind off those damn clothes. Lily got to her feet and walked to him, smiling. "What are you fixing us for lunch?" She put her arms around his neck and brushed her body against his.

Nash stepped backward, frowning. "No. They were wearing these when they left the lodge."

"Were they?" She tapped her index finger against her lips. "I can't remember."

"I do."

"Oh, stop making such a fuss over nothing," Lily groused, pretending to be cross. The man was too damn observant. She'd have to be more careful with the two of them confined to such close quarters.

"Something funny's going on here," Nash insisted.

"You don't see me laughing." Lily headed to the kitchen. "I'm starving. Let's eat."

She heard Nash return to the bathroom as she opened the fridge and took out a pack of crabmeat and mayonnaise. The bathroom door creaked open and she felt his eyes on her back. Lily ignored him and rummaged for the loaf of bread and a bag of chips.

"Lily," he said, a command to face him.

She continued puttering with the food. "What?"

Nash pulled at her right elbow, guiding her to turn around. The implacable, sober set of his jaw warned that this conversation wasn't over.

"You're keeping something from me."

She opened her mouth, but Nash placed a finger on her lips.

"Don't bother to deny it. I've told you things I've never told anybody. Can't you trust me in return?"

Lily froze, conscious of the utter stillness. The only sound in the kitchen was the mechanical hum of the refrigerator. Guilt spiraled in her mind like an eddy. Oh, how she wanted to tell him everything, but she couldn't. Sure, he'd confessed to some supernatural abilities, but it wasn't like he shape-shifted into another kind of creature.

His eyes stared into her own, open and pure. "All I ask from you is honesty. I've learned from my past that if you can't have that with someone, then there's nothing real between you. So what about your past, Lily? Have you been honest with the men you've been with over the years? Or did you keep a part of yourself hidden while secretly enjoying their devotion?"

His words seeped into the dark corners of her heart and mind, slipping through years of denial and justifications. Shame scalded and she glared at him, angry he brought it into the open. "That's not true," she denied, not wanting to see the truth. 'I can't help it if men fall in love with me."

"But it pleases you, doesn't it? Heady stuff, having all the men chase you, wanting to be your lover."

Lily pursed her lips. "Is that how it feels to you when all the women fall at your feet?" she snapped.

"It used to," he admitted quietly. "Gets old, though,

over the years. And I'd give anything if I'd never encouraged Connie and Rebecca. They wanted more from me and I had nothing to give. I should have ended it with both of them when I knew I wasn't in love."

She thought of Gary, how he had dropped his steady girlfriend when she'd crooked her finger his way. She remembered all the men she'd enticed. True, it hadn't taken much effort on her part, but she could have kept to herself. But no, loneliness had driven her to pursue men for the momentary excitement and temporary satisfaction.

What perfect cosmic justice if she'd fallen for the one man who couldn't love her in return.

"Have you ever been in love?" she asked wistfully.

"For the first time, I think I could be."

Lily sucked in her breath, dizzy with joy. It could really happen for her; she could love and be loved in return. "Nash—"

"So tell me what's going on around here. What are you hiding? I need the truth."

"I—I can't," she stammered. "If it were only me... perhaps I could. But too many people could be hurt."

An entire race, to be precise.

His eyes shuttered and his lips compressed. "I see."

Nash turned and walked away, taking all her hopes and dreams with him. Lily raised a hand to catch his arm but let it drop by her side. There was nothing more to be said except...

"I'm sorry," she said to his retreating back.

He kept walking.

Lily gripped the edge of the countertop. She'd been so close... Pain lanced her heart. *So this is love. Damn, it hurts.*

The screen door squeaked open and then banged shut. Nash's footsteps sounded across the wooden porch floor and then all was silent again. Lily peeked out the window and watched him settle into a rocking chair, feet propped on the railing.

Day one alone with Nash and she was blowing it. Lily numbly put up the uneaten food, appetite gone. She returned to the den and sank onto the sofa, acutely conscious of Nash on the porch, probably brooding on what a disappointment she was.

The trill ring of his cell phone went off and he answered, voice low and muffled. Had there been any developments in finding the stalker? Lily strained to hear.

Nash unfolded his feet and jumped out of the chair; his voice had risen to a louder, faster rate, but she couldn't make out the words. Whatever it was, the news wasn't good. Nash propped an arm against a column and dropped his head.

Lily scrambled to her feet. It had to be news from Tillman or Landry. Was someone else hurt? She opened the door and saw Nash let the cell phone drop to his side.

"What's happened?" She edged between him and the porch column. "Nash?"

He lifted his head, eyes dead with pain. "It's Grandfather. He's had a heart attack."

"Is he—?" Lily faltered, unable to go on.

"He's in the hospital. Critical condition."

She stepped into his arms and rubbed his back. "I am so, so sorry."

He clutched her close for a heartbeat and then set her aside. "I've got to go."

"Of course." She took the cell phone dangling loosely in his left palm and checked the time. "Fifteen minutes until the noon ferry. Let's get packing."

His face was rigid, his spine stiff as a column of stone. "You don't have to come with me."

Lily bit her lip. She couldn't let him freeze her out of his life, especially not now, when he needed a friend. "Don't be ridiculous."

He shrugged. "Suit yourself."

The pungent scent of antiseptic cloyed at Lily the moment she entered the hospital lobby. It followed her down a maze of tight passageways and into the crowded ICU waiting room.

She rubbed her temples, wishing she were a lady in the days of yore with a hanky doused in rosewater to hold over her nose. Hours of this olfactory torture and her head would hurt so badly she'd be admitted as a patient.

As if. No telling what kind of funky biology the docs would flush out of her mer body.

Denim-clad legs brushed against her bare knees.

"Excuse me, ma'am," someone mumbled.

Lily looked up at the same moment the middle-aged man caught her eye. His mouth widened slightly and he didn't move.

"No problem," she mumbled, lowering her face to gaze at the white linoleum. She didn't want to deal with any advances right now. With a swish of denim, he moved on and she surreptitiously watched as he poured a cup of coffee into a foam cup.

Her mouth salivated with the need for a drink. Her body required at least twice the amount of daily liquid intake needed by humans. Unfortunately, she hadn't noted any water fountains or vending machines en route to the waiting room and she didn't want to risk going to the cafeteria to buy a bottle of water.

Coffee it was, then. No sense taking a chance on missing Nash when he finished his visitation. She couldn't stand his anger and disappointment. There had to be some way to appease him while protecting her family. Lily got up and poured a cup of the hospital-provided coffee. Maybe it would help take the edge off the chill in the cold room.

She wandered over to a back window and sipped, taking in an uninspiring view of the parking deck. Somewhere in the cavernous lot, they'd whipped into the nearest empty space and hightailed it inside, arriving breathless and flushed. Nash was assured his grandfather had survived the ordeal but was weak. They'd ushered Nash down a hallway and through a set of double doors that locked behind him and she had no idea when he'd return.

The cold sterility of the room made Lily want to shrink into herself for warmth. Harsh light bounced around gleaming walls alternately painted white or a sickly institutional green she associated with prisons or morgues. She'd never been inside a hospital before and sincerely hoped to never again have to enter its artificial, claustrophobic confines. Lily longed for the open sea, enveloped by the primordial water dancing with life in every microscopic drop.

As she waited, she absorbed the special subculture of an ICU waiting room. A few people sat alone, staring at a book or their cell phones, clearly giving the message they wanted to be uninterrupted with their misery. Most everyone else huddled in small groups, talking of trivial matters while continually caressing one another's shoulder or offering little kindnesses. Lily turned again to look out the window.

Elevator doors constantly pinged open and shut behind her as staff and families alike scurried about their business. An unexpected hush descended and Lily turned, curious at the sudden silence. Her gaze followed the crowd and she spotted the reason.

The Bosarge women—Mom, Shelly and Jet—emerged from the elevator. Lily noticed their striking beauty in a way she never had before. Jet's dark hair and eyes created an exotic panache, while Shelly and Mom bookended either side of her with their pearly skin and Nordic blond hair streaming in thick waves down to their hips. Jet wore a scarf, and Mom's and Shelly's hair was artfully arranged over their necks' gill markings. But more than their beauty, they possessed an energy about them that was deep and flowing and magnetic.

"There she is." Adriana gracefully floated to Lily's side, leaving a ripple of male interest in her wake.

"You got here quick," Lily said, grateful for their company.

Jet rolled a small suitcase along the bare linoleum. "And armed with provisions."

Ever the nurturing one, Shelly placed an arm across Lily's shoulder. "How is Nash's grandfather? Any word?"

"He survived, but they want to keep him longer. Nash is with him now."

Jet unzipped the suitcase and pulled out a pink cotton sweater. "Landry warned me that hospitals are usually as chilly as a meat locker."

"Bless you." Lily donned it at once and accepted the bottle of water Shelly held out. She guzzled it down immediately, parched throat allayed from thirst.

"The smell in this place is atrocious." Adriana frowned and scrunched her forehead. "It's giving me a headache."

"Try sitting in here for an hour and see how you feel."

Mom rubbed Lily's arm. "Poor baby. See what happens when you mix with—" She darted a furtive glance at everyone studying the four of them from the corners of their eyes. She lowered her voice to a whisper. "When you get mixed up too long with humans."

"It's not all bad," Jet muttered.

Shelly slipped Lily a wink. Those two were clearly happy to be "mixed up" with their human husbands.

Adriana addressed Jet with an imperious lift of her chin. "Now do you believe me when I say an underwater birth is the right way to go?" Lily grinned. At least Mom's attention was distracted by Jet's pregnancy.

As if sensing her daughter's unspoken thoughts, Adriana rounded on Lily. "And you must realize that the proper thing for you do is to—"

"—take my rightful place with my own kind," Lily groaned, careful to keep her voice down.

"How much longer are you going to stay here?" Adriana asked. "If Nash is visiting with his grandfather, is there any need for you to remain?"

Lily bristled. "I want to be here when Nash comes out. I can't walk out on him."

"Write a note or something. Too much longer in this hospital and your head will explode from the noxious smell. You need fresh air."

Really, Mom was so obvious in her attempts to steer her away from Nash. Lily pursed her lips to staunch an angry retort.

Adriana's face softened. "Don't be angry. You've always been overly sensitive to odors, even more than the rest of us. I'm only looking out for my only daughter."

Jet's sharp inhalation drew Lily's attention. Their Mom's remark had hit a painful spot. Technically, Jet was Adriana's niece, but Mom had raised her since she was a newborn when her sister—Jet's biological mother—had died in childbirth.

"Really, Aunt Adriana!" Shelly's normally serene face reddened in anger.

Adriana's eyes filled with tears and she placed a hand over her mouth, as if to take back the words.

But the damage was done.

Jet placed a hand on her protruding belly, as if calming her own baby from distress.

"Excuse me."

The older gentleman in jeans who'd brushed against Lily earlier approached with tentative steps. "I don't mean to intrude but I couldn't help overhearing you mention the need for fresh air. The hospital has a lovely outdoor garden area for families."

"I can't leave," Lily protested. "I'm waiting for my boyfriend to finish his visitation."

"Send him a text message to call when he's available," Shelly said. "The break will do you good."

Lily wavered.

"You'll be better able to comfort Nash if you don't greet him with a splitting headache," Shelly added.

Some fresh air *would* be renewing. "Okay," Lily agreed. "For a little bit."

The man smiled kindly. "Take the elevators to the lobby and turn left. You'll see a door on your right marked Therapeutic Garden."

"Thanks," she said, giving him a grateful smile. They headed to the elevators and snagged one with no one else inside.

"We didn't drag you away for your health," Jet said as the elevator doors clanged shut.

Lily's heart quickened. "Have Tillman and Landry found out something about the stalker?"

"I wish," Adriana cut in. "I'm afraid it's more trouble. Carl Dismukes is turning into a real problem."

Chapter 13

Lily's shoulders sagged in disappointment as they exited the elevator. How she'd love to have good news for Nash after all his worry over Sam's health.

An orderly pushing a steel cart loaded with surgical supplies stopped in the middle of the hallway and blocked their path, staring at them as if hypnotized.

"We're looking for the therapeutic garden. Could you direct us?" Adriana asked, attempting to break the spell.

He limply raised an arm and pointed like a marionette doll, never breaking his stare. "Th-that way."

Lily and Shelly moved to the orderly's right, while Adriana and Jet passed to his left, like a wave bypassing the solid boulder formed by man and cart.

"There it is. Hope no one else is about so we can really talk." Jet pushed open a glass door, allowing Adriana and Shelly to pass through.

Lily stopped at the entryway. "I'm stealing Jet for a

moment. We'll be right back." Ignoring Adriana's frown and Shelly's knowing nod of approval, Lily pointed at an empty alcove banked with a row of chairs. "We need to talk a minute."

Jet scowled. "If this is about what Mom said earlier, there's no need. I'm used to it."

"This is between us." Lily walked to the alcove and sat, patting the empty chair beside her. After a moment's hesitation, Jet came. Her tall, athletic frame and normally fast, purposeful gait somewhat marred by the bulk of her pregnant belly, she settled into the chair butt-first, a hand holding the back of it for support. Lily still couldn't get used to the idea that her wayward, fiercely independent sister was the first of them to make the leap into motherhood. Shelly she could buy, with her nurturing nature. Being only half-merblood, her cousin's need to be at sea was easily satisfied with the occasional full-moon swim.

But Jet?

"You seem to get a little bigger every day," Lily remarked.

Jet settled her hands over her swollen abdomen, a satisfied smile transforming her face with tender grace. "Landry likes to tease me about it, but he's so proud and excited he's about to burst."

Lily marveled at the changes in her sister these past months. "Are you happy, Jet? Truly happy?"

Jet's brown eyes narrowed and snapped. "Of course I am. Did Mom put you up to this little talk? She doesn't believe I'm capable of making my own decisions on how I want my baby delivered and raised. I suspect she even wants me to return to the sea, as well. But there's no going back to my old way of life. And, thank you very much, I couldn't be happier."

Now *that* sounded like the old Jet she knew.

"Mom goes about showing it the wrong way, but she wants what's best for you."

Jet huffed. "Fooled me. And if she makes one crack about my child being a TRAB, I'll never forgive her."

For merfolk, a TRAB, or traitor baby, was the result of mixing mer and human races and was increasingly considered taboo. Centuries of interbreeding had reduced their pure-blooded population to dangerously low levels.

Lily nervously tugged and twirled the ends of her hair. Jet's baby had more than the TRAB stigma. The child would also inherit her paternal grandfather's Blue Clan blood. That clan was mostly shunned in the merworld because of their ferocious nature, not just toward humans, but also to their own race. They were an aggressive, power-seeking tribe that sought to overtake and rule the undersea kingdom.

As if Jet could read her mind, she scowled at Lily. "Even if I mated with a merman, our children would still be considered tainted. You are her pure-blood, true daughter, not me."

Lily swallowed hard, wishing they were kids again with none of the emotional baggage that had driven a wedge in their relationship.

Once Lily had hit puberty, a shadow had darkened their former childhood camaraderie. Lily had been slammed with attention from all sides, and not only from males of both human and mer species. She'd had the adulation of all the mermaids for her siren's voice and beauty. Worst, Adriana showed a partiality that must have deeply hurt Jet.

"No matter what happens, Mom does love you."

"Not as much as she loves you."

There. It was now a spoken thing between them.

Lily didn't deny it. "I'm sorry." She bit her lower lip, trying to quell its tremble. "Truly," she added miserably.

"It doesn't matter." Jet's gaze dropped to her belly.

"Of course it matters." Lily's face burned with shame, recalling the many occasions when she'd made the situation worse with her selfish need for attention.

She placed a tentative hand on her sister's knee. "I'm sorry," she said again.

Jet looked up and arched a brow. "You've certainly changed."

"I'm trying to be a better person. Hopefully a little older and wiser."

"It's Nash, isn't it? I do believe you've fallen in love for the first time in your life."

"Yes," she whispered. For once, someone else's needs and happiness outweighed her own. Even if he returned to his travels and she returned to the sea, she was forever changed. "It's scary," she confessed.

Jet slowly nodded. "Even scarier than the stalker threat, I'll bet. Is he worth the danger?"

"Oh, yes." Lily's answer was swift, unequivocal.

"Then fight for him."

Understanding and affection flowed and crested between them in a new way.

"Thank you, Jet. Forgive me?"

"You're my sister."

Lily grasped her hand and Jet squeezed it in return.

"Are you two finished?" a voice called from the doorway. Adriana waved them forward.

"We're coming," Lily answered, helping Jet rise from her chair.

Adriana disappeared behind the door and Jet gave Lily a rueful smile. "Don't worry about me and Mom. We'll make our peace. She is who she is. Now that I have

Landry and our baby's on the way, I'm satisfied. And very, very happy."

"I'm glad."

In spite of the unresolved danger, the sadness at Sam Bowman's health and the uncertainty of Nash's feelings toward her, Lily felt a lightness in her body and heart. Whatever problems she faced, she had her family behind her. The Bosarge women stuck together.

"We have a huge problem," Adriana announced as they seated themselves at a round picnic table in the shade of an old oak tree.

Lily scanned the tranquil outdoor area that featured a bubbling water fountain and a labyrinth of blooming flowers. Therapeutic indeed, a real sanctuary from the artificial, intense hospital world fraught with illness and death.

With a sigh, she faced her family. "Okay, what's Carl Dismukes done now?"

"The man won't go away," Shelly said. "We thought that after Tillman forced him to retire, that would be the end of his threats. But no, he's going to make trouble in the sheriff's election next month. Last week, he went to Tillman's office with a stack of papers documenting the money Tillman's father embezzled when he served as sheriff. Dismukes says he's going to drag his father's reputation through the mud."

Lily leaned her elbows on the table. "I don't get it. Carl was in on the whole embezzling scheme, too."

"He's doctored all the documents to cast blame solely on Tillman's dad," Shelly explained.

"That's rough, but Tillman's dad has been dead for years. I don't mean to be rude, but it's not like the scandal could hurt him."

"Its guilt by association," Jet cut in. "People will think 'like father, like son.' It would ruin Tillman's chance at reelection."

"Maybe." She considered Jet's agitation. "And if Tillman goes down, your husband's job as deputy is jeopardized."

"Right. He could probably get back his old FBI job in Mobile, but that would be…problematic. I don't want to leave Bayou La Siryna."

Lily nodded. Here in the bayou, Jet could come and go as she pleased without detection. She came to their homestead almost daily and slipped out to sea through their secret portal.

But the situation didn't seem all that dire. Not compared to the life-and-death dramas going on in the hospital or her own danger from an unknown enemy. Easy to see why Jet and Shelly were upset, but why was her mother taking it so hard? It wasn't as if she were especially fond of her human sons-in-law.

She faced Adriana. "What's got your tail twisted in a knot?"

"You haven't heard the worst part. I thought once Jet quit illegally selling marine treasure on the black market, the past would stay buried. But the ever-resourceful Carl is threatening to expose that little secret, as well."

"But—" Lily frowned at Jet. "I thought Landry had taken care of all that."

Jet nodded. "He did. Dismukes can't prove anything from my past. But that's not the point."

They all stared at Lily expectantly. She was obviously missing something here. Lily threw up her hands. "Spell it out for me."

Adriana took charge. "Carl wants us to start providing him more marine artifacts to sell. If we do, he won't expose Tillman's father during the election. And even though he can't prove Jet once was involved in shady business, he's lived here long enough that he knows influential people in Bayou La Siryna. He'll trash Jet and Landry's reputation."

Dread curdled in Lily's stomach. Would they never be free of this man?

"I don't care about my reputation," Jet said.

Adriana stared pointedly at Jet's belly. "You're starting a family. Do you want your children to grow up here and be stigmatized for your past mistakes?"

Jet's hands fisted so tightly her knuckles turned white. "This is all my fault. If I wasn't pregnant, I'd take care of him right now."

"Carl is a disgrace." Adriana shook her head. "Blackmail and betrayal to fellow humans, I understand. But he has merblood in him and our kind is bonded together to protect one another from exposure. I could return to sea and alert the merfolk. There are some who would be willing to travel here and take care of the matter. They'll force Dismukes to stop…or else."

"That might work," Shelly mused. "We can play along with him, give him a few trinkets and buy time until help arrives."

"You can't be serious!" Lily said. "We can't buckle under to his demands. Not even once. And contact the merfolk to do our dirty work? Unacceptable."

Her mother fixed her with a pointed stare. "Then what do you propose we do?"

"We need to confront him at sea, on our own turf." Lily's thoughts whirled as she stared at each mermaid relative across the table.

Shelly. Being only half-mermaid, her cousin was the weakest link. And her nature was much too kind for dirty business. When Shelly had had her own crisis with a serial killer, Melkie Pellerin, Lily and Jet had been forced to handle the matter.

No help there.

Jet. Much as she was willing, and the physically strongest of them all, her sister was in no condition to take any risks for several weeks. She shouldn't even have to endure this emotional strain while carrying a baby.

Mom. Adriana was mentally tough and had no compunction enforcing the merfolk code of secrecy. But even though she was in good shape, Mom was getting on in years and it wasn't fair to expect their mother to protect them anymore. She'd already aided them once before when Jet's ex-boyfriend, Perry Hammonds, had kidnapped Jet and held her hostage.

Which left…

"I'll take care of Carl Dismukes," Lily said at last. She knew exactly how to get him alone at sea. It should be easy enough to scare the wily old bastard then. Frighten him so bad he'd realize the Bosarge women were out for blood.

His blood.

"How?" Jet asked bluntly. "Dismukes isn't a criminal fugitive like Perry was. If he disappears or dies like Perry, there'll be questions and a lengthy investigation." Jet's stare was hard, accusing. "You can't kill him."

Murder? Lily sprang to her feet, outrage crackling through her spine. "I'm not going to kill Dismukes! Why would you say such a thing?"

No one answered. Silence pounded her eardrums and swished through her brain like the pressure from floating at the bottom of the deepest ocean.

"Well," Adriana said drily. "We've always wondered exactly how Perry died the day you rescued Jet. You were alone with him undersea when Jet swam away. And you were the last person to see him alive."

They think I killed him.

The thought reverberated in her mind, loud and forceful as a whale's bellow. Lily inhaled raspy and loud, her panicked lungs unable to suck in enough oxygen. She pressed her trembling lips together and tried to paste on her Mona Lisa smile, a reflex built from years of masking emotion.

It didn't work.

How could they believe her capable of murder? Lily couldn't take their avid stares. She sat down and picked at a small sea-glass chip on her bracelet, staring down as if she'd never seen it before. Churned and battered by the currents, it had been buffed from a shard of broken glass—garbage—to a piece of art. The muted teal absorbed Lily's attention. Perhaps she could capture that tone in a watercolor, mix the blues and greens together, followed by an opaque wash...

A warm touch on her forearm startled Lily out of her reverie.

"No one's judging you," Shelly said. "We're curious about what happened down there."

Lily met the kind eyes of her cousin. They might look almost like twins, but they couldn't be more different in temperament. Whereas Shelly was a soft-hearted peacemaker, Lily was rigid and unyielding in her ideas of justice.

Evil deserved no mercy. But she'd never made herself jury and executioner. Except that one time...

"An eye for an eye," Shelly nodded, as if reading her mind. "Like when you clawed out one of Melkie Pellerin's eyes that night we captured him for the police."

"But I didn't kill the killer." Lily jerked away from

Shelly's touch. She shuddered, remembering the serial killer that had stalked the bayou for several years. He'd gotten away with murder until Shelly observed him dumping the body of a victim one night at sea. "He was fortunate to only lose one eye. His victims suffered far worse."

Shelly crossed her arms. "If I hadn't stopped you, I believe you would have killed him."

"Then you would be wrong." Lily rubbed her face, feeling as weary as an old woman. If her own family believed her so cold-blooded... Well, she had nothing.

Jet thrust her face within inches of her own. "Did you kill Perry or not?" she asked in her forthright manner.

That bastard. Perry of the roving hands, who'd groped and leered at her every time Jet left the room. Yet she would never tell Jet. That little secret was as dead and silent as Davy Jones's locker at the bottom of the sea.

"'Cause if you did—" Jet ran her hand through her black hair and exhaled loudly "—I don't care. You saved my life."

No, she hadn't laid a hand on Perry. But she hadn't helped him, either. Guilt and shame scalded her nerves at the memory of Perry under the ocean, swallowing handfuls of sea water, panicked from oxygen deprivation. Her only crime was one of omission. She'd drifted nearby, observing his agony for a couple of seconds before rushing in to save him. Had those two seconds made the difference between life and death? Her brain said no, but the question haunted her.

"I didn't lay a finger on him," Lily spat out, immediately on the defensive. "He drowned."

"Sure, he did." Jet drummed her fingers on the picnic table. "Very convenient. Had Perry lived, he would have blackmailed us to bankruptcy...or worse."

"Worse?" Shelly asked, brows furrowed.

Jet stood and paced. "We were probably worth more to him alive. As a circus act." She stopped and faced Lily again. "Thank you."

They don't know me at all. Damn her famous composure. "I didn't kill anybody!" Lily's scream echoed like a receding wave in the stunned silence.

"Shh." Adriana put her index finger to her lips and glanced about the garden.

Lily pushed away from the table, eager to flee, but her knees shook and she slowly stumbled past them, feeling invisible—like the ghost from Christmas past in a roomful of strangers.

Death stalked her in the tight maze of hallways as patients were wheeled by in stretchers. It haunted the fearful eyes of family members in waiting rooms. Life was so fragile, so fleeting.

Lily quickened her pace, overcome with an urgent need to see Nash, to feel tucked into the haven of his embrace.

Stubborn, stubborn, stubborn. Sam Bowman was worse than a headstrong mule when it came to modern medicine. Nothing Nash or the doctors said earlier today could shake his resolve at refusing another heart operation.

"I done tried it before and I'm not doing it again. The spirits told me the end is drawing near and I aim to spend what's left of my life fishing and roaming my own property and dying in my own bed."

Nash unwrapped a barbecue sandwich, knowing he needed to eat but not having much of an appetite. Nothing was more physically and emotionally draining than sitting for hours and hours at a hospital. He'd rather brave climbing a Peruvian mountain in a sleet storm.

Lily appeared equally exhausted. Her face was drawn and pale and she kept rubbing her temples.

"Headache?" he asked.

"The worst. I think I'm allergic to hospitals."

"You didn't have to come." He was surprised she had after their argument. But he had to admit her presence had been comforting, even if he was still angry. And at least he knew she was safe as long as he was with her for protection. "Let me get you some aspirin." He half rose from the sofa but she waved him to sit back down.

"Um, no. I don't take pills. I have a weird metabolism. A little food and wine will help."

She picked at her basket of fried shrimp, appearing to take as little enjoyment of the takeout food as he did.

A few more bites of the barbecue and Nash gave up on it. He took a long swallow of beer and stared moodily out the window of his grandfather's cottage.

"It's his decision, you know," Lily said quietly. "And who's to say it's the wrong one? Seems like he's outlived all his family."

Irritation spiked his gut. "I'm still here. Dad and my brother are still alive."

"But he hardly sees y'all. You're spread all over the country, living your own lives."

"He could come visit us. Over the years, I've sent him dozens of invitations to join me. Places like Hawaii and Alaska and South America, all at my expense. He refuses to leave the bayou." Nash realized he was shouting and calmed himself. "It's like he's obsessed with this damn place."

"It's his home. And you've told me he's held in high

regard by your tribe. They come from Mobile and farther for his help when they're sick or need council."

"All the more reason to live as long as possible," he snapped. "He helps everyone except himself."

Nash had brought up that exact point in his futile attempt to convince his grandfather to undergo another heart operation. But Sam was having none of it.

"Another healer will take my place," he'd said. "Someone who can be guided by the animal spirits and Mother Earth better than I ever could. A man born to this destiny but who has yet to discover all his gifts."

There had been a certain directness in his grandfather's eyes when he'd spoken those words that had shivered through Nash like the burning cold of frostbite. *He couldn't possibly mean— No way— I don't want this— No, no, NO.*

But Sam hadn't pushed the point. He'd closed those burning black eyes and murmured, "I need to rest. Come back in the morning."

Lily set down her glass of wine and strolled over to a small gallery of black-and-white photos mounted above the fireplace. She pointed to the largest, a woman in her mid-thirties with long black hair braided in two plaits, dressed in a plain white shirt adorned with a beaded and feathered necklace. The woman's expression was sober, intense. "Your grandmother, right?" Lily asked.

"Momma Nellie," Nash confirmed. "She died when I was quite young. I only remember her as a quiet woman, always cooking and doing her beadwork."

Lily idly traced a finger over the beaded bracelet on her wrist. "How did she die?"

"Boating accident. She'd gone out fishing alone one morning and the boat capsized. Her body was found three days later. Grandfather doesn't talk much about it, but I believe he's mourned her all these years. As far as I know, he's never even looked at another woman."

Lily's arms hugged her waist. "Drowned. How horrible. She couldn't swim?"

"No. I can't understand how someone can live near the ocean all their lives and never learn. Like you."

She ignored the jab. "Perhaps staying in Bayou La Siryna makes Sam feel closer to his Nellie."

"Maybe. And he places importance on living in the land of his ancestors."

She turned and pierced him with a direct gaze, an arrow that fissured his soul. Nash recalled the intensity of his sun ritual, when he'd felt the love and protection of all who had come before him and walked the same path in the same place.

"Don't you feel it, too?" she asked.

Against the backdrop of the darkened window, her hair glowed in a tangle of golden curls, bright as lighthouse beams in a storm.

Your destiny.

The seagull's message slammed into him anew.

"No," he denied peevishly. "There's nothing special about Bayou La Siryna."

This was all a trap. He was being hemmed in on all sides—his grandfather's expectations, the communion of his ancestors, but most of all, by the call of Lily. It was too much, too fast. He was being sucked in like quicksand. The longer he stayed in the bayou, the deeper he was drawn into the pit until the roots of the prevalent majestic oaks tangled around him deeper, tighter, until at last there would be no escape. The swampy miasma would swallow him up until it smothered and choked him into surrendering his freedom.

She walked to him and stopped an arm's length away. "You don't mean that," she said, her voice all honey and harmony.

"Why do you stay here? You have enough money to live anywhere. Why this marshy swampland?"

"It's been home to my kind—I mean, my family—forever."

Not knowing better wasn't a valid reason for exploring the world. He'd traveled it for years now, made a name for himself, been successful in a tough, crowded field. His life had been fine until some unknown enemy had slithered into his personal life, silent and deadly as a water moccasin.

Nash couldn't shake the feeling that the unknown woman was nearby, lying in wait, coiled and poised to strike. And this time—the third time—she would kill Lily, sink her poisonous fangs into that fair skin. His brain ran in circles again—that endless groove of searching his past romantic relationships for clues. If only he could read people like he did animals and nature.

"I should leave," he said, his voice guttural and harsh. "And so should you."

"You're thinking of the stalker again."

"Not a stalker—a killer. Call it what it is."

"Your grandfather needs you," Lily reminded him. "*I* need you."

He studied her sea-blue eyes. So blue and bottomless he could drown in them if he let himself dive into those tempting deep pools. She was like the bayou—mysterious, full of secrets and a living link to memories of his carefree childhood.

Lily stepped closer, toe to toe with him. "Did you hear me, Nash? I need you. Don't go. Not yet."

And then she kissed him, her soft flesh pressed against

his, reminding him of their joining earlier this morning. But this time, instead of the purity and openness and sunlight of the beach, it was night and moonbeams and a sweet seduction into an unknowable magic.

One day she would regret he ever returned to the bayou. They were hurtling toward some dangerous day of reckoning; he sensed it with every glimmer of a gift that had been passed on through his Choctaw ancestors. If only she could trust him with her secrets, the way he had shared his own.

But for now, it was night and she was life and feminine energy and alive—and he'd spent all day with sickness and death and worry. So he drank in Lily's comfort, rejuvenated by her essence. Nash returned the kiss, marveling at how perfectly they complemented one another in every way.

He abruptly pulled away and took her hand. A pause—a look, that unspoken communication that was timeless between men and women—and she followed as he led her to his bedroom. They undressed slowly under the flickering moonbeams pouring through the window. Her naked body filled him with awe—he'd never tire of the sight as long as he lived.

And this time their joining was tender. Nash took his time, determined to postpone his ultimate pleasure until he'd touched and tasted every part of her creamy, sleek body. He didn't stop until her moans of demand could no longer be denied. He covered her body with his own and entered, sinking deep into her core, until they both found their release.

And so the night went on. He made love to Lily many times, as if it were the only night they were promised to spend together. When the first light of morning dawned,

Lily lay in his arms, her mouth slightly curved upward in an innocent, trusting smile.

Whatever it took, Nash vowed to protect her from the danger that stalked.

Chapter 14

Gusting winds trembled the Spanish moss in the tall oaks, making the trees appear like old bearded men shaking their heads. The sky dulled from turquoise to smutty gray and scented the breeze with an electric charge that promised rain.

Not great weather for deep-sea fishing. Which meant that her chances of confronting Carl Dismukes alone on his boat were probably slim this morning. But she had to try.

Giving Nash the slip hadn't been easy. She'd sat with him and his grandfather most of the morning before announcing she had a few errands to run. Nash made her promise that she would keep a family member with her for protection.

She'd lied, of course. This job was something she needed to do alone.

Lily parked her car next to the storage shed, got out

and glanced back at her house. The old Victorian appeared the same as always—solid, feminine in its curved lines, inviting. Grand without being so majestic as to attract undue notice from the townsfolk. No hint that it had been trespassed, yet Lily wondered if it would ever seem as safe and secure as it once had.

How had the intruder broken in? All their doors were double-bolted, had been since the incident with the serial killer last year. They'd all believed their world was secure again, their haven in the bayou permanently restored. Until someone had trespassed yet again.

And then there was Dismukes.

The first raindrops sprinkled as Lily unlocked the shed. As she quickly secured it behind her after she entered, the familiar musk smell of enclosed spaces washed over her, comforting in its familiarity. This space had never been violated by outsiders. To the rest of the world, it appeared to be an ordinary detached shed, a stainless-steel safeguard against strong winds and the occasional hurricane.

Inside, the room was empty save for a shoe rack and a pegged rack for clothes, bags and robes. In its center was a hole about the size of a manhole cover on a paved street. Lily stripped naked and hung up her clothes, glad to be rid of their lingering antiseptic scent.

She picked up an oilcloth sporran from one of the pegs and discarded the items in it that she wouldn't need for this trip—a few scavenged pearls and antique coins, a couple of seashells that had caught her eye, a small golden trinket to remind her of the sun while in the darkest realms, seaweed string for tying fish together and pulling back her hair while hunting, a mirror and various other knickknacks. Her sea purse was nearly as stuffed as the leather one she toted on land.

Lily carefully drew out a slender abalone vial and unscrewed its coral stopper. Excellent—it was more than half-full with a liquid neurotoxin harvested from seasnake venom. This she would bring. She withdrew her knife from its leather case and examined the edges, satisfied it was sharp. This she would also bring. Last, she unclasped an airtight clamshell, ensuring that it was filled with sand. The shell was secured on a leather chain that could be worn like a necklace. She placed it in the sporran and belted it around her waist. These three items were all she needed to carry.

The sound of the ocean was louder inside than outdoors, the crash of waves reverberating off the steel walls. Splattering rain echoed on the tin roof, casting an illusion that the storm was already in full swing. During heavy rainfall, the effect was like being trapped inside a steel drum during an air raid.

Compacted sand squished between her toes as she approached the portal. Generations of Bosarge women had used this same portal for shifting from land to sea and back again. Curiosity about land dwellers had always run high, and many mermaids and mermen had chosen to live among humans over time. Many of Bayou La Siryna's citizens unknowingly carried distant merblood in their veins. Lonely, remote bayous had always appealed to merfolk as a portal because they afforded the needed privacy to mingle undetected.

She entered the water feetfirst, legs instantly melding into a fishtail that shimmered with a glow that cast rainbow prisms on the shed's walls and ceiling, as if someone had switched on a jeweled candelabra. Down she went, until the narrow tunnel widened. Lily swam out of the tiny undersea cave and into the Gulf waters.

Briny tang coated torso and tail in welcome and Lily

luxuriated in its caress, as if the ocean were lover and mother and friend. She flipped and rolled, playful as a dolphin. Bubbles and billowing hair swilled about her body, drawing the attention of a few rainbow runner fish that brushed against her arms and tail. The eternal swish of the currents roared in her ears, a muffled static to the chirps and hums of sea creatures teeming below on their eternal quests for food and mates.

Too bad today wasn't a mere joy swim.

Lily quit the acrobatics and used her sonar senses to set her course. Past experience had taught her where Carl best liked to anchor down for fishing. With his enforced retirement, the man's passion for fishing was indulged almost daily. An impending storm wouldn't deter him as quickly as most humans. He was one-eighth merman, so in any boating disaster he had the advantage of being an exceptional swimmer and could even stay submerged underwater for a good length of time. Perhaps as long as ten minutes, Lily guessed from various accounts she'd heard from other mermaids.

Still, he was no match for her at sea. Especially with her advantage of surprise.

Distant churning vibrations signaled a boat ahead, exactly where Carl preferred to fish most days. Lily swam closer, the roaring of the motor louder, more strident, churning a thick maze of foamy bubbles.

Abruptly, the motor cut off and silence reigned. A fishing cable plunked in the water ahead with a bit of shrimp dangling at the end as bait.

Lily circled underneath the boat and studied the hull. Made of white fiberglass and at twenty-five feet long and eight and half feet wide, it fit the dimensions and color of Carl's vessel, which she'd observed many times in previous swims. She swam near twin one-hundred-fifty horsepower motors with their ominous black blades, careful to keep a safe distance in case it roared to life. She read the Yamaha label, which was the brand Carl used. Yet she had to be 100 percent certain this was Dismukes and that he hadn't brought a friend out on this expedition, although that was a rarity.

She sped out fifty yards from the boat and calculated the risks. First, the location was too far from shore for anyone to spot her from land. Two, she'd only raise her head above water for an instant. Three, she'd perform this final check on the boat's stern. More than likely, Carl's back should be to her while he cast his fishing lines.

With a mighty swoosh of her tail, Lily wiggled up and broke surface. The nictating membrane in her eyes instantly adjusted to air and she spotted Dismukes's profile. His white hair fell in a damp, untidy mess about his long, angular face. He was bare-chested and she was surprised that despite his age, he had good muscle tone in his chest and back.

No matter. This was her chance and she was taking it.

Lily sped forward, deadly and silent as a torpedo, slowing only as she neared the boat's low-sided stern. She took one last quick peek at Dismukes, who was absorbed in baiting the troll lines. The opportunity would never be greater than this moment. She slithered up and over the low side as soundlessly as possible, tail instantly morphing to legs. Lily curled into a ball, casting an anxious eye to the boat's bow.

Dismukes's back was to her. Success! No doubt the low rumble of thunder now tumbling in from the west had helped shield any noise from her landing. Heart hammering, she glanced around the interior for something to throw over her naked body. She shouldn't give a damn about modesty, but couldn't bear the thought of his crude leering.

Lily spotted a beige cotton shirt on the floorboard underneath an empty cooler. Carefully, she pried it loose. Fish blood and slime were smeared across the front and it smelled as awful as it looked. But it was long and oversize, which was what mattered. She slipped it on, grateful that it fell midthigh. It was damp on one side from the steadily increasing rain, but it would have to do. She unsheathed the buck knife from her sporran, hung the clamshell necklace over the front of the shirt and left the sporran flap open in case she needed quick access to the poison vial, her last desperate weapon for self-defense.

Lily padded forward on bare feet until Dismukes was within six feet. "Are the fish biting?" she called out.

Carl jumped and swung forward, jumbo shrimp scattering down his legs. A fishing pole clattered to the floorboard.

"Wh-What?" he sputtered, the whites of his eyes exposed in fear.

Lily took momentary pleasure at his terror. After all he'd put her family through over the years, he deserved that and so much more.

He looked past and around her, evidently checking for any more unpleasant surprises. "How?" Carl shook his head. "You swam out here." His gaze swept the sea. "Alone?"

"Maybe," she brazened. "Or maybe there are a dozen mermaids below, ready for my signal to sink your precious boat."

Carl's spine stiffened and his face resumed a cunning edge she always associated with him.

"Nah, you're alone." His lips curled into a sneer as he pointed at the weapon held loosely in her right hand.

"Gonna take more than a buck knife to scare me, little girl."

Show no fear. "We'll see." Lily kept her voice cool, face composed. She raised her right hand and waved it loosely, the sun sparkling on the knife's metal surface. "Nice vessel. Folks around here always wondered how you could afford a sixty-thousand-dollar boat on a county deputy's salary. I'd say you owe me and my family a huge thanks for past services rendered."

"That what you sneak on board for? To force me to be polite? Okay, then. Thank you. Now get the hell off my boat."

"Not until I get what I came for."

"Which is?"

"To make you understand my family won't be blackmailed anymore."

"Jet and Shelly put you up to this?" He spat off the boat's side. "Bitches. Shelly's a weakling. And now that Jet's knocked up, they elected you to do the dirty work."

Crude old bastard. "The balance of power has shifted in the bayou. Tillman and Landry are the head honchos now, and you're a nobody. Stay away from us."

"Or else?" He raised a shaggy gray eyebrow and grinned, as if she'd delivered the punch line to a joke.

"Don't underestimate our kind's ability to protect one another. We're not without our own defenses. Once we spread the word to other merfolk about your threats, these waters will swarm with some pissed-off mermaids and mermen."

"So what?"

"Look at you. You're out here almost every day—even in *this*." Lily raised a hand skyward, indicating the storm. "Keep messing with us and you'll have to give up your passion for boating. You will never be safe at sea again."

"Passion, you say?"

His words came out garbled, husky—not his usual raspy bark. Carl's face had gone funny, too. His eyes were glazed and he wouldn't meet her gaze. Lily glanced down, following the path of his eyes, and immediately realized what had distracted Carl.

Rain had plastered the grimy cotton shirt to her breasts, exposing the outline of her nipples and the thatch of hair between her thighs. She needn't have bothered putting on the filthy rag, for all the protection it offered.

So much for modesty.

"Look at my face, you pervert."

Instead, his gaze drifted lower. Lily fought the impulse to cross her hands in front of her thighs. *Don't let him know it bothers you. He wants to humiliate you, gain the upper hand.* "Enjoying the view?" she asked, acting as if she could give a rat's ass.

"I ain't looking at nothing that half the men in Bayou La Siryna haven't done seen."

Fury lanced, as sharp as if her mermaid tail had slashed against needle-pointed coral. She'd been offended when her family thought she'd murdered Perry, but now Lily believed she truly had it in her to kill. The knowledge of the poisonous vial in her sporran made her hands itch to fling it in Dismukes's lecherous face.

Stay calm. Think. "Too bad you'll never get further than the looking stage, asshole."

He chuckled and gave a wink. "I've had my eye on you for years. Maybe we can work out our own little deal."

"No deals." She gripped the knife tighter. "I'd rather die than let you touch me."

"Methinks you protest too much." He stepped forward. "I could satisfy you more than that Indian dude you're sleeping with. Slut like you probably likes it a little on the rough side, I bet."

"Shut up." She was getting nowhere talking.

"Does he know you're a freak of nature? Play nice with me and it'll stay our little secret."

"I've told him," she lied.

He grinned and advanced another step, almost in arm's reach. "You're bluffing."

Lily scooted backward and fumbled with the necklace clasp, not daring to break his stare. She emptied the clamshell and cupped the sand in her left palm.

Carl's bushy gray brows drew together. "What the hell you got there?" he asked incredulously. "Sand?"

Lily mentally tested the wind. It was blowing against her back, right in Dismukes's direction. *Perfect.* She flung it into his eyes as hard as she could.

Carl stumbled and rubbed at his face, grinding the gritty sediment farther into the tender tissue of his eyeballs. "You little bitch!"

Now was her chance. Lily lifted a knee, preparing to kick him in the groin while he was blind and helpless.

Damn. She couldn't do it, not yet, anyway. At one time, Lily wouldn't have hesitated. Behind the mesmerizing voice and serene face lay a steel determination no one suspected, save her family. It was why she was here, after all. But she remembered how calmly, and with such dignity, Nash had dealt with Gary and his friends at the restaurant. Maybe there was a way to get Carl off their backs without resorting to violence. Quickly, she gathered up a length of coiled rope on the deck and tied Carl's hands behind his back. By the time he realized her plan, she had him good as handcuffed.

Tears streamed down his face, his body's natural reaction to the irritant in his eyes. Lily waited until his vision returned and then slowly curled her lips into that Mona Lisa smile she'd perfected over the years. That mask that hid all traces of inner turmoil. *Be strong. Show any mercy or weakness and it's game over.* She had to do this or none of them would ever be free from his greed. He would ruin her family and Lily couldn't bear it if that happened.

"Look at me, Carl. Here's how it's going to be. You aren't going to destroy my family. We'll never work for you again. You're going to go away quietly because to expose us is to expose yourself. Understand?"

"Why should I listen to you?" he said with a sneer.

"You have one week to leave Bayou La Siryna."

He raised an eyebrow. "And if I don't?"

"You didn't act concerned about me contacting other mermaids about your threats. But what if I told you I could rally some of the Blue Mermen Clan this way?"

Carl paled and worry lines creased his brow.

"Ah. You *have* heard of them, I see. One of their clan—a particularly vicious one named Orpheous—is quite enchanted with me. He and his friends wouldn't hesitate to kill you. All it would take is one word from me."

"But—"

"No buts. Live out what's left of your miserable life someplace far from here and keep your mouth shut. Because if you don't, the Blue Mermen will find you. And anytime you're at sea you'll always be wondering who's underneath, ready to pull you under, never to be seen or heard from again. Because I promise you, we'll do it."

A bolt of lightning flashed in the gray sky and thunder cracked loud as a shotgun blast. She gathered her knife from the floorboard and circled behind Carl. With two slices, she cut through the rope's binding and tucked the knife back into her sporran. Carl swung around with a fist raised.

Lily waved an index finger in his face. "Not a good idea," she sang in her sweetest siren's voice.

He slowly lowered his hand and his shoulders slumped in defeat.

"Better hurry to land," she added. "The storm has arrived."

And she dove under, heading home.

Nash paused at the closed door, puzzled by the laughter and murmurs of many voices on the other side. He checked the room number—408—which he'd been told was his grandfather's new room after being moved from intensive care. He pushed open the door and entered, surprised to find a dozen or so men and women packed inside.

Raymond, his grandfather's closest friend, stepped forward and shook his hand. About Sam's age, Raymond was tall and gangly. Just as Nash remembered as a kid, he still sported the same turquoise bolo tie whether dressed in a business suit or jeans.

"Thanks for calling me last night, Nashoba. I alerted the rest of the tribe that he was at the hospital and many wanted to come pay their respects."

Nash nodded at the assemblage, deeply touched by their concern for Sam. He glanced around at the unusual bevy of gifts—no flowers or fruit baskets in sight. Instead, a few eagle and crow feathers were strategically placed by the window and at the foot of Sam's bed. A colorful dream catcher adorned the standard-issue medical cot and on the nightstand sat open bowls of fresh crumbled tobacco and sage. The rich, earthy aroma mingled with the scent of food. Lots of food. Every square inch of flat space on the dresser, shelf and windowsill was stacked with aluminum-covered casserole dishes.

Sam sat up in bed, looking much healthier. He'd changed out of the hospital gown and wore a short-sleeved denim shirt and cargo pants. He was down to just one IV stuck in his arm. Although his color was better, Nash could read the fatigue in his eyes, and the lines in his face seemed more deeply etched, as if the heart attack had aged him overnight.

Nash approached the foot of the bed and nodded. "How are you, Grandfather?"

"Better," he answered. "Ready to go home."

Nash knew not to bring up the operation in front of present company. To argue the point would insult his grandfather's dignity.

"Docs say he can be released in the morning," Raymond piped in. "I'd be honored to stay at Sam's cottage a few days or as long as he needs to regain his strength."

Nash clenched his jaw to refrain from arguing that his grandfather should undergo further surgery. Raymond was not to blame for Sam's stubbornness.

"Thank you for your kindness," he said, clasping Raymond forearm to forearm.

Sam spoke up, his voice proud. "This is my grandson, Nashoba. Many of you have not seen him since he entered manhood."

Shame gutted Nash, quick and deep. He should have visited more often instead of insisting his grandfather travel to meet him.

Raymond raised his arms at the crowd. "Time to go and let them visit in private. Sam needs to get some rest, as well."

A scraping of chairs and the whoosh of people gathering their belongings, and then one by one they shook Nash's hand and waved goodbye to Sam.

Alone, he stared at his grandfather and shook his head. "Is there no talking you into having another operation?"

"My mind is set and I'm at peace," Sam said firmly. "I have prayed to my God and the spirits have answered."

Nash conceded defeat. Sighing, he pulled up a chair close to Sam's cot. "Then I suppose I have no choice but to accept your decision." His throat constricted, remembering how kind his grandfather had been on those summer visits long ago. The bayou had been his childhood refuge, a place to escape his parents' constant bickering and the hustle of city life, which he'd detested. All during the long school years he looked forward to exploring the Alabama backwoods and hearing his grandfather's tales of the Choctaw.

"I'm sorry," Nash said, throat burning with regret. "I should have visited more." He swallowed painfully. "Come sooner."

Sam grasped his shoulder with surprising strength. "None of that now. I understood the circumstances."

He'd been thirteen when his parents divorced, and his mother had spitefully refused to let him visit his paternal relatives in a misguided attempt to punish Nash's father for his many infidelities. For his part, Nash's father was too wrapped up in his own life to want to return to Bayou La Siryna. To him, the place he grew up in was dull and he couldn't wait to leave at the soonest opportunity.

Still, Nash wished he hadn't been so set on traveling and building his own career. He should have visited more once he was older and on his own.

"I, um, spoke to Dad last night. He'll be flying out in the next couple of weeks, as soon as he wraps up his latest business trip." Nash had urged him to come sooner, but his father was insistent he had other matters to finish first.

"It will be good to see him again," Sam said, removing his hand and settling against his pillows.

Nash hoped that whatever distance had come between his father and grandfather could be healed before it was too late.

The room seemed too quiet now after the earlier crowd of well-wishers. Sam's eyes had closed, but Nash didn't think he'd fallen asleep yet. "Grandfather?" he asked tentatively.

Sam's eyes opened. "Yes?"

"Tell me one of your stories again like you used to." Nash didn't want to ever forget them. He yearned for the closeness they'd once shared. "Unless you need to rest," he added quickly.

The deep lines on his grandfather's face softened and he smiled softly. "Which one?"

"You choose."

"The most important one is that of the Okwa Nahollo."

"The white people of the sea."

"With skin the color of trout," Sam said with a nod. "There are places deep in the swamp where the water changes to a clear white color. That's where they live. It is said that if you near this mysterious pool of clear water, they will take you down below to their home under the sea. Should you stay with them more than three days, you may never return to land."

"I wonder how this legend came to be," Nash mused.

His grandfather regarded him with a profound intensity. "Legend? It's true."

Surely Sam didn't expect him to believe these old tales like he once had as a child. "Okay," Nash said mildly. Now was no time to scoff.

"They exist. And a day will come soon when you see this truth."

What kind of medication was his grandfather taking? He seemed lucid enough—but mermaids? Really.

"Since you've returned, haven't you felt and seen things more deeply? Haven't the land and its creatures revealed anything to you?"

Nash immediately thought of the crows and seagulls telling him Lily was of two spirits. "I have," he admitted.

"I'll tell you more of the Okwa Nahollo, things that aren't part of the general legend. It's a truth that the waters have whispered to me over the years."

Nash's skin prickled. "Go on."

"As our people were being rounded up for the Trail of Tears, the sea dwellers heard their wails. Those who chose, those who believed, escaped capture and removal. The Okwa Nahollo allowed them to come live with them undersea. There they were free, far from the government men who hunted them down."

Nash said nothing. His grandfather would never lie to him, so he must truly believe this had happened. It was probably what came with old age, a great imagination and too much time alone in the bayou.

"It's true," Sam insisted. "But you must discover this for yourself."

"Sorry, but you're right. To believe such a legend, I'd have to see a mermaid with my own eyes."

Sam closed his eyes once more and whispered, "Maybe you already have."

Chapter 15

"Where were you all day?" Nash had asked the moment she arrived at the hospital.

"Family business," Lily offered cryptically. "How's Sam?"

"Downgraded from ICU to a regular bed. He may even be released in the morning." Nash delivered what should have been good news with an air of impatience.

"I see. So you couldn't talk him into the operation?"

"No. His mind is good and made up."

Lily squeezed his arm in sympathy. Privately, she couldn't blame Sam for opting out. He'd lived a long life and deserved to meet his end on his own terms.

It had taken a long time to load up Nash's truck with the avalanche of food. Sam Bowman would be set for at least a couple of weeks. Even though it was human food and not her preference, the combined scent of turkey, corn bread, dressing and homemade pies created a homey, cozy kind of smell.

The truck jostled over the bumpy road to the Bowman cottage, which was worse than usual because of the earlier downpour. Although the storm had passed, it was dark for late afternoon, courtesy of a few lingering clouds that muddied the sky to a potash gray. Lily kept a check on the backseat, making sure none of the packaged food overturned. A comfortable silence settled in, for which she was grateful. The confrontation with Carl had left her exhausted and anxious. Had she done enough? Too much?

The jangling ring of her cell phone startled Lily and she scrambled in her pocketbook to find it. "Hello?" she answered breathlessly.

Click.

"Hello?" she repeated.

Silence.

"Who is it?" Nash asked sharply.

"Could just be a bad signal out here." Her fingers trembled as she pulled up the recent calls menu. It was a local number but not one she recognized. She pressed the number and waited.

"Whoever it is, they aren't answering," she said flatly. *Oh, hell, here we go again.*

"Let me see." Nash grabbed the phone and frowned at the screen. "Recognize the number?" he asked.

"No," she admitted.

"Son of a bitch." Nash handed the phone back to her and slammed a hand against the steering wheel. "I'll call Tillman as soon as we reach the cottage. See if he can do anything."

"It's not the same phone number from the last incident." Lily tried to infuse some optimism in her voice. But the memory of the slashed canvases sent a renewed surge of anxiety rippling down her spine. At least with Dismukes, the enemy was in the open.

"Big deal. It'll turn out to be from a throwaway phone again."

Nash's frustration and bitterness was palpable, his body rigid with anger.

It was so much worse for him, even though the threat was directed at her. He'd been dealing with this for so long, Lily couldn't fathom the pain he must have endured, was still enduring.

"Tillman and Landry will find whoever—"

The phone rang again and Lily dropped it in her lap as if it were a live thing with the power to sting. "Same number as before," she said, inhaling sharply.

Nash scooped it up and pressed the answer button. "Who are you?" he demanded. "You fucking coward." He dropped the phone in the console in disgust. "They hung up again." He accelerated the truck, branches and shrubs scraping noisily against its sides. He drove as if speeding to an encounter, desperate to confront danger head-on.

"At least she knows I'm not alone," Lily offered. "Maybe—do you suppose—we could set a trap? We could make her think I'm alone one evening while you secretly lie in wait."

"Not a chance."

Nash's tone was implacable, but Lily couldn't let go of the idea. If Nash wouldn't do it, perhaps she could talk her brothers-in-law into it. The sooner, the better.

"I don't like waiting for her to catch me," she insisted. "This might be the safest option."

"Absolutely not." Nash pulled up to the cottage and abruptly slammed on the brakes. He turned to face her, dark eyes gleaming with intensity. "Get it out of your head. Understand?"

I understand what needs to be done. "Okay," she agreed at once.

Nash narrowed his eyes. "I mean it," he ground out in a voice hard as diamonds.

"I said *okay*." Lily scrambled out of the truck and slammed the door. He didn't have to be so testy on the subject.

With an impatient sigh, Nash got out and they each gathered armfuls of the gifted food from the back of the truck. In a silence that was no longer peaceful or comfortable, they climbed up the cabin steps.

A sheet of notebook paper was pinned to the door with a message written in large red block letters.

"No trespassing. Go Home Lily."

She stared at it stupidly, the words sinking in slow, burning like hot lava. The roar of thousands of crickets and cicadas buzzed in her brain. What was it Sam used to say? Something about crickets signaling that bad prayers and wishes were being cast upon you. She glanced behind her and then to the tree line past the yard. Was there someone out there now, waiting for a chance...one unguarded moment to snatch her into the darkness?

Nash swore under his breath, and she caught the sentiment, if not the exact words. He set the casserole dishes on a porch rocker and took the load from her arms, as well. Nash grabbed a large tree branch that had fallen near the porch steps and roughly pulled her behind his body as he tested the lock. "Stay behind me," he ordered.

"Be careful," she whispered against the soft cotton of his T-shirt. She pressed her head between the hard blades of his broad shoulders, inhaling his musky sandalwood scent.

The door was securely shut, so he fished keys from his jeans pocket and unlocked it. They entered, Nash's palm curled tightly on the branch, ready for battle. Lily peaked around his shoulder. The small den appeared undisturbed, same as always. She let out a whoosh of relief as some of the tension unfurled from her tight muscles. "It looks okay," she ventured, stepping to his side.

"Stay close," he said shortly.

Lily willingly followed as he walked, silent and deliberate, into every room, checking closets, windows and under beds.

Nothing.

"Looks like she wasn't able to break in," Lily said. "We're safe."

"For now."

Frustration laced his words and Lily suspected he was disappointed not to uncover an intruder. He wanted to find the culprit and end her deadly games.

"Let's get the food put away and leave," he said, glancing at the clock over the fireplace. "We can catch the last ferry out to the island if we hurry."

"You think she'll come back tonight?"

"I'm not taking any chances while you're with me." Nash abruptly pulled her to him and wrapped her in a fierce embrace. "I won't let anyone hurt you. Ever." His breath was fiery and fervent as he kissed the top of her scalp.

He released her as quickly as he had gathered her close. "Stay in the kitchen while I bring everything in."

They made quick work of storing everything, placing a few casseroles in the fridge and most everything else in the freezer. Lily opened a large plastic bin, grateful to find it filled with a fish stew. They could eat this tonight on the island.

Supper in hand, they returned to his truck. Lily stared back at Sam's cabin, a new worry wiggling in her brain like a worm. "If Sam's released in the morning, you'll need to stay with him while he gets his legs under him."

"He's got a friend that's going to stay with him."

"Do you think they'll be safe?"

"I do. The killer only came here to find you. But I'll warn them to be careful. My grandfather has several shotguns and the two of them are both excellent hunters."

"He shouldn't have to worry. The stress can't be good for his heart."

"I know. I've done him more harm than good coming back."

She studied his profile, noting the grim set of his jaw. "I don't believe that. He's thrilled you're here. Besides—" she pointed at the warning note he'd carefully removed from the cottage door and placed in the backseat "—that might give Tillman and Landry a clue to the woman's identity. With any luck, they'll find her soon."

"Doubtful. But we'll pay them a visit in the morning after I check on my grandfather."

His mood stayed somber as they again traversed the muddy potholed road, rushing to catch the last ferry ride of the day. What a nuisance having to depend on a boat when she could easily swim to the island alone. If he only knew... Lily reached out a hand and placed it on his thigh, wondering what he'd think if he saw her shape-shift to mermaid form. When this ordeal was over, and if he decided to stay in Bayou La Siryna, she would have to reveal her secret. He'd been so open with her about his own supernatural abilities—maybe he had it in him to accept hers, as well. *Lots of ifs and buts and maybes.* No point borrowing more trouble with speculations on the future when the present swirled with danger.

The moon beckoned like the call of a long-lost lover. Lily stole a glance at Nash, sprawled on his back, chest moving rhythmically up and down in deep slumber.

Their evening had been subdued, each absorbed in their own troubles. Their earlier rift over revealing secrets remained a wedge between them. She'd tried to cajole him out of his gloom, but he stayed reserved and she'd felt so removed from him, at least until they'd made love. Their shared passion remained unmarred from the outside world and all its problems. One pure thing, intimate and open. And she'd come oh-so-close to telling him she loved him. But when she did, Lily wanted the timing to be perfect, unfettered by secrets and danger.

She stared out the window, the moon tugging at her restless thoughts. How she craved a swim. Night was the best time of all undersea, when silver beams danced on the water's surface and starlight flickered above with pinpoints of light.

Dare she chance it?

It would be a relief to go undersea and erase the memory of today's harassment and especially the underwater confrontation with Carl. A reclaiming of her territory of sorts.

Ever so slowly, Lily disentangled her legs from beneath the sheet while keeping an eye on Nash. She eased off the bed and padded across the hardwood floor to the kitchen, then paused at the open doorway.

He hadn't moved. She could see him in the darkness, her mermaid nature accustomed to vision in the ocean's dark depths, the same eyesight that allowed her to see at night while on land. Nash's eyes remained closed, his breathing regular. Lily silently passed through the kitchen and to the separate bedroom on the other side of the lodge. He'd be less likely to hear any squeak from the other room's door. Gently, she crept out and waited to hear if she'd disturbed his slumber. If he sought her, she'd tell him she'd stepped out for some fresh air.

A few minutes of silence passed, and she was confident he hadn't heard anything. Lily ran sure-footed to the shore, tossing off her silk nightgown in the island breeze. Not even the softest of material felt as freeing or soft as the night wind against bare flesh.

She ran and ran until shore met sand, then slipped into sea, the transition to siren seamless and instant. Sediment and seaweed swirled, roused from the day's storm. Tonight the ocean was all astir, tumbling with power. Lily absorbed its energy, became one with its vital force. She drifted with the strong undertow, allowing it to draw her farther, deeper. Not fighting, not thinking, not plotting nor scheming as she had to do on land. Here, she was queen of the sirens, the pride of the merfolk, secure in her power.

Could she really give all this up? Did she want to?

Niggling doubts crept in, disrupting her mindless swim. The easiest path would be to leave the bayou with its endless problems and dangers. Her mother would be delighted and her own kind would welcome her return. With them, there would be no secrets or need for subterfuge. She could mate freely and do her duty in helping repopulate their dwindling species. Why resist her natural siren's call?

Lily propelled upward, fishtail beating back and forth, arms lifted, parting a path through the Gulf current until she was within a foot of the water's surface. She floated on her back and sought sight of the moon.

There. It shone a pale green, full and ripe in a pregnant beauty. Dark clouds drifted over its face, giving an illusion that it winked at her, sharing a secret, acknowledging its very own child of the waters.

The same ink-black clouds hid the stars, blanketing their beauty. Even so, Lily felt their burning presence, which refused to be muted by mere puffs of drifting nebula.

This must be how Nash experiences Earth. The very soil sings to him, and all land's creatures recognize he is one with them, a fellow brethren of land. He has more power than he knows, if he would but accept his gifts.

Nash's face flashed in her mind's eye, obscuring the moon. It was strong—harsh, even—sporting high cheekbones, an aquiline nose and a squared plane along his jawline.

I love him.

Totally, completely, unequivocal as any law of nature. Every cell in her body craved his touch, whether on land or at sea, as human or as mermaid. Nash was anchor and home in the world.

Could he learn to love her, as well? Or would he leave one day soon and return to his travels? Much as she loved him, she couldn't follow him down that road, even if he asked. To leave Bayou La Siryna and her portal was unthinkable. The bayou straddled land and sea, allowing the freedom to shape-shift between two worlds. She was a mermaid and needed the sea, even if it was restricted to this slice of the Gulf of Mexico.

Fight for him, Jet had advised.

And so she would. But only if he loved her, too, and could be satisfied keeping Bayou La Siryna as a home base. Nash was worth every danger. Always and forever.

Peace came with resolution and Lily swam for shore, longing to return to his bed, to feel his body pressed against her own. At the shallow sand bed that marked the meeting of ocean and earth, she glided in, tail fin dissolving as her body rolled onto shore. She arose, human legs wobbly at first until the adjustment to solid footing on ground, the earth steady and sure beneath the flesh of her soles.

The white of her nightgown whipped in the breeze at eye level, and a ghost cloud descended from the heavens. Lily narrowed her eyes and saw that the gown was attached to a human arm. Her gaze traveled the length of the arm to the man standing less than six feet in front of her—solid and strong as an oak tree.

Nash.

Oh, shit. Not now, not like this.

"Enjoy your swim?"

Angry disbelief surged through Nash and he marveled that he could even speak. *What the hell?* Was this a mirage or some kind of magical illusion? His world shook as if an earthquake rumbled beneath, tectonic plates shifting the natural order of the universe. He inhaled deeply, grounding himself against the maelstrom of this revelation.

No, it was real. He'd seen what he'd seen.

"You're a—" He sputtered and halted. Lily was— He couldn't bring himself to say the *M* word, much less think it.

She stood before him, eyes wide, wet and sleek as a dolphin, bits of seaweed clinging to her golden hair and pale skin. *Pale as trout.* His grandfather's tale of the Okwa Nahollo rang in his head, leaving him dizzy and disoriented. *Maybe you've even seen one and not known*, he'd said.

Lily took a tentative step forward, hand outstretched, pleading. "Oh, Nash. I didn't mean for you to find out so soon. And not like this."

He steeled himself against the anguish in her voice and eyes and stepped backward. Her hand fell to her side.

"I don't believe you were ever going to tell me," he ground out harshly. "You've lied to me from the beginning." Even as a child, she'd lied. He saw that now.

"I had to. Please try to understand. It's not just my secret. It's one I share with all my kind. Exposure to humans can mean our death."

"So you were toying with me all this time. Playing with me, treating me like a dumb animal you could pet and then abandon." He remembered all the local men and their crude remarks about the easy Lily Bosarge. "I'm the latest in your long string of conquests."

Her face grew even paler, white as the fabric of the nightgown he held in his hands. Nash bunched the silky folds in his fist and raised it toward her in accusation. "I woke up and when I couldn't find you in the lodge I went searching. Do you have any idea how scared I was? I was afraid the killer had found you."

"I—I'm so sorry. I didn't think you would—"

"You're damn right, you didn't think. And when I found *this*—" he shook the gown like it was some vile thing "—I thought maybe there'd been an accident. That you had drowned."

"I get it. You're angry I slipped away." She grew more composed, face smoothing into its usual calm. "You have every right."

"Damn straight."

"Now can we discuss the real issue?"

Her voice was sensible and matter-of-fact, as if she were dealing with an unreasonable child. Anger washed over him anew. "Fine. Let's talk about the fact you're a liar, a sneak."

"That's not what I meant and you know it." Gone was the sorrow and regret in her eyes. They glittered now with defiance as she lifted her chin. "You witnessed the change."

His mind balked at the image of Lily washing up on the beach. At first, he'd been terrified, certain she had drowned. And then a large mass behind her had shimmered, reflecting a rainbow of colors in the moon's light. Enough light to see that the object was a fishtail that began at the curve of her hips and narrowed down to a split fin. The colors he'd seen were pixilated scales where legs should have been. Seconds later, the shimmering mass had dimmed and become two columns of pure white. Lily had arisen on the sand like a ghost in the night.

He'd been rooted. Torn between relief she was alive and dismay at her dual nature and utterly, utterly astonished. Was this what the crow and seagull had been trying to tell him? *Two spirits*. Which was the real Lily? A creature of the sea, or the warm-blooded woman who was his lover?

His mind grappled with the warring emotions and he chose anger. Familiar, safe, old-fashioned anger that masked vulnerability and powerlessness.

"I don't want to talk about your—*change*," he spat out, mocking her euphemism. "Maybe the real issue here is trust and your lack of it. I opened up to you—told you things I've never shared with anyone. And there you sat with your big secret, never saying a word."

The confident defiance slipped and her chin quivered. "I was going to tell you."

"When?"

"Later. After the killer was caught and everything returned to normal."

"Normal?" He laughed bitterly. "Nothing about my

life is normal. You were the one good thing I had going for me."

Tears streamed down her face, almost undoing him.

"I'm still me," she said, placing a hand over her heart. "Lily."

The anger melted, replaced with an unbearable sorrow. "It feels like I don't even know you anymore," he said softly. "What other secrets do you hide?"

"Just one."

His heart took a nosedive off a cliff and he averted his face from hers, seeking balance.

She moved close and touched his arm. "Nash, look at me."

He gazed at her. Even now, wet and covered with bits of seaweed, she was the most beautiful woman he'd ever met.

"I love you."

The truth was there in her eyes. "Don't," he said, broken. "I'm a man who's brought you nothing but trouble."

"That's not true. You've taught me what it truly means to love another. I didn't know before if that was possible for me." She placed both her hands in his. "I don't expect you to tell me you love me, too. You've had a shock tonight. But answer me this—does my mermaid nature repulse you? Do we still have a chance?"

Nash drew in a deep breath. Repulsed? No. There had been beauty and magic in her mermaid body. No matter what form she took, Lily was lovely. Even now, the close proximity of her body made his blood pound with desire.

"You could never be anything but beautiful in my eyes," he admitted.

She dropped her head against his chest and he wrapped his arms around her slender waist.

"That's all I need to hear for now," she whispered.

Another cloud passed over the moon, pitching the world in black shadows. Still, he didn't let go of Lily.

Was this love?

His mind was confused, torn, uncertain of everything he once held as fact. There would be no answer to this question tonight. For tonight, he would keep her close, filled with wonder and an aching need to discover the real Lily.

Chapter 16

Lily tossed aside the sketchpad. She couldn't focus on anything except Nash. Besides, what was the point? Her best paintings had been ruined and her dreams of artistic recognition had been ripped apart as surely as the shredded canvases. It'd been a foolish ambition anyway.

"Problems?" Shelly asked in wry amusement. Her cousin didn't bother opening her eyes as she rocked on the front porch, the wooden floorboard creaking at a lazy pace. "Relax," she advised. "Sit a spell with me and enjoy the breeze. I love this island. It's so peaceful."

"So remote," Lily grumbled.

Shelly cocked open one eye. "Getting a little stir-crazy, are we?"

"You try sitting around here all the time." Lily stood and sighed heavily. "I'll go bring us more iced tea. You want anything to eat? We've got leftover fish stew and corn bread."

"Nah, I'm meeting Tillman for lunch in a bit."

Lily pushed open the screen door and entered the tiny kitchen. The lodge seemed deserted without Nash. *Don't get used to him hanging around forever*, her heart whispered in warning. She opened the fridge, removed the pitcher of tea and returned to the porch.

Shelly held out her glass and Lily poured more tea in it before refreshing her own glass. She sat in the rocker next to Shelly and tried to relax. Images from last night rattled around her brain in photographic clarity: Nash's grim face as he held her nightgown on the beach, their bodies intertwined in the moonlight later that night and the mysterious flicker in his eyes as he'd left on the morning ferry.

Where did they go from here?

She and Shelly fell into a syncopated rocking pattern that soothed her agitation.

"Do you want to talk about it?" Shelly's voice broke the companionable reverie.

Lily stared at her cousin, who was physically almost her mirror image. "Talk about what?" she hedged.

"Nash, of course. And how you've fallen completely in love with him."

"Jet must have told you." There weren't many secrets between the three of them.

"Nope. Figured it out all on my own."

"I'm that obvious, huh?"

"Only because I know you so well." Shelly took a long swallow of iced tea. "The feeling's mutual, right? I've seen the way he looks at you."

"He hasn't said so, but I'm hopeful."

"A man couldn't help but fall for you with that siren's voice."

"It's more than that," Lily said sharply. "He knows me—knows everything."

Shelly's eyes widened. "You mean—"

"He caught me swimming last night."

"Why did you take such a risk?" Shelly stopped rocking and her fingers tightened around her glass. "You must have wanted him to find out."

Lily opened her mouth to deny it, then clamped it shut. Maybe she subconsciously had wanted to force the issue.

Shelly bit her lip. "Hope he doesn't tell anybody."

"He won't," Lily said, bristling. "Nash wouldn't do that to me. To us."

"I hope you're right."

Lily frowned at her cousin's skepticism. "It's not like you didn't spill the beans with Tillman. And Jet did the same thing with Landry. Why shouldn't I be allowed to do the same?"

"But Nash is only here to do a photo assignment and visit his grandfather. It's not like he's staying."

The reminder was like a slap and something in her face must have communicated the hurt. Shelly got out of the chair and gave her a quick hug.

"Forget what I said. I just don't want you to get hurt, Lily."

"Too late." She attempted a wobbly smile.

Shelly ran a hand through Lily's hair. "Whatever the difficulty, the two of you can work it out. You deserve love as much as the rest of us. Don't give up on it."

"Jet said much the same." Lily got out of the rocker, restless. "Isn't it almost time for the noon ferry? I'll walk with you to the landing."

"Are we good?" Shelly asked with a tentative smile.

"We're good," Lily assured her. "Go gather your things."

Shelly scooped her pocketbook from the coffee table and they began the short walk to the ferry landing.

"I almost forgot to tell you some great news," Shelly said. "Your mom called this morning and reported that Dismukes's house has a for-sale sign in the front yard."

Relief washed through her. "One problem solved, a dozen more to go," she quipped.

"How'd you do it?" Shelly slanted a look of admiration.

"We had a little heart-to-heart talk while he was deep-sea fishing. The details aren't important." She didn't want to talk about or think about the encounter. "So what's the game plan for this afternoon? I'm sure Mom or Jet will show up next to babysit me."

"They went shopping in Mobile this morning for baby clothes, but said they'd be on the noon ferry to take my place. Don't be annoyed. You shouldn't be alone until Tillman finds the stalker. Besides, none of us want to face Nash's wrath if we left you unguarded."

Lily stifled a sigh. She'd much prefer to be by herself until Nash came on the last ferry. Mom would get on her nerves about returning to sea and Jet had enough to do running her antiques store. Lily could have gone to the hospital with Nash this morning and helped him get Sam settled back at his cabin, but she'd wanted them to have time alone together.

They arrived at the landing in time to see Ned pulling in the boat with only a handful of passengers.

Shelly frowned. "I don't see Mom and Jet." She dug her cell phone from her purse and entered her password. "Damn. I missed a call. They left a message saying they're running late and asked if I could stay with you the rest of the day."

"It's okay," Lily said quickly. "You go on and have lunch with Tillman. I'll be fine."

"No way. I'll call and cancel. He'll understand."

Lily again stifled a sigh and watched as Ned guided the boat to the small wooden pier where passengers exited onto the island. A flash of red hair blazed like fire in the harsh sun and a friendly, familiar face grinned at her from the boat.

"It's Opal," Lily said with a start, waving back at her friend. "I can't believe she's here."

Shelly paused from punching in numbers on her phone. "Who's Opal?"

"Nash's assistant. I met her earlier, but she left to go on another assignment."

They watched as Opal climbed out of the boat and strode down the short wooden walkway. A camera was slung across one shoulder and she carried a small tote bag.

"Problem solved," Lily said cheerfully. "You can go to your lunch with a clear conscience."

Shelly eyed the redhead pushing past an elderly couple with binoculars and a bird guide book. "You sure?"

"Positive." Lily waved an index finger in front of Shelly's face. "Better watch it," she said with a mocking grin. "You're getting as suspicious and paranoid as Jet."

"Okay, okay. Call me later."

"Stop being a mother hen," Lily said firmly. "I'm in no danger."

After a myriad of paperwork and a last-minute dire warning from the doctor on duty, Nash drove his grandfather home. Once there, Sam insisted on sitting up in his favorite chair on the back porch, which he claimed was the most comfortable spot in the small cabin. Nash pulled up a chair beside him.

"You feeling okay?" He studied Sam's face, searching for signs of fatigue.

"A little tired," he admitted. "But there is no pain and for that, I'm grateful. There will be no suffering when the spirits come to take me with them."

"Let's hope it's not for a long time."

"My time is near. Very near. And I have much to tell you."

Nash shifted uncomfortably in his seat and sincerely hoped his grandfather wasn't going to spring some shocking revelation. Discovering Lily was a mermaid last night still had his mind spinning. But he straightened in his chair and focused on Sam. He could at least do that much for his grandfather. "I'm listening."

"I have one last story to tell you. But first, why don't you share what's on your mind? Something has filled you with confusion."

Sam was as perceptive as always. Nash rubbed his face. It would help to talk over what he'd witnessed, but he didn't want to give away Lily's secret. "I can't go into specifics," he said carefully. "But last night I saw—" He drew a deep breath. If anyone would believe this wild tale, it was the man seated beside him. "I saw a mermaid."

Sam nodded and kept his face turned to the woods in the backyard. "Here? Or on the island?"

"The island." It was easier to talk with his grandfather's profile to him instead of his direct gaze. Nash also stared straight ahead.

"Then it wasn't the Okwa Nahollo, but some other manner of being that is closely related to our white people of the sea."

"You said you'd seen one of them before, but I didn't

believe it. Not that you would lie," he added quickly. "I thought you'd imagined it."

"No one would believe such a thing unless they saw it for themselves. I knew the day would come soon when you'd observe one firsthand."

"Shocked the hell out of me and I'm not sure I handled it well."

"Lily understands this."

Nash leapt to his feet. Sam had known it before he did. "You've known all along about her and didn't warn me?"

Sam calmly motioned for him to sit back down. "Some truths a man must discover for himself. Didn't the birds deliver a message?"

He slumped back down in the chair, bemused and bewildered. "They said Lily was of two spirits and that she was my destiny. Whatever that means."

"What do *you* think it means? Learn to search your own heart for answers. Be honest and fierce in seeking truth."

The trapped feeling he'd experienced before returned and the screened-in porch was like a cage. His world narrowed to the narrow slab of concrete flooring surrounded by metal screens. *No!* The spirits—fate—some supernatural force—were trying to snare him for their own mysterious reasons and he wanted no part of it. *Screw them.* He was his own man.

Nash rose to his feet again. "I need some space," he said shortly, heading to the door.

"Wait." Sam motioned for him to return to his seat. "Let's finish our talk first."

Reluctantly, Nash returned and sat, folding his arms across his chest. "How did you know about Lily? Oh, wait." He held up a hand. "The spirits told you."

Nash tried to keep the sarcasm contained inside, but

the words came out with a sardonic edge nonetheless. Sam had to have picked up on it, but he answered with his usual dignity.

"I've suspected for years that the Bosarge women were of the sea. You must observe and seek signs in the smallest of details, consider the behavior of your subject and keep an open mind. After all that, ask the spirits for help in interpreting all the information you've gathered. I did all three before I reached my conclusion."

Keep an open mind. He would try. The smallest details... Nash struck a palm against his forehead. "The tiny scars on each side of Lily's neck must be some sort of gill markings."

Sam nodded. "Go on."

"The pale skin." He pictured Lily's naked legs with their subtle mica shine. "Pale skin that glitters. Must be a small vestige of her mermaid fishtail." Nash stopped and stared at his grandfather. "I can't think of anything else."

"You're missing the biggest clue, but we'll come back to that. Can you identify any of Lily's actions and habits that could have helped you uncover her secret earlier?"

"Only in hindsight. I see now how she lied, but I thought she was merely reserved, overly private."

"If someone is guarded with friends and lovers, it is wise to ponder why. Here's what I have noticed. The Bosarge women have always lived in an isolated area and kept to themselves. No man has ever lived with them in that house. I suspect that somewhere on the property is a hidden portal where they come and go."

"That's some mighty big speculations based on little that is fact."

"And that's where your spirit guides can assist. But first you must do the groundwork and be open to that which is unlike any other reality you've experienced. If you do, you'll find the bayou is filled with magic."

Despite his reluctance to entertain the supernatural, a stirring of wonder fluttered in Nash's gut. "You told me you once saw the Okwa Nahollo. How did it happen? You must have caught one unaware, like I did with Lily."

Sam rocked in his chair, silent, his profile stern and unyielding as carved granite. But to Nash's astonishment, salty tears flowed down the deep crevices of his lined face.

"I didn't come across one unaware," he said. His grandfather's voice was gruff but sturdy. "Many, many years ago, she came to me. I was out fishing late one afternoon by the small nearby inlet, as is my custom. I grieved for my loss and she heard. My Nellie came for me."

Nash's breath caught and the skin on his arms and legs prickled. "Grandmother?"

Sam closed his eyes, reliving the moment. "I heard distant chanting in the old Choctaw tongue. It didn't come from the sky or float across the wind, but from underneath a clear white pool of water. As I stared at this calm patch, a mass of black tendrils drifted near the surface. I walked into the water up to my knees for a closer look." Sam paused and swallowed hard, opening his eyes again. "It was my Nellie, her long dark hair swirling about her pale, pale face, so different from the olive color I remembered. Her deep brown eyes were darker, too, like large, black pearls, but I recognized her instantly."

Nash's mind tumbled with a thousand questions. "What did she want? Did she speak?"

"The water parted and she came halfway out, exposed only to the top of her hips. And then she spoke, her voice as familiar and dear as always. She had heard my grief as I fished every night and she daily begged the Okwa Nahollo for a chance to console me until at last they granted her wish."

Incredible. Nash stood and paced the small porch, trying to wrap his mind around the strange tale. "But she died. Drowned in a boating accident." He stopped suddenly and whirled to face his grandfather. "Did the Okwa Nahollo kill her? Did they deliberately capsize her boat and drag her underneath to become one of them? My God, how you must hate them!"

"You misunderstand. They saved her life, took pity on the human whose lungs filled with water and could not breathe. They offered Nellie life, not death. And they accepted her as one of their own, just as they did with our ancestors who sought asylum rather than be forced on the Trail of Tears."

Nash propped a shoulder against a porch railing and stared at Sam. His tears had dried and a gentle light lit his eyes and a slight smile played along his lips. "I don't get it," Nash said slowly. "I would think it would be hell knowing your wife lives only a fifteen-minute hike away, yet you can never be with her as man and wife are meant to be."

"I had many, many years with Nellie on land. And two unforgettable nights with Nellie under the sea—the woman I thought was lost to me forever. The spirits showed me great favor. I am grateful for the blessing."

If you stay with the Okwa Nahollo three days or longer, you can never return to land, his grandfather had once told him. "Maybe you should have stayed the third night," Nash said around the painful lump in his throat. "You could have been with Grandmother all this time."

"I was needed with my people here."

Nash shook his head. "It was too great a sacrifice."

"You must do what the spirits have called you to do. We all have our duties." Sam pinned him with a pointed stare. "Destiny denied leads to days filled with sorrow and regret."

Lily is your destiny, the seagull had proclaimed.

"Duty and destiny," Nash said heavily, the very words like shackles chaining his soul. "I've been told my destiny. Now I suppose you're about to tell me my duty." Of late, Sam had been hinting at it more frequently and directly.

"You have the gift to heal. It's a blessing, not a curse."

"Go on," Nash said between pinched lips. "Say it. You want me to stay in Bayou La Siryna and take your place."

Sam reached out to the porch railing for support and rose slowly, straightening his arthritic knees. Yet, as usual, he maintained a dignity accorded a wise man who had lived an honorable life.

Nash both respected and envied his grandfather's noble bearing. He could never, ever measure up to this man he admired. It wasn't fair that this was demanded of him.

"There is always a choice." Sam placed an aged hand on Nash's shoulder. The weight felt heavy, an anchor forcing him down. "Choose wisely."

Nash twisted out of his grasp. "Okay, now I *really* need to get out of here for some fresh air." He jerked open the porch door and walked down the steps.

"Take your time, Nashoba. I'll be waiting."

He turned around at the bottom of the wooden steps, suddenly remembering an unanswered question. "You said I missed the biggest clue that Lily was a mermaid. What was it?"

"Her siren's voice. Its effect on us is slight since our heritage is intertwined with the Okwa Nahollo. Your Lily is a beautiful woman, but the men in this town are unnaturally attracted to her charms."

For the first time, the thought of Lily's past relationships angered Nash and he chided himself for the useless jealousy. He had his own past of easily accepting the attentions of many women and then as easily letting them go. *Just like my father*, he thought with disgust. His dad's numerous affairs had been the root of his parents' divorce.

Sam cut through his thoughts, as if sensing their direction. "Haven't you ever wondered why women are so drawn to you? I suspect male siren blood has been passed in our family from generations of intermingling with our Okwa Nahollo neighbors."

It excused nothing. Behavior trumped biology and he was responsible for controlling his actions. It had taken the deaths of two women to drive that point home.

He walked, almost ran, to the woods and up the red dirt path littered with pinecones, instinctually seeking solitude and the peace of nature. The bracing scent of pine and the musky odor of oak moss clamored for notice above the pervading ocean smell.

Nash leaned against the tall column of an oak and let his senses absorb it all. The whispering of the wind rattling through the trees like the sky's breath of life, the ground vibrating from small animals scurrying about their business, the soles of his feet tingling with earth energy from a tangle of tree roots expanding ever deeper in its thirst for life-sustaining water. The pores of his skin welcomed the sun's heat and his blood pounded in time to the breaking waves at sea.

Something broke the tranquil pattern. Something *not right* drew him to explore a dense thatch of scrub. A high-pitched chirping of distress beckoned Nash in a plea for help that could not be ignored.

A tiny bird ruffled its wings and Nash separated the shrub's branches for a closer look. Two marble-sized black eyes regarded him with both hope and terror. "I won't hurt you, little one," Nash promised. He disentangled the bird from where it was pinned beneath brambles. An agitated squawk from above told him momma bird was nearby. He guessed the little one had dropped from its nest and was too badly hurt to do more than roll about in the tangle of branches and vines. Gently, Nash freed the baby bird and held it in his cupped palms. A faint, erratic heartbeat fluttered against his fingers.

Now what?

He closed his eyes and willed that the bird be spared. Warmth and energy flared in his hands as if providing a miniature incubator. The bird ceased its struggle and its heartbeat slowed to an even pace, pulsing stronger. Nash opened his eyes and the bird hopped to its feet, tiny claws scratching into the flesh of his hands. He flattened his palms to provide a launching pad. The bird shifted from one foot to another, testing its balance. Then it flapped its delicate wings and was airborne in a flurry of fuzzy feathers. Nash watched as it flew upward to a nearby pine, where momma bird and the rest of her brood welcomed him with noisy tweeting.

Nash bent one knee up, propped an elbow on it and rested his forehead on the tips of his fingers. He felt drained, shaken and—profoundly humbled. *I have the gift. So where do I go from here?* He stood up and looked skyward, shaking his head. "Not so subtle, spirits," he called out.

A small brown feather stuck to one sweaty palm. He peeled it off and tucked it into the drawstring medicine bag belted at his waist. It would stay with him the rest of his days, a reminder of his first healing.

He slowly made his way out of the woods and returned to the cabin. His grandfather was halfway across the backyard, waving a cell phone. Nash frowned and quickened his pace. "Go sit down," Nash yelled. "I'm coming." Sam shouldn't be exerting himself like this; he should be resting. He hurried to Sam's side and took his arm, leading him to the porch. "Don't scare me like that," he chided. "Whoever called can wait."

Sam breathed heavily, as if he'd just completed a marathon. "It's—"

"Sit down and rest before you give me the message."

Nash settled him in his chair and waited as his grandfather collected his breath.

"Sheriff Angier called," he rasped. "Who is Opal Wallace?"

Nash's heart hammered. *Not another accident.* "My assistant. The woman who set up the island shoot."

Sam's eyebrows drew together and he affixed his sternest gaze on Nash. "You never mentioned her name."

"So?" What the hell was going on?

"Opa. *O-p-a*," Sam spelled out. "Choctaw for *owl*."

"Oh-kay," Nash drawled. "I'm in the dark here." Bewilderment flashed to unease. "Has something happened to her?"

"No, no." Sam fluttered a hand in front of his face as if clearing cobwebs. "But don't you remember all I've taught you about the animals? Owls are a sign of evil. Impending death."

The unease flared to an alarm that Nash tried to quell. "That's a superstition. Why did Angier call about Opal?"

"She's here."

"Huh. I wasn't expecting her back for another week."

"She's not *back*, Nashoba. Sheriff says this Opal never left Bayou La Siryna. She's been here all along."

The sweat on the back of his neck chilled and stung like ice chips. "But...why would she stay?" He felt as if he were moving in slow motion, half-buried in thick mud. His mind sludged through the implications. None of them good.

Sam gave a slow nod. "Now you know your enemy."

Chapter 17

Lily grinned at her friend's wild muddy-red hair blowing in the breeze like an out-of-control forest fire. The temporary purple streaks of color she'd put in were gone. "I thought you were in the Appalachian Mountains taking photos of wild herbs. We weren't expecting you back for another week."

"Nah, it turned out to be easier than I anticipated. Didn't have to tromp about the trails much searching for specimens. It's as if I was meant to be back on the island with—*oomph*." Opal's right foot twisted free from her sandal and she stumbled in the sand.

Lily put out a hand and steadied her.

"Drats." Opal bent over, slipped both feet out of her old but still serviceable Birkenstocks and carried them in her hands.

Lily noticed Opal's wide freckled feet were unpedicured. Her gaze traveled upward and took in the cut-off shorts with loose threads dangling haphazardly. She wore an old faded T-shirt, a faded khaki cloth bag slung diagonally across her body and not a single piece of jewelry. It was one of the things Lily liked best about her—Opal didn't bother with artifice. Her warm, friendly smile said take me or leave me, and it was her most endearing feature.

Opal wiggled her brows. "Do I pass or fail inspection?"

Lily cocked her head to one side, as if seriously considering the question. "Pass. You look great. Fresh-faced and lively as usual."

"And you look amazing as ever." Opal gave a theatric sigh. "It's so unfair. If you weren't my friend I'd hate that about you."

Lily laughed. "I've missed you. Even tried to call you a couple of times but couldn't get through. Figured you were in the boonies with no signal."

They resumed their way to the lodge.

"I'd have called or at least texted you if I could have. So what are you doing out here today?" Opal asked. "More drawing? Or has Nash recruited you as his assistant in my absence? Looks like I might have been squeezed out of a job."

"Don't worry. I'd be the world's worst assistant. I talk too much when he's trying to sneak up on the birds."

"Has Nash managed to get the mating shots of the rail clappers?"

"Probably not. He's been...distracted lately."

Opal winked. "I can guess why."

"No, it's not *that*," Lily said ruefully, climbing the porch steps. "Come inside, and I'll bring you up to speed on everything." She stopped suddenly and Opal slammed into her back. "Sorry. Just wondered if you'd rather sit on the porch."

Opal glanced backward, apparently watching the retreating backs of the elderly bird-watching couple as they headed toward the woods. "Let's go inside," she said. "More privacy that way."

Lily snorted. "I think you've forgotten how remote this place is."

Opal made her way to the sofa and flopped down, propping her tanned legs on the coffee table and slinging the tote bag beside her.

"Make yourself at home," Lily said unnecessarily. "Want some iced tea?"

"Tea? Let's drink something a little more fortifying. How about a glass of wine?"

"I don't think we have any."

"Sure you do. There are bottles of sangria in the cupboard below the sink."

"There are? I hadn't noticed." Lily scurried to the kitchen.

"Pour it over some ice, will you, sweetie?" Opal called from the den. "I'm parched."

"No problem." Lily opened the cupboard and, sure enough, there were a couple of sangria bottles. She fixed a glass of ice and carried it to the living room along with the wine. "I'm glad these are the twist-off tops. I haven't noticed any corkscrew openers here."

Opal straightened and put her feet on the floor. "Nothing but the low-end stuff for my gourmet tastes," she joked. "Hey, aren't you going to join me?"

"It's a little early in the day."

"Oh, come on. Don't make me drink alone. What kind of hostess are you, anyway?"

Lily hesitated. Oh, what did it matter? It wasn't like she was going anywhere. "Okay. Be right back."

Opal smiled. "Take your time. We'll have some fun girl talk all afternoon. When do you expect Nash to return? I assume he's out taking shots."

"He's not here. His grandfather isn't doing well. Nash is staying with him until Sam's friend arrives later in the afternoon."

"Oh, that's too bad. What happened?" Opal waved a hand. "Get your drink first and then you can tell me."

Lily returned to the kitchen and grabbed a glass. This would be fun. She'd never had a wine-and-girl-talk kind of day. Glass in hand, Lily went to the den, where Opal paced.

"There you are," Opal said brightly as Lily poured herself some sangria. She stood next to Lily and clinked their glasses together. "Cheers. Here's to a revealing afternoon."

"Revealing? Oh, you mean like sharing confidences, I suppose."

Opal took a sip. "Mmm. So good. Drink up."

Dutifully, she tasted the wine, her mouth exploding with the sweet tang of blackberries and citrus.

Opal returned to the sofa and patted the seat beside her. "Come tell me what happened to Nash's grandfather."

"Poor man had another heart attack and was in the hospital until they released him this morning." Lily sat down and kicked off her shoes, then tucked one leg beneath the other. "Sam has refused another bypass surgery and nothing Nash says can change his mind."

Opal shook her head. "Never underestimate the stubbornness of a man, huh? Nash taking it hard?"

"Yeah." Lily took another swallow of the sangria. "He's pretty crushed." Here she was having company all day and lazing about while he cared for Sam. "As a matter of fact, I should call and see how they're doing." She scanned the coffee table for her cell phone.

It wasn't there.

"Where's that damn phone?" she muttered. "I could have sworn I left it right there."

"Maybe you took it in the kitchen when you got the glasses," Opal suggested helpfully.

Lily stood and frowned. "I don't think so, but let me see. Be right back."

"You might want to check your bedroom and the porch while you're at it," Opal called from behind. "I'll call your number so you can hear it ring." Opal rummaged through her bag for her phone.

"Great. Thanks."

Back in the kitchen, she checked the countertops. Not there. With a sigh of exasperation, she went to the bedroom, checking nightstands and the dresser top. Still no phone. Lily peeked in the bathroom and then to the unused back bedroom. She must have left it on the porch earlier when she was talking to Shelly. Lily retraced her steps and passed back through the den.

Opal held up her phone. "It's ringing. Think you might have turned the ringer off?"

"I never do that. Don't hang up— I'm going on the porch to look."

Outside, her gaze swept the porch, but there was no sign of it and no ringing, either. Lily lifted chair cushions and searched the floor, thinking it might have dropped. Damn it, she'd lost another one. Lily jerked open the screen door and stalked back to the sofa.

"No luck?" Opal said with raised brows, turning off her phone.

"None." She flopped next to Opal and crossed her

arms over her stomach. "I can't believe it. This is the third time in the past year."

Opal patted her arm. "Don't be upset. I'm sure it will turn up. Here—" She picked up Lily's glass and held it out. "Relax. You'll find it later. No sense getting all worked up."

"I guess," Lily said with a sigh. "Sure is frustrating, though." She sipped the wine, willing it to mellow her sour mood. A hint of bitterness mingled with the fruity taste. Lily raised the glass to her nose and sniffed. "Can sangria go bad? This has a weird aftertaste."

Opal laughed. "Nah, you're probably used to the gourmet stuff and not this cheap shit I picked up at the gas station." She raised her glass. "The more you drink, the better this will taste."

Lily followed Opal's cue and downed another mouthful. A flavor of bitter almonds lingered, but it wasn't too bad.

"Anything else go on while I was away? Twyla give you any more trouble?"

"Yes and no. There's been trouble, but Twyla's not to blame. We're actually friends now—or at least not enemies."

"Tell me about it."

Lily recounted the break-in and hang-up calls, drinking more of the sangria. It was like she couldn't get enough liquid—her mouth was parched and her tongue wanted to stick to the roof of her mouth. Opal said something, but Lily couldn't focus enough on the words to catch their meaning. She stared into Opal's blue eyes until the color shifted, became alive and splashed like seawater spilled into a miniaquarium. And she was in that water, her mermaid fishtail swishing back and forth.

Back and forth.

Lily's stomach roiled with motion sickness.

"I feel funny," she said. "That sangria doesn't agree with me."

He had to get to Lily and warn her about Opal. Nash checked the time on his cell phone and cursed. "The noon ferry's already run. I should have insisted Lily stay with me today."

"I'm sure she's fine," Sam said. "You told me she promised to have a family member stay with her."

Nash barely listened to his grandfather's reassurances as he speed-dialed Lily's number. It rang and rang and rang. He punched in Tillman's number, who picked up on the first ring.

"Nash? We've got a problem. Landry and I've been reviewing the old case files the past few days. We decided to focus on Opal since she came to Bayou La Siryna with you. After a thorough background check, we now suspect Opal Wallace is the person who broke into Lily's house and may be responsible for the deaths of Rebecca Anders and Connie Enstep."

"Why?" he asked quickly. A small, still-rational part of his brain wanted something more concrete than Sam's association of her name as a sign of evil. He'd known her for years, had never once suspected his friend and assistant might be the cause of so much grief.

"Did you know she was once a person of interest in the murder of her foster brother, Thomas Drake? They apparently had a secret long-term affair and when he tried to break it off, Opal stalked him. A restraining order was issued and Drake died four months later. An autopsy revealed he'd been poisoned by white snakeroot. The case has never been solved."

"Shit." His skin crawled as if a hundred hairy tarantulas had been loosed on his body.

"There's more," Tillman continued. "Not long after Drake's death, Opal was committed to a state psychiatric hospital for an acute psychotic episode. Given her prior arrest, the background of mental health issues and the fact she's lied about her whereabouts, I'd say she's our prime suspect."

"What do you mean, Opal lied about her whereabouts?"

There was a pause and Nash tensed, anticipating more bad news.

"Opal never left Bayou La Siryna. She's been holed up in a motel right outside of town."

Hearing it from the sheriff instead of his grandfather seemed more damning and official. All doubt fled. Nash jumped to his feet as adrenaline flooded his system. "Then go take her in! What are you waiting for?"

"We can't. She's on Herb Island. She disembarked on the ferry as Shelly boarded."

"Damn it! Who's with Lily now?"

"No one except Opal. Lily thought she'd be safe with her."

Nash balled his left hand into a tight fist. Lily was alone with a psychotic killer. It was hard to imagine Opal as a killer, but the facts were too incriminating to think otherwise. "How soon can we get over there?" he growled.

"I've been trying to call Ned, but can't reach him. The next scheduled ferry is hours away. In the meantime, our office is contacting everyone we know with a boat large and sturdy enough to get out there. I know you're worried. I would be, too. Landry and I are doing everything possible—"

"Call me when you find someone," Nash said, cutting him off. "I'm going with you." He turned off the phone and faced his grandfather's worried eyes. "Lily's alone on the island with Opal and no one can get out there for hours. If something happens to her—" He couldn't go on, couldn't form the horrible words. "I never suspected Opal. Never. I thought she was my friend. And she never made a pass at me or indicated she had feelings for me. She told me once she was having a long-term affair with a married man. Like an idiot, I believed her story."

"Don't blame yourself." Sam placed a hand on his shoulder. "You aren't the first person to ever be deceived and betrayed by a false friend."

"It's all my fault." Nash's fingers curled into his palms. "I led Lily straight to a killer and there's nothing I can do to save her."

"There is a way to the island," Sam said. "But you may not like it."

"Poor baby." Opal stroked Lily's head. "Your hair's so pretty." She ran her fingers through the long locks. "And silky, too."

Lily closed her eyes and relaxed into the comforting touch of fingers stroking her scalp and the nape of her neck. The nausea subsided, replaced by a deep lethargy. She felt weighted down and longed to curl into a ball and sleep. For days.

"I wish I had your hair."

Lily yawned and roused herself. "There's nothing wrong with your red hair. It suits you."

"It's a curse," Opal said. The words came out loud, harsh. "I mean—" she gave a small laugh "—I wish I looked exactly like you. There's this guy... Well, he doesn't ever notice me *that* way. Know what I mean?"

Lily opened her mouth, but Opal cut in before she could speak.

"Of course you don't know what I mean. All men love the lovely Lily."

The singsong bitterness in Opal's voice made Lily's spine prickle with unease. Maybe Opal was like the other human women after all. And here she'd thought she'd found a true friend.

Opal laughed again, her face returning to its plain, open warmth. "Sorry. It's the alcohol talking." She poured them both another glass and raised hers in the air. "To friendship."

"I don't want any more." Her voice sounded weak and plaintive, as if she were a small child protesting something forced upon her.

"Fine. I believe you've had enough now," Opal said gently. "You look paler than usual. Feeling a bit strange, my dear?"

The room went fuzzy, the edges of everything blurred like one of her impressionistic watercolors. Maybe she had landed inside one of the paintings. Maybe her own body would become wave-washed until all that remained of Lily Bosarge would be an indistinguishable smudge on a forgotten canvas. She tightened her hands, welcoming the sharp pain of her nails digging into her palms.

"I'm still here," she said, sounding like a lost, confused child even to her own ears.

Opal smiled, but there was no warmth or comfort in it. Something about her expression hardened, became cruel. She ran a finger down the faint scar on her right cheek. "You see this atrocity?"

"It's barely visible," Lily protested, overcome with the need to cajole the stranger beside her. Where was that damn cell phone? Lily swiped her hand across the coffee table as if the phone would magically materialize. She'd left it right there, she knew she had.

An explosion of glass on the hardwood floor echoed in her head, like shock waves from a dynamite detonation. Lily clasped her hands to her ears and watched a rivulet of sangria spill over the edge of the table. It slowed to droplets, like blood dripping from an IV. "I need my phone. I need to call Nash and—"

"Shut up!" Opal hissed. "You shut the fuck up."

All traces of friendship were wiped out. Opal's eyes deepened to a blue blackness of fury and her thin lips pursed. A wall of hate smacked Lily's body like a wet towel, sharpening her hazy senses. Understanding flashed. "You're the killer," she whispered. "It's been you all along. You hate me because you're in love with Nash. You put something in my drink…"

"Yeah, genius. I hate you." Opal threw her glass against the wall and it exploded. Tiny glass shards and sangria cascaded downward in slow motion, like a red waterfall. Lily couldn't stop staring at it, all the while willing her mind to concentrate on reality. "What did you put in my drink?"

"A little angel's trumpet, my dear."

The answer filtered through her drugged trance, though the sound was distant, as if it had come from the abyss of an underwater volcano.

Opal's voice had abruptly reverted to a calmer tone and pitch, but Lily scrambled to stay on guard. *Once a monster is out of the bag, it can't go back in.* A hysterical giggle bubbled out of her throat.

"That's right. Let the drug take hold. It will make everything so much easier." Opal thrust her face in front of Lily, studying her dispassionately. She was like a hawk zeroing in on some small, helpless prey, certain of victory.

"What's angel's trumpet?" Lily asked, struggling to understand what was happening to her mind and body.

"A poisonous flower, also known as hell's bells or the zombie cucumber." Opal took hold of Lily's right arm and jerked her to a standing position. "I boiled one of the leaves and made a special tonic." With her free hand, Opal opened the shoulder bag slung securely across her body and pulled out a glass vial half-filled with a sickly yellow liquid. "I've plenty more if I need it, so you better be a good girl."

She slipped the vial back into the bag and Lily saw it was filled with more vials and clear packets of dried herbs and flowers. A witch to-go kit. Lily giggled even as the horror mounted. She pointed at the bag, laughing. "It's like a poison sample pack, a murder-on-the-go kit, a witchy traveling broom tote or a— Ouch!"

Opal's fingers dug into Lily's upper arm, sharp as talons, forcing her to walk toward the back door on wobbly legs. All the while, she kept up a one-ended conversation, delivered in the patient tone of a teacher instructing a student.

"I selected it just for you," she droned on. "It has a hallucinogenic effect and often makes one euphoric and submissive. Came in handy with Nash's other lovers, too. It was all so easy to set up the drug overdose for one and then the car accident for the other. The best thing? It's not a substance likely to ever be checked for in an autopsy."

How had she not seen the crazy beneath Opal's friendly facade? Even through the drug haze, everything clicked into place. Lily's heart kicked into high gear, as if it were trying to hammer a hole out of her chest. No doubt another side effect of the angel's trumpet. The door opened and Lily took heart at the sound of the ocean. If she could only reach the water... But even if she changed to mermaid form, there was no way of gauging what affect the drug would have on her mermaid metabolism.

She tripped going down the porch steps, but Opal's grip tightened, preventing a fall, preventing escape. Lily dragged her feet in passive resistance, but Opal was firm—and relentless.

"Where are we going?" she asked. The dry mouth was worse; her entire palate felt encased in sand, her tongue swollen and useless.

Opal ignored the question. "There won't be any pain, not much, anyway. The end will be quick, like it was for Connie and Rebecca." Opal clucked her tongue, chiding disapproval. "If you all had minded my warnings and stayed away from Nash, you could have lived. I'm not unreasonable."

Nash. Lily's heart pounded erratically. If she died, he'd feel responsible and devastated. She had to try to save herself.

"Opal, this makes no sense. He doesn't love you. Killing me won't change that."

"Third time's the charm," she quipped, unperturbed. "He'll realize he loves me and that the rest of you sluts never mattered."

Holy Triton, the woman's so delusional she can't fathom logic. The nonchalance rattled Lily. There was no reasoning with a person living in a fantasy world.

Their march continued onto a small trail in the woods. Lily stumbled along, weak and disoriented. It felt like this was happening to a different person and her body and brain were disconnected.

Opal began singing—a children's melody. The mirthful, familiar tune was warped into something eerie and sinister. She'd heard it recently but couldn't place where.

"Ring around the rosie

Pocket full of posies
Ashes, ashes
We all fall down."

A glow of candles and the sweet odor of incense... Yes, that young girl, Annie, had sung it at Tia Henrietta's. Annie had tried to warn her. Now Opal was the one singing, turning the light ballad into a funeral dirge as they slowly made their way through the woods.

"Ring around the rosie
Darkness befalls thee
Ashes, ashes
They all must drown."

Opal stopped the demented warbling and came to an abrupt halt. "We've arrived."

They'd reached the end of the trail. A few feet ahead a small two-person canoe was tethered to a tree by a thick rope.

Lily stared incredulously at the faded green canoe. "You're taking me out on *that*?" She tried to hide the relief but laughter tripped out of her belly, great gut-wrenching guffaws that left her clutching her stomach. "Y-you're taking me out t-to sea?" Lily gasped in between the laughter, swiping at the tears running down her face.

Opal gave a twisted smile as she untied the rope and pointed for Lily to board. "That's a good girl. Enjoy the mind trip. Keep laughing right up until the end."

She clamped her talons on Lily's arms again and forced her onto the boat. Lily did her best to avoid getting her feet wet. *Can't shift to my fishtail yet. Best wait until we go in a little ways.* Opal gave a rough push and Lily's butt landed on the metal slab that served as seating. She gulped in air, trying to stop laughing, but she couldn't get her body to obey her mind's command. *Mustn't let the monster know she's playing right into my hands.*

Opal withdrew the oar beneath Lily's feet and gave the canoe a push-off from shore before scrambling in and seating herself directly opposite Lily. In the tiny space, her knees crammed painfully into Lily's.

A little farther out and I'm home free. She could feel the muscles in her face contort into a wide, foolish grin that Opal would attribute as a harmless effect of the drug. *But you don't know how that drug will affect shape-shifting.* Still, she liked her chances.

"Won't be so funny when you hit water," Opal said smugly. "We both know you can't swim. Oh, you might manage a doggie paddle for a bit, but you'll tire after a few minutes. And I'll be right here, sitting in the canoe, watching. Waiting."

The canoe headed out to sea as Opal paddled; the freckled skin of her face and chest disappeared as she reddened with exertion. Lily hung on tightly to the sides as it rocked in the waves, preparing for the right moment to jump overboard. *Soon.* A little deeper.

She barely listened as Opal began singing, gasping between the words. Same tune as before, different lyrics.

"Leaves of angel's trumpet…"

She exhaled, arms straining as the oar dipped into the water.

On an inhale, Opal drew the oar into the air and nodded her head at Lily.

"Soon I'm gonna dump it…"

The boat surged ahead and Opal dipped the oar on the other side of the canoe and pushed, still singing.

"Die, bitch. Die, bitch.

Lily must drown."

Chapter 18

"I'll do anything to save Lily," Nash said. "Anything. It's my fault she's in danger."

"It will require a huge sacrifice on your part," Sam warned. "And a giant leap of faith."

It took all Nash's patience not to snap at his grandfather. He inhaled deeply, trying to quell the hope that there might be a way. Knowing Sam, he might suggest a flaky scheme like astral travel or some such. "Just tell me your idea."

"There is an ancient ritual passed to me from the spirits. It will grant you power to access the island undersea. But in exchange for this ability, there's a price."

He must be crazy. Undersea access? The glimmer of hope that had lit Nash's spirit died. "That's not possible."

"After everything you've seen and heard, after proof of your healing gift—" At Nash's sharp inhale, Sam nodded. "Yes, a spirit revealed to me that you saved a bird not ten minutes ago. And after all this, you still can't keep an open mind? You disappoint me, Nashoba."

His grandfather's words stung like a poisoned arrow, filling him with bitter regret. "I'm sorry, I want to believe there's a way, but it's ludicrous. How can I possibly—"

Sam turned his back on Nash's explanation and walked away, his steps labored, shoulders drooped. Nash easily outpaced him and blocked his path.

"Grandfather, I've never told you this, but you were the man I always looked up to as a boy. I admire and respect your wisdom and dedication to our people. But I'm not like you. This is all new to me. It's a big adjustment. Please, if there's a way to save Lily, I want to try."

Sam's eyes, dark as crow feathers, assessed his grandson. "When you entered this earth, the spirit of the wolf howled in recognition. You were born to be a protector, a spiritual man with special gifts. In the old days, you would have been the tribe's greatest hunter and provider. The ability for stealth, tracking and connection to the natural world and its signs are skills you've adapted for today's world. It's aided you in your career of capturing wildlife on film. But only you can decide whether to now accept your heritage."

A strong breeze picked up and Nash's attention was drawn past his grandfather to the trees beyond them, where limbs and leaves tussled, an alive, canopied shelter for birds and beasts. The rustling increased, became an agitated whisper for his ears alone. *Stay.*

He'd never sought any of this. But how could he deny offering help to those who needed him to intercede with the spirit world? *I was born and selected for a reason.* Nash's resistance faded and he was filled with peace. "I accept and I believe."

The wind softly settled down like a sigh.

His grandfather's face lit with pride. "You've chosen wisely. But before we begin the ritual, you must know the price. In return for revealing and granting you a special power, the spirits demand that once the ritual is completed, you may never leave Bayou La Siryna."

"Never?" The sacrifice was harsh, a complete abandoning of his adventurous lifestyle and ambitions. The storied career he loved, had worked so hard to build, would be ruined. He'd be stuck in this hot, small Southern town the rest of his days. Surely, there must be a little leeway here. "Not even for a few weeks now and then?"

"Never." Sam's voice was solid as the earth's core and as inflexible. There was no compromise, no bending fate.

"So that's why you've never left this place," Nash said slowly. "It wasn't because you didn't want to visit me, but because you were bound to the bayou." *All these years, he loved me as I loved him.* A hurt Nash didn't realize he'd harbored in some dark recess of his soul came to the surface and melted like ice in the noonday sun.

"I've always loved you through the years, Nashoba."

Nash nodded but couldn't speak. He hugged his grandfather and held tight, knowing Sam would understand what was in his heart, as he'd done when Nash was a child. His grandfather's dignified posture softened slightly and he briefly returned the hug. Nash pulled away. "I've made my decision."

"You're going to try and rescue Lily," Sam stated. "No regrets?"

"None." He pictured her face and body as they made love, so giving and free. Life without Lily was unthinkable. Nash wasn't sure when that had happened, but he guessed it was the day she had walked to him, naked and open, after his morning sun ceremony. And she belonged to this bayou as surely as he. "Lily's my destiny," he said simply.

Sam nodded. "Wait for me at the same place we did the healing for Kevin. The circle is already set. I have to go inside first and get the talisman."

Nash walked across the yard to the circle laid out with large stones and shells. His skin itched with impatience to begin. Every second that ticked by put Lily in more danger. He paced inside the sacred circle and tried to ground himself in preparation for whatever was to come.

The cell phone in his back pocket buzzed. Nash hastened to answer, hoping for news that Tillman had secured a boat. A message from Lily lit the screen.

"Gone boating. See you later."

His brow wrinkled as he concentrated on the brief message, feeling more alarmed than comforted. The only boat on the island was a two-person metal canoe tied to a rope at the back of the woods. As far as he knew, Lily didn't even know it was there. Besides, why the hell would a mermaid go boating? Made no sense.

Opal knows about that boat. A flash of conversation flickered in his brain. The three of them had been picnicking under a shade tree when Opal suggested they all go for a swim to cool off. *I can't swim*, Lily had said. Facts scrambled about his mind, seeking arrangement: Opal and Lily were together—Shelly had relayed that news. Opal thought Lily couldn't swim, so why get on the small craft with no life jackets? If Lily could send a text, why hadn't she responded to his earlier calls?

The logical conclusion left his palms sweaty. *Opal sent this.* And if she had, the crazy bitch was about to kill again, only this time it would be death by drowning. Nash tried to take heart, knowing that if such was Opal's plan, it had a major defect. Pushing Lily overboard would be tossing her to safety.

He speed-dialed her number but, as he expected, there was no response.

Sam emerged from the back porch.

"We need to hurry," Nash shouted, stuffing the phone back into his jeans. "I think I know how Opal intends to kill Lily."

"I'll be quick," Sam promised. "You will have time to save Lily."

Nash eyed his approach with impatience and curiosity. Sam clasped a ten-inch knife in one hand and a bag of cornmeal in the other. "What's the knife for? Animal sacrifice?" he asked, only half joking.

His grandfather didn't smile. "There will be some pain."

Holy crap. The knife is for cutting my flesh. Nash squared his shoulders, determined to show no sign of weakness.

As before, Sam walked the circle's inner boundary and tossed the cornmeal skyward, appealing to the spirits for their blessing and expressing gratitude for past blessings received. As instinctual as breathing, Nash silently prayed to all the brave Choctaw warriors who had walked this land before him and whose spirits lingered yet.

He stood rigid and proud in the middle of the circle as Sam set down the empty bag of cornmeal and faced him.

"Take off your shirt and unfasten your hair," he instructed.

Nash shed his T-shirt and took out the leather band that secured his long hair in a ponytail. His tribe had once been infamous for their many tattoos; maybe his grandfather was about to carve one on his chest as a symbol of his unity with them.

Sam raised the knife upward with both hands. "By the Spirits, I ask that the blood of the Okwa Nahollo that lives on in Nashoba Bowman be magnified a thousand times a thousand times. May he breathe underwater and navigate the seas as he does on land."

He paused, closing his eyes and tilting his head to one side, as if listening to an answer. Nash strained to catch what was being communicated, but an unnatural stillness settled. The breeze died, and he couldn't hear a single bird or sense any animal movement. Even the constant crash of the tides seemed far, far away. A dark cloud passed over the sun, darkening the sky enough that the moon's outline was visible.

Sam opened his eyes and lowered the knife. "Do you vow never to reveal this mystery to anyone except tribe members and only as the need arises?"

"Yes."

His grandfather positioned the blade so that it lay flat across his palms. It was more than just a knife; Nash recognized it at once. For as long as he could remember, the knife had been mounted above the fireplace, ensconced in the center of a grapevine wreath decorated with white shells and eagle feathers. He'd been warned never to touch it because it was a sacred, ancient relic passed down through generations. For those deemed worthy by their ancestor spirits, it held great power.

Let me be found worthy. I have to reach Lily.

"Place your right hand on the knife and swear by your honor."

Nash positioned his hand so that it rested atop most of the blade and the handle, a bone carving of a woman with long flowing hair. The steel was as warm and throbbing with life as the bird he'd cupped in his palm earlier, whereas the handle was as cool as a stream of flowing water.

"I swear never to break the code of silence."

"And you must swear that from this day forward, you will remain in Bayou La Siryna, never a day's travel away from your ancestral home."

If he was too late, if Lily died, he'd be imprisoned here to a lifetime of loneliness, much as his grandfather had lived in his later years. *I have to try. She's everything to me, in life and in death.* "I swear to stay forever."

Sam's eyes softened in sympathy.

He understands what this costs me. The knife trembled in Nash's hands and he saw that his grandfather's was shaking. With great effort, Sam again raised the knife upward in both hands. Shoulders and biceps strained, as if it weighed a hundred times its weight.

He was growing weaker. Rituals drained his energy and Nash feared that his grandfather's heart was overtaxed. He gripped Sam's forearms, helping him keep the knife raised.

The dark cloud blew away, the moon's outline disappeared, and the woods resumed its usual animal chatter. Full sunlight reflected off the blade's metal in a blinding flash.

"It is time," Sam pronounced.

Nash withdrew his support and Sam placed the edge of the hot blade to one side of Nash's neck.

"The pain will be brief," he promised. "And there will be no blood."

Sharp heat slashed across a couple of inches of his flesh. Nash kept his eyes fixed on the ocean, visible past his grandfather's shoulder. He clamped his jaw tight, refusing to utter a sound. Twice more his grandfather carved the same vertical lines directly beneath the original cut.

His knees wanted to buckle at the burning wave of pain and Nash stiffened his spine to stay upright.

"And now the other side," Sam said. "Almost done."

Again? Nash braced for the new onslaught.

His grandfather made quick work of it. Three new cuts were carved on the opposite side, in the same location as the first set of markings. His gut cramped in agony and he staggered. A faint drumming sounded in his ears, gradually increasing in tempo and volume until it drowned all other sound. His body vibrated in time to the pounding cadence until it abruptly halted, leaving his ears ringing in the sudden silence.

The pain was gone, exiting his body the exact moment the drumming stopped. Nash tentatively pressed his fingertips against the set of cuts on his right side. He traced three small lines of raised skin that felt like scar tissue. He lowered his hand and stared, expecting blood. But as his grandfather had promised, there was none.

"It's done." Sam's voice was weak and he drooped in exhaustion. "The gill slits are in place."

Gill slits. He remembered the faint scars on Lily's neck, same placement as his own now. His eyes narrowed at the tattoos on Sam's neck. And he understood. "Those tattoos cover your markings. That's how you lived undersea two days with Grandmother."

Sam gave a slight nod.

"But who did the cutting?"

"I did. Nellie provided this knife and told me what must be done."

Nash marveled at his grandfather's courage. His own initiation had been much easier.

"Now you can breathe underwater and swim to Lily."

"But how will I find her? How quick can I get there?"

"Enter the sea and all will be revealed. The spirits say this is the fastest way to get to the island." Sam's voice was so soft it was almost a whisper. "Go."

Nash hesitated. "Will you be okay?"

"Raymond will arrive shortly."

Nash noticed that he'd deftly evaded the question. He was frantic to reach Lily, every cell in his body screamed *run*, but what if Sam had another heart attack before Raymond showed up? "Maybe I should wait with you."

Sam shook his head. "No. The outcome will be the same whether I'm alone or not."

"You mean—?"

His grandfather silenced him by placing an index finger to his lips. "The time is near. Go in peace, Nashoba. I am well pleased with you."

Nash read the truth in his grandfather's eyes. *I'll never see him again.*

A brief clasp of the forearm and pat on his shoulder and Sam made his goodbye. "My spirit will always be with you."

He watched as his grandfather walked away, his steps slow but back straight and head held high. Overwhelming sadness rooted him to the spot.

A blue jay flew within inches of his face, beating its wings. *Scraa, scraa. Save Lily*, it screeched. Adrenaline trumped the temporary paralysis and he ran for the sea. Nash entered the water wearing only his boxers. At waist-deep level, he dove under a wave and swam as he'd always done. Eyes closed, mouth shut, arms forward, legs kicking behind. Nothing was different. His legs were still legs, no morphing into a fishtail. At last, his lungs burned for oxygen and he rose to the surface and gulped in air.

Shit. What the hell kind of idiot was he to believe his

grandfather's fanciful legends? Nash turned his head in all directions, searching for the help he'd been promised. Water surrounded him in all directions—not even a damn seagull in sight. Nash treaded water, debating his options.

He could return to land in hopes Tillman had secured a boat. But by the time they headed out, they were probably going to get there too late. Or, he could continue swimming, but even if by some miracle he was able to swim the distance, he'd arrive exhausted and weaponless and still too late.

All hope rested on the undersea route.

Nash sank in the water again and pushed forward, repeating the same, familiar motions. This time, he tried to ignore the screaming of his lungs. But it was no good. He broke surface and sucked oxygen long enough to break into a litany of cursing.

It took his last ounce of strength to push his head above water once more. Salt stung his eyes and he coughed up water. He glanced back to the barely visible shoreline and realized he couldn't return now if he tried. All around, the ocean stretched to infinity and the sun shone as brightly as it had when he started. Time and distance tangled into a Möbius strip he couldn't unravel. He'd never been so disoriented with the earth.

Think. Grandfather has never lied to me. I've seen and spoken to the spirits, sensed my ancestors roaming the bayou and fallen for a mermaid. Anything is possible. Before the ritual, he'd sacrificed his career and future happiness by agreeing to never leave the bayou. Now, he would sacrifice his life.

Nash sank below the surface and opened his eyes, bracing for the sting of salt. Light green water danced with swirls of tiny black specks and bits of shell and there was no sting. First hurdle passed. His body instinctually wanted to rise for air, but he fought the impulse. *My eyes adjusted, so why not my lungs?* Yet he couldn't bring himself to try until the last reserve of oxygen withered.

The moment was upon him. Life and death suspended in the next breath. *Now!* Nash opened his mouth and inhaled. The sea rushed in—and bubbled out on an exhale. He took another breath, then a third.

It worked! Nash placed fingers on each side of his neck where Sam had cut through flesh. Tiny currents of air flowed in and out. The ritual had opened superficial skin that had blocked the gills from functioning. Unknown to him, the ability had always been there, hidden under a thin dermal layer, awaiting discovery. Nash glanced down, curious to see if he sported a fishtail. But his legs were still human.

He swam forward with speed. *Must find Lily.* But which direction was the island? He couldn't tell. On a clear night, he might have been able to swim close to the surface and use the stars as a compass. But only the sun lit the sky. His grandfather said the spirits would help in navigating, but he saw and sensed nothing. Nash swam on, alert for a sign he was on the right track.

Look below.

Nash quit paddling, uncertain if he'd heard a voice or if the message had come from within. He gazed down at the darkness.

Come deeper.

The command was a vibration that rumbled in his gut and he obeyed at once. Down, down, down into the black, blind as a baby in a womb. Gradually, his eyes became accustomed and he made out shapes, which became clearer still—groups of fish, bits of driftwood, rocks and shells littering the ocean floor.

Phosphorescent globs of light appeared suddenly like

a colony of giant fireflies. But the long, slender columns of light didn't flicker and they were tall and thin like bioluminescent strings of stalactites. Several of the lighted forms neared, coalescing into a ghostly human form. They were white, with elongated bodies and slender legs almost twice the length of humans'. Their long, silver hair billowed like clouds; the solid black of their eyes emphasized the paleness of their skin.

The Okwa Nahollo had arrived.

Perhaps they had been here from the start, ready to assist once he'd fully surrendered to the sea. Wonder paralyzed him at the appearance of the gossamer beings. Their figures rippled in the current and one of them drifted closer, lifting a hand and circling her fingers, beckoning him to follow.

Nash gathered his wits and nodded to show he understood. The pale people of the sea surrounded his body, swimming alongside him like a protective battalion. Cocooned in their midst, he felt no fear. Although he moved as fast as possible, they drifted effortlessly around him and were probably capable of much greater speed.

A shorter, younger one approached, just out of arm's length. A male child, probably in his early teens. The boy grinned at him and pointed to his chest. Thin black lines were etched in some kind of pattern. It took Nash several moments to grasp the design through the rippling water, but with a start he recognized it depicted the seal of the Choctaw Nation—an unstrung bow, with three arrows and a smoking pipe at its center. The tattoo's color had faded but marked the boy as one who had once roamed on land. Nash wondered if he'd drowned long ago and was taken in by the Okwa Nahollo, or if he was an ancestor who'd chosen to live undersea to escape the once-wretched conditions of reservation life.

Hurry. Almost there.

The message came from a point directly ahead, and Nash refocused on his mission. *Don't let me be late. I have to save Lily.*

Abruptly, they shifted upward and he followed. By degrees, the darkness lightened until he saw sunlight flickering on top of the water. He estimated they were within twenty feet of the surface when the Okwa Nahollo halted.

We dare go no farther.

A woman drifted closer and pointed upward.

There.

Above him was a dark object, about eight feet long, wider at the middle and narrowed into a point at both ends. A paddle dipped down, stirring the water, guiding it farther from shore.

His canoe.

Chapter 19

The singing stopped and Opal staggered to her feet, the paddle held out to her side in the position of a baseball player at bat, ready to swing.

"Get out," she hissed.

Lily shielded her face with her hands. "Okay, okay. Please don't hit me." She stood, drugged legs clumsy and awkward as she stepped up onto the raised bench where she'd been sitting.

Now. Jump.

She took one last glimpse at Opal's red, sweaty face, eyes focused in deadly intent, the bird of prey swooping in for the kill. Lily couldn't resist a smile of satisfaction. "Joke's on you."

Opal flushed an even deeper shade of crimson and her mouth twisted in fury. The paddle swooshed toward her, so close Lily felt it stir the air.

She expertly dove into the sea, legs together, toes

pointed and nary a splash left behind as she descended. *Take that, Opal.* Elation and relief made her giddy. Or was it the drug? She giggled—and swallowed a mouthful of salty water. Lily coughed and tried to draw a breath, but more water immediately clogged her lungs. *What's happening?* Panicked, she looked down, dismayed to find useless human legs where her fishtail should have been. She kicked frantically while parting the water with her arms.

Air. She needed air. Without it, her head would explode. Her lungs were a furnace, burning a hole through her chest. Lily clamored near to surface level, where Opal's face wavered above the churning water, peering down, paddle clutched in both arms, ready to strike.

But she had no choice but to break through for air. Her head bobbed up and she coughed up a mouthful of liquid before sucking in oxygen, the painful rasp of her inhalation loud as a siren. Another desperate gulp and then a sickening thump connected against her right cheek. Pain blazed and she fought the blackness of passing out.

Lily moved beneath the boat's hull, out of striking range. She lifted her hands and clung to the hull, trying to rock the boat and force Opal overboard. But she was too weak. *I'm going to drown, after all.*

The irony of a drowned mermaid registered before the darkness obliterated all thought.

Nash watched Lily's dive overboard. *She's safe.* He swam toward her, eager to reunite. This ordeal was almost over.

He got within a few yards before he realized something was terribly wrong. She hadn't transformed. Lily's face contorted with agony and she shot back up. Opal was there waiting and delivered a vicious blow that felt like he'd been struck, as well. Blood oozed from the side of her face as he covered the distance between them. She grasped the bottom of the canoe for a moment and then her hands dropped to her sides. She was sinking. Graceful even while unconscious, alabaster skin alit with a subtle pink-and-silver sparkle, lovely formed limbs slowly swaying as directed by the ocean current, long blond hair cascading above her elegant face like a staged spotlight.

An underwater ballet of death.

Nash grabbed Lily by the waist and pulled her by the canoe's side. She was so, so heavy, a dead weight in his arms. They broke surface and he positioned her torso over his right shoulder, thumping firmly between her delicate shoulder blades. Lily heaved water and drew a short breath before vomiting once again.

The wretched sound filled him with joy. He dared hope that he'd arrived in time. His body almost sagged and lowered back down in the sea from overwhelming relief.

"Wh-what? How did you... Nash?"

He'd entirely forgotten Opal. She plastered her body on the opposite side of the wobbling canoe, gaping as if a sea monster had bobbed up from the ocean's depth. The oar fell harmlessly from her hands. He scanned the canoe's interior, searching for a gun or knife, but there were no weapons. Not surprising—that wasn't Opal's modus operandi anyway. He searched for the shoreline and saw they weren't more than fifteen yards out. The canoe was small and he'd have to contend with Opal's possible interference if he tried to board. Lily's chest rose and fell against him, her breathing shallow but steady.

Land it was.

It seemed he'd been swimming for hours. Despite the adrenaline rush that had pushed him on the long journey, his body had used up its last reserve of energy. The hormone crash was sudden and complete. His legs became useless appendages and he barely kept Lily's head above water.

From underneath, dozens of cold hands imprinted upon his back and legs, guiding and pushing his and Lily's broken bodies. In short order his feet and knees crunched against rock and shell. Nash sat in the shallow water, catching his breath, Lily cradled in his lap. A crowd of Okwa Nahollo floated nearby, in such large numbers it appeared as if a cloud had fallen from the sky and lay suspended beneath the water.

The youngest boy broke away like a wandering wisp of smoke and waved goodbye.

"Thank you," Nash called out, unsure if they could hear. He touched a hand to his heart and patted it, a final gesture of gratitude. These were his people—his kin—and the allies and friends who had saved his ancestors. And now they had saved him and Lily, as well. Without their help, his life would have become unbearably lonely.

The columns of light departed in a brilliant ripple, leaving no trace of their presence.

"What was that?" Opal screamed. She'd seen them—or seen enough that she appeared shell-shocked. She stood on the canoe, staring at him as if he were a ghost. "How did you get here? I don't understand what's happening."

Nash ignored the questions and dismissed all thought of Opal. She wasn't going anywhere and he'd deal with her later.

He looked into Lily's wan face, fear forming a tight band across his chest. She was breathing but remained unconscious. He tenderly pushed away tendrils of hair plastered against her face. An open gash cut across her right cheek, marring the perfect beauty of her alabaster complexion. He lowered his lips and kissed her forehead, which felt cold and clammy. Nash desperately sought something he could do to help her. Perhaps her lungs still contained water—he'd heard of it happening before when people drowned hours later from accidents. They called it "dry drowning" from fluid buildup in their lungs.

It couldn't hurt to try to pump more water. Nash laid her in the sand on her stomach, head turned so that the undamaged side of her face didn't grind into sand. Straddling her back, he pressed his hands into her spine and several minutes later was rewarded with a trickle of brackish water that ran out of her mouth. He continued the ministrations until he was certain there was nothing more he could do.

Lily coughed and her eyes fluttered open, seeking to understand where she was, what had happened. Nash scrambled to lie beside her and she focused on him, smiling as if it cost her great effort. "You came for me." Her voice sounded bruised and gravelly, holding nothing of its usual siren's cadence.

"You're safe," he promised. "Help's on the way." Speaking of which—where the hell was Tillman? Nash had no idea how much time had passed.

He glanced back again at Opal, frowning when he saw she was paddling their way. He rose to his feet to intercept her before she got anywhere near Lily. For all he knew, the crazy woman might yet have a knife or gun stashed somewhere.

Nash waded up to his thighs in the water and raised his hand for her to stop. Opal stared at him with a wild, pleading look. She was a stranger to him, this woman he'd worked with for years, had considered a friend.

"Please don't be angry with me. We went for a little ride and she fell overboard. I tried to save her."

"Liar," he spat out. "I saw you hit her with the paddle. You were trying to kill her."

Opal stretched out a hand, beseeching. "No, I was trying to help Lily, get her to grab on to the oar so I could pull her in."

"Game's over, Opal. I know who and what you are now. So do the cops."

Her eyes flickered nervously past his shoulder, and at her sharp inhalation, Nash glanced behind.

Lily had pulled up onto her knees and rocked back and forth on all fours like a crawling child attempting its first tentative steps.

The sight enraged him. "What did you do to her?"

"Nothing. I—"

"Stop lying. I know what you've done. You killed Rebecca and Connie." Nash tried to control the fury long enough to find out what she'd done to Lily. It had to be something more than throwing her in the water. If that was all, Lily would have shape-shifted and swam away. "I'm asking you for the last time. What did you do? Slip her some kind of poison or drug?"

Opal jumped out of the canoe and waded forward. "Please. Nash, forget her. She's nothing." Tears ran down her face and she sobbed, her whole body shaking. "I did it all for you. Can't you understand? I love you."

Horror and revulsion hit him with the frigid shock of an ice bath. Its chill numbed and then burned along his nerve endings.

"You love me, too," she insisted, stumbling and almost falling into the water. She righted herself and surged forward. "You come to me every night in my dreams and tell me so."

Before he could realize her intention, Opal lunged forward and flung herself at him, wrapping her arms about his waist and sobbing into his bare chest. He smelled the sweat of her desperation.

Nash stepped backward and grabbed her forearms, peeling her off his body. She was surprisingly strong, clinging like a leech sucking blood.

She stared at him, imploring. "Make love to me like you do when you come to me in dreams. This was supposed to be *our* time. None of the others ever loved you the way I do. Can't you see that?"

All he could see was what a fool he'd been. The face of his friendly, slightly homely, competent assistant and friend was erased forever. It was as if in the past he'd viewed Opal through a diffused camera filter that had cast a haze on the truth. Now that the filter was removed he could read the sharp longing in her eyes and the clear gleam of delusion that twisted her lips and face.

It was diametrically opposed to the revelation of the real Lily. Lily's true nature made her appear even more beautiful, more vulnerable, more sweet. The crows had recognized her dual human/mermaid nature and communicated that Lily was his true destiny. Too bad the birds couldn't detect evil in humans.

"You're delusional," he told Opal curtly. "The cops are on the way. You'll spend the rest of your life in prison or locked up in another psychiatric hospital. Until they arrive, all I want to hear from you is what you gave Lily."

Her eyes flashed in an instant, igniting to fury. "Lily, Lily, Lily!" she screamed, writhing, breaking one hand free from his grasp. "What about *me*, Nash?"

Opal beat her chest so hard he wouldn't be surprised if a rib cracked. He released her other arm and stepped back.

"You're supposed to love me. *Me!* Everything I did, I

r you." She gouged her face and neck with her fingernails, leaving a track of blood as savage as if she'd been mauled by a bobcat.

After all the years he'd thought of Opal as a friend, a competent assistant and talented photographer in her own right, after all that time—he'd never really known her. Never suspected the torment and savagery hidden underneath the sunny, calm exterior.

She twisted her face to one side and lifted her chin. "It's because of this, isn't it?" She jabbed an index finger into the slight scar that ran from ear to mouth. "You think I'm hideous. Not worthy."

Nash gritted his teeth, impatient with Opal's ranting. He lunged toward her and snatched her right arm above the elbow. "Tell me the drug you gave Lily or, so help me, I'll beat it out of you."

She threw her head back, bursting into maniacal laughter. "Go ahead. Do it. I'd rather be hit than ignored."

Nash pushed her away in disgust. The woman was hopeless.

A reed-thin voice spoke from behind. "Angel's trumpet," Lily said. She stood, swaying slightly. "A hallucinogenic she slipped in my drink."

Nash rushed to Lily's side and put an arm around her waist to prevent a fall. Lily leaned into him. "I'm better," she whispered. "It's starting to wear off."

He held on to her tightly, grateful she was in his arms again and appeared stronger. Another minute and he would have been too late. He shuddered and Lily weakly ran her hands down his back, reversing their roles and acting as comforter, strengthening his mind and spirit.

A scream pierced the air and they broke apart.

Opal's hands were clasped against her ears, eyes and

mouth widened in pain. "No, no, no!" she shrieked, as if the sight of he and Lily together was driving her crazy.

She stumbled back to the canoe, which had drifted a few yards out, and awkwardly heaved herself on board.

"Surely she doesn't think she can escape to sea on that thing," he muttered as the sound of a large motorboat approached in the far distance. About time. Lily needed medical attention.

Opal jerked her head in the direction of the sound and then stood unsteadily on the canoe, facing him from a good fifteen yards out. She continued staring at him as her hands reached into the shoulder bag slung across her body and scrambled through it.

A gun? Nash moved in front of Lily, shielding her from danger.

Opal extracted two thin glass vials. She quickly unstopped the lids and swallowed the contents in two gulps.

"What the hell are you doing?" Nash yelled, instinctively moving toward her.

"Drinking the last of the angel's trumpet and poisonous juice from white baneberry. That should do the trick." Her voice was flat and her eyes vacant.

"For God's sake, Opal." He couldn't help feeling sorrow for her—for the friend he'd thought she'd been.

"My life is nothing without you," she continued in the same matter-of-fact monotone. "I'd rather die than see you—" Opal bent over, clutching her chest "—with another woman."

Nash ran until the water hit midthigh, and then he started to swim.

Opal turned her back on him and dove under.

He glanced over his shoulder at Lily, who motioned him to go on. "I'm fine," she called. "Get her."

Undersea again, Nash's eyes adjusted. The Okwa Nahollo were gone, but he had no trouble spotting Opal's pale, thrashing legs and arms, her mass of red hair swirling in the current like spilled blood. He made his way over and grabbed an arm, pulling her toward the surface.

She fought him. Resisted with a panicked fury that might not understand he was trying to save her life. Nash placed his face within a foot of Opal's—hoping she would recognize him and cease struggling.

Her eyes were wide-open, bulging and bloodshot. Nash pointed up, gesturing he wanted to pull her to air.

Opal flailed her arms and legs, still fighting him off.

To hell with trying to communicate. Nash grabbed underneath her arms and swam up, Opal twisting like a snake in his grasp. When he reached the canoe, Nash flung himself inside, one hand still firmly gripping Opal's ankle. Her body went limp and he pulled her into the boat, muscles heaving with the dead weight. She lay facedown and he turned her over. Opal's eyes stared unblinking into the sun overhead.

Dead.

Nash attempted to save her as he had Lily, but whatever concoction had been in those vials Opal had swallowed had swiftly done its work.

His enemy had been found and silenced, but Nash took no pleasure in it. So many people had been hurt over the years. If only he'd realized sooner what was happening right beneath his nose. He never once suspected Opal was mentally ill and that he was the focus of her obsession. She'd befriended his past girlfriends and claimed to have a secret lover, a married man. And all this time he and the police had looked for suspects among women he had dated and rejected. What a tortured, miserable life she must have secretly lived.

The roar of the motorboat was upon them.

He stared at the stranger who'd claimed to love him. Opal's top had wedged under her armpits, exposing her freckled chest and plain, white bra with a safety pin attaching a broken strap on one side. Nash pulled down the T-shirt to cover her. "I hope you are finally at peace," he whispered before standing.

He waved his arms, shouting in the wind, "Over here."

Chills racked her body in waves and the sound of the men grew fainter as they shouted commands and lifted Opal's limp body onto their boat. The roaring in her head drowned out everything and her peripheral vision narrowed. *Must sit down.* Lily sank onto the sand and shivered. The sun held no warmth and its light faded, leaving nothing but pinpoints of light and dark specks. Where was Nash? She needed him to hold her, to share his body heat and reassurances everything was all right.

But it wasn't.

It was as if her body had roused itself only long enough to see that Nash had survived and Opal had been captured. Now it was spent and she was so cold, so tired. Her body was betraying her again, as it had done undersea when it was unable to shape-shift. She closed her eyes against the spinning landscape that made her stomach rumble with nausea.

Blessed heat bore down on her shoulders. Someone had placed a blanket on her. She huddled into it and opened her eyes to a blur of people—brown uniforms with silver star-shaped badges and men dressed all in blue with stethoscopes dangling from their necks.

"Lily, can you hear me?"

Nash squatted in front of her. His face was so intent and drawn it made her want to cry.

"I'm here,' she said, realizing as she spoke that her throat was still parched and burning.

A man in blue crowded him to the side and put a blood-pressure cuff on her sleeve. He listened intently to her heart rate and nodded. "Steady, but weak. Let's get her to the hospital."

No! "No hospital," she rasped.

Tillman dropped to a knee and waved the medic away. "Lily, you have to go."

"You know I can't."

"It's okay. Nash told us about the angel's trumpet. They'll do a chest X-ray to make sure there's no fluid remaining, and then pump your stomach in case any of the drug remains. I promise I won't let them draw blood or run other tests."

A strong hand engulfed hers and squeezed. She knew it was Nash without even looking.

"I'll be with you every minute," Nash vowed.

Lily nodded and closed her eyes again as he scooped her into his arms and lifted her. His warm breath whispered in her ear.

"Chi hollo li."

She had no idea what the words meant, but it washed her soul in immediate solace.

Chapter 20

Sunbeams lit every shadow in the bayou and sparkled atop the calm Gulf waters, inviting folks in Bayou La Siryna to luxuriate in the fine summer afternoon.

Weather not at all fitting for a funeral. Lily closed her eyes against the sun's determined brightness as she stood by the cottage window. It was the second funeral in as many days, although the first should more properly be called a burial instead, because no one had come to mourn Opal Wallace. A plain wooden casket and a tiny stone marker in the county pauper's cemetery were all that marked her life's end.

But Samuel Chula Bowman's service had filled the funeral home. All morning, lines had formed around the building with people coming to pay their respects. Lily had never suspected that the quiet man who'd lived so far in the backwoods was this universally well-known and loved.

A sudden tingling crept up the nape of her neck. Someone was watching her. Lily turned from the window and caught Nash staring at her from across the room, brows drawn in concern.

He shouldn't have to worry about her when this day was so difficult for him. Lily forced a smile and circulated among the few guests that remained at Sam's cottage, picking up empty paper plates and refreshing drinks as needed. It seemed like it should be late evening instead of late afternoon, and she was weary. The fatigue from the angel's trumpet had eased but hadn't entirely gone away, even after a week had passed.

She'd been pronounced fit at the hospital after getting her stomach pumped and spending a few hours hooked to an IV that replenished her body with fluids and vitamins to treat dehydration. Nash had been busy arranging his grandfather's burial, so she'd returned to her own home every night. Mom had at once moved back in with her to play nurse. The attention had been nice—for the first few days.

But lately her mom's nervous gaze and hovering left Lily feeling smothered. Jet and Shelly weren't much better. They visited daily and the three women huddled together often, speaking in hushed tones. If she ventured too close, they stopped talking and studied her quizzically.

Finally, the remaining guests took their leave.

Lily gathered up the last of the dishes and took them to the kitchen sink. As she rinsed and placed them in the dishwasher, she kept glancing out the window, eyes drawn to the small patch of blue on the horizon. A deep sigh escaped. Although she had twice ventured into the sea this past week with her family, her mermaid fishtail hadn't emerged.

Lily feared it never would.

"You've been working too hard," Nash scolded, nuzzling his lips by her ears. His arms wrapped around her waist from behind, and she leaned into his warm strength. "Why don't you lie down for a nap and I'll finish up here?"

Lily sighed again. She was so sick of being sick. Sick of taking naps, sick of worrying. But even worse, now that the funeral was over, how much longer would Nash continue to stay in Bayou La Siryna? They hadn't addressed anything in the past week. The little strength she'd had, Lily had spent giving police statements or helping Nash with funeral arrangements.

"Hey, you." Nash guided her body around so that she faced him. "Why the long sighs?"

"Sorry. Don't pay attention to me. You're the one having a tough day. I know how much you loved Sam."

"I miss him, but he lived a long time and was prepared for death. At least, as much as anyone can be." Nash's voice was grave but controlled.

"I never knew his middle name was *Chula*. Is it a Choctaw name?"

He nodded. "It means *fox*. Fit my grandfather perfectly. He was wise, shrewd and concerned with family."

"Just as *Nashoba* fits you. Like the wolf, you're my protector. If you hadn't come when you did..." Lily shuddered.

His face tightened. "I can't stand to think about what might have been. If I had been a second later—"

"About that," Lily cut in. "How did you appear out of nowhere? I know the story you gave Tillman and Landry about a friend loaning you a large commercial vessel. Must have been a ghost ship, because no one saw it."

"Lucky for me, the local sheriff's department is run by your BILs," he joked. "So convenient."

She didn't smile. "I may not be on my game lately, but I've noticed you won't give me a straight answer whenever I ask you questions about that day."

A guarded expression darkened his green eyes. "What do you remember?"

"Lots of my memory is hazy. The doctors say that's not an unusual side effect from a hallucinogenic drug. I clearly remember losing my cell phone and pouring sangria for me and Opal. After that—" She paused, struggling to bring events into focus. "I only remember a few details, like stumbling through the woods and hearing a children's song. I remember being frightened and Opal's face above me when I was underwater. Then there was pain, and when I woke up I was lying in the sand and you were with me."

"Anything else?"

Lily rubbed her temples, trying to grasp wisps of broken details. But it was like trying to remember a dream after awakening. A snatch of memory floated through her mind like a cloud being swept away by the wind, yet a tiny trace remained… "Wait. There is something else. I was being pulled through the water and you were holding me. But—oh, this will sound crazy—"

"Don't say that. You're not crazy. Go on," he urged.

She wished she'd kept her mouth shut. "Okay, here goes. I thought I saw white shapes all around us, like undersea ghosts. Only I wasn't scared, their presence felt comforting. I sensed…they were helping us."

Lily waited for him to laugh, to tell her the ghosts were merely part of a drug-induced fugue. But his face was set, eyes hard as agate. "Nash?" She touched his chest. "What is it?"

He looked past her and stared out the window. He didn't want to tell her what had happened on the island. But why? It made no sense. "What are you hiding? Tell me."

"I can't." His voice was clipped, and he avoided her eyes.

Hurt burned at the back of her throat. "You can trust me," she said quietly.

Nash stuffed his hands in his dress slacks and faced her. "Damn it, Lily. It's not a matter of trusting you. I took an oath of silence and I won't break my word. Don't ask it of me."

"An oath to whom?" She frowned and shook her head. "I don't get it."

He stood immobile and unyielding and silent.

The divide between them was sudden and absolute. For the first time, Lily truly understood how keeping secrets had the potential to destroy faith and love between a man and woman. Nash must have felt this way when she wouldn't tell him her true nature. Yet he hadn't abandoned her even when he'd come face-to-face with her lies the night she'd shape-shifted from land to sea, unaware he waited for her.

Lily slowly stretched out a hand over the gaping chasm between them. "Okay," she whispered.

His eyes softened with hope and the tight muscles in his shoulders relaxed. "Okay? You can live with my silence on the matter?"

"Without you, I would have no life."

He crossed the distance between them in a heartbeat and she was in his arms. His fierce strength was more precious to her than ever before. He kissed her and she melted into his fire, giving and taking and yet needing more, needing all of him, heart and soul and body. Nash groaned into her mouth and she pressed her hips into his arousal.

"My sweet Lily," he murmured, running hot kisses down her neck and the hollow of her throat.

His hands cupped her breasts and she moaned. It seemed like forever since they'd made love. "I've missed you," she said breathlessly. "Missed this."

Nash leaned down and rested his forehead on hers, his breath hot and sweet against her face. His heart thumped wildly beneath the hand she rested on his broad chest.

"God, I've missed you, too." His voice was husky and raw. "But are you sure you're up for this? You've been so sick—"

Lily kissed his lips, stopping his protests. "Not that sick," she laughed shakily.

The desire in his eyes reflected her own passion. That age-old look of understanding and intimacy that passed between man and woman flashed silently in the charged stillness. Nash held out his hand and she accepted it, following her lover to the bedroom.

Much, much later, when the August Alabama sun began dipping beneath the treetops, Lily lazily rested her head on Nash's lap as they rocked on the back porch glider. She wore nothing but one of his oversize T-shirts and panties. He'd changed from his earlier formal wear to an old T-shirt and gym shorts, and in Lily's eyes he looked as sexy in the casual outfit as he had in the suit.

She closed her eyes, enjoying the soft stroke of his fingers running through her tumbled hair. The breeze was cool and ocean waves tumbled in the distance like a lullaby. She drifted toward slumber, her mind blank and peaceful, body sated from lovemaking.

"Did you try to go in the water today?"

Nash's voice jolted her back to reality.

"Yesterday. It was a no-go. Mom keeps assuring me that I'll be able to shape-shift again in time." She yawned and stretched her feet and arms like a cat awakening from a nap. She'd probably been sleeping as much as any cat for days now.

"If my grandfather were still alive, I bet he could heal whatever's wrong."

Lily sat up and settled in his lap, hope flaring her to attention. "How?"

"He said all illness was caused when someone's soul was injured. For healing, he connected to caring spirits, power animals and plant life. Sam believed health was the result of restoring a person's spiritual power."

"And you think my soul was injured by the attack?"

"I think it's possible."

She remembered Sam involving Nash in the ceremony for Twyla's son. "And he was grooming you to take over for him one day, wasn't he?"

"Yes. But I couldn't ever live up to his work. He'd been healing for years. It was something he felt called to do ever since he was a young man."

Lily cupped his face with her hands, fevered with excitement. "I believe in you, Nash. Heal me."

"Don't get your hopes up," he cautioned. "I'm not sure I can."

"Try. Please. You have a connection with the spirits—I've seen it in you."

"I'm willing, but—" He stopped. His muscles tensed beneath her, his gaze locked on something beyond the porch. Nash raised a hand over his brows, shading his eyes from the sun.

Lily scrambled off his lap and followed the direction of his stare. "What is it?"

"There," he said, whispering as if afraid of disturbing something. He pointed to the far right side of the tree line in the backyard.

"I don't see anything."

"Right there, under the cypress where Sam used to chop wood in the shade. His old wheelbarrow is still leaning against the magnolia."

She squinted into the dark greenery. "There's nothing there. Wait. Is that…a fox?"

"It is." His voice was hushed, deep with excitement. "Unusual to spot one this early in the evening. They're nocturnal hunters. Stay here."

She waited as he went to the porch and pushed open the screen door. His movements were slow and silent, cautious not to startle the fox.

The animal didn't move other than twitching its long black bushy tail tipped in white. It regarded Nash intently with its pointed face and intelligent eyes. His fur was a reddish color with a white underbelly and paws dipped in black.

Lily's skin tingled. *Chula.* Did Nash really think this could be Sam?

Nash came within a few feet of the fox and stopped as if hitting an invisible wall. He slowly hunched down until almost eye level with the fox.

Lily rubbed the goose bumps on her arms, watching them stare at one another in some sort of silent communication. At last Nash stood and raised one arm, elbow bent, a gesture that could mean goodbye or "message received." Or both. The fox turned and trotted off into the woods, tail held high.

She could wait no longer. Lily ran out the door, down the steps and across the yard. "Well? Was it Sam? What did he say?"

"Seems you got your wish. I'll contact the spirits for a healing. Your body needs to be made whole so you can be fully at one with land and sea again." A rueful smile played on his lips. "Don't get your hopes too high, Lily. This is all new to me, but I'll do my best."

She wanted to jump up and down and fist-pump the air. This would work; she knew it deep in her soul. But for Nash's sake she restrained her enthusiasm and tried to match his somber mood. After all, this was serious business and sacred territory. "I understand. When do we start?"

"Now."

Lily headed to the circle of stones where Twyla's son had had his healing. She was moving at a dignified pace, but she wanted to skip with joy.

"Not here," Nash said. "For this, we must go to shore." He turned and walked in the opposite direction and she followed.

He moved with a slow but steady gait and she stepped into place beside him, glancing from time to time at his preoccupied, silent profile. She didn't attempt conversation, sensing that Nash was mentally preparing for the healing. Twilight deepened the shadows but he walked sure-footedly, eyes focused on the distance. They scrambled down a clump of brush, arriving at a small patch of sandy soil where the sea gently lapped at the shore.

Wordlessly, Nash stripped out of his clothes and she followed his lead. Still silent, he waded into the water up to his knees.

Lily hesitated, not sure if he needed to be alone. Nash turned and held up an index finger. "Wait here."

He dove under, disappearing in the green depths. She ached to join but dared not risk ruining the process. This might be her only chance to become a mermaid again.

She'd never imagined losing her ability to shape-shift. It felt as if part of her soul were amputated. Niggling doubts crept in. What if this didn't work after all?

She studied the water where Nash had submerged. It seemed too long since he'd dove under. She waited and waited, growing more anxious with every second that passed. Nash needed air. No human could hold their breath this long. Was he in danger? Lily shifted from one leg to the next and then paced, eyes constantly scanning the empty surface of the sea. *Where are you? Come back to me.*

She couldn't stand it any longer. Lily stepped forward, intent on saving Nash. But she halted at the sight of a mass of white floating in the distance. It looked as if someone had dumped piles of white sheets into the sea.

Just like before, when Nash had pulled her to land. Wonder enveloped her senses.

The underwater ghosts had returned.

A human form glided under the water's surface. Nash arose and stood before her, his long black hair plastered against his olive skin. His eyes bore into hers. With a start, she realized the color of his eyes wasn't leaf-green as she'd imagined. They were the exact hue of this bayou water.

He came to her and clasped his wet hands in hers, holding tight. "The Okwa Nahollo have agreed to help. Don't be afraid. They've been the Choctaw's friends and neighbors for generations. They are similar to you, but not the same. They don't have fishtails or shape-shift, and their bodies are light as air."

"They helped us before. Out there on the island."

"Yes. It's what I couldn't speak of this morning until I asked their permission to reveal everything to you. You can never, ever tell anyone about their existence." His voice grew sharper. "Including your family."

"I won't," she promised.

Nash withdrew his hands and touched fingertips along either side of his neck. "We now bear the same markings. I breathe underwater, same as you." He dropped his hands and continued. "I have a distant heritage with the Okwa Nahollo, something I was unaware of until recently. The opening of these gills was my grandfather's final blessing, granted to save your life."

Lily reached up and traced his neck markings with wonder. "So that's how you did it," she breathed. "You changed your very nature for me." Her vision blurred with tears. "It must have hurt like hell. Are you happy with the change? Do you regret it?"

Calloused hands gently swiped the tears from her cheeks. "I am at peace. This is my home now. Forever."

Her mind tumbled with questions. Joy and hope and sadness mingled in a cauldron of confusion. She wanted him to stay so desperately, but not like this. Never against his own will. The sacrifice was too great and he might come to despise her over the years. "Is that the price you had to pay for changing? You're forced to stay in Bayou La Siryna the rest of your life?"

"It was my decision. With my grandfather's death, our people need a new healer and the spirits chose me."

"But it seems so unfair. What about your career? You love to travel and—"

Nash brushed his lips over the top of her scalp. "Hush. That isn't the only reason I stayed. I've traveled enough. It's time to explore new territory." He faced her again, placing his hands on the sides of her hips, grounding the two of them together on this spot of land where land and sea joined. *"Chi hollo li."*

His deep, serious voice rolled the unfamiliar words like a caress, wrapping her soul in joy. She had heard them once before but couldn't remember when or why, only that Nash had said them. *"Chi hollo li,"* she repeated slowly. "What does it mean?"

"It's Choctaw for *I love you*."

"Oh, Nash!" Lily buried her face in his damp, broad chest. "I do believe I've loved you since I was a child and you found me when I was lost in the woods. I was so scared, but I knew that you would find me."

"And so I always will." He pulled her from his body and stepped back. "The Okwa Nahollo await us. You will be a mermaid once again, fishtail and all." He held out his hand. "Come."

Lily took his hand and they ran, laughing and splashing into the water. At waist level, they faced one another and embraced, sinking into the sea as one.

Together.

Epilogue

Three months later...

"Surprise!"

Lily blinked, confused by the bright light from the gargantuan chandelier above and the attention of the large crowd of well-dressed citizens packed inside the grand opening of Jet's new downtown shop. Her Pirate's Chest antiques store had done so well she'd purchased the vacant space next door for expansion. For weeks, a construction crew had been hard at work under a veil of secrecy.

The intent scrutiny of the crowd was puzzling. She stiffened her back, grateful to feel Nash's reassuring squeeze at her elbow. Her eyes sought out and found her family, grinning at her in some secret delight. Jet and Landry, Tillman and Shelly, and Mom cuddling her first grandchild, six-week-old Adrian Fields.

Jet raised a hand and dramatically swept it toward the left wall, as if she were Vanna White displaying a grand prize on *Wheel of Fortune*.

Lily's breath caught as she spotted the paintings. *Her* paintings. Dozens of them ornately framed and individually spotlighted by brass sconces. The walls were painted in the palest shade of sea-foam green, which subtly suggested an ocean backdrop for her watercolor seascapes.

It was beautiful—perhaps perfect—yet she felt exposed and vulnerable at the sight of her intimate work on public display. Her right hand picked at the hem of her little black dress that skimmed mid-thigh. Automatically, she reverted to the Mona Lisa smile she hid behind to conceal her emotions.

A dreadful silence hung as she fidgeted with the hem of her dress. What if they all hated her work? Mocked her efforts as blatantly amateurish? She'd be an embarrassment to Nash and her family. It would even top all the years of ostracism and ridicule she'd endured from the Bayou La Siryna townsfolk.

Twyla swept forward, confident and elegant, holding a glass of wine in one hand. She flashed Lily a dazzling smile and flanked her side. "Welcome, Lily," she said, her voice carrying over the room. "We hope y'all enjoy our little surprise tonight. So many people have worked hard to make it possible. Your fiancé, Nash, your family and all your friends and new admirers. We're surprised and honored to have such a talent right here in Bayou La Siryna."

Applause erupted and everyone crowded around, talking at once.

"Remarkable."

"Who could have guessed?"

"I want to buy one."

Twyla held up a hand for silence. "There's more. Come back to the gallery next month for an amazing display of underwater photography taken by Nashoba Bowman. Best of all, the photos were taken right here in Bayou La Siryna's slice of the sea."

Lily turned to Nash, who smiled broadly and winked. He bent down and whispered in her ear. "See? Told you your paintings are exceptional. We make a good team."

The Mona Lisa mask melted and she bid it adieu. Happiness bubbled inside and she uncorked it like a bottle of vintage champagne. A genuine smile lit Lily's face as she nudged Twyla and pointed to her wineglass. "How about finding me a glass, as well? I could sure use it."

Twyla snapped her fingers and nodded toward the back of the room. At the signal, three men dressed in navy blue tuxedos moved forward, carrying silver trays of drinks, and passed them out to the crowd. A waiter approached her and Nash and they each accepted one. Before she could raise it to her lips, Nash held his glass in the air and silenced the crowd.

"Here's to Lily Bosarge," he said, the pride evident in his voice. "A fantastic artist and the woman I am proud to call my future wife."

More applause rang out and she scanned the beaming faces of everyone she held dear. Her circle of friends had widened exponentially over the past few weeks, due in large measure to Twyla's influence. Trusting another human female after Opal's betrayal hadn't been easy, but Twyla had won her over with many acts of kindness. Lily turned to her and clinked their glasses together. "To my first and truest friend."

She sipped the wine, knowing that *this* time there would be no ugly hidden surprise lying in wait.

Nash rubbed her neck and gave a playful squeeze. "Hey, I thought *I* was your truest and dearest friend."

"You're that and so much more." Unmindful of the audience, Lily rose up on her toes and kissed him square on the mouth.

And that drew the biggest applause of the night, among much laughter and teasing. Lily cast a quick glance at her mother. Adriana slowly nodded, a silent gesture of acceptance of her daughter's decision to seek her own happiness in her own way. There would be no more talk of returning to sea and living with the merfolk.

Lily had to acknowledge her sister's clever stroke of genius in naming her son Adrian in honor of their mother. Adriana had been present at the home birthing and had fallen instantly and totally gaga over the tow-headed baby boy. Lily stifled a grin, recalling Landry's grumbling that his mother-in-law seemed in no hurry to ever leave the bayou. But he was so besotted with Jet, he'd suffer anything to make her happy.

Just as Nash was equally determined to lavish her with love and affection.

All of them had followed their hearts. And all of them had fought and won against great odds. And if sometimes Shelly was haunted by dreams of an escaped one-eyed killer on the loose, or if Jet remembered an ex-lover launching a spear at her undersea—the reward of love was worth the trials.

As for herself, the image of Opal's determined face as she raised an oar, poised to strike, would sometimes return with a clarity that set her heart pounding erratically. But the horror of that day was fading as she and Nash planned their future and lived each day grateful for the opportunity to be together. Tillman and Landry were solid and serious and had the power of the law on their side.

With Nashoba she'd found a protector, a healer and a forever love.

Amid the gallery exhibition's noisy camaraderie and cheer, Nash pulled her aside and gazed down with his intense green eyes, searching her heart. "Are you truly happy, Lily?"

More than I ever dared dream. "With you—always. *Chi hollo li.*"

* * * * *

THE WORLD IS BETTER WITH *Romance*

Harlequin has everything from contemporary, passionate and heartwarming to suspenseful and inspirational stories.

Whatever your mood, we have a romance just for you!

Connect with us to find your next great read, special offers and more.

f /HarlequinBooks
🐦 @HarlequinBooks
www.HarlequinBlog.com
www.Harlequin.com/Newsletters

HARLEQUIN

A *Romance* FOR EVERY MOOD™

www.Harlequin.com

SERIESHALOAD2015

HARLEQUIN®
A Romance FOR EVERY MOOD™

Love the Harlequin book you just read?

Your opinion matters.

Review this book on your favorite book site, review site, blog or your own social media properties and share your opinion with other readers!

Be sure to connect with us at:
Harlequin.com/Newsletters
Facebook.com/HarlequinBooks
Twitter.com/HarlequinBooks

HREVIEWS

HARLEQUIN®

A *Romance* FOR EVERY MOOD™

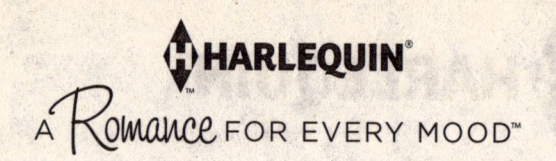

JUST CAN'T GET ENOUGH?

Join our social communities and talk to us online.

You will have access to the latest news on upcoming titles and special promotions, but most importantly, you can talk to other fans about your favorite Harlequin reads.

Harlequin.com/Community

- Facebook.com/HarlequinBooks
- Twitter.com/HarlequinBooks
- Pinterest.com/HarlequinBooks

HARLEQUIN®
A Romance FOR EVERY MOOD™

Stay up-to-date on all your romance-reading news with the *Harlequin Shopping Guide*, featuring bestselling authors, exciting new miniseries, books to watch and more!

The newest issue will be delivered right to you with our compliments! There are 4 each year.

Signing up is easy.

EMAIL

ShoppingGuide@Harlequin.ca

WRITE TO US

HARLEQUIN BOOKS
Attention: Customer Service Department
P.O. Box 9057, Buffalo, NY 14269-9057

OR PHONE

1-800-873-8635 in the United States
1-888-343-9777 in Canada

Please allow 4-6 weeks for delivery of the first issue by mail.